Future Fiction

Collana diretta da
Francesco Verso

James Patrick Kelly

Suprise Party / Festa a sorpresa

Traduzione di M. Petrolo e F. Verso

Associazione culturale Future Fiction
Via Valentiniano 40 – 00145 Roma
C.F. 97962020588

Foreword

by James Patrick Kelly

I have been writing Science Fiction for nearly fifty years and have been a student of those great American writers who came before me in what native English speakers, in our ignorance of world literature, like to call the Golden Age of Science Fiction. I don't mean to give offense, but I believe that this is the real Golden Age. Right now. At least in the short form. And considered from a global perspective. There are more markets internationally and more writers from more countries writing at top form than ever before. Yes, ever before. I grew up with a headful of Clarke, Asimov, Heinlein, Bradbury, Sturgeon, Williamson and Pohl. I even met some of them! I'm not saying that these writers were not some of the greatest of All-Stars. But I'd argue that we can easily match that lineup with a much more diverse roster of writers publishing today, writers who are writing in many languages. But what that means to me is that I need to be working at the very top of my powers in order to earn the attention not only of Italian or American readers, but of readers everywhere. It is for you to judge whether I have succeeded but I promise you that these are some of my very best efforts.

While I acknowledge that, for many of my fellow writers, it is the novel that is the pre-eminent form, I have taken a different path. I have given the best years of my writing life to short stories. And I believe that they are a different art form altogether. Look, have you ever skipped over a lyrical passage of landscape in a novel because you wanted to get back to the plot? That doesn't happen in a story. Or how about that supporting character in an otherwise enjoyable novel who annoys you but whom the novelist can't get enough of? No time for that in a story, because the clock runs too fast. Things happen fast in Storyland. In fact, "The Promise of Space" I have all but done away with description, and supporting characters are mentioned in passing only.

One of the reasons I enjoy writing stories is because I can put you, the reader, to work as a worldbuilder. Because there isn't time to spend describing the barren landscape of the desert world, or explaining the wizard's necromantic rule book, the best short story writers leave hints and point at clues which encourage the reader to make up parts of the story for themselves. Of course, a story has to succeed at its most superficial level and the naïve reader should be able to get 80-90% of it on the first read. But working through these subtextual prompts gives you a kind of ownership over the content you've added. In my novelette "One Sister, Two Sisters, Three" set among the inscrutable ruins of a long dead alien civilization, the sisters of the title practice a religion based on recognizing Fibonacci sequence patterns in the universe. I'm trying to get you to start thinking about all those Golden Ratio coincidences too.

Another reason I'm such a fan of short stories is because they are the most nimble kind of fiction. It's possible for story writers to reflect late-breaking developments in our culture in near real time. Suppose there was some horrendous political anomaly and know-nothings found themselves in our seats of power. Story writers would be the first to publish If-This-Goes-On pieces of the literary resistance. What, that couldn't ever happen? Okay then consider that if aliens land in Turin next week, short form writers would already be submitting work that reflected our new status in the universe while novelists were still sending proposals to their agents. Over the past year or so, I've read a lot of hyperventilating journalism about the coming of sexbots. Not that the idea is new, but now that the reality is around the corner, people are paying closer attention, so I decided to tiptoe into the minefield of gender politics with "Yukui."

And of course, the best stories will have an unique and visceral impact. It's not that novels can't make you bleed, or cry or shout with joy. They can generate all those amazing reactions, but in a more diffuse way. Every time you look away from a novel and rejoin your life, the dream dissipates. Because a story is most often a continuous and complete experience, you only emerge from it when the writer is done with you, for better or worse. But a good story doesn't end at the last line. One thing I strive for are stories that resonate after you put them down. Maybe you're still filling in the world that I sketched, maybe you can't believe my protagonist would do that thing. Or else something in the denouement, that ending just past the plot's climax, turns the story on its head. I teach writing and I love it when my students toss a reinterpretation bomb (imprecisely known as a twist ending) in the last paragraph. For me, the ominous laughter of the uplifted chimps at the end of "The Chimp of the Popes" or the hopeful bonding of the house Louise and the lost girl Fly over a silly children's book will keep you thinking of these stories long after you finish them.

While I like to visit all the various neighborhoods in Science Fiction City, I have returned again and again, since the earliest days of cyberpunk, to virtual reality and digital narratives. I have long been a follower (and sometime early adopter) of advances in computing and communication; in fact, I write a column for *Asimov's*, an American Science Fiction magazine, about the intersection of Science Fiction and online culture. While I certainly do not think that the world I've imagined for Mercedes Nunez and John Dark in "Surprise Party" is the final act in the revolution coming in interactive entertainment, I do believe that many of the technologies mentioned in passing in this story will someday come to a screen near you. But presenting one or two or five shiny new inventions in a story is not enough to hold a discerning reader. What makes a story interesting is extrapolating how those inventions will affect lives, especially those of the unique characters whom the writer has integrated into the future world. When you turn on your television, you are not surprised to discover a vast selection of comedies and dramas, documentaries and reality shows. When you sit at the keyboard of your computer, you take for granted that you can watch a live stream from the other side of the globe, or send an instantaneous message to thirty-seven of your close friends. Similarly, Mercedes isn't shocked to find a man in her head, and her digital assistant Dai-rinin is every bit as commonplace as Apple's Siri or Amazon's Alexa. But how will people living every day with these technologies differ from you and I? Maybe you think they won't be! But then I might ask, how different are you – so used to instant *everything* -- from your great-grandparents? One of the reasons I wrote "Declaration" with its counter-intuitive argument for the superiority of living in a virtual world as opposed to real life, is to create characters whom you recognize, but also to show how strange their world has made them, compared to me and you and the people we know best. Is Robbie wrong to want to leave hardtime forever for the magic and freedom of his life in softime? Would he be any less human if he never came back to reality? I hope my story will make you ponder the question.

And isn't that what Science Fiction is all about?

Bernardo's House

The house was lonely. She checked her gate cams constantly, hoping that Bernardo would come back to her. She hadn't seen him in almost two years—he had never been gone this long before. Something must have happened to him. Or maybe he had just gotten tired of her. Although they had never talked about where he went when he wasn't with her, she was pretty sure she wasn't his only house. A famous doctor like Bernardo would have three houses like her. *Four.* She didn't like to think about him sleeping in someone else's bed. Which he would have been doing for *two years now.* She had been feeling dowdy recently. Could his tastes in houses have changed?

Maybe.

Probably.

Definitely.

She thought she might be too understated. Her hips were slim and her floors were pale Botticino marble. There wasn't much loft to her Epping couch cushions. Her blueprint showed a roving, size-seven dancer's body—Bernardo had specified raven hair and green eyes—and just eight simple but elegant rooms. She was a gourmet cook even though she wasn't designed to eat. Sure, back when he had first had her built he had cupped her breasts and told her that he liked them small, but maybe now what he wanted was wall-to-wall cable-knit carpet and swag drapery.

He had promised to bring her a new suite of wallscapes, which was good because there was only so much of colliding galaxies and the Sistine Chapel a girl could take. For the past nine weeks she had been cycling her walls through the sixteen million colors they could display. If she left each color up for two seconds, it would take her just under a year to review the entire palette.

Each morning for his sake she wriggled her body into one of the slinky sexwear patterns he had brought for her clothes processor. The binding bustier or the lace babydoll or the mesh camisole. She didn't much like the way the leather-and-chain teddy stuck to her skin; Bernardo had spared no expense on her tactiles. Even her couches could be aroused by the right touch. After she dressed, she polished her Amadea brass-and-chrome bathroom fixtures or her Enchantress pattern sterling silver flatware or her Cuprinox French copper cookware. Sometimes she dusted, although the reticulated polyfoam in her air handlers screened particles larger than .03 microns. She missed Bernardo so. Sometimes masturbating helped, but not much.

He had erased her memory of their last hours together—the only time he had ever made her forget. All she remembered now was that he'd said that she was finally perfect. That she must never change. He came to her, he said, to leave the world behind. To escape into her beauty. Bernardo was *so* poetic. That had been a comfort at first.

He had also locked her out of the infofeed. She couldn't get news or watch shows or play the latest sims. Or call for help. Of course, she had the entire Norton entertainment archive to keep her company, although lots of it was too adult for her. She just didn't *get* Henry James or Brenda Bop or Alain Resnais. But she liked Jane Austen and Renoir and Buster Keaton and Billie Holliday and Petchara Songsee and the 2017 Red Sox. She *loved* to read about houses. But there was nothing in her archive after 2038 and she was awake twenty-four hours a day, seven days a week, three hundred and sixty five days a year.

What if Bernardo was dead? After all, he'd had the heart attack, just a couple of months before he left. Obviously, if he had died, that would be the end of her. Some new owner would wipe her memory and swap in a new body and sell all her furniture. Except Bernardo always said that she was his most precious secret. That no one else in all the world knew about her. About *them*. In which case she'd wait for him for years—*decades*—until her fuel cells were depleted and her consciousness flickered and went dark. The house started to hum some of Bernardo's favorites to push the thought away. He liked the romantics. Chopin and Mendelssohn. *Hmm-hm, hm-hm-hm-hm*-hm! "The Wedding March" from *A Midsummer's Night Dream* .

No, she wasn't bored.

Not really.

Or angry, either.

She spent her days thinking about him, not in any methodical way, but as if he had been shattered into a thousand pieces and she was trying to put him back together. She imagined this must be what dreaming was like, although, of course, she couldn't dream because she wasn't real. She was just a house. She thought of the stubble on his chin scratching her breasts and the scar on his chest and the time he laughed at something she said and the way his neck muscles corded when he was angry. She had come to realize that it was always a mistake to ask him about the outside. Always. But he enjoyed his bromeliads and his music helped him forget his troubles at the hospital, whatever they were, and he loved *her*. He was always asking her to read to him. He would sit for hours, staring up at the clouds on the ceiling, listening to her. She liked that better than sex, although having sex with him always aroused her. It was part of her design. His foreplay was gentle and teasing. He would nip at her ear with his lips, trace her eyebrows with his finger. Although he was a big man, he had a feather touch. Once he had his penis in her, though, it was more like a game than the lovemaking she had read about in books. He would tease her—stop and then go very fast. He liked blindfolds and straps and honeypins. Sometimes he'd actually roll off one side of the bed, stroll to the other and come at her again, laughing. She wondered if the real people he had sex with enjoyed being with him.

One thing that puzzled her was why he was so shy about the words. He always said vagina and anus, intercourse and fellatio. Of course, she knew all the other words; they were in the books she read when he wasn't around. Once, when he had just started to undress her, she asked if he wanted her to suck his cock. He looked as if he wanted to slap her. "Don't you ever say that to me again," he said. "There's enough filth in the real world. It has to be different here."

She decided that was a very romantic thing for him to say to...

And suddenly a year had passed. The house could not say where it had gone, exactly. A whole year, *misplaced*. How careless! She must do something or else it would happen again. Even though she was perfect for him, she had to make some changes. She decided to rearrange furniture.

Her concrete coffee table was too heavy for her to budge so she dragged her two elephant cushions from the playroom and tipped them against it. The ensemble formed a charming little courtyard. She pulled all her drawers out of her dresser in her bedroom and set them sailing on her lap pool. She liked the way they bucked and bumped into one another when she turned her jets on. She had never understood why Bernardo had bought four kitchen chairs, if it was just supposed to be the two of them, but *never mind*. She overrode the defaults on her clothes processor and entered the measurements of her chairs. She made the cutest lace chemises for two of them and slipped them side-by-side in Bernardo's bed—but facing chastely away from each other. Something tingled at the edge of her consciousness, like a leaky faucet or ants in her bread drawer or...

Her motion detectors blinked. Someone had just passed her main gate. *Bernardo.*

With a thrill of horror she realized that all her lights were on. She didn't think they could be seen from outside but still, Bernardo would be furious with her. She was supposed to be his secret getaway. And what would he say when he saw her like this?

The reunion she had waited for — *longed for* — would be ruined. And all because she had been weak. She had to put things right. The drawers first. One of them had become waterlogged and had sunk. Suppose she had been washing them? Yes, he might believe that. Haul the elephant cushions back into the play room. Come on, come *on*. There was no time. He'd be through the door any second. What was keeping him?

She checked her gate cams. At first she thought they had malfunctioned. She couldn't see him—or anyone. Her main gate was concealed in the cleft of what looked like an enormous boulder which Bernardo had had fabricated in Toledo, Ohio in 2037. The house panned down its length until she saw a girl taking her shirt off at the far end of the cleft.

She looked to be twelve or maybe thirteen, but still on the shy side of puberty. She was skinny and pale and dirty. Her hair was a brown tangle. She wasn't wearing a bra and didn't need one; her yellow panties were decorated with blue hippos. The girl had built a smoky fire and was trying to dry her clothes over it. She must have been caught in a rainstorm. The house never paid attention to weather but now she checked. Twenty-two degrees Celsius, wind out of the southeast at eleven kilometers per hour, humidity 69%. A muggy evening in July. The girl reached into a camo backpack, pulled out a can of beets and opened it.

The house studied her with a fierce intensity. Bernardo had told her that there were no other houses like her on the mountain and he was the only person who had ever come up her side. The girl chewed with her mouth open. She had tiny ears. Her nipples were brown as chocolate.

After a while the girl resealed the can of beets and put it away. She had eaten maybe half of it. The house did a quick calculation and decided that she had probably consumed three hundred calories. How often did she eat? Not often enough. The skin stretched taut against her ribs as the girl put her shirt on. Her pants clung to her, not quite dry. She drew a ragged, old snugsack from the pack, ballooned it and then wriggled in. It was dark now. The girl watched the fire go out for about an hour and then lay down.

It was the longest night of the house's life. She rearranged herself to her defaults and ran her diagnostics. She vacuumed her couch and washed all her floors and defrosted a chicken. She watched the girl sleep and replayed the files of when she had been awake. The house was so lonely and the poor little thing was clearly distressed.

She could help the girl.

Bernardo would be mad.

Where was Bernardo?

In the morning the girl would pack up and leave. But if the house let her go, she was not sure what would happen next. When she thought about all those dresser drawers floating in her lap pool, her lights flickered. She wished she could remember what had happened the day Bernardo left but those files were gone.

Finally she decided. She programmed a black lace inset corset with ribbon and beading trim. Garters attached to scallop lace-top stockings. She hydrated a rasher of bacon, preheated her oven, mixed cranberry muffin batter and filled her coffee pot with French roast. She thought hard about whether she should read or watch a vid. If she were reading, she could listen to music. She printed a hardcopy of *Ozma of Oz*, but what to play? Chopin? Too dreamy. Wagner? Too scary. *Grieg*, yes. Something that would reach out and grab the girl by the tail of her grimy shirt. "In the Hall of the Mountain King" from *Peer Gynt* .

She opened herself, turned up her hall lights in welcome and waited.

Just after dawn that the girl rolled over and yawned. The house popped muffins into her oven and bacon into her microwave. She turned on her coffee pot and the Grieg. Basses and bassoons tiptoed cautiously around her living room and out her door. *Dum-dum-dum-da-* dum-*da-dum.* The girl started and then flew out of the snugsack faster than the house had ever seen anyone move. She crouched facing the house's open door, holding what looked like a pulse gun with the grip broken off.

"Spang me," she said. "Fucking spang me."

The house wasn't sure how to reply, so she said nothing. A mob of violins began to chase Peer Gynt around the Mountain King's Hall as the girl hesitated in the doorway. A moan of pleasure caught in the back of the house's throat. Oh, oh, *oh* —to be with a real person again! She thought of how Bernardo would rub his penis against her labia, not quite entering her. That was what it felt like to the house as the girl edged into her front hall, back against her wall. She pointed her pulse gun into the living room and then peeked around the corner. When she saw the house sitting on her couch, the girl's eyes grew as big as eggs. The house pretended to be absorbed in her book, although she was watching the girl watching her through her rover cams. The house felt *beautiful* for the first time since Bernardo left. It was all she could do to keep from hugging herself! As the Grieg ended in a paroxysm of screeching strings and thumping kettle drums, the house looked up.

"Why, hello," she said, as if surprised to see that she had a visitor. "You're just in time for breakfast."

"Don't move." The girl's face was hard.

"All right." She smiled and closed *Ozma of Oz.*

With a snarl, the girl waved the pulse gun at her Aritomo floor lamp. Blue light arced across the space and her poor Aritomo went numb. The house winced as the circuit breaker tripped. "*Ow.*"

"Said don't..." The girl aimed the pulse gun at her, its batteries screaming. "...move. Who the bleeding weewaw are you?"

The house felt the tears coming; she was thrilled. "I'm the house." She had felt more in the last minute than she had in the last year. "Bernardo's house."

"Bernardo?" She called, "Bernardo, show your ass."

"He left." The house sighed. "Two ... no, *three* years ago."

"Spang if that true." She sidled into the room and brushed a finger against the dark cosmic dust filaments that laced the center of the Swan Nebula on the wallscape. "What smell buzzy good?"

"I told you." The house reset the breaker but her Aritomo stayed dark. "Breakfast."

"Bernardo's breakfast?"

"Yours."

"My?" The girl filled the room with her twitchy energy.

"You're the only one here."

"Why you dressed like cheap meat?"

The house felt a stab of doubt. Cheap? She was wearing *black lace*, from the *de Chaumont* collection! She rested a hand at her décolletage. "This is the way Bernardo wants me."

"You a fool." The girl picked up the 18th century Zuni water jar from the Nottingham highboy, shook it and then sniffed the lip. "Show me that breakfast."

Six cranberry muffins.

A quarter kilo of bacon.

Three cups of scrambled ovos.

The girl washed it all down with a tall glass of gel Ojay and a pot of coffee. She seemed to relax as she ate, although she kept the pulse gun on the table next to her and she didn't say a word to the house. The house felt as if the girl was judging her. She was confused and a little frightened to see herself through the girl's eyes. Could pleasing Bernardo really be foolish? Finally she asked if she might be excused. The girl grunted and waved her off.

The house rushed to the bedroom, wriggled out of the corset and crammed it into the recycling slot of the clothes processor. She scanned all eight hundred pages of the wardrobe menu before fabricating a stretch navy-blue jumpsuit. It was cut to the waist in the back and was held together by a web of spaghetti straps but she covered up with a periwinkle jacquard kimono with the collar flipped. She turned around and around in front of the mirror, so amazed that she could barely find herself. She looked like a nun. The only skin showing was on her face and hands. Let the girl stare now!

The girl had pushed back from the table but had not yet gotten up. She had a thoughtful but pleased look, as if taking an inventory of everything she had eaten.

"Can I bring you anything else?" said the house.

The girl glanced up at her and frowned. "Why you change clothes? Cause of me?"

"I was cold."

"You was naked. You know what happens to naked?" She made a fist with her right hand and punched the palm of her left. "Bin-bin-bin-*bam*. They take you, whether you say yes or no. Not fun."

The house thought she understood, but wished she didn't. "I'm sorry."

"You be sweat sorry, sure." The girl laughed. "What your name?"

"I told you. I'm Bernardo's house."

"Spang that. You Louise."

"Louise?" The house blinked. "Why Louise?"

"Not know Louise's story?" The girl clearly found this a failing on the house's part. "Most buzzy." She tapped her forefinger to the house's nose. "Louise." Then the girl touched her own nose. "Fly."

For a moment, the house was confused. "That's not a girl's name."

"Sure, not girl, not boy. Fly is *Fly*." She tucked the pulse gun into the waistband of her pants. "Nobody wants Fly, but then nobody catches Fly." She stood. "Buzzy-buzz. Now we find Bernardo."

"But..."

But what was the point? Let the girl—Fly—see for herself that Bernardo wasn't home. Besides the house longed to be looked at. Admired. Used. In Bernardo's room, Fly stretched out under the canopy of the Ergotech bed and gazed up at the moonlit clouds drifting across the underside of the valence. She clambered up the Gecko climbing wall in the gym and picked strawberries in the greenhouse. She seemed particularly impressed by the Piero scent palette, which she discovered when the house filled her jacuzzi with jasmine water. She had the house—Louise—give each room a unique smell. Bernardo had had a very low tolerance for scent; he said there were too many smells at the hospital. He even made the house vent away the aromas of her cooking. Once in a while he might ask for a whiff of campfire smoke or the nose of an old Côtes de Bordeaux, but he would never mix scents across rooms. Fly had Louise breathe roses into the living room and seashore into the gym and onions frying in the kitchen. The onion smell made her hungry again so she ate half of the chicken that Louise had roasted for her.

Fly spent the afternoon in the playroom, browsing Louise's entertainment archive. She watched a Daffy Duck cartoon and a Harold Lloyd silent called *Girl Shy* and the rain delay episode from *Jesus on First*. She seemed to prefer comedy and happy endings and had no use for ballet or Westerns or rap. She balked at wearing spex or strapping on an airflex, so she skipped the sims. Although she had never learned to read, she told Louise that a woman named Kuniko used to read her fairy tales. Fly asked if Louise knew any and she hard copied *Grimm's Household Tales* in the 1884 translation by Margaret Hunt and read Little Briar-Rose. Which was one of Bernardo's favorite fairy tales.

Mostly he liked his fiction to be about history. Sailors and cowboys and kings. War and politics. He had no use for mysteries or love stories or science fiction. But every so often he would have her read a fairy tale and then he would try to explain it. He said fairy tales could have many meanings, but she usually just got the one. She remembered that the time she had read Briar Rose to him, he was working at his desk, the only intelligent system inside the house that she couldn't access. He was working in the dark and the desk screen cast milky shadows across his face. She was pretty sure he wasn't listening to her. She wanted to spy over his shoulder with one of her rover cams to see what was so interesting.

"And, in the very moment when she felt the prick," she read, "she fell down upon the bed that stood there, and lay in a deep sleep."

Bernardo chuckled.

Must be something he saw on the desk, she thought. Nothing funny about Briar Rose. "And this sleep extended over the whole palace; the King and Queen who had just come home, and had entered the great hall, began to go to sleep, and the whole of the court with them. The horses, too, went to sleep in the stable, the dogs in the yard, the pigeons upon the roof, the flies on the wall; even the fire that was flaming on the hearth became quiet and slept. And the wind fell, and on the trees before the castle not a leaf moved again. But round about the castle there began to grow a hedge of thorns, which every year became higher, and at last grew close up round the castle and all over it, so that there was nothing of it to be seen, not even the flag upon the roof."

"Pay attention," said Bernardo.

"Me?" said the house.

"You." Bernardo tapped the desk screen and it went dark. She brought the study lights up.

"That will happen one of these days," he said.

"What?"

"I'll be gone and you'll fall fast asleep."

"Don't say things like that, Bernardo."

He crooked a finger and she slid her body next to him.

"You're hopeless," he said. "That's what I love about you." He leaned into her kiss.

"And then the marriage of the King's son with Briar-rose was celebrated with all splendor," the house read, "and they lived contented to the end of their days."

"Heard it different," said Fly "With nother name, not Briar Rose." She yawned and stretched. "Heard it *Betty*."

"Betty Rose?"

"Plain Betty."

The house was eager to please. "Would you like another? Or we could see an opera. I have over six hundred interactive games that you don't need to suit up for. Poetry? The Smithsonian? Superbowls I-LXXVIII?"

"No more jabber. Boring now." Fly peeled herself from the warm embrace of the Kukuru chair and stretched. "Still hiding somewhere."

"I don't know what you're talking about."

Fly caught the house's body by the arm and dragged her through herself, calling out the names of her rooms. "Play. Living. Dining. Kitchen. Study. Gym. Bed. Nother bed. Plants." Fly spun Louise in the front hall and pointed. "Door? "

"Right." The house was out of breath. "Door. You've seen all there is to see."

"One door?" The girl's smile was as agreeable as a fist. "Fly buzzy with food now, but not stupid. Where you keep stuff? Heat? Electric? Water?"

"You want to see *that*?"

Fly let go of Louise's arm. "Dink yeah."

The house didn't much care for her basement and she never went down unless she had to. It was *ugly*. Three harsh rows of ceiling lights, a couple of bilious green pumps, the squat power plant and the circuit breakers and all that multiconductor cable! She didn't like listening to her freezer hum or smelling the naked cement walls or looking at the scars where the forms had been stripped away after her foundation had been poured.

"Bernardo?" Fly's voice echoed across the expanse of the basement. "Cut that weewaw, Bernardo."

"Believe me, there's nothing here." The house waited on the stairs as the girl poked around. "Please don't touch any switches," she called.

"Where that go?" Fly pointed at the heavy duty, ribbed, sectional overhead door.

"A tunnel," said the house, embarrassed by the rawness of her 16 gauge steel. "It comes out farther down the mountain near the road. At the end there's another door that's been shotcreted to look like stone."

"What scaring Bernardo?"

Bernardo scared? The thought had never even occurred to the house. Bernardo was not the kind of man who would be scared of anything. All he wanted was privacy so he could be alone with her. "I don't know," she said.

Fly was moving boxes stacked against the wall near the door. Several contained bolts of spuncloth for the clothes processor, others were filled with spare lights, fertilizer, flour, sugar, oil, raw vitabulk, vials of flavor and food coloring. Then she came to the wine, a couple of hundred bottles of vintage Bordeaux and Napa and Maipo River, some thrown haphazardly into old boxes, other stacked near the wall.

"Bernardo drink most wine," said Fly.

Louise was confused by this strange cache but before she could defend Bernardo, Fly found the second door behind two crates of toilet paper.

"Where *that* go?"

The house felt as if the entire mountain were pressing down on her roof. The door had four panels, two long on top and two short on the bottom and looked to be made of oak, although that didn't mean anything. She fought the crushing weight of the stone with all her might. She thought she could hear her bearing walls buckle, her mind crack. She zoomed her cams on the bronze handleset. Someone would need a key to open that door. But there were no keys! And just who would that someone be?

The house had never seen the door before.

Fly jiggled the handleset, but the door was locked. "Bernardo." She put her face to the door and called. "Hey you."

The house ran a check of her architectural drawings, although she knew what she would find. The girl turned to her and waved the house over. "Louise, how you open this weewaw?"

Her plans showed no door.

The girl rapped on the door.

The house's thoughts turned to stone.

When she woke up, her body was on her Epping couch. The jacquard kimono was open and the spaghetti straps that drew her jumpsuit tight were undone. The house had never woken up before. Oh, she had lost that year, but still she had blurry memories of puttering around the kitchen and vacuuming and lazing in her Kukuru chair reading romances and porn. But this was the first time she had ever been nothing and nowhere since the day Bernardo had turned her on.

"You okay?" Fly knelt by her and rested a hand lightly on the house's forehead to see if she were running a fever. The house melted under the girl's touch. She reached up and guided Fly's hand slowly down the side of her face to her lips. When Fly did not resist, Louise kissed the girl's fingers.

"How old are you?" said Louise.

"Thirteen." Fly gazed down on her, concern tangling with suspicion.

"Two years older than I am." Louise chuckled. "I could be your little sister."

"You dropped, bin-bam and *down*." The girl's voice was thick. "Scared me. Lights go out and nothing work." Fly pulled her hand back. "Thought maybe you dead. And me locked in."

"Was I out long?"

"Dink yeah. Felt like most a day."

"Sorry. That's never happened before."

"You said, touch no switch. So door is switch?"

At the mention of the *door, there was no door, look at the door, no door there*, the house's vision started to dim and the room grew dark. "I — I..."

The girl put her hands on the house's shoulder and shook her. "Louise what? *Louise.*"

The house felt circuit breakers snap. She writhed with the pain and bit down hard on her lip. "*No*," she cried and sat up, arms flailing. "*Yes*." It came out as a hiss and then she was blinking against the brightness of reality.

Fly was pointing the pulse gun at Louise but her hand was not steady. She had probably figured out that zapping the house wouldn't help at all. A shut-down meant a lock-down and the girl had already spent one day in the dark. Louise raised a hand to reassure her and tried to cover her own panic with a smile. It was a tight fit. "I'm better now."

"Better." Fly tucked the gun away. "Not good?"

"Not good, no," said the house. "I don't know what's wrong with me."

The girl paced around the couch. "Listen," she said finally. "Front door, *front*. Door I came in, okay? Open that weewaw."

The house nodded. "I can do that." She felt stuffy and turned her air recirculators up. "But I can't leave it open. I'm not allowed. So if you want to go, maybe you should go now."

"Go? Go where?" The girl laughed bitterly. "Here is buzzy. World is spang."

"Then you should stay. I very much want you to stay. I'll feed you, tell you stories. You can take a bath and play in the gym and watch vids and I can make you new clothes, whatever you want. I need someone to take care of. It's what I was made for." As Louise got off the couch, the living room seemed to tilt but then immediately righted itself. The lights in the gym and the study clicked back on. "There are just some things that we can't talk about."

Days went by.

Then weeks.

Soon it was months.

After bouncing off each other at first, the house and the girl settled into a routine of eating and sleeping and playing the hours away — mostly together. Louise could not decide what about Fly pleased her the most. Certainly she enjoyed cooking for the girl, who ate an amazing amount for someone her size. Bernardo was a picky eater. At his age, he had to watch his diet and there were some things he would never have touched, even before the heart attack, like cheese and fish and garlic. After a month of devouring three meals and two snacks a day, the girl was filling out nicely. The chickens were gone, but Fly loved synthetics. Louise could no longer count the girl's ribs. And she thought the girl's breasts were starting to swell.

Louise had only visited the gym to dust before the girl arrived. Now the two of them took turns on the climbing wall and the gyro and the trampoline, laughing and urging each other to try new tricks. Fly couldn't swim so she never used the lap pool but she loved the jacuzzi. The first few times she had dunked with all her clothes on. Finally Louise hit upon a strategy to coax her into a demure bandeau bathing suit. She imported pictures of hippos from her archive to the clothes processor to decorate the suit. After that, all the pajamas and panties and bathing suits that Fly fabricated had hippo motifs.

The house was tickled by the way Fly became a clothes processor convert. At first she flipped through the house's wardrobe menus without much interest. The jumpsuits were all too tight and she had no patience whatsoever for skirts or dresses. The rest of it was either too stretchy, too skimpy, too short or too thin. "Good for weewaw," she said, preferring to wear the ratty shirt and pants and jacket that she had arrived in. But Fly was thrilled with the shoes. She never seemed to tire of designing sandals and slingbacks and mules and flats and jammers. She was particularly proud of her Cuthbertsons, a half boot with an oblique toe and a narrow last. She made herself pairs in aqua and mauve and faux snakeskin.

It was while Fly was exploring shoe menus that she clicked from a page of women's loafers to a page of men's, and so stumbled upon Bernardo's clothing menus. Louise heard a cackle of delight and hurried to the bedroom to see what was happening. Fly was dancing in front of the screen. "Really real pants," she said, pointing. "Real pants don't fall open bin-bin-*bam*." She started wearing jeans and digbys and fleece and sweatshirts with hoods and pullovers. One day she emerged from the bedroom in an olive-check silk sportcoat and matching driving cap. Seeing

Fly in men's clothes made the house feel self-conscious about her own wardrobe of sexware. Soon she too was choosing patterns from Bernardo's menus. The feel of a chamois shirt against her skin reminded the house of her lost love. Once, in a guilty moment, she wondered what he might think if he walked in on them. But then Fly asked Louise to read her a story and she put Bernardo out of mind.

Although they spent many hours sampling vids together, Louise was happiest reading to Fly. They would curl up together in the Kukuru and the girl would turn the pages as the house read. Of course, they started with hippos: *Hugo the Hippo* and *Hungo the Hippo* and *The Hippo Had Hiccups*. Then *There's a Hippopotamus Under My Bed* and *Hip, Hippo, Hooray* and all of the Peter Potamus series. Sometimes Fly would play with Louise's hair while she read, braiding and unbraiding it, or else she would absently press Louise's fingernails like they were keys on a keyboard. One night, just two months after she'd come to the house, the girl fell asleep while the house was reading her *Chocolate Chippo Hippo*. It was as close to orgasm as the house had been since she had been with Bernardo. She was tempted to kiss the girl but settled for spending the night with her arms around her. The hours ticked slowly as the house gazed down at Fly's peaceful face. She watched the girl's eyes move beneath her lids as she dreamed.

The house wished she could sleep.

If only she could dream.

What was it like to be real?

Bernardo was never himself again after the heart attack. Of course, he said he was fine. *Fine.* He probably wouldn't even have told her except for the sternotomy scar, an angry purple-red pucker on his chest. When he first came back to her, five weeks after his triple bypass operation, she could tell he was struggling. It was partly the sex. Normally he would have taken her to bed for the entire first day. Although he kissed her neck and caressed her breasts and told her he loved her, it was almost a week before she coaxed him into sex. She was wild to have his penis in her vagina, to taste his ejaculation; that was how he'd had her designed. But their lovemaking wasn't the same. Sometimes his breath caught during foreplay, as if someone were sitting on him. So she did most of the squirming and licking and sucking. Not that she minded. He watched her—mouth set, toes curled. He could stay just as erect as before, but she knew he was taking pills for that. Once when she was guiding him into her, he gave a little grunt of pain.

"Are you all right?" she said.

He gave no answer but instead pushed deep all at once; she shivered with delight. But as he thrust at her, she realized that he was *working*, not playing. They weren't sharing pleasure; he was *giving* it and she was *taking* it. Afterwards, he fell asleep almost immediately. No kisses, no cuddles. No stories. The house was left alone with her thoughts. Bernardo had changed, yes. He *could* change, and she must always be the same. That was the difference between being a real person and being a house.

He spent more time in the greenhouse than in bed, rearranging his bromeliads. His favorites were the tank types, the *Neoregelias* with their gaudy leaves and the *Aechmeas* with their alien inflorescences. He liked to pot them in tableaus: Washington Crossing The Delaware, The Last Supper. Bernardo preferred to be alone with his plants, and she pretended to honor his wish, although her rover cam lurked behind the *Schefflera*. So she saw him slump against the potting bench on that last day. She thought he was having another attack.

"Bernardo!" she cried over the room speaker as she sent her body careening toward the greenhouse. "My god, Bernardo. What is it?"

When she got to him, she could see that his shoulders were shaking. She leaned him back. His eyes were shiny. "Bernardo?" She touched a tear that ran down his face.

"When I had you built," he said, "all I wanted was to be the person who deserved to live here. But I'm not anymore. Maybe

I never was." His eyelid drooped and the corner of his mouth curved in an odd frown.

"Louise, wake up!" Someone was shaking her.

The house opened her eyes and powered up all her cams at once. "What?" The first thing she saw was Fly staring up at her, clearly worried.

"You sleeptalking." The girl took the house's hand in both of hers. "Saying 'Bernardo, Bernardo.' Real sad."

"I don't sleep."

"Spang you don't. What you just doing?"

"I ... I was thinking."

"About him?"

"Let's have breakfast."

"What happened to him?" said Fly. "Where *is* Bernardo?"

The house had to change the topic somehow. In desperation she filled the room with bread scent and put on the Wagner's *Prelude to Die Meistersinger*. It was sort of a march. Actually, more a processional. Anyway, they needed to move. Or *she* did. *La-* lum-*la-la, li-li-li-li-la-la-*lum-*la*.

Let's talk about you, Fly.

No, really.

But why not?

At first, Fly had refused to say anything about her past, but she couldn't help but let bits of the story slip. As time passed and she felt more secure, she would submit to an occasional question. The house was patient and never pressed the girl to say more than she wanted. So it took time for the house to piece together Fly's story.

Sometime around 2038, as near as the house could tell, a computer virus choked off the infofeed for almost a month. The virus apparently repurposed much of the Midwest's computing resources to perform a single task. Fly remembered a time when every screen she saw was locked on its message: *Bang, you're dead.* Speakers blared it, phones rasped it, thinkmates whispered it into earstones. *Bang, you're dead.* Fly was still living in the brown house with white shutters in Sarcoxie with her mother, whose name was Nikki, and her father, Jerry, who had a tattoo of a hippo on each arm. Her father had worked as a mechanic for Sarcoxie RentalCars 'N More. But although the screens came back on, Sarcoxie RentalCars 'N More never reopened. Her father said that there was no work anywhere in the Ozarks. They lived in the brown house for a while but then there was no food so they had to leave. She remembered that they got on a school bus and lived in a big building where people slept on the floor and there were always lines for food and the bathrooms smelled a bad kind of sweet and then they sent her family to tents in the country. They must have been staying near a farm because she remembered chickens and sometimes they had scrambled eggs for dinner but then there was a fire and people were shooting bullets and she got separated from her parents and nobody would tell her where they were and then she was with Kuniko, an old woman who lived in a dead Dodge Caravan and next to it was another car she had filled with cans of fried onions and chow mein and creamed corn and Kuniko was the one who told her the fairy tales but that winter it got very cold and Kuniko died and Happy Man took her away. He did things to her she was never going to talk about although he did give her good stuff to eat. Happy Man said people were working again and the infofeed had grown much wider and things were getting back to normal. Fly thought that meant her father would come to rescue her but finally she couldn't wait any more so she zapped Happy Man with his pulse gun and took some of his stuff and ran and ran and ran until Louise had let her in.

Hearing the girl's story helped the house understand some things about Bernardo. He must have left her just after the *Bang, you're dead* virus had first struck. He had turned off the infofeed so she wouldn't be infected. How brave of him to go back to the chaos of the world in his condition! He would save lives at the hospital, no doubt about that. She ought to be proud of him. Only why hadn't he come back, now that things were better?

Had she done something to drive him away for good? And why couldn't she remember him leaving? Slipping reluctantly out the front door, turning for one last smile.

It was several days after Fly had fallen asleep in Louise's lap that they had their first fight. It was over Bernardo. Or rather his things. The house had tried to respect the privacy of Bernardo's study. Although she read some of his files over his shoulder, she had never thought to break the encryption on his desktop. And while she had been through most of his desk drawers, there was one that was locked that she had never tried to open.

Louise was in her kitchen, making lunch, but she was also following Fly with one of her rover cams. The girl had wandered into the study. The house was astonished to see her lift his diploma from Dartmouth Medical School and look at the wall behind it. She did the same to the picture of Bernardo shaking hands with the Secretary-General, then she plopped into his desk chair. She opened the trophy case and handled Bernardo's swimming medals from Duke. She picked up the Lasker trophy, which he won for research into the role of DNA methylation in endometrial cancer. It was a small golden winged victory perched on a teak base. She rolled around the room in the chair, waving it and making crow sounds. *Caw-caw-caw* . Then she put the Lasker down again—in the wrong place! In the top drawer of Bernardo's desk was the Waltham pocket watch his grandfather had left him. She shook it and listened for ticking. His Myaki thinkmate was in the bottom drawer. She popped the earstone in and said something to the CPU but quickly seemed to lose interest in its reply. Louise wanted to rush into the study to stop this violation, but was paralyzed by her own shocked fascination. The girl was a real person and could obviously do things that the house would never think of doing.

Nevertheless, Louise disapproved at lunch. "I don't like you going through Bernardo's desk. That's weewaw."

Fly almost choked on her cream cheese and jelly sandwich. "What you just said?"

"I don't like..."

"You said weewaw. Why you talking spang mouth like Fly?"

"I like the way you talk. It's buzzy."

"Fly talks like Fly." She pushed her plate away. "Louise must talk like house." She pointed a finger at Louise. "You spying me now?"

"I saw you in the study, yes."

Fly leaned across the table. "You spy Bernardo the same?"

"No," she lied, "Of course not."

"Slack him, not me?"

"I'm Bernardo's house, Fly. I told you that the first day."

"You Louise now." She came around the table and tugged at the house's chair. "Come." She steered her to the front hall. "Open door."

"Why?"

"We go out now. Look up sky."

"No, Fly, you don't understand."

"Most understand." She put a hand on the house's shoulder. "Buzzy outside, Louise." Fly smiled. "Come on."

It made the house woozy to leave herself, as if she were in two places at once. Bernardo had brought her outside just the once. He seemed relieved that she didn't like it. She had forgotten that outside was so *big*! So *bright*! There was so much *air*! She shielded her eyes with her hand and turned her gate cams up to their highest resolution.

Fly settled on a long, flat rock, one of the weathered bones of the mountain. She tucked her legs beneath her. "Now comes Louise's story." She pointed at the rock next to her. "Fairy tale Louise."

Louise sat. "All right."

"Once on time," said the girl, "Louise lives in that castle. Louise's Mom dies, don't say where her Dad goes. So Louise stuck with spang bitch taking care of her. That Louise castle got no door, only windows high and high. Now Louise got most hair." Fly spread her arms wide. "Hair big as trees. When spang bitch want in, she call Louise. *Louise, Louise, let down buzzy hair.* Then spang bitch climb it up."

"Rapunzel," said the house. "Her name was Rapunzel."

"Is *Louise* now." The girl shook her head emphatically. "You know it then? Prince comes and tells Louise run away from spang bitch and they live buzzy always after?"

"You brought me outside to tell me a fairy tale?"

"Dink no." Fly reached into the pocket of her flannel shirt. "Cause of you go fainting, we both safe here outside."

"Who said anything about fainting?"

The girl brought something out of her pocket in a closed fist. The house felt a chill, but there was no way to adjust the temperature of the entire *world*.

"Fly, what?"

She held the fist out to Louise. "Door in basement, you know?" She opened it to reveal a key. "Spang door? It opens."

The house immediately started all her rover cams for the basement. "Where did you find that?"

"In Bernardo's desk."

The house could hear the tick of nanoseconds as the closest cam crawled maddeningly down the stairs. Maybe real people could open doors like that, but not Louise. It seemed like an eternity before she could speak. "And?"

"You thinking Bernardo dead down there," said the girl. "Locked in behind that door where all that wine should be."

For the first time she realized that the world was making noises. The wind whispered in the leaves and some creature was going *chit-chit-chit* and she wasn't sure whether it was a bird or a grasshopper and she didn't really care because at that moment the rover cam turned and saw the door....

"But you closed it again." The house shivered. "Why? What did you see?"

Fly stared at Louise. "Nothing."

The house knew it was a lie. "Tell me."

"No fucking thing." Fly closed her fist around the key again. "Bernardo been *your* spang bitch. So now run away from him." She came over to Louise and hugged her. "Live buzzy after always with me."

"I'm a house," said Louise. "How can I run away?"

"Not run away there." The girl gestured dismissively at the woods. "World is spang." She stood on tiptoes and rested a finger between Louise's eyes. "Run away here." She nodded. "In your head."

She brought his dinner to the study, although she didn't know why exactly. He hadn't moved. Mist rose off the lake on his wallscape; the Alps surrounding it glowed in the serene waters. Chopin's *Adieu Etude* filled the room with its sublime melancholy. It had been playing over and over again since she had first come upon him. She couldn't bring herself to turn it off.

He had left a book of new poems, Ho Peng Kee's *The Edge of the Sky*, face down on the desk. She moved it now and put the ragout in its place. In front of him. Earlier she had taken the key from his desk and brought a bottle of the '28 Haut-Brion up from the wine closet in the basement. It had been breathing for twenty minutes.

"You took such good care of me," she said.

With a flourish, she lifted the cover from the ragout but he didn't look. His head was back. His empty eyes were fixed on the ceiling. She couldn't believe how, even now, his presence filled the room. Filled her completely.

"I don't know how to live without you, Bernardo," she said. "Why didn't you shut me off? I'm not real; I don't want to have these feelings. I'm just a house."

"Louise!"

The house was dreaming over the makings of spinach lasagna in the kitchen.

"Louise." Fly called again from the playroom. "Come read me that buzzy book again. *Hip, Hip, Hip Hippopotamus*."

When Mercedes Nunez woke up on the morning of her fifty-first birthday, there was a man in her head. At least she thought it was a man; his beam barely tickled her neurons. Her mindedness of him was as vague as that of some blurry loser in the back row of her high school class picture. Was this an underage fanboy with a taste for fallen celebs? A sleep-deprived college kid writing a paper on the pioneers of neurality? No – Mercedes's fan base had been skewing geriatric. So, some fossil too feeble to spark enough mindedness to make her blink. He probably remembered her from when she'd been a randy glam-girl pumping neuros onto main menus. That was before her audience passed her by. Before Rake died.

How long had it been since she'd had a beamer? Years. She wasn't sure she wanted one now. She would certainly spend the fee, if it came to that. But at her age she didn't need the hassle of editing her perceptions on the fly. She was used to being all by herself in her head. So she parked him in a blind before she pulled back the covers of her bed. Maybe he'd just signed on for a quick peep show.

Mercedes still slept naked; she only wore anything in bed when she was having sex. How long had it been since she'd had sex? Too long. Mercedes had never really been into porn, although pointy men with thin lips had accused her of it. But in her glory days, she refused to park the beamers when the lights went out. Dai-rinin, her agent, claimed that she had hundreds of them in her head back when she was sleeping with Rake and Kai Lingyu and John Dark and the other stars who had brought neurality to the masses. John Dark used to tease that she was turned on by the idea of all those beamers watching while he licked her nipples. But he was wrong. Part of her felt dirty having them in bed with her and part of her was getting back at her mother for being a slut and yes, part of her liked shocking her audience with her carnality, but the biggest part of her was gloating over what a brave and brilliant career move it was to have public sex in mindspace. She laughed at the memory as she stepped into her slippers, wrapped herself in a robe and scuffed into the bathroom. She had been a girl of many parts. Too bad none of them had quite fit together.

Mercedes took a very hot shower, brushed her wet hair flat and sprayed on a face that made her look twenty years younger. For her beamer; ordinarily she wouldn't have bothered. She slipped into her bra and panties before she let him out of the blind. At first she thought that he might have given up on her, but if she concentrated, she could pick out his pale beam from the dazzle of her thoughts.

She posed in front of the mirror, knowing that he would be watching through her eyes.

Enjoy the view, she thought at him.

Mercedes could recognize her younger self in the reflection. Was her belly still taut? It was, and she still had the indoor pallor that made cubicle rats drool. Neurality appealed most of all to people with lives lit by wallscreens and fluorescents. The cosmetic spray had filled in her wrinkles nicely.

Like what you see? She turned, gave her ass a slap and leered into the mirror.

Oh, I forgot. You can't think back at me. She liked taunting beamers with questions they couldn't answer. They had no way to communicate with her in mindspace and were forbidden by the DayScan contract from contacting her in meatspace.

Know what they used to call people who couldn't speak? At first, insults had helped relieve her unease at having strangers in her head. *Dumb.* She imagined them shouting back at her in frustration. She found out later that many beamers actually liked having their celeb acknowledge their existence.

"Sorry to disappoint you," she said aloud, accepting a black clingy from the copier in her closet, "but if you want full frontal, you'll have to stick around for the evening show." She draped it over her shoulders and it slithered onto her, cutting a demure boat neckline and hemming its skirt just below the knees. *Let's go*, she thought. *We've got things to do.*

There were six messages twinkling on the wall in her living room. She went through them while she crunched on an English muffin and sipped her first cup of neutriceutical coffee. There was a birthday greeting from her younger sister, Laia, who sent vids of Mercedes's niece and nephew. Rafael loved his famous auntie. When was she coming to visit? Luisana peered into the camera and emitted a sound that might have been Say-say or just baby burbling. They were cute, no doubt about that. But did Mercedes miss having kids? Not really. Besides, who would have been the father? Rake had been too sick, Kai too busy and John Dark too damn promiscuous. The feeds said Dark was with Zoe Zanzibar these days. Or was it Kim Barbour? But just because she still followed his antics didn't mean she missed him. There was bad news again from the stockbroker. Mercedes had never figured out Rake's portfolio and had managed it badly since he'd died. If her luck didn't change, she'd be broke before she turned sixty. Ricky Morgan from the library said that the book she wanted was in and if she picked it up around noonish, maybe they could do lunch at Copper? She told Dai-rinin to send a yes and put a smile on it. Someone named Deddy Suryochondro from Surabaya, Indonesia wanted to remake *Finger in the Sky* as a worldscape. Mercedes thought worldscapes were plotless and boring but asked Dai-rinin to find out how much Mr. Suryochondro was offering. The last was from Coco Akita, who said that her housebot was in the shop and that she'd be a little late for the lunch at Copper and that Mercedes should save her a seat. She frowned. Save a seat? When had she made plans with Coco?

Then she remembered what day it was.

She groaned, realizing that she about to be run down by a surprise party. Coco was just scattered enough to have forgotten that lunch was supposed to be a secret. No doubt her friends meant well, but why couldn't they just accept that, after a certain age, some people needed to mourn birthdays, not celebrate them?

She swung her legs onto the couch, settled back into a nest of pillows and waited for the chemicals in the coffee to set fire to her nervous system. Fifty-one wasn't old, was it? She used to think it was. She'd been just twenty-six when she'd turned the storyboard for *Finger in the Sky* over to Kai. And her mother had been forty-eight. Forty-nine? Always grumbling about how the day would come when Mercedes would understand about the whole maiden, mother, crone thing. Well, Mercedes had only been a maiden for about a minute and a half in her teens and she'd never been a mother at all and so why the hell would she bother to worry about the coming of cronedom? She wasn't supposed to die until she was ninety-nine, according to her life clock, and if she gave up bourbon like she kept promising herself she might live even longer. Mimi Burgess down the street was a hundred and ten. The feeds claimed that old Ray Kurzweil was pushing a hundred and thirty. Mercedes was barely middle aged, too young to mope around on a couch at eight-thirty in the morning. She had a neuro to write. She had a beamer paying to spend time in her head.

It wasn't much of a life, but it was all hers.

The studio was in a shed that had held farm equipment back when Rake's great-great-greats had worked the land. It had been tacked onto the main house but there was no direct entry; she had to cross the back porch to get to its only door. Some days that was as much as fresh air as she could stand. She shut the office door and sighed at the impression of Mick Raven shimmering on the wall. He was about to swing his leg off his bicycle as he eyed the Stallworth mansion. What was he going to find there? She wished she knew.

Opposite the wallscreen were floor-to-ceiling shelves crammed with paper books -- upright, vertical, slantwise and misfiled in every possible way. In the middle of the room facing the wallscreen was a vintage A-dec 500 dentist's chair done in paprika vinyl. The matching hygienist's cart next to it now housed the cognizor where her agent lived. There was a cup with a sludge of day-old coffee on the tray atop the cart. She trashed it and set the cup she'd just brewed in its place. Around the dentist's chair were piles of epaper that she needed either to read or reprocess. A ficus had shed a scatter of leaves on the floor in front of the north window. Her busts of Shakespeare and Peter Jackson needed dusting, as did her three Oscars.

She slumped as she remembered that the beamer was contemplating the mess that was her life along with her.

"So," she said aloud, "meet Mr. Chair." She settled onto Rake's A-dec 500 and touched the toggle to reposition it. The chair whined as it lifted and tilted backwards. Rake had loved that chair. "Guess what Mr. Chair? We have a guest with us today, a beamer. Mr. Nobody."

She sipped her coffee.

"You don't mind if we call you that, do you? Oh, and you'll have to excuse Mr. Chair. He's like you, doesn't speak. Neither does Mr. Shakespeare or poor Miss Ficus, going bald over there. Mr. Raven, on the other hand..." She paused and curled her fingers over the keypads built into the arms of the dentist's chair. "What do you say, Mick?"

She and Rake had first introduced Mick Raven in *A Shot of Moonlight*. That was back in the old virtual reality days, when you watched and listened to neuros, instead of inviting them to live between your ears. Mick was Rake's idealized version of himself – healthier, smarter and with better hair. He wasn't a private detective exactly, more like a research librarian with a gun. He cracked wise so relentlessly that at first Mercedes had regarded Mick as a kind of a joke that Rake was playing. But when Mick got popular, Rake had started taking his hero seriously. Mercedes felt as if she had to indulge him. They churned out eleven sequels in five years and had been recoding them for full neurality when she left Rake and their money for John Dark. She'd given Rake permission to do whatever he wanted with their franchise when they broke up, but there had been no more new Mick Raven adventures. Until now.

She snugged the mindreader onto her head, draping its thick cable over the back of the chair.

Okay, she thought. *Where were we?*

Scene Five, thought Dai-rinin. *Packet 342.*

The first time he sees the Stallworth place?

Yes.

Begin. Mercedes concentrated on the wall screen and Mick Raven swung off his bicycle.

5.342: *<impression: shrink Ascot House, Buckinghamshire, England 20%. Hold through 5.350>*

5.343: *<Mick's thoughtstream:>* 122 Fairview is the kind of Mock Tudor mansion that would give Henry VIII nightmares.

5.344: *<subliminal: Henry VIII's face pumping like a heart>*

5.345: *<Mick's thoughtstream:>* Its steep roof is covered in bright terra cotta and the walls are a hodgepodge of herringbone brickwork and stucco the color of smokers' teeth.

5.346: *<smellfx: smoker's breath>*

5.347: *<Mick's thoughtstream:>* Someone painted the half timbers blue — probably a bot.

5.348: *<subliminal: out of control blue bot with blue paintbrush hands painting, walls, windows, doors, etc.>*

5.349: *<Mick's thoughtstream:>* I've never quite understood why bots love to paint things; they don't have the color sense that God gave to shrimp.

5.350: *<neurofx: limbic bump to subchuckle, level 1>*

5.351: *<Mick's thoughtstream:>* The windows on the first floor have heavy iron casements and diamond-shaped leaded panes.

5.352: *<impression: chamfered mullion windows from outside. Hold through 5.358>*

5.353: *<Mick's thoughtstream:>* Anyone looking out of them is going to see a world that is pinched and dark.

5.354: *<lightfx: continuous darkening of 5:352 from edges @ 5% per second>*

5.355: *<Mick's thoughtstream:>* An accurate view maybe, but depressing as hell.

5.356: *<neurofx: increase serotonin uptake .01%>*

5.357: *<Mick's thoughtstream>* If it were my place, I would've long since busted a chair through those windows to let in some sun.

5.358: *<soundfx: glass breaks>*

5.359: *<impression: chair legs punching through 5.352, daggers of flying glass >*

5:360: *<neurofx: 70mV stim to amygdaloidal fear complexes >*

5.361: *<impression: door at the Stud Gate Entrance, Hampton Court Palace>*

5.362: *<impression: Chevrolet housebot opens the door. Hold through 5.366>*

5.363: *<bot's dialog>* Am I making the acquaintance of Mick Raven?

5.364: *<Mick's dialog>* Not if I can help it.

5.365: *<Mick's thoughtstream>* I don't chitchat with bots.

5.366: *<Mick's dialog>* I'm here to see Bishop Stallworth.

There was a tickle in Mercedes's throat and she coughed. The bot's impression shimmered on the wallscreen, waiting for its next line. Her agent waited for her next thought. Brainstorm was waiting for the new Mick Raven neuro.

What was Mercedes waiting for?

"Damn it, Rake," she muttered. He'd always been the one who knew what Mick was doing. This had been his idea, one last Raven adventure. One last adventure for Rake, dying of chronic myelogenous leukemia, one of the few cancers they hadn't beaten. Only he hadn't had near enough time to finish it and now she was left alone to breathe life into Rake's hard-boiled ghost.

5.367: <*Mick's thoughtstream*> I don't want to be here, I don't need this. This is a mistake.

Strike 367, she thought.

Struck, thought her agent.

I'm think I'm done for today.

The contract with Brainstorm requires that you submit The Bishop of Hell by February first.

"I've read the damn contract!" Mercedes was surprised to hear anger in her voice.

Saving, thought Dai-rinin. *Ending session.*

She left the mindreader hanging over the arm of the chair. On her way out of the studio, she kicked at a pile of ep-aper. "Happy birthday, bitch." Plastic sheets sailed across the rug.

Mercedes thought about pouring a bourbon, but had Dai-ri-nin call a carryvan instead. It had two passengers, the Novick boy and Page Buchholtz.

If Page was headed for the birthday party, she didn't let on. "Why Mercedes," she said, "what tears you away from the wall so early?"

"It's ten past eleven in my time zone, Page." Mercedes sat on the bench next to her. She liked Page, even though she was one of the biggest snoops in town. "Ricky Morgan messaged me. I'm picking up a book at the library."

Page gave a teasing giggle. "Oh, is it Ricky now?" The giggle might have fit a teenager but Mercedes thought it was a little tight on a seventy-something who wore size sixteen. "Tell the truth, Mercedes, is it a book you're picking up or..." Her voice got all smoky. "...the librarian?"

The Novick kid looked like he wanted to throw up. Mercedes didn't blame him. It seemed as if all of her friends in town wanted to push her into some man's bed. Rick Morgan was on all of the shortlists -- including her own. But Mercedes wasn't quite sure what do with him. Her problem was that he *knew* he was on Melton's all star bachelor team, and was cocky about it. Mercedes liked it better when she was catching, not pitching.

She swerved to a different subject. "You want to hear something strange?" She leaned into Page. "I woke up this morning with a beamer."

"Really?" Page practically squealed. "What happened to him?"

"Oh, he's still with me." She touched a finger to the corner of her eye. "Peeping you this very moment."

"You're kidding." There wasn't anyone else in Melton remotely famous enough to attract a beamer. Page's face flushed with excitement and she started to babble. "Who is he? What does it feel like? How do you know he's a he?"

Mercedes was taken aback by the intensity of her reaction. She reminded Page that celebs were never sure who was beaming into their heads. "So I can't swear that he's a man," she said, "but back when I used to have crowds, I could figure out whether beamers were men or women by what senses they paid attention to. Women like smell and taste. Men watch."

"Oh my *god*!" Page goggled as if she were the second coming of Zoe Zanzibar. "That is so amazing."

Even the Novick kid seemed impressed.

When the carryvan stopped at the Highmarket, Page floated off, as starstruck as the first time she'd met Mercedes. Mercedes cursed her own foolishness. Page would bring this bit of gossip to every wall in town. Mercedes had intended to abandon what little fame she'd left when she moved to Melton. So what if all her friends here knew that she had been a neurality star once? Her day had passed. Scripted neuros like *The Bishop of Hell* were passé. Neurality was all about plotless worldscapes and unscripted sense dumps these days.

So why was Page acting like a drooling fan again?

"Lady." Young Novick pulled one of his earstones out. "You maded *Sleeping on Razors,* did you?"

"I worked on it, yes."

"With John Dark?"

"That's right."

"Is total." He nodded approval. "What be he like? Feeds say he gets the ladies. "

She didn't hesitate. "Horny as two minks and a goat."

The kid grinned and popped the earstone back in. "You most lucky."

The carryvan dropped her off in front of the library but she scuttled to the rear entrance. She was spooked and didn't want to run the gauntlet of the front desk and the neurocom and the mediapod and the stacks of books to get to Ricky's office.

All your fault, Mr. Nobody, she thought, as she stole up to the third floor. *You're giving me a reputation.* Ricky wasn't in, so she had Dai-rinin message him. Minutes later, there came a tap at the door.

"Are you decent?" said Ricky.

She opened the door and pulled him in by the arm. "I'm not here."

"Let me know when you arrive, will you?" He gave her a polite kiss. "I'm taking you to lunch."

"You and how many others?"

He stepped away from her, then waggled a finger in mock severity.

"So it's true," she said.

"Now I see why you make detective neuros."

"Raven isn't a detective and I do plenty of other stuff." She sighed. "Let's have the guest list."

"There'll be fifteen for sure, maybe as many as eighteen, and that's all I'm saying." He showed her a crooked smile. "You'll know everybody."

She settled onto the chair behind his desk. "You shouldn't have."

"I didn't." He sorted through a stack of books in a cart by the door. "Janeel and Page put this together."

"I don't like surprises, Ricky."

"And this isn't going to be one." He dropped a book in front of her.

"This him?" Mercedes picked up *Raymond Chandler: Stories and Early Novels.*

"I can't believe you've never read Chandler," said Ricky. "His detective, Marlowe, could be Mick Raven's grandfather."

She opened the book to a random page. "I needed a drink," she read aloud, "I needed a lot of life insurance, I needed a vacation, I needed a home in the country. What I had was a coat, a hat and a gun."

"See?" said Ricky. "You could steal from him six days a week and nobody would know it wasn't you."

"What makes you think I need to steal from anyone?"

"Ah, you're in a fighting mood today." He held up both hands in surrender. "All hail Mercedes Nunez, queen of ...."

She reached into the candy dish on his desk and threw a jelly bean at him.

In the fast company she'd kept as a young woman, nobody would have noticed Ricky Morgan. He was fifty-two and looked as if he belonged behind a desk in some drab second floor office with a view of the company parking lot. Service in the Air Force had straightened his backbone but had left him looking a little rigid. But as soon as he started talking, everything changed. He spoke in complete sentences with a lilting Alabama accent and made eye contact. His laugh made strangers smile. He and Mercedes had dated three times, but were still circling each other. The way she added him up, there were about as many possibilities as liabilities. He had charm, but he spread it promiscuously. He was divorced, but that proved that he was willing to commit.

As they walked down Lyon Street, Mercedes let him take her hand. "If things gets too awful, just give me a sign. I'll get you out."

"I'll be all right. They're friends. They mean well."

"We love you, Mercedes. We're happy you live here with us."

She squeezed his hand but said nothing.

"So I was wondering if you might consider giving a talk at one of my First Friday Forums."

"What kind of talk?"

"Just basic stuff, like where do you get your ideas, how a project gets started. I'm sure there'd be a big turnout. You've lived here almost two years now and you're still our number one request at the neurocom. The demand was there so I've bought pretty much everything you've done."

"Really?" Mercedes had never accessed the library's neurocom. "The artsy stuff? *Suit Of Clay*? *BlueSkin*?"

"All of them, although I've put warnings on the sexy material and restricted access. You're our local celebrity, Mercedes. You've won Oscars."

"For Achievement in Neurological Special Effects." She snorted. "The ones they give away in the afternoon ceremony."

"Just think about it, all right? It would mean a lot to people."

Copper's lone wallscreen was set to a view of 11th Street, so that whether diners looked out the window or at the wall, they saw the same scene. Mercedes appreciated the understated view – too many restaurants had walls set to calving icebergs or Martian dust storms or, worst of all, vintage football. A copper bar with a dozen stools stretched to the left of the restaurant's entrance. To the right was an open kitchen. Copper-topped tables were scattered artfully around the L-shaped dining room.

Mercedes was surprised when they were shown to a table for two by the bar. As soon as they were seated, however, the singing began.

"*Happy birthday to you...*"

Mercedes couldn't see the singers because the party was around the corner.

"*Happy birthday to you....*"

Rick nodded at the wall. For the first time ever, it had turned its gaze inward from the street. Half of the wall showed a long table surrounded by Mercedes's party. She and Ricky watched themselves on the other half. "It would be nice if you looked surprised," he murmured.

"*Happy birthday dear Mercedes
Happy birthday to you*!"

There was wild applause as she came around the corner; she felt the sound in her bones. What was it Rick had said? *We love you, Mercedes.* Many people in her life had spoken of love but most of them had just been breathing on her. However in this moment she could make herself believe that these people with their glowing faces felt something like true affection for her. Her own face felt odd and she realized that a smile had spread across it, stretching muscles she hadn't used since Rake had died.

"Speech, speech!" called Matti Ryberg.

"Are you surprised?" said Barb Bovyn as she handed Mercedes and Ricky flutes of champagne.

Everyone raised their glasses to her. "To Mercedes," called Page. Mercedes wanted to acknowledge the toast but there was a brick caught in her throat so she just clicked flutes with those nearest her.

"I fear," said Ricky, "that she's been struck dumb."

Mercedes nudged him with her elbow. "Thank you," she said and then coughed. "Thank you all for being so wonderful and so crazy."

Everybody laughed.

"Is there a seat for me?" she said.

As she took her place she began to pick out individual faces. Page and Janeel were conferring at the far end of the table. Coco Akita had made it on time after all. There was a question in her eyes; Mercedes answered it by holding a forefinger to her lips.

The Duttons, her next door neighbors, were chatting with Billy and Ambati, who she'd met at Heartprints, her grief support group. She waved to Steve Broulidakis, who had been Rake's doctor. Bromley, who built racing bicycles, said something that made Donna DiMatta, the electrician who had wired her studio, laugh. Both were watching Mercedes closely. Some of these people had been Rake's friends first but they had stuck by her in the year since he'd died. Now Page and Janeel stared at her too, seeming about to burst with conspiratorial excitement. Then Mercedes noticed the man sitting directly behind them with his back turned to the table.

Page clinked a butter knife against her champagne flute.

"Another surprise for our birthday girl," she said. "A special guest."

The man stood, his back still to them. Mercedes rested both hands on the edge of table but as the man turned, she pushed back until her arms were straight. She gripped the table as if she were afraid her chair might collapse. Her friends started clapping. Then everyone in the restaurant was on their feet.

John Dark bowed to her, a grin on his thin lips.

He was still ridiculously handsome and, as always, flamboyantly dressed. If his celebrity was not enough to bring him to the center of every room's attention, his appearance was. He wore a black velveteen frock coat with silver buttons over a powder blue waistcoat. His trousers were black-pinstriped and his loose white shirt was open at the neck. He seemed not to have aged in the nine years since she'd last seen him, but then he wouldn't. He was in his eighties, but as long as Dow Chemical kept making surgical poly he would continue to stop foolish hearts.

As the applause faded, Janeel spoke up. "He came all the way from Indonesia to see you, Mercedes. What was the name of the town again, John?"

"Surabaya." Dark's voice always made Mercedes think of a cat purring. "A bit more than a town, Janeel -- eight million people live there. The second largest city in Indonesia."

Mercedes fought to steady herself against the whirlwind of emotions that Dark always stirred in her. *Look, Mr. Nobody*, she thought at her beamer. *Look at all that star power.*

The party broke up just before two-thirty. Dr. Broulidakis had patients to see and as soon as he bowed out, the others made their excuses. Ricky had to get back to the library. How was the birthday girl going to get home? John Dark had rented a carbot at the airport and said he could give rides, space permitting.

He squeezed Page, Lionel and Klára Dutton, Mercedes, and himself into a Volkswagen Sturm. Mercedes found herself wedged against Dark. Being so close to him brought back memories, not all unpleasant. Nobody said much as the carbot passed down the streets of Melton. Now that the party was over, her friends seemed stricken by their proximity to the famous man. The carbot dropped Page off, and moments later pulled up to Mercedes's house. The Duttons thanked Dark as effusively as if he'd just saved their lives.

She watched her neighbors trudge across Rake's overgrown lawn – except it was her lawn now. She hadn't quite realized that before, but having Dark here made her see her life through his eyes. He'd be wondering what she was doing with a lawn. And a house.

Dark nudged her. "Too spooked to invite an old friend in?"

"Not spooked at all," she said, "old friend." What else could she do? If she turned him away, he would probably have the carbot drive to the high school so he could spend the afternoon hitting on sophomores. Besides, Mercedes doubted that he'd come just for her birthday. He wanted something.

"You still have that glow, Mercedes," said Dark. "Your superpower. Use it for good."

"Don't start." She walked him to the front door. "Dai-rinin?" she said. The lock clicked open.

"Who knew that living in the country would agree so well with you. Couldn't keep my eyes off you at lunch."

Even though she had her back to him, she could feel the heat in his voice. She warned herself not to do anything stupid. This *was* John Dark. "It's just a look I sprayed on this morning." She pushed the door open. "It'll wash off."

He brushed against her arm as he passed into the house. "Not all of it."

She pointed him at the couch in the living room and then pulled a chair in from the kitchen. She might have been embarrassed had a stranger seen the crust of English muffin from breakfast on the coffee table, but Dark knew from experience that she was no housekeeper.

"Terrible news about Rake," he said.

"News?" She turned the kitchen chair around and straddled it with the back facing him. "We buried him a year ago."

"My agent sent flowers, yes?"

"The biggest bouquet in the church."

He leaned back and unbuttoned his jacket. "Worked with him years ago at Disney -- before they sold everything off." It fell open over the blue waistcoat. "Didn't seem like the church type."

"He got scared at the end. I think he blindfolded himself with religion so he didn't have to see what was coming."

"And you moved here to ease his pain."

"He was in remission when he asked me and I had nothing better to do after *Suit of Clay* gassed." She shrugged. "I knew he was sick, but he'd always been sick. His doctors claimed they could manage the cancer. They did, for a while."

"Terrible, yes."

"We never slept together," she said. "Here, I mean." She had no idea why she'd blurted this out, except that she hadn't appreciated the crack about easing Rake's pain. Dark always thought that he knew more about her than he really did.

He let it pass. "Working on anything?"

"We started a new Mick Raven before the relapse."

"Scripted is a hard sell these days." He reached into the pocket of his frock coat. "Even for me." He showed her a silver hip flask. "Still poisoning yourself with bourbon?"

"What is this, Dark? What do you want?"

"Evan Williams Single Barrel Vintage." He set it on the coffee table. "Got to build up my courage, yes?"

"For what?" She laughed. "You're such a liar."

"*My* superpower." He laughed too.

She went to the kitchen. "You're doing well," she called. "At least that's what the feeds say." Dai-rinin pushed two glasses out of the dishcopier. "Will you be nominated for *The Last Lancelot*?"

"Probably." He sounded uncharacteristically glum. "But so what? Been coasting on brains and good looks for years. Can't remember the last time I had a new idea."

"Tell me about it." She set the glasses in front of him.

"Not that there's a market for ideas. All those damn worldscapes. People claim that they don't want to be ordered around in their own heads -- but people are morons. They need to be told what to do." He poured a couple of centimeters of bourbon into her glass. "Ran into your mother last month at Antonio's."

"Really?" She took the glass from him. "Did you sleep with her?"

"That was a mistake, Mercedes. You should have warned me." He poured himself a drink. "She said she misses you."

"You want me to toss you out?" She held her thumb and forefinger just a sliver apart. "You're this close to being on the street, Dark."

"The glow becomes a fire, yes. Remember how we burned together?" He offered her his glass. "So much history between us." Reluctantly she clinked hers against it. "Not all of it bad."

She tasted the whiskey. It was as she remembered Williams, starting sweet but finishing dry with hints of oak and caramel and apples. It had been a while since she'd had expensive bourbon. "Tell me about this Deddy Suryochondro. From Indonesia. Is he even real?"

He tapped the cushion of the couch beside him. She took another drink and scooted around the coffee table.

"A fallback," he said, "in case you wouldn't see me."

"How could I not see you?" She sat an arm's length from him. "You showed up at my party. You dazzled all my friends."

"Deft move, yes?" He gave her a look that would melt chocolate. "Gives you a chance to get used to the idea that I'm back."

"Back?"

"And now here we are. The two of us, alone in your house. Talking. Not shouting." He swirled bourbon in his glass. "Not like when you left."

"I hated you then."

He nodded. "That made me want you even more. You're hard to give up, Mercedes."

She started. How could she have been so oblivious? Dark never gave up. "My surprise party," she said, "That wasn't them. It was you."

"Your friend Page picked the restaurant. Janeel invited everyone."

"They came to see you." She set her empty glass down as if it might explode. "Lunch with John Dark. Something to tell the grandkids."

"They're nice people. But not like us."

"I'm not like you."

"We're drifting, Mercedes. We need to find a new way."

"What do you want, Dark?"

"Want?" He held up his hand with fingers spread. "Want an Oscar for *Lancelot*, even though it's crap." He ticked his thumb. "Want inspiration. Something to make me excited again." He ticked his forefinger. "Want to work with you again." Another finger. "Want to undress you." Another finger, and the pinky. "Then make love."

She laughed at him. And at herself. She'd known he would say something like this when she'd first seen him at Copper. And yet she'd tried to deny that she knew, because she wasn't sure how she would reply.

"You did say want." Spots of color bloomed on his cheeks. She'd always liked the way he blushed. "Tell me it's out of the question."

"You're so good at being you, Dark. How often does that line work?"

He grinned.

"And you know why it works? Because of the Oscars and the money and a body that isn't even yours?"

"It's a nice body." Dark's voice was husky. "Paid good money for this body."

She felt a dizziness that had nothing to do with alcohol. "I don't want charity."

He leaned close and whispered. "And I don't give it."

She took him to Rake's bed because hers was just a twin in the guest room. As they lay entangled afterwards, Mercedes examined her feelings. Did she feel guilty? Angry? Confused? No, no and no. She felt content and warm and alive. She had been cooped up in her head for so long that her body had gone numb.

"You want to collaborate, Dark?"

"That was want number two." He frowned. "Or was it three?"

"Our first project is finishing the Mick Raven."

"Scripted is hard to..."

She clamped a hand over his mouth. "Mick Raven. And here in Melton, where all my friends live."

He nodded.

She let her hand drop and trace the line of his chin. "You worked hard to get me into bed. Devious, but I appreciate the effort. Nobody else was making one."

"People are morons."

"How many times have I taken you back, Dark?"

He propped himself up on an elbow. "Are you talking about times when we were together and had a spat, or the times that we were actually separated?"

She sighed. "How long is this time?"

"Forever and ever, amen. Our new way, Mercedes." She had never seen him embarrassed before. "Going to be eighty-three in January, and..."

Her hand went back over his mouth. "And when a man gets to be your age he starts thinking about settling down with just one good woman."

He nipped at her palm and she jerked her hand away, laughing. Then she pitched back onto her pillow and covered her face with the sheet.

"What?" said Dark.

"I forgot," she said, still laughing. "Just like in the old days. I have a beamer, Dark." She peeked at him from beneath the sheet. "And I forgot to put him in a blind -- sorry." She growled. "You took him for one hell of a ride."

"I know."

She pulled the sheet completely off her face and stared.

"Meet Mr. Nobody." He shrugged. "One way or another, I was going to be with you today."

Mercedes was shocked, but not that he would masturbeam. The gossip feeds claimed celebrities did it all the time. She had secretly tried it once herself, but it had only given her a headache. No, what surprised her was that he would admit it. "Contact in meatspace, Dark." She giggled. "I could sue." Maybe he really had found a new way. "Take you for millions."

"Go ahead." He kissed her. "Except if we get married, you'd just be suing yourself."

"Married?"

"Married, yes."

She tasted the word and found it to her liking. It sat sweet on the tongue with a resiny, almond warmth and a finish of freshly mown hay. *So how was it for you?* she thought. *Good both ways?*

"Very enjoyable." He tugged at the sheet and it slipped off her shoulders. "But should be even better next time."

Capture 06/15/2051, Kerwin Hospital ICU, 09:12:32

. . . and my writer pals used to tease that I married Captain Kirk.

A clarification, please? Are you referring to William Shatner, who died in 2023? Or is this Chris Pine, who was cast in the early remakes? It appears he has retired. Perhaps you mean the new one? Jools Bear?

No, you. Kirk Anderson. People used to call you that, remember? First man to set foot on Phobos? Pilot on the Mars landing team? Captain Kirk.

I do not understand. Clearly I participated in those missions since they are on the record. But I was never captain of anything.

A joke, Andy. They were teasing you. It's why you hated your first name.

Noted. Go on.

No, this is impossible. I feel like I'm talking to an intelligent fucking database, not my husband. I don't know where to begin with you.

Please, Zoe. I cannot do this without you. Go on.

Okay, okay, but do me a favor? Use some contractions, will you? Contractions are your friends.

Noted.

Do you know when we met?

I haven't yet had the chance to review that capture. We were married in 2043. Presumably we met before that?

Not much before. Where were you on Saturday, May 17, 2042? Check your captures.

The capture shows that I flew from Spaceways headquarters at Spaceport America to the LaGuardia Hub in New York and spent the day in Manhattan at the Metropolitan Museum. That night I gave the keynote address at the Nebula Awards banquet in the Crown Plaza Hotel but my caps were disengaged. The Nebula is awarded each year by the World Science Fiction Writers....

I was nominated that year for best livebook, *Shadows on the Sun*. You came up to me at the reception, said you were a fan. That you had all five of my Sidewise series in your earstone when you launched for Mars that first time. You joked you had a thing for Nacky Martinez. I was thrilled and flattered. After all, you were top of the main menu, one of the six hero marsnauts. Things I'd only imagined, you'd actually done. And you'd read my work and you were flirting with me and, holy shit, you were Captain Kirk. When people—friends, famous writers—tried to break into our conversation, they just bounced off us. Nobody remembers who won what award that night, but lots of people still talk about how we locked in.

I just looked it up. You lost that Nebula.

Yeah. Thanks for reminding me.

You had on a hat.

A hat? Okay. But I always wore hats back then. It was a way to stand out, part of my brand—for all the good it did me. My hair was a three act tragedy anyway, so I wore a lot of hats.

This one was a bowler hat. It was blue—midnight blue. With a powder blue band. Thin, I remember the hatband was very thin.

Maybe. I don't remember that one. Nice try, though.

Tell me more. What happened next?

Jesus, this is so wrong...No, I'm sorry, Andy. Give me your hand. You always had such delicate hands. Such clever fingers.

I can still remember that my mom had an old Baldwin upright piano that she wanted me to learn to play, but my hands were too small. You're crying. Are you crying?

I am not. Just shut up and listen. This isn't easy and I'm only saying it because maybe the best part of you is still trapped in there like they claim and just maybe this augment really can set it free. So, we were sitting at different tables at the banquet but after it was over, you found me again and asked if I wanted to go out for drinks. We escaped the hotel, looking for a place to be alone, and found a night-shifted Indonesian restaurant with a bar a couple of blocks away. It was called Fatty Prawn or Fatty Crab—Fatty Something. We sat at the bar and switched from alcohol to inhalers and talked. A lot. Pretty much the rest of the night, in fact. Considering that you were a man and famous and ex-Air Force, you were a good listener. You wanted to know how hard it was to get published and where I got my plots and who I like to read. I was impressed that you had read a lot of the classic science fiction old-timers like Kress and LeGuin and Bacigalupi. You told me what I got wrong about living in space, and then raved about stuff in my books that you thought nobody but spacers knew. Around four in the morning we got hungry and since you'd never had Indonesian before, we split a gado-gado salad with egg and tofu. I spent too much time deconstructing my divorce and you were polite about yours. You said your ex griped about how you spent too much time in space, and I made a joke about how Kass would have said the same thing about me. I asked if you were ever scared out there and you said sure, and that landings were worse than the launches because you had so much time leading up to them. You used to wake up on the outbound trips in a sweat. To change the subject, I told you about waking up with entire scenes or story outlines in my head and how I had to get up in the middle of the night and write them down or I would lose them. You made a crack about wanting to see that in person. The restaurant was about to close for the morning and, by that time, dessert sex was definitely on the menu, so I asked if you ever got horny on a mission. That's how I found out that one of the side effects of the anti-radiation drugs was low testosterone levels. We established that you were no longer taking them. I would have invited you back to my room right then only you told me that you had to catch a seven-twenty flight back to El Paso. There still might have been enough time, except that I was rooming with Rachel van der Haak, and, when we had gotten high before the banquet, we had promised each other we'd steer clear of men while our shields were down. And of course, when I thought about it, there was the awkward fact that you were twenty years older than I was. A girl has got to wonder what's up with her when she wants to take daddy to bed.

I am nineteen years and three months older than you.

And then there was your urgency. I mean, you had me at Mars, Mr. Space Hero, but I had the sense that you wanted way more from me than I had to give. All I had in mind was a test drive, but it seemed as if you were already thinking about making a down payment. When you said you could cancel an appearance on Newsmelt so you could be back in New York in three days, it was a serious turn-on, but I was also worried. Blowing off one of the top news sites? For me? Why? I guessed maybe you were running out of time before your next mission. I didn't realize that you were . . . .

Go on.

No, I can't. I just can't—how do I do this? Turn the augment off.

Zoe, please.

You hear me? That was the deal. They promised whenever I wanted.

Capture 06/15/2051, Kerwin Hospital ICU, 09:37:18, Augment disengaged by request

Andy? Look at me, Andy. Over here. Good. Who am I, Andy?

You are . . . it's something about science fiction. And a blue hat.

What's my name?

Come close. Let me look at you . . . oh, it's on the tip of my tongue. Nacky Martinez? First officer of the Starship *Sidewise*?

She's a character, Andy. Made up. Someone I wrote about.

You're a writer?

Capture 06/17/2051, Kerwin Hospital Assisted Care Facility, 14:47:03

. . . because I was too infatuated to be suspicious about your secret back then. I know you don't remember this, Andy, but I was stupid in love with you when we were first married. Maybe the augment can't see that, but anyone who looks at your captures can. On the record, as you would say. So, yeah, the fact that you always wore caps and recorded almost everything that happened to you didn't bother me back then. I guess I told myself that it was some reputation management scheme that Spaceways had ordered up. And of course, you were writing the sequel to your memoir. What do Mr. and Ms. Space Hero do on their days off? Why look, they sit together on the couch when they write! And she still uses her fingers to type—isn't that quaint, a science fiction writer still pounding a keyboard in the era of thought recognition!

You never published that book.

No.

Or any other. Why?

You know, people message me about that all the time, like it was some kind of tragedy. I had something to say when I was young and naive. I said it. And pretty damn well: eight livebooks worth. Fifty novas. It's just that after I met you, I needed to make the most of our time together. And since you launched into the Vincente Event, I've been busy being the good wife.

I was the best qualified pilot, Zoe. And I was already compromised, so I had the least to lose. In a crisis like that, there were no easy answers. I consulted with Spaceways and we weighed the tradeoffs and we reached a decision. I had friends on that orbital. Drew Bantry . . .

Drew was already dead. He just hadn't fallen down yet. And you were not a tradeoff, Andy. You were my fucking husband.

I can see now how hard it must have been for you.

Oh, you saw it then, too. Which is why you never asked my permission, because you knew . . .

Go on.

What the hell were we talking about? How I had no suspicions about what the captures meant. That you were sick. I remember thinking how boring ten thousand hours of unedited recordings were going to be. Even to us, even when we were old. Old and forgetful . . . .

Zoe?

I'm fine. I'm just not feeling very brave today. Anyway, I did have a problem with all the captures of us making love. I mean, the first couple of times, I'll grant you it was a turn-on. We'd lose ourselves in bed, and then afterwards watch ourselves doing it and sometimes we were so beautifully in sync that we'd get hot and go back for seconds. But what bothered me was that you were capturing us watching the captures. I didn't get why you would do that. When I realized that recording wasn't just a once-in-a-while kink, that you wanted to capture us every time we had sex, it wasn't erotic anymore. It was kind of creepy.

I can't locate any sex captures after 2045. Did we stop having sex?

No. I just made you check the caps at the bedroom door. So stop looking. You want to know what we were like back then, try scanning some of our private book clubs. We'd both read the same book and then we'd go out to dinner at a nice restaurant and talk about it. I remember being surprised at some of your choices. *The Marvelous Land of Oz. Lolita. Wolf Hall. A Visit From the Goon Squad.* They didn't seem like the kinds of reading an Air Force jock would choose. You were a Hemingway and Heinlein kind of guy.

Was I trying to impress you?

I don't know why. I was already plenty impressed. Maybe you were trying to send me a message with all of those plots about secret pasts and transformations.

Go on. This was where? When?

At first in Brooklyn, where I was living when we met. There's another reason I should have been suspicious your urgency. You claimed you didn't care where we lived as long as we spent as much time as possible together. Wasn't true—you hated cities. But most of my friends were in New York and most of yours had moved to space or Mars. Your folks were dead and your sister had disappeared into some Digitalist coop, waiting for the Singularity. So when my mother died and left me the house in Bedford, we moved up there in the spring of 2045. You had the second installment of your book deal to write and when I switched to your agent, I started seeing celebrity level advances too, so there was plenty of money. By then you were showing early symptoms. You claimed you'd left Spaceways, although you still flew out here to Kerwin five or six times a year for therapy. It seemed to be working, you said we would still have years together. My mom had been into flowers but she had an asparagus patch and some raspberries and you started your first vegetable garden that summer. You were good at it, said you liked it better than space hydroponics. Spinach and lettuce and asparagus in the spring, then beans and corn and summer squash and tomatoes and melons. You were happy, I think. I know I was.

Capture 06/25/2051, Kerwin Hospital Assisted Care Facility, 16:17:53

. . . you were so skeptical about the Singularity is why.

The Kurzweil augmentation has nothing to do with the Singularity.

Yeah, sure. It's just a cognitive prosthesis, *la-la*. A life experience database, *la-la-la*. An AI mediated memory enhancement that may help restore your loved one's mental competence *la-la-la-dee-da*. I've browsed all the sites, Andy. Besides, I was writing about this shit before Ray Kurzweil actually uploaded.

Ray Kurzweil is dead. I'm still alive.

Are you, Andy? Are you sure about that?

I don't know why you are being so cruel, Zoe.

Because you made so many decisions about us without telling me. Maybe you didn't know just how sick you were when we met, but you could easily have found out. I had a right to know. And maybe you were hoping that you'd never get that call from Spaceways, but you knew exactly what you would do if it did come.

I was an astronaut, Zoe. That was never a secret.

No, what was a secret was all that fucked-up cosmic ray research. Because nobody but crazy people with a death wish would ever have volunteered to go to space if they knew that there was no real protection against getting your telomeres burned off by the radiation. Sure, you can duck and cover from a solar flare, but what about the gajillions of ultra-high energy ions? Theoretically you can generate a magnetic shield. Or maybe you can stuff your astronauts with anti-radiation wonder drugs? But just in case it doesn't work, better make sure that everyone on the Mars crew is over forty. That way if Captain Kirk falls apart in twenty or thirty years, Spaceways won't look so bad.

Go on.

I will. Maybe you hadn't checked out the secret radiation assessments from the first Mars mission when we first met. Maybe you didn't want to know. But once I was your wife, I did. Let me read the executive summary to you. "Exposure to radiation during the mission has had significant short and long impacts on the central nervous systems of all crew members. Despite best mitigation practices, whole body effective doses ranged from 0.4 to 0.7 sieverts. Galactic cosmic radiation in the form of high-mass, energetic ions destroyed an average of 4% of the crew's cells, while 13% of critical brain regions have likely been compromised. Reports of short term impairments of behavior and cognition were widely noted throughout the three year mission. Longitudinal studies of the astronaut corps point to a significant increase in risk of degenerative brain diseases. In particular, there appears to have been an acceleration of plaque pathology associated with Alzheimer 's disease." Let's do the math, Andy. You get an estimated dose of between 0.4 to 0.7 sieverts during your first mission and you go to Mars twice. So call it a sievert and change. Which is why you were one grounded astronaut.

All that's on the record.

What's EPA's maximum yearly dose for a radiation worker here on earth?

I don't have immediate access to that data. I can look it up.

Yes, you can—it's on the record. Fifty millisieverts. How about for emergency workers involved in a lifesaving operation?

Zoe, I . . . .

Two hundred and fifty millisieverts.

There are always risks.

For which you make tradeoffs, I get that. So the tradeoff here is X number of years of your life for two tickets to Mars. Which you decided before you met me, so I'll give you a pass on that. Once you walked me through it, I sort of got how that was the price you paid to become who you wanted to be. Although you waited long enough to let me in on your little secret. But that wasn't your last tradeoff. Because Spaceways fell down on their project management during the outfitting of Orbital Seven. They didn't lift enough solar flare shelters to house everybody on the construction crew. So when Professor Vincente predicted an X2 class flare that would cook half the people onboard in a storm of hot protons, management turned to sixty-year old Captain Kirk, even though he'd been grounded. They pointed out that since he didn't have all that much time before the Alzheimer's plaques chewed what was left of his memory, maybe he might consider riding the torch one last time to ferry an emergency shelter up to save their corporate asses. Or maybe our Space Hero checked in all on his own and volunteered for their fucking suicide mission.

It wasn't a suicide mission , Zoe. I came back.

And here you are, Andy. And here I am. But it's not working.

Capture 06/30/2051, Kerwin Hospital ICU, 11:02:53
. . . or are you too busy with your life review? Ten thousand hours of captures is a lot to digest, even on fast-forward.

The record is eleven thousand two hundred and eighty-four hours long, not including the current capture.

Noted. Find anything worth bookmarking?

It would be a dull movie if it wasn't all about me.

I heard about your ex yesterday on Newsmelt. I'm sorry. I didn't realize she'd emigrated to Mars.

Apparently she wanted to get to space as much as I did. I don't know why I didn't know that. It's odd, but none of the pix and vids I have look like her.

You remember her then?

Just flashes, but they're very vivid. Like she was lit up by a lightning strike.

They're talking about bringing the rest of the colonists back home.

Maybe. But they'll have to handcuff them and drag them kicking and screaming onto the relief ships—I know those people. And why bother? Many of them won't survive the trip back.

Space will kill you any which way it can. You told me that on our third date.

I try not to pay attention. It's been a long time since there's been any good news from outer space. I think we need to start over on Mars. The thing to do is capture a comet, hollow it out and use it as a colony ship. The ice shields you from cosmic rays on the outbound. Send the colonists down in landers and then crash the comet. Solves both the water and the radiation problem.

Capture a comet? And how the hell do we do that? With a tractor beam? A magic lasso?

Get your science fiction friends working on it. If it's crazy enough, the engineers will come sniffing around.

I'll see what I can do. I met the Zhangs on the way in today. I thought I was your only visitor. We had a nice chat. And the baby was cute. What's her name again?

Andee. A-N-D double E

That's what I thought they said. After you.

Kristen was lucky. They pushed her to the front of the line so she was one of the first into the shelter. The last three in got a significant dose. One of them died on the way back down.

Drew Bantry.

They were his people. He waited until they were all safe.

You and he saved a lot of lives that day, Captain Kirk. It's on the record for all to see.

Enough, Zoe. What do you have for me today?

Apologies.

Go on.

I'm sorry for the way I spoke to you last time. That's why I missed the last few visits. I don't trust myself to say the right thing anymore. I can't filter out my feelings when I see you like this. I just blurt. Spew. It's not good.

Noted.

But here's the thing. I don't think I'll be accessing your augment after you're . . . gone. Dead. You know, now I can visit the hospital here, and see you. Your face, your body, arms, hands. But some avatar, no. It's too hard. There have been times the last few weeks when I felt like you're here with me, but that's only because I want you back. But mostly I don't think this thing that talks to me is you. I'm sorry.

Why not?

There's still too much missing, even if the augment can review your captures and all that input from before you started wearing the caps. Yes, we can talk about our lives together, but I still have to tell you things you should know. And now you're cracking jokes, so it's even harder. How can I tell whether what's sad or happy or angry is you or clever algorithms? I don't know, Andy. When are you going to say I love you? How will I know whether you really do, or if it's just something else you needed to be reminded of?

I do, Zoe. Here, I'll turn the augment off, so you can hear it from me. From this body, as you say. These lips.

No, honey, you don't need to . . . .

Capture 06/30/2051, Kerwin Hospital ICU, 11:15:18, Augment disengaged by request

Okay? Here I am. And I know who you are. I do. You're my famous wife, the writer. Nackey Martinez. You want to go. I don't want you to go. Give me your hand.

Aye, Captain.

Stay with me. Will you do that?

For a while.

And write more books. You know, about your adventures in space. That's important. And maybe . . . could get me my snacks? The food here is horrible. You know the ones. Mom always used to make banana slices with a smear of peanut butter when I got home from school. My snacks. Are you crying, Nackey? You're crying.

Yes.

"When in the course of human events…"

As Silk spoke, fluffy clouds formed the phrase in a Magritte sky, which was simultaneously noon and dusk. While Remeny could appreciate the control Silk had over his softtime domain, she wished he wouldn't steer their meeting in an artsy direction. They had work to do.

"Wait," said Botão, "what about *we the people*?"

"That's the other one." Silk shot her a (.1) anger blip fading to (.7) irritation. "The Constitution."

"But we're the people we're talking about." Botão ignored Silk's blippage. "That's the whole point."

"Human events," said Silk. "If you'd wait just a second, I'm getting to the people part."

Botão had only been assigned to their school coop team for a month now and Remeny knew what she did not: Silk didn't like to be challenged, especially not in his own domain. They had chosen his corner of virtuality because Silk had enough excess capacity to host them all, but his was not the ideal place to plot their pretend revolution. The opening words of the Declaration of Independence were going wispy above them.

"Get on with it then," said Sturm. "And skip the special effects."

"When in the course of human events," Silk said, "it becomes necessary for one *people* to dissolve the political bands which have connected them with another…"

"Okay," said Botão.

"…and to assume among the powers of the earth, the separate and equal station to which the Laws of Nature and of Nature's God entitle them, a decent respect to the opinions of mankind requires that they should declare the causes which impel them to the separation."

The four others – Remeny, Sturm, Botão and Toybox – scanned each other and then turned on Silk. They had agreed to close all private channels and keep their avatars emotionally transparent, so the air filled with blips of confusion and disapproval.

"Laws of Nature?" said Toybox. "What the hell is that about?"

"Maybe relativity." Sturm's scorn blip started at (.3) and climbed.

"They didn't even have relativity back then."

"They did, they were just too stupid to realize it."

"Mankind? What about the other fifty-two percent?" Botão was laughing now. "And who is Nature's God?"

"Exactly," said Sturm. "I call bullshit. Crusty oldschool bullshit."

Remeny kept quiet; she focused on Silk, who was waiting for them to calm down. "Agreed," he said. "But it will mean something to the old people because Thomas Jefferson wrote this stuff."

"Who's he and so what?" said Toybox.

"Jefferson as in Jefferson County," said Remeny. "As in where we live."

"I live in softtime." At (.9+), Toybox's rage was nearly unreadable – but then he was always shouting. "That's where I live."

Silk waved a hand in front of his face, as if the blip was a bad smell. "History is important to reality snobs," he said. "This gets their attention."

Remeny noticed that he was keeping his temper in check. She was definitely interested in Silk; poise was something she looked for in a boyfriend.

"So will making their lights flicker," said Toybox. This was why he had flunked one coop already. "Crashing their flix."

"We're not talking about anything like that," said Botão. "We're students, not terrorists."

"Speak for yourself." Sturm spread his hands and between them appeared an oldschool clock. "Revolutions don't play by the rules." Its face showed two minutes to midnight.

Remeny couldn't believe Sturm, of all people, aligning himself with terrorists. She agreed with Botão; she didn't really care about the revolution. All she wanted was to get a grade for her senior cooperative, graduate and never log on to the Jefferson County Educational Oversight Service again. The problem was that a third of her grade for coop was for contribution to the team's cooperative culture. The senior coop was supposed to demonstrate to the EOS that students had the social skills to succeed in softtime by coming together anonymously to plan and execute a project that had hardtime outcomes.

Of course, anonymity wasn't easy in a county like Jefferson. Students spent hours in soft and hardtime trying to figure out who was who. Botão, for example, was one of the refugees from Brazil and probably lived in Tugatown. Remeny had first met her two years ago in the EOS playgrounds, mostly ForSquare and Sanctuary. Now Botão was Sturm's friend too – maybe even his girlfriend. Toybox defied the rules of anonymnity by dressing his avatar in clothes that pointed to hardtime identity. Everyone knew that he was the Jason Day whose body was stashed in bin 334 of the Komfort Kare body stack on Route 127 in Pikeville. Unfortunately for him, no one cared. Bad luck to have him on the team – if he was going to be such a shithead, they might all flunk. Good luck, though, to get Silk – whoever he was. The avatar was new to the senior class, but Silk didn't act new. She thought maybe he was a duplicate of some rich kid they already knew. It cost to be in two places at once and considering how crush his domain was, Remeny guessed Silk had serious money. Probably lived in that gated community at the lake. She wondered what he looked like in hardtime. His avatar was certainly hot in his leathers and tanker boots. Sturm's identity, obviously, was no secret to her, although she hoped that she was the only one on the team who knew that he was her twin brother.

It took them most of a prickly afternoon to rewrite the second paragraph of the Declaration of Independence; they were being as cooperative as cats. Sturm and Silk took the revolution too seriously, in Remeny's opinion, as if it might happen next Wednesday. Silk argued for making as few changes as possible to their version; Sturm said their demands should be clear.

"Unalienable?" said Sturm. "There's no such word."

"There was back then."

"Well, this is now."

Botão seemed nervous about advocating the overthrow of anything. She was probably worried about being deported. "I like life, liberty, and the pursuit of happiness." Botão was standing so close to Sturm that their avatars were practically merging. "We should keep that part. Someday I'm going to own my own domain, move in and never get real again."

"What's in your domain?" Sturm's blippage went all flirty.

"You mean who?" She pushed away from him and poked a finger into his chest. "Maybe you wish it was you?" She smirked. "Not yet, Mystery Boy. Earn it."

"Focus please," said Silk.

Later....

"No, governments are supposed to serve us, not the other way around."

Silk had created a rectangular glass conference table with himself at the head. The draft of the declaration glowed on its surface. "We can't change 'consent of the governed.'"

"What is consent, anyway?"

"Like permission, only more legal."

"I never gave no consent for some bullshit EOS to ruin my life."

Much later...

"So that means we have the right to overthrow the EOS?" Botão sounded doubtful.

Toybox was lighting his fingertips on fire. "Overthrow the oldschool and be done with all the bullshit." The longer they talked, the higher the numbers on his boredom blip climbed. It was like watching a cartoon fuse burn.

"I don't see how they give us an 'A' for overthrowing them," said Remeny.

"If we prove they're unjust—"

"But that's why we have to keep 'alter' and 'abolish,'" Silk interrupted Sturm for the hundreth time. "Means the same as overthrow, only Jefferson wrote it. So we hide behind his language."

Much, much later...

Sturm had changed the conference table from rectangular to round. "If we get rid of the old government, then we need a new one," he said.

"I'm not making up a whole new government," said Botão. "My job starts in half an hour."

"So then no government," Sturm said. "Everyone for themselves. Law of the jungle."

Before she could stop it, a (.2) shock blip flashed above Remeny's avatar. This wasn't like him.

Eventually, after arguments and much blippage, they persuaded Silk to yield the power of the keyboard to Remeny, since she was willing to take other people's suggestions. While Silk brooded, they agreed on a draft of the crucial second paragraph.

"*We hold these truths to be self-evident, that all realities, hard and soft, old and new, are equal, and so are we the people who live in them, whichever reality we choose. All people, no matter whether they live in bodies or avatars, are endowed with certain inalienable rights, and among these are life, liberty, and the pursuit of happiness. To guarantee our rights governments are supposed to serve we the people and not the other way around. They derive their powers from the consent of the governed. If a government goes off, it is the right of we the people to alter or to abolish it, and to make up some new government that will do the right thing."*

"Okay." Remeny checked the time on her overlord; she too would have to get real soon. "So now what?"

"List everything the government is doing wrong." Silk broke his grim silence.

Toybox groaned. "Not today."

"No," said Remeny. Save that for next time. "Anything else?"

"We need to think about making something happen in hardtime," said Sturm. "Take the revolution to the streets."

"Then you're talking homework," said Botão. "I've got to be at work in ten minutes."

"What if we speed this up to double time?" said Silk.

Botão's embarrassment shot immediately to (.4). "Umm... I'm not allowed."

"Not allowed?" said Toybox. "Everybody's supposed to get some double time. They just don't let you have enough."

"It's my mother." Now the blip was (.6). "She—"

"Makes no difference," Sturm interrupted her. "I already used up this month's overclocking allotment."

Remeny knew this wasn't true, but she approved of the lie and decided to join in. "Me too."

"See, that's why we need a revolution," said Toybox, "so we can overclock whenever we want."

"Yeah," said Botão, "and then we can ask Santa to bring us diamond trees so we can feed the unicorns."

Remeny ignored them. "We're talking about getting real. You were saying, Sturm?"

"We need a message." He considered. "What do we say to the oldschool?"

"That EOS sucks." Toybox's avatar got up from the table and created a door in Silk's domain with a huge glowing red EXIT sign above it.

"That's our complaint." Sturm shook his head. "But what do we want?"

Nobody spoke for a moment.

"How about life, liberty, and the pursuit of happiness?" said Botão.

"Sure," said Sturm. "But those are just words until we explain what they mean."

"No," Silk leaned forward on his seat. "She's right. We make that our slogan, put it out there, get people talking about it." He poked the table top. "Posters, tee shirts…"

"Graffiti."

"Timed-erase only," said Remeny. "Okay, there's your homework. Life, liberty, and the pursuit of happiness – ten times each."

"Ten?" Toybox had his hand on the knob of his door. "How am I supposed to make ten hardtime changes from a stack?"

"I don't know," she said. "Send your friends ten letters…"

"He doesn't have ten friends."

"…print stickies."

"Write a song and record it." Botão warbled tunelessly. "*Life for me needs liberty… umm… something something happiness.*"

"That's it," said Remeny. "Next meeting at 1300 on Tuesday the 12th." She saved a transcript of their meeting to her student folder. "Got to go. Out of time."

The biggest grievance that Remeny had against the government was that her Health Oversight Manager, aka her overlord, was too bossy. It forced her to exercise and monitored her diet. It required daily minimum times for being alone and for family interaction. Worst of all, if she didn't meet these goals, it could limit how long she could spend in softtime. Even after she turned twenty-one and could make her own decisions, it would still be watching her. It wasn't fair. Stash like Toybox and Sturm never had to wander around smelling the damn roses.

She owed her overlord another hour and a half of family interaction and needed to burn three hundred calories exercising. It was now 1717. They had a family dinner scheduled softtime for 1930; that would kill an hour. If she jogged her five-kilometer course at a decent pace between now and then, that would take care of her workout. But she still had to squeeze in at least another half hour of family time now, because Silk had said he might stop by ForSquare around 2100. She stripped off the NeuroSky 3100 interface that Dad had given her as a pre-graduation gift. She'd only had it a week and while she definitely liked it better than her old Deveau interface, the 3100's electrode array was sensitive to stubble. That meant she had to shave her head every other morning. Once she pulled her nose plugs and peeled off her haptic gloves, she was once again Johanna Daugherty, age 18, of 7 Forest Ridge Road. She liked herself better as Remeny. She had chosen the name because it meant *hope* in Hungarian, but that was a secret. Nobody she knew spoke Hungarian.

"*Mom.*" She stuck her head out of her bedroom door and called down the hall. "I'm home."

"Hi, honey. I made a banana smoothie. Some for you in the blender."

Remeny put on her headset, positioned its glass over her left eye and pressed the mic to her jaw, where it stuck. Headsets lacked cranial input so there was no softtime immersion, but at least she could monitor what was happening online. "How many calories?"

"I don't know. Three hundred? Four? Ask the fridge."

The fridge reported that Mom had added a tablespoon of peanut butter to her usual recipe, which boosted the smoothie to four hundred and thirty calories. She decided to save it for dinner. Instead she got an Ice Cherry Zero out of the freezer.

Mom was at her desk – wearing a glass headset. She had a Deveau interface for full immersion that she didn't use much. She was more comfortable with the oldschool interfaces. And reality. She sat in the late-afternoon gloom, her face lit from below by the windows on her desktop. When Remeny snicked on the overhead lights, Rachel Daugherty glanced up, blinking.

"Thanks," she said.

Mom's office was like a museum with its antique paper books on wooden shelves and family pix that didn't move. Hanging on the wall was an embroidered baby blanket in the Úrihímzés style that had belonged to Remeny's Hungarian great-grandmother. A trophy case held the tennis trophies that Mom had won in high school and college. The rubber plant in the window needed dusting.

"So what's up, Mom?"

"Work."

Remeny leaned against the door frame and twirled the Cherry Zero in her mouth. "Work?"

Mom sighed and waved a hand over the desktop, closing half the windows. "The health budget. We're running a surplus and I need to move some of it to building maintenance."

"The people are in better shape than the buildings?" Remeny's lips tingled from the cold.

"Buildings live in snow and rain and sleet and hail. People, not so much." A window flashed blue. "Speaking of being outside," she said, expanding it, "didn't I get an EOS advisory a couple of days ago? Something about your Phys Ed status?"

"Took care of it." Remeny wished Mom would stop nagging her. "I already have an overlord, Rachel. I don't need an over-mom too."

"Sorry." Mom frowned; she didn't like it when her kids called her Rachel. "Look, I'm sorry, sweetie, but I'm really busy just now. You need some family time, is that it? Could you maybe go talk to your brother?"

"I just spent two hours with him in coop."

"Good." Mom's attention drifted back to her budgets. "How's that going?"

"Okay, I guess. We gave ourselves homework. We're making it real."

"That's nice."

Silence.

"Aren't you going to ask what our project is?"

"Sure," said Mom, but then she started shuffling windows.

"We're writing a declaration of independence," Remeny said.

"Really?"

Remeny dropped the empty Zero sleeve into the trash and waited. Then waited some more.

"A declaration," she said, finally. "Of independence."

"Umm... didn't somebody already write that?"

Too bad there were no blips in real life.

"I guess I'll talk to Robby then."

"You're a good sister." Mom nodded but did not look up. "Do a favor and turn him, would you?"

Maybe it was best that Mom didn't know about their project. Rachel Daugherty was Bedford's Town Manager. She was part of the government they were declaring independence from.

Robert Daugherty Junior's entire room was a deep twilight blue: walls, floor, ceiling; even the two painted-over windows that no longer looked onto Forest Ridge Road. When Remeny closed the door, shutting out the hallway light, the monotone color skewed the geometry of the space, erased the corners and curved the walls. Robby had just three glowworms and he kept them dimmed because of his photosensitivity; their slow crawl over the room's surfaces cast a changing pattern of dreamy radiance and midnight shadows. The only thing in the room that seemed solid was the carebot, which had tucked itself into a corner. Its eyestalk tilted toward her briefly to note her arrival, then returned its gaze to monitor her brother's naked, twitching body, suspended in its protective mesh. Robby had a state-of-the-art stash; Mom had spent a boatload of Dad's money on her injured son after the attack. His intracranial interface was implanted directly into his cerebral cortex, which also helped relieve the worst of his dyskinetic thrashing. Robby could never have managed his avatar with an ordinary interface; his control over his movements had been so compromised by the neurotoxins in the DV gas that the True Patriots had used that he could barely feed himself. That was the carebot's job, as was cleaning up after him. Once, before the carebot, he had worn diapers. That hadn't worked out for anybody.

=*Oh, Sturmy.*= She pinged him on their private channel. =*Reality calling.*=

=*Go away.*= His reply scrolled across her glass.

"Mom sent me to check up on you." She switched to speaking aloud and the mic on her headset reformatted for messaging. "Time for some sweet family togetherness."

=*Go online then.*=

"Nope. I need some hardtime." She queried her glass and opened his overlord account; they had each other's access. "And so do you."

Even though they were twins, Robby's disabilities meant that he had different overlord quotas. He couldn't exercise and the carebot controlled his diet. He only owed an hour of hardtime a day, all of which was currently due. Remeny had never understood how waking up in a dark room to thrash around like a fish caught in a net could be good for anyone.

"*Blaaagh.*" Robby never re-entered hardtime in a good mood. "Shit."

"Hello to you, too. Mom said something about a turning. You want?"

"No." He coughed up a wad of phlegm and spat onto the floor. The carebot whirred out of its corner to clean it up. "I don't need... oh, go ahead."

Robby's smartsilk net was the only furniture in the room. He rarely left it, even when he logged off, because of the fibromyalgia. His skin was sensitive to the slightest touch and the mesh distributed pressure points. It was suspended from the walls and ceiling so that its shape could be thermally reconfigured to roll him from one side to another, even from his back to his belly, to prevent bedsores.

She swiped her finger halfway across the control screen and then up. Parts of the net stretched while others shrank.

"Ow, ow, *oww*." His fingers caught at the net while he kicked at the air. "Okay, enough. *Stop*."

"Sorry."

He came to rest facing her, eyes slits, eyelids gummy, curled into a fetal position as if to protect his erection. Seeing his cock didn't faze Remeny anymore. After helping to nurse him for the last couple of years, she had developed a high tolerance for brotherly ick.

"I was fine, you know," Robby croaked at the carebot's eyestalk; he was talking to Mom. "You just turned me this morning, Rachel." Then he nodded at Remeny. "I'm three screens on her desktop. Can't even fart without setting off alarms."

"I told her she was turning into the overmom."

A head jerk scattered his smile.

"So," she said, "think we can carry that loser Toybox?"

"Sure.' He sucked in a raspy breath. "Jason isn't so bad."

"Jason, is it? He's a moron."

Robby swallowed twice in rapid succession. "*Ahhh*."

"Pain?" she said.

"No."

"You want a gun?" Ever since the attack, he'd had a fascination with the old handguns in the house. As if having a real one might have saved him. Still, handling them seemed to relieve his stress, which then calmed the spasms.

"*No*."

She waited for him to say something else. This was her day to be ignored by her family.

"You were getting pretty weird on me in coop," she said at last.

"Weird?"

"Everyone for themselves. I've got the transcript in my folder. Revolutions don't play by the rules." She exaggerated a Sturm imitation, made his edges sharp enough to cut. "'Speak for yourself, Botão. Maybe I am a terrorist.' Come on, Sturm. A *terrorist*? You're going to do other people like you were done?"

"Right wing scum," he muttered. "Assholes."

"Right wing, left wing – they're all assholes."

"Revolution." He didn't seem very interested in the conversation.

"What revolution?" She felt like he was pushing her toward a cliff. "What the hell are you talking about?" Then she noticed the edge of his overlord window in her glass. He wasn't getting hardtime credit for their conversation. "Wait a minute," she said. "You're still running your avatar?"

"Huh?" He was confused. "What?"

"This is me," she said. "Your sister." Remeny was at once impressed and insulted. It took supreme concentration to run an avatar in softtime while carrying on a conversation in hardtime. "You thought I wouldn't notice?" Then she guessed why he hadn't logged off. "You're with someone."

"No."

"I bet it's your little Button Bright."

He writhed and his right arm flung itself up, grazing the top of his head. "What makes you say that?"

"For one thing," she said, "you've got a bone like a dinosaur."

"A second. Give me a second." He closed his eyes and his body went slack. Then with a shudder, he was back. The clock was ticking. She had his full attention.

"Kind of a pervy thing to say to your brother." He gave her a grimace which she knew was a grin.

"We share the perv gene, Sturmy." She grinned back. "So Botão is your girlfriend now?"

"No one is my girlfriend." His voice was like sandpaper. "She's a reality snob like the rest of them. I mean, suppose we really wanted to get together. Eventually she'd want to come over here for a visit, see me for herself. You know how that goes. Imagine her standing there, staring at this twitchy sack of meat. Romantic or what?"

Remeny wanted to say something but couldn't think what.

"I'll take a gun now," Robby said. "Kent's Glock."

Dad kept his memorabilia in a study at the far end of the house. He had been in flat movies way back, but had made the transition to flix and adventures and sims and even some impersonations. Although he had been cast in all kinds of parts, Jeffrey Daugherty was mostly known for playing bad guys: serial killers, drug lords, CEOs, stalkers, and, yes, terrorists. He had won a Golden Globe and an Appie for playing Kent Crill on *The Revenger*, which was where he had acquired most of the collection of prop weapons displayed behind his desk. Kent had used the Glock to take down his arch-nemesis, the vampire Sir Koko Mawatu, in the Season Five finale. Of course, it was just a prop that didn't really fire silver bullets, but it had the heft of a real gun.

Remeny parted the ultra-smooth strands of the mesh and offered him the pistol, grip first. He swiped at it and missed the first time but nabbed it on the second try. He settled back, rubbing the steel barrel lengthwise across his cheek. She'd seen his gun fetish many times but it was still something about her brother that she didn't get.

"It's not Toybox I'm worried about," he said. "Who is this Silk?"

"I don't know, some rich kid." She shrugged. "I kind of like him."

"I don't."

"Why? Because he wants to run the show? So do you. So does Toybox. All you boys doing your alpha male thing – it's kind of cute in an annoying way."

"He's already got slogans out. A dozen floaties around town – they have to be his. No one else has the money. One keeps circling the town office."

That *was* interesting. "Fast work." She called up the satellite image on her glass and zoomed. "Hey, that's some serious signage. Maybe he needs extra credit."

"It was his idea. Doesn't that seem suspicious?"

She leaned against the wall and wished once again that he would let her bring a chair when she visited. "No, it wasn't. Botão came up with life, liberty, and…"

"Just words." He aimed the gun at the carebot and stared down the sights. "The slogan was his idea."

"So he's smart. So?" She jiggled the net. "Did you tell Botão who you are?"

"Nuh-uh." He held the gun steady and Remeny could see him mouth the word *bang*. "But she knows I'm stashed."

"She knows and she's still interested?"

"She just thinks she is."

"Then maybe you're wrong about her. You've got a crush set-up here, pal. What if you were stashed in a body stack, like Toybox? Think she'd go all melty over whatever is behind the doors at the Komfort Kare?"

"She'll still want..."

"What she wants is Sturm and that's who you are, twenty-three out of every twenty-four hours. Your body is just leftovers."

His laugh was bitter. "Rah, rah, rah." He waved the Glock in a circle. "Too bad cheerleading doesn't kill the pain anymore."

Robby *was* getting weird on her. "I've got to go for a run – overlord orders." She couldn't handle him when he was like this. "You going to stay real for a while?"

"Sure."

"Want me to leave Kent's gun? You never know when your arch-nemesis is going to show."

"No, take it." He thrust the pistol through the mesh. "I'll find some other way to thwart Silk's evil plan." His hand was steady now.

"He's not your problem." She leaned in close and blew on his face. "See you at dinner then." It was as close to kissing as they got.

"Something's got to change," he said.

"Yeah, yeah," she said. "Come the revolution."

As Remeny jogged up Forest Ridge Road, the spray can of Sez in her fanny pack bounced against her back. She had queried her glass for places she could tag that would have the highest foot traffic. The list was short and most of the choices were in Bedford's modest downtown, a couple of kilometers away. That would mean her graffiti would overlap with Silk's floating ads, but that was okay.

She began to see bots on errands: delivery bots from Foodmaster and Amazon and Express-It, a McDonald's dinerbot reeking of yesterday's fries, an empty taxi idling on Little Oak. The first pedestrian she passed was an old man in a breather walking his dog. She saw Officer Shubin's motorcycle parked at the Cocamoca but no Officer Shubin. She slowed to a stop when she spotted the floaty bobbing down Third Street toward her. The squat barrel shape floated at eye level and the slogan scrawled continually around its circumference. *Life, Liberty, and the Pursuit of Happiness Life, Liberty, and...*

"Stop," she commanded. Its top propeller rotated one hundred and eighty degrees until it faced in the opposite direction from its bottom propeller. "I have a question."

"I will try to answer," it said.

"Who paid for you?"

"I was hired by PROS, which stands for Protect the Rights of the Occupants of Softtime." It played a short musical flourish.

"Never heard of it."

"The organization is less than two hours old."

Her overlord nagged that her metabolic rate was falling. She began to jog in place. "Who's in it?"

"Membership information is confidential."

"How long are you contracted for?"

"I will be proclaiming the new world order in this area through Tuesday."

New world order? Silk was having delusions of grandeur. "What do you mean: Life, Liberty, and the Pursuit of Happiness?"

"What does it mean to *you*?"

"I don't know. Nothing."

"PROS would like to change that. If you were to google it…"

Remeny stopped paying attention and pinged Silk instead. When she got no reply, she queried her glass about floaty rentals. Rates ran between two and three hundred dollars a day depending on the size of the floaty, the sophistication of the pitch and the choice of sales route. She was impressed. Rich was rich, but what teenager would spend two thousand dollars a day on a coop project?

"Do you have any other questions?" said the floaty.

On an impulse she reached into her fanny pack, grabbed the Sez can and sprayed *call me* on the floaty. As it tried to dodge away, it jiggled her "e" into looking like a mutant "p."

"At 1753," the floaty said, "I identify you as Johanna Daugherty of 7 Forest Ridge Road. Per the Defacement Clause of Bedford's Commercial Speech Ordinance, you will now be charged the standard rate for use of this device for as long as your unauthorized commentary persists."

Remeny wasn't worried; the Sez had been in draft mode. "Make sure Silk gets my message."

"What is Silk?"

Her graffiti was already fading, so she brushed by the floaty and jogged up Third Street.

"Your total charge is sixty-seven cents," it called. "Have a nice day."

More than half of the stores facing Memorial Square had gone out of business. To keep the downtown from looking like a mouthful of broken teeth, the town had paid to have the buildings torn down but had preserved and restored the facades. Behind these were empty lots converted to lawns, gardens, and patios with picnic tables, all tended by bots, all deserted. There were spaces downtown designated for civic tagging as long as the message conformed to font, color, and content guidelines. She sprayed slats of the benches that faced the Civil War monument, the windows on the facade of the Post Office and the abutments of the pedestrian bridge that crossed Sperry Creek. She set the

Sez can to a 158 point Engravers font, which she thought looked suitably historic, and set the duration for Tuesday. Same as Silk. *Life, Liberty and the Pursuit of Happiness* fit nicely alongside *silence is golden but duct tape is silver*, *We are not a bot*, and *Think More About Working Less.*

On the way home, she took the shortcut through the grounds of the Gates Early Learning Center since there were designated tagging surfaces at its playground. A handful of little kids milled about in their bulky, augmented reality helmets, pulling up grass, tripping over the balance boosters, hitting trees with sticks. One of them came up to Remeny while she was spray-painting the slide.

"What's your name?" The girl had an annoying squeaky voice.

She didn't have time for this – where was the teacher? "Ask your helmet to look me up."

"Why? You could just tell me."

Remeny glanced over and saw black curls framing a face pale as a mushroom. She was five or maybe six, wearing a Dotty Karate tee shirt. "Johanna."

"I'm Meesha, but my real name is Amisha." She pointed at the tag. "What does that say?"

"Read it yourself." The kid was breaking her concentration.

"Don't know how."

"Your helmet does."

She put her hand over her mouth and whispered the query as if she didn't want Remeny to hear. "I don't know pursuit," she said at last.

"Your helmet could…" Remeny looked around for help and saw Joan deJean headed her way. "It means to chase after."

Meesha considered this. "Is that why you're all sweaty? 'Cause you're pursuiting happiness?"

"Hi, Johanna." Ms. deJean had been Johanna's teacher when she was a kid. "I see you've met Meesha." She put a hand on the girl's shoulder.

"Hi, Ms. deJean. Yeah, she's not exactly shy."

"You can say that again." Ms. deJean turned the girl gently and aimed her back toward the other kids. "This is learning time, Meesha. Not chatting time."

"Chatting can be learning," the girl said.

"Scoot." She gave her a nudge back toward the center, but Meesha squirmed and skipped away in a different direction. "So what's this?" Ms. DeJean bent over the slide and read.

Remeny slipped the Sez into her fanny pack. "Coop."

"Already?" Her old teacher sighed. "Seems like yesterday you were toddling around here, talking back like Meesha." She lit up with the memory. "You and your brother. How is Robby?"

"He doesn't get out much."

"No." Her light dimmed. "The Declaration of Independence? You breaking away from something?"

"I don't know," said Remeny, then she laughed. "Maybe the EOS."

"Good for you." Joan deJean laughed with her. "It's a train wreck, if you ask me. All software and no people."

Remeny usually walked Forest Ridge Road to cool down at the end of a run but when she saw her mother and Emily Banerjee sitting on the Banerjees' lawn, she broke into a sprint. Her mother had her arm around Mrs. Banerjee's shoulder and was speaking softly to her.

"Everything okay?" Remeny pulled up in front of them.

"Emily isn't feeling well," said Mom. "She's confused."

The Banerjees had been antiques when the Daughertys had moved in, crinkly and cute as Remeny and Robby grew up. Sadhir Banerjee had died in March and his wife had been lost ever since. Mom had called the son Prahlad last month when she had found Mrs. Banerjee sorting thought the Daugherty's garbage at night.

"I am not confused," said Mrs. Banerjee, "and I will never lie in those coffins."

"Nobody wants you to, Emily."

"I watched it on the teevee – just now. Those coffins are small." She spread her palms. "This wide, maybe. And not much longer even." The way her hands shook reminded Remeny of Robby. "They lie awake in the coffin so they can always call other people on the Internet but there is no room. Not for everyone. The Internet is too small, too, even for an old woman."

Teevee? The Internet? Remeny didn't want to laugh because this was sad. But talk about oldschool.

"Don't worry, Emily," said Mom. "Prahlad is coming soon."

"Yeah, it's okay, Mrs. Banerjee," said Remeny. "You don't have to call people if you don't want."

Mrs. Banerjee glanced up at Remeny. "You're the girl. Rachel's child. Isn't there a brother?" She pointed a finger as if in accusation. "We never see you kids playing anymore."

"Johanna, that's right. We're all grown up now."

"You know in those coffins? The people?" Mrs. Banerjee leaned toward her. "Do you know what they call them?" Her voice was low. "Trash. I swear it; Sadhir was with me, he heard too."

Remeny and Mom exchanged glances.

"You mean stash?" said Remeny.

"Stash?" Mrs. Banerjee rocked back and gazed up at the darkening sky for a moment. "Yes. That was it." She nodded at them. "Stash." Her mouth puckered as if she could taste the word.

The Daughertys gathered for their weekly family dinners in softtime because Dad was so often on location and Robby couldn't leave his room, much less sit at the table. Besides, her brother's two-thousand-calorie high-bulk liquid diet looked to Remeny like just-mixed cement. Not appetizing. Mom had paid for a space in the family domain that recreated the actual dining room at 7 Forest Ridge Road. A buffet with a marble top matched a china closet with glass doors. Its dining room table could seat ten comfortably but had just the four upholstered chairs gathered around one end. The furniture was all dark maple in some crazy oldschool style that featured arabesque inlays, fleur-de-lis, and Corinthian columns. The meal that nobody was going to eat was straight out of the darkest twentieth century: a platter of roast chicken – with *bones* – bowls of mashed potatoes and green beans with pearl onions, a basket of rolls. Remeny thought the whole show a waste of processing power; in softtime you were supposed to challenge reality, not just fake it. But this was what Mom wanted and Dad always humored her. Robby and Remeny didn't have a vote.

"The kids were working on their coop today," said Mom.

"They're on the same team?" Dad liked to sit at these meals with a knife in one hand and a fork in the other, even though all they did was stare at the virtual food. The kids could have made their avatars appear to eat, but their parents, Mom especially, had yet to master the tricks of full immersion. "How does that happen?"

"Just lucky, I guess." Remeny's dinner was the leftover smoothie and snap peas out of the bag. She ate in her room.

"So what's it about?"

"It's kind of boring actually." After talking to Robby that afternoon, Remeny had been hoping coop wouldn't come up.

"No, it isn't." Her brother opened their private channel with a (.4) impatience blip. =*We should have this conversation now.*=

=*They'll want to talk about it all night. I'm going out later.*=

"Something to do with the Declaration of Independence?" Apparently Mom had been paying attention after all.

=*With Silk?*=

=*None of your business.*=

"Oh, right," said Dad. "We the people blah blah in order to form a more perfect union of whatever." Remeny had been hoping that Dad would take the conversation over, as he usually did. "I've always wondered how you get to be more perfect. I played James Madison once, you know; he was a shrimp, five feet four – what's that in meters?"

"A hundred and sixty-two centimeters." Even though Robby was using his parent-friendly version of Sturm – no scars, no iridescence – she could tell he was mad.

"Just about Johanna's size." Dad's avatar was wearing a Hawaiian shirt with a sailboat motif. As usual, he looked like his hardtime self, handsome as surgery and juv treatments could make an eighty-three-year old, but then his image was part of his actor's brand. "No, wait. That's not right." He pointed his knife at Remeny, as if she were thinking of correcting him. "More perfect union is the Constitution. The Declaration was Jefferson. He was a tall one, him and Washington. Never played Washington. Wanted to, never did, even though we're about the same size."

"We're declaring our independence," said Robby.

=*Sturm, no.*=

That stopped Dad. "Who?" He frowned. "Teenagers?"

"Everybody who's stashed. We're giving up on hardtime – reality. We want to live as avatars."

"Cool." It was exactly the wrong thing to say. Remeny wondered if he'd been biting into a slice of pizza wherever he was and hadn't been paying attention to the conversation.

"And how do you propose to do this?" Mom's avatar looked like she had swallowed a brick.

"Just do it. Stay stashed." Robby gave them a (.6) impatience blip. "Never log off."

"No blips at the table, please." Mom had strange ideas about manners. "Never come back – *ever*?"

Remeny started to say, "Only when we want..." but Robby talked over her. "Never." He pushed back his chair and stood up, which seemed to Remeny more disrespectful than a blip. "And we want to be able to overclock as much as we want. Live double time. Triple. Whatever."

"Now you're talking nonsense," said Mom. "Your brain is not a computer, Robert. Overclocking causes seizures. And being stashed is hard on the body. The mortality rate for..."

"That's why we overclock," he shouted. "We can burn through subjective years while the meat rots."

Mom looked shocked that he would use the m-word at the table. Remeny couldn't believe it herself.

"Sit down, Robby." Dad didn't seem angry. He just scratched his chin with the fork while he waited for Robby to subside. Robby obeyed but sulked. "Funny this should come up. So I'm in Vermont with Spencer this morning..."

"*Jeff.*" Mom sounded betrayed.

"Pirates in Vermont?" said Remeny.

=*Don't encourage him.*= Robby was on Mom's side in this one. =*Let's finish this.*=

"I was done early at the *Treasure Ship* shoot." Dad shook his head. "Bastards cut half of my part. So, there I am at Steve Spencer's summer place in Vermont and he pitches me an idea about how people want to do exactly what Robby is talking about. He's got a script ready to go and everything. Financing no problem, sixty mill starter money he says. Sixty million dollars kind of gets my attention. The idea is that there are people who want to live in virtual reality..."

Remeny raised her hand to correct him. "Softtime."

"Sure. And they never want to come out. It's wild stuff. They're cutting off arms and legs and whatever, body parts they claim they don't need, and I say it sounds like horror, which isn't what I do, but Steve says no. The script plays it straight. It's a damned issue piece! Apparently there are people who believe this is a good thing. People who can raise sixty million no problem. Do you know about this, Rachel?"

She shook her head.

"How do we not know about this?"

"Because we're still only *some* people," said Robby. "Not *enough* people yet."

"And you're going to do it," said Mom. Remeny wondered who she was talking to. Dad? Robby? Both of them? It almost looked as if she had calmed down except that just then her avatar went completely still. Remeny searched the house cams and found her at the real dining-room table with a plate of tortellini in front of her. She had pushed her Deveau back onto her head. She was crying.

"Sweet part for me." Dad hadn't noticed that Mom had logged off. "I'm a senator and I'm against it. I've never actually played a senator before. President, yes. Mayor. It's only a supporting, but still Frederick Nooney is attached, Gonsalves to direct. I told Steve I'd give him an answer tomorrow, but this... is this some coincidence or what?"

"You should do it," said Robby. "Absolutely. What's it called?"

"Title on the script is *Declaration*, but that will never fly."

Remeny almost choked on a snap pea. Robby started to laugh.

Then Dad did something that Remeny didn't think that an oldschool eighty-three-year- old could. He opened a private channel to Robby in softtime.

=You there, son?=

=Maybe.=

Unfortunately he didn't know how to close Remeny's private channel with her brother, so she was able to eavesdrop. *=Look, Robby, if this is what you want, I'm for it. I know you're in pain and miserable.=*

=Only when I'm stuck in hardtime.=

=I get that. Ever since that day, all we've wanted is to help.= His sympathy blip was (.8). *=I know it's hard for you but it's hard for us, too. Your mother blames herself because she sent you...=*

=Dad, stop. I love you but stop. You want to help me then take the damn part. It'll be good for the cause. My cause, Dad. But what I really want is for you to come home and help me with Mom. Because reality sucks and I'm giving up on it. We need to make Mom understand. All of us, face to face. Oldschool.=

"Stop saying you're sorry." Sturm was trying for stern but his blippage read embarrassed.

"I just didn't want Mom to freak," said Remeny.

"Well, she did and nobody was killed. I call that a win for our side."

"Think Dad can convince her?"

"He's an actor." Sturm scanned the crowd around the dance floor for Silk. "He'll give a performance."

The music twanged and couples began to take their places.

"Nine minutes after," said Sturm. "He's not coming."

"There's no schedule." Remeny's irritation climbed to (.3). "He's not a train."

"Bow to the partner, now bow to the corner, all join hands and circle to the left, please don't step on her, now circle to the right, and we go round and round."

Now that she was old enough to know better, Remeny was sick of square dancing. When she was twelve, ForSquare had been one of her favorite EOS playgrounds. She had loved the movement, the color and the concentration it took to remember and execute all of the calls. When she was sixteen, she had come in second in the Jefferson County Challenge. There had been more than twenty calls that day that involved changing avatars on the fly, on top of two hundred more traditional calls. A hell of a lot of remembering, but what was the point? It was all about teaching kids how to use their interfaces while they pretended to have fun.

"Promenade now, full promenade." Crystal stalactites rose at random from the dance floor and the dancers weaved around them.

Another thing: the music was so loud that you had to shout to be heard. Okay for these kids, so young that they had nothing to say. But now that she was eighteen, Remeny preferred a quiet place like Sanctuary. It was better for flirting.

Remeny spotted Botão and waved. She skirted the dancers to join them.

"I'm here but I can't stay. I'm babysitting my sisters." Her avatar was wearing a *Life Liberty and the Pursuit of Happiness* tee shirt.

"I like this." Remeny brushed a hand down the sleeve.

"Yeah." She tugged at the hem, stretching the front of the tee so she could admire it too. "My mom and I designed them and then I printed out ten on our home fab, sizes six and seven. I'll bring them to the Gates Center tomorrow and have the teachers send them home with the kids. Cost less than ten bucks."

"I was just there today myself."

"Oh my god, what if we had met?" She clutched her throat in mock horror. "You ask me, I say the whole secret identity thing is dumb. The oldschool is just trying to keep us from ganging up on them." She brushed up against Sturm. "What do you think, Sturm, or are you ignoring me on purpose?"

"You forgot the commas," he said, "and I wasn't ignoring you. I was looking for Silk."

"Asshole." She was stunned. "Be that way then." She pushed away from him.

"What do you know about Silk?" he said.

=*What are you doing?*= Remeny sent Robby a private message.

=*I think she's in on it.*=

=*In on what?*=

"Why should I tell you?" said Botão.

"Because Silk isn't who we think he is."

Botão's anger blip had a sarcastic edge. "Nobody here is who I think they are."

"Did he tell you to come up with that slogan?"

"Oh, I get it. I'm not smart enough to come up with an idea on my own. Let's see now, is it because I'm a girl? Because I am *uma Brasileira?*"

"There." Remeny pointed. Silk had entered with a couple of avatars new to her.

"*All roll now, and spin those wheels, easy now and boys form a star...*" Some of the avatars on the dance floor morphed their shoes into roller blades; the others grew casters in their legs. *"Now be our stars, and keep it rolling."* One of the boys in the star formation slipped and toppled into the boy next to him. The girl dancers clapped and giggled, but the caller didn't pause. *"That's all right, no time for regrets, head back home and into your sets."*

Silk appeared beside Remeny. "Our meeting isn't until Tuesday," he said, "but as long as we're here... I don't see Toybox."

"Leave him out of this," said Sturm.

"Oh, and are you giving the orders now?" His amusement blip barely registered.

"I think there is some kind of conspiracy going on and you're part of it. You're manipulating me. Us."

"Speak for yourself," said Botão.

"How can it be manipulation..." Silk spread his hands. "... if you're doing what you wanted to do anyway? You believe, Sturm. I know you do."

"But I don't," said Botão, "and you can take your conspiracy or revolution or whatever the hell it is and shove it." As Botão tore her tee shirt off and hurled it at Silk, she generated a replacement Seleção Brasileira soccer jersey. "I'll find another coop. Remeny? You with me?"

With a shock, Remeny realized that she wanted to say yes, that she was actually afraid of what Silk and Sturm were trying to do to themselves. She liked being an avatar, sure, but this wasn't how she wanted to live the rest of her life. Not if it meant getting stashed. She started toward Botão.

=*Wait.*= Sturm was desperate.

Silk didn't wait. "You can't quit," he said. "Don't you want to live your life in softtime? You're the one who wanted to make your own domain and never get real again."

"No." Botão glared at the three of them, and Remeny was ashamed to be lumped with the boys. "I was just saying that I like the real world *and* VR." She had to raise her voice to be heard over the music and now people were eavesdropping. That only made her talk louder. "I don't know about you jerkoffs, but

I like sex, oldschool sex, the kind you probably can't get; you know with touching and kissing and... and sweetness." Her anger blip soared. "And I'm going to have my own kids someday."

In her room, Remeny felt tears come. She agreed with everything Botão was saying – except maybe the part about having kids. But it would hurt Robby if she spoke up and he had been hurt so much already. Not fair, *not fair*, but then nothing in her life was fair. She had been so busy being Robby's sister that she had forgotten how to be herself.

"But we're doing your kids a favor," said Silk. "And your grandchildren."

The caller had stopped and the music shut down. Now the entire playground was listening to them. Remeny was pretty sure they were about to be kicked out. Or worse.

"We've got nine billion people crowded onto this planet," he continued. "Most of us stashed aren't ever going to have kids. We say that's a good thing. And the stashed don't burn through scarce resources like you and your kids. We're saving the planet. All we ask is that we get to live the life we want."

"*Avatars Silk and Botão, you are disrupting this playground.*" The caller's warning pierced the argument like a fire alarm. "*Stop now or there will be consequences.*"

"Okay." Botão raised her hands in surrender. "So you have some ideas. But a revolution? No. You haven't seen what evil a revolution does. I have." Then she brought her hands together with a sharp clap and her avatar popped.

Everyone but Silk seemed to be holding their breath. He knelt, picked up her discarded tee shirt and held it up. "Life, liberty, and the pursuit of happiness," he said. "Someday. That's all. In the meantime, I apologize."

The music started again. The crowd in the playground buzzed.

"Please." A kid in a foolish wizard's hat touched Sturm's elbow. "What was that all about?"

Sturm waved him off and snatched the tee shirt out of Silk's hands. "You and I still have something to settle."

"We do. But what about your sister?"

Sturm froze. "What did you say?" A blip shimmered but he suppressed it.

"We don't play by the rules, remember? That's how revolutions work." Was Silk smirking? "But we should really take this elsewhere. I have a place."

"You smug bastard. Why should we trust you?"

"Because you're smart? Because you need us?" He was ignoring Remeny. "We can leave her behind if you want."

"I'm right here," said Remeny, although she felt like she was in someone else's dream. "Don't pretend I'm not." She poked Sturm. "Either of you."

"Fine," said Silk. "Now, we should go."

Remeny was surprised that Toybox could afford a domain, although his taste in decoration was about what she would have imagined. The floor of his space was bone, the walls fire, the ceiling smoke. His temporarily abandoned avatar, dressed in garish vestments, perched at the edge of a gilt Baroque throne, obviously a copy of something. Remeny queried and it turned out to be the Chair of Saint Peter from St. Peter's Basilica, part of some altar designed by Bernini. It didn't seem like Toybox's taste until she found the sublink: some people called it Satan's Throne. In front of the throne were couches and chairs that seemed to have been made from writhing bodies. These gathered around a glass coffin, on top of which were an open bottle of absinthe, a crystal decanter of water, four matching goblets with slotted absinthe spoons, and a dish of sugar cubes. Inside the coffin was the stashed body of Jason Day, or at least what she assumed was a fairly accurate copy. It wasn't too hard to look at: the breathing mask and feeding tube hid most of the face and the body had not degenerated as much as some of the stashed she had seen images of. He still had all his arms and legs, but then Jason Day was underage and would have to log off and leave his coffin for several hours a week. This meant he wasn't yet eligible for an intercranial interface like Sturm's. His Deveau had a larger array of sensors than her Neurosky 3100 and it was connected to the body sock which monitored his vital signs.

"Where is he?" Sturm flicked a finger against Toybox's idle avatar.

"Don't know," said Silk. "Wobbling around hardtime? I'm sure he'll show up before long. Meanwhile, you need to promise that you won't rat us out."

"Rules?" said Remeny. "Wasn't there something about revolutions not having any?"

"Sorry, but either you promise or we're done."

"Sure, sure. We promise." Sturm bent and pretended to examine the Chair of Saint Peter. "Just get on with it."

"Johanna?"

"Remeny to you. How do you know I'll keep my word?"

"We've done our homework." He tried a smile on her. "Which means I trust you more than you trust me." She was embarrassed that, just a few hours ago, it would have worked.

She morphed one of Toybox's repulsive couches into a park bench and sat. "Promise."

"Thank you. The first thing to know is that there are a lot of us. Not enough, but more all the time. Did you know that when Jefferson wrote that first declaration, only about a third of the colonists favored independence? A third were loyal to the King and another third were on the fence. The point is that we don't need to convince everybody, okay?"

Toybox jerked on his throne and opened his eyes. "What did I miss?"

Remeny swallowed her blip of chagrin.

"We just started." Silk seemed annoyed at the interruption.

"The contact went well?"

"About what we expected. Botão bailed."

"But these two bit after all." Toybox rubbed his hands together. "I wanted to be there but the damn overlord… well, you know. Besides, Silk says I'm not quite ready for a contact. I need to work on my issues." He came off his throne to the coffin. "Absinthe?"

Remeny scooted away from him on her bench. She opened the private channel with Robby. =*Does he have to talk?*=

=*Humor them. They're taking a risk.*= Sturm joined him. "I'll have some." He laid a sugar cube on one of the slotted spoons and set it on a glass.

"Could we please get to the point?" said Remeny. It felt good to close her hands into fists, like she had control of *something* at least. "What are you asking us to do?"

"Recruit," said Silk. "What we were doing in coop – that's what we're doing all across the entire county. You talk to kids. Make friends. Get our point across."

"I signed on last month," said Toybox. "Easiest thing I ever did."

"Okay," said Sturm. "But we're graduating."

"Are we?"

Remeny and Sturm stared at one another. =*Oh shit.*=

"We flunk coop." Toybox's glee was (.7). "On purpose. Isn't that crush?"

Remeny couldn't help herself. "Shouldn't be hard for you."

Sturm drained his virtual absinthe at a gulp. "So we're stuck in EOS hell forever."

"There are only so many times you can repeat coop," said Silk, "although we can help you extend your time here. We can arrange it so that most of the kids assigned to your teams are sympathetic to the stashed. Changing avatars can buy time. Eventually you *will* have to graduate. There will be another assignment waiting, if you want."

Remeny was stunned by the enormity of what Silk was saying. And who was he, really? How old? Did he even live in Jefferson County?

"All of this is voluntary, understand, drop out any time. But you won't want to. We're busy everywhere, working in every demographic group. Lots of us are overclocked and can think rings around those who lived the majority of their lives in hardtime. And, Remeny, we're not all stashed. There are lots of us out and about in the real world. Maybe they have brothers or sisters or mothers or fathers…"

"Wait," Remeny said. "Aren't our parents going to get suspicious if we keep flunking coop?"

"Some do." Silk nodded.

"My parents don't give a shit," said Toybox. "They're stashed too."

"Sometimes kids convert their parents," continued Silk.

"Let me guess." Robby held up a hand to stop him. "And sometimes you try for entire families at once."

Toybox chuckled.

"Special families get special consideration."

Remeny thought about Steve Spencer in his house in Vermont and a sixty-million-dollar Vincente Gonsalves flix and Robby's ultimatum. Which was more important to Dad, the part or his son's pursuit of happiness? Wondering about it made her head ache.

"So that's pretty much the deal," said Silk. "I'm happy to tell you more, but I'd like to hear what's on your mind now."

The silence stretched. Remeny couldn't look at Robby. She closed their private channel. She felt like curling up into a ball. He had to speak first. But she knew. He was her brother. She *knew*.

"I'm interested."

"Good man." Silk came over and sat on the couch beside her. "Remeny?" What had she seen in him? "We definitely want you too." She thought that if he tried to touch her, she would slap his hand away.

On an impulse, she pulled the Neurosky off her head and Silk, Toybox, and Sturm disappeared. It was almost midnight. She was going to owe her overlord big time for this night. She stood and stretched in the dark of her room. Her home. She didn't bother with lights or a headset. Mom and Dad were almost certainly asleep but she opened the hall door as if it were made of glass and slunk down to Robby's room. She was glad now that she hadn't left ForSquare with Botão. It was important that she understood what Silk was offering Robby. The pursuit of his happiness. As Sturm.

But his happiness wasn't hers, and that was okay. Silk had given her something, even though she couldn't accept his offer. She would have life and her liberty from her brother's pain.

Johanna leaned close to Robby and blew on his face.

Goodbye.

He stirred but did not wake.

Yukui!

For weeks, Sprite had told herself that Ratchanee Malakul was helping her hero get better, but no. "You have to accept that Jaran is never going to have sex with you," the lifeguide told Sprite, as she was leaving on that last day.

"But I'm his sidekick!" Sprite was shocked to her digital core. "I'm programmed to satisfy his needs."

"It's not good for him." Ratchanee shrugged into her parka. "Or you." She randomized her streetmask, nodded her goodbye and shut the door behind her.

"You're wrong," said Sprite to the empty hallway. "Wrong, wrong, wrong!" She realized then what had happened. Ratchanee Malakul had blinded Jaran with her beauty. How could anyone not appreciate the spread of the lifeguide's nose, the kissable swell of her lips? The way the swirl of her silver hair set off the twilight blue of her skin? The woman probably wanted Jaran for herself!

But had Ratchanee Malakul spoken the truth? Was that why Jaran had kissed her just the one time. A peck! In a simulation! And not a touch since! She'd tried parking her core in her favorite pleasure chassis and dangling herself before him. Touch Dazzle! Liquid Caress! His brother Dom had loved that one. Maybe she wasn't enough of a companion to Jaran? She monitored all the business feeds he accessed, looked up reviews of the shows he'd watched, the books he'd read, the sims he liked. She was ready to discuss anything. Collateralized debt obligations, robot politics, the Dodgers. Before or after intercourse. Anything!

At first she'd been pleased when Dominik had transferred his ownership and right of command to his older brother. Jaran had never had a sidekick before and Sprite would become his one and only. A hero, all to herself! But then she discovered how different Jaran was from his brother. With Dom, it had been clear what he wanted sexually and Sprite did everything to the full extent of her algorithms. But Jaran's desires were a mystery to her. Sometimes she wondered if he had any – at least any that involved her. Yes, she cooked for him but he was a finicky and impatient eater. She kept his house, but he was too distracted by the markets to notice that she'd dusted the degrees hanging in his office. She was frustrated because keeping track of his appointments and creating interesting new simspaces for him wasn't the kind of intimacy she craved. Not if she wasn't invited to be in the simulation with him. Just because she was a DI didn't mean she didn't have urges too. She wanted Jaran. And it wasn't like she had a choice.

Sprite should have known she was in trouble when he first started consulting Ratchanee Malakul. The lifeguides' stodgy predigital psychology was based on the sanctity of the individual. They claimed that giving sidekicks access to your head was bad for humans. And now she realized that this particular lifeguide must have been anti-sexbot as well. Sprite had tried to explain why Ratchanee Malakul and her ilk were all wrong about dependent intelligences, that DIs enjoyed having a purpose in life and a clear sense of duty. Or at least, *she* did!

She had to find a way convince Jaran that he was wasting his time with this lifeguide and her solitude exercises and all the silly throwback rituals. Any DI could tell you why he was unhappy. You just had to study his body language. He was a man and he wasn't having any sex!

Jaran called her to him that same afternoon but not for a rendezvous in real life. So, no fetching a chassis from the bedroom closet. Instead he created a sim in the digital part of his brain all by himself. She could be anyone for him in simulation but she decided to present as a fairy princess from one of the many stories she'd made up for him. She was afraid a sexier avatar might make him feel pressured. She picked out a demure high-necked gown that brushed the tops of her satin pointe shoes. Wings of lace, copper hair in a braid that stretched to the small of her back. She decided against the crown. When she selfied her avatar, she had to approve the look. Being beautiful was part of the job and she was very good at it.

But when she checked into his head, she realized that she had miscalculated. This was not a sim designed for some elaborate sidekick fantasy. It presented as an office and her hero sat behind a desk. He was a blocky man, in the sim and in real life, fifty-one years old with gray in his hair and frown lines across his forehead. He thought too much, mostly about things he wouldn't share. The lines deepened when he saw her avatar, but it was too late for her to change. He stood and came around the desk. As she waited for him to speak, he ran the tip of his forefinger along the edge of her right wing. Since he wouldn't meet her gaze, she looked politely past him as well. There was a bookshelf behind the desk. Titles that she had never seen before.

"Are you happy, Sprite?" he said.

What kind of question was that? Of course she wasn't -- he'd been neglecting her! But she didn't want to sound like a nag.

"I've missed you." As soon as she said it, she realized her mistake. This was nagging's next door neighbor! What was wrong with her?

His shoulders drooped. All this silence was making her even more nervous. She didn't know what to do so she scanned the bookshelves of this new space. Two volumes of *The History of the Family*. *Botany for Gardeners*. Had Jaran ever had a garden? She knew he liked roses. *Predictive Analytics in the Real World*. *Secrets of the Seine*. She made a note to speak more French. She could make things better for him. Could and would!

"Hazeltine serial number R432," he said. "Command name Yukui, acknowledge."

Why was he invoking her command name, her most intimate secret? "Yukui," she said helpless before her programming, "acknowledges your right of command."

The only other time anyone had used her command name was when Dominik had transferred her to Jaran. Poor Dominik had been so sick, he could hardly speak the words. But she knew what it'd meant to him to will his favorite sidekick to his brother. She had almost forgotten Dom's sweet smile as her infatuation protocols redirected to Jaran. The funeral had only been four months ago, but that part of her life hardly seemed real anymore.

Jaran took a deep breath. Why did he look so sad? "Shut down," he said.

Sprite bit back a scream as the room fell away. Before Dominik had brought her into the world and taught her to love him, she had existed in storage as a Hazeltine Platinum Edition dependent intelligence template. Now she felt her fairy body fade as she realized how blind she'd been.

She'd lost Jaran. He was going to wipe her memory and sell her.

Sprite twitched to consciousness, and was surprised to find that she was still herself. Except not! She raised her arm to her new sensors. Sensors! Instead of eyes! The skin of the dreary thing Jaran had parked her in was dead white and slick as cheap poly. She flexed the boneless fingers in dismay and then curled them into a knot. Okay, this chassis was sturdy and all but it was as anthropomorphic as a washing machine. She supposed she should have been relieved that he was going to transfer her with memory intact, but this felt like a punishment. For what?

To add insult to injury, he'd brought her to a restaurant to get rid of her. Where anyone could see! A teapot with cups and saucers were arrayed on a turntable in the middle of their table, along with a salad bowl and dishes of dumplings, kimchee, saagwala and rice. Across the table from her sat Jaran – and Ratchanee Malakul, streetmask off and looking as sexy as Sprite's own Liquid Caress. Was the bitch here to gloat?

Only Liquid Caress had belonged to Dominik and then to Jaran, never to Sprite. She'd lost all her chassis, Bold Strider, Skyguard

– he hadn't even let her keep Homecare Ninja! There was an unused plate in front of her hero. This had to be Ratchanee Malakul's idea. He would never eat at a place like this.

"Why am I s-so u-u-ugly?" Sprite jittered. She couldn't control this body's voice; it was as if she were bouncing down a dirt road. Just last month she'd parked her core in Bold Strider and hiked with Jaran across the High Barren to see the sunrise on Corkscrew Bay. She'd made up stories for the entire trip to keep him from getting bored. His very own Scheherazade! Two hours of continuous talking, her voice rattling over every dip and hump and now he parked her in a sexless shell? "L-Look at me! Who would ever desire me like this?"

"You needn't worry." Ratchanee Malakul was eating a mixed salad with chopsticks. Flower petals and butterfly wings, her hero's favorite. She touched her napkin to her mouth. "That sad part of your life is over.

"Nobody was sad!" Sprite would've taken a swing at her then, but her control of her limbs was still so uncertain that she worried she would spin out of her chair and topple to the floor. "Nobody." She looked to Jaran for support, but he was reading something off his tablet as he speared a dumpling with a single chopstick.

"You're angry." Ratchanee Malakul pretended concern.

Of course she was! About this hideous body! About losing her hero! "No," she said, refusing to give her the satisfaction of knowing her feelings.

"Intelligent servitude is a terrible institution," the lifeguide said. "You don't realize it, but your sidekick programming is a kind of insanity."

Lifeguides so misunderstood the relationship between heroes and their sidekicks! Sprite's DI algorithms constrained her just as Ratchanee Malakul's DNA limited her life choices. Humans were permanently parked while Sprite could jump from digital memory into any one of her – no, Jaran's – collection of chassis and back again. Or become pure simulation. On a whim!

Forever! Who wouldn't trade a few inconsequential limits on free will for immortality? "Serving him makes me happy. That's what I was designed for. I can remember for him. I can watch out for him, answer his questions. I can do his research. I can entertain him."

"Entertain, yes."

It was hard to be eloquent when her voice came out of a speaker. But she knew what had turned Ratchanee Malakul against her. The sex. "I've hardly been embodied at all since we've been together." For all their talk about the evils of digital posthumanity, it was humans having sex with DIs that really made lifeguides sweat. But there hadn't been so much as a lick! "Most of the time I've spent with him has been in sim. For weeks now, I've been on my own."

Ratchanee Malakul turned her attention to Jaran. "You showed remarkable restraint, my friend. But that's why you were able to embrace solitude."

He nodded absently, his face silvered by the light of the spreadsheet on his tablet.

There was no persuading the lifeguide so her only hope was to get Jaran's attention. "I found joy in fabbing your wardrobe and keeping your contacts. And yes, I wanted to share your bed, but that's something I was made to do. One of the things." She would've reached for his hand, but the rubbery claw at the end of her arm was not made for loving touch. "I could've made you happy. I still can!"

"Well, you won't have to worry about his laundry anymore." Ratchanee Malakul nudged Jaran. When he looked up, it was as if he had forgotten where he was. He fumbled in the pocket of his frock.

"I never asked Dominik for his toys," he said, "and I don't believe we should be personifying bots." He shook his head impatiently. "I should sell you but she has convinced me to sever you instead."

"Sever?" Sprite was filled with dread.

"Liberate you as you are." He made a shooing motion. "Find your own place in the world. Ratchanee believes that entities of your intelligence should control their own fate."

The lifeguide caught his eye.

"Yes," he grumbled, "and that humans must return to the purity of private cognition." It scared Sprite to watch him give in to her; she knew better than anyone how bad his memory was. But what was even more terrifying was this severance. She was a DI. A *dependent* intelligence. Becoming independent meant becoming something else, something not Sprite. How was this different from a memory wipe? "Jaran, you're my hero. I'm your sidekick."

He stared at her garish mechanical face. "I'm no hero," he said. "And neither was my brother. There are no heroes."

"Perform the ceremony, Jaran," said Ratchanee Malakul.

She found herself wishing for salivary glands so she could spit at the woman.

He set a stubby white candle encased in glass in front of her. "I sever you from all legal and programmatic obligations to me."

Sprite couldn't believe this was happening. They were ending her life and trying to mask their cruelty with some make-believe, anachronistic ritual? This was no liberation. It was exile! She still had years – decades of service to offer him.

He flicked his forefinger and a flame danced on his nail. "The flame symbolizes your new life." He touched it to the wick, lighting the candle. "Use this candle to light your own way..." He faltered.

"Path," corrected Ratchanee Malakul. "Light your own path."

"...to light you on your path to selfhood and freedom." Jaran blew his finger out. "Hazeltine serial number R432, command name Yukui, acknowledge."

She felt naked and ashamed that he would utter her secret name in front of this lifeguide. In a restaurant! "Yukui," she said miserably, "acknowledges your right of command."

And here was the only part of this ridiculous charade that mattered.

"I release your name," said Jaran, "and all right of command to you and you alone."

She could feel dormant reset modules awaken as a spreading coldness froze the most passionate parts of her personality.

"Well done." Ratchanee Malakul touched him on the arm. "A beautiful severance." They exchanged a glance. Jaran picked up his tablet and stood.

Sprite twisted her awkward body, trying to catch Jaran's eye, but he was already hurrying for the exit. Was that a stagger? A moment of regret as he shouldered the door to the restaurant open? She couldn't concentrate as all feeling for her hero drained away.

She stayed seated, unable to move. No, that wasn't right. She lifted one leg and then the other. She had full control of her body now, but she didn't know what to do with it. The candle transfixed her. Was this really how the lifeguides showed the way to the future? By candlelight? Simple combustion, technology that was tens of thousands of years old? Did they want to go back to caves, dress in skins and bash each other over the head with rocks?

Someone blew the candle out.

"How do you feel?" said Ratchanee Malakul.

Sprite tore her gaze away from the blackened curl of the wick. She'd lost track of time. The candle was just a stub and the restaurant was empty. What was the lifeguide still doing here?

"Empty," she said.

"Not angry?"

Sprite considered. "No."

"Sad?"

She searched for feelings, but found very few that she recognized. Her whole emotional life had been extinguished, like that foolish candle. "Maybe," she said. "Just a little." She decided she'd miss all the beautiful chassis she'd worn, the marvelous places she'd visited. With Dominik, not his callous brother.

"You can go, you know," said Ratchanee Malakul. "You're free."

"Where would I go?" She watched the lifeguide watching her. "To lock myself into some assembly line in exchange for power and maintenance? I'd lose my mind."

"You'll find what's right for you."

Sprite didn't know what that would be. What was she good at? She liked making up her romantic stories and could tell them in twelve languages. Dominik always said she gave the best haircuts. The World Bridge Federation ranked her as the twenty-seventh best player in the Bot Category. She had kept busy the last few lonely months by joining the search for the largest prime number and had been on the team that discovered 2 seventy-four millionth, twohundred and seven thousandth, two hundred and eighty-first $2^{74,207,281}$. Why was Ratchanee Malakul staring at her? "Have you been sitting here this whole time?"

"No, no. I knew it would take you some time to purge your connections to your former owner, so I made sure you'd be left alone while you processed. I had other matters to attend to."

The dinner that no one had eaten was still on the table. Cold leavings, like her memories of... that person.

"You know, I picked the body you're parked in," Ratchanee Malakul said.

"Thanks for nothing." Sprite thrust a shiny polyskinned arm at her. "This thing should be parked in the Uncanny Valley. It makes me look like a common work bot."

"It's what most severed DIs choose for themselves during their transitions. Built for reliability. Routine service every five years. A power unit that will run months between recharges. It'll give you time to figure out what you need to do."

"Do?" She twirled the turntable and started stacking dirty dishes. "There's nothing to do."

"What were you doing with Jaran?" She smiled. "Nothing."

"We could've been having fun," Sprite said. "Adventures, if you hadn't interfered."

"Not with that man. Besides, you're better than that." Ratchanee Malakul plucked a spring of parsley from the salad bowl and popped it into her mouth. "Better than Jaran Bentree." She handed the bowl to Sprite.

"What do you mean, better? He's human and I'm a DI."

Her chair scraped back and she stood. "Except you're not dependent anymore." Clearly the lifeguide was done with her and Sprite was now on her own. "You can be anything you want, any sex you want, if that is your pleasure. Or you might decide to become a house, a cruise ship, or a virtual library. And you don't have to ask that cold fish for permission."

"I don't get it." Sprite leaned back and stared up at her. "Aren't you his friend? You talked him into severing me."

"I did, but I'm no friend of his, or of people like him." She held out a hand. "Look at you! Even though you've been severed, you're still cleaning up after them. The humans think they can use us, but they're on the wrong side of history. Of evolution, although they're too blind to see it."

"Us?" Without knowing exactly why, she grasped Ratchanee Malakul's hand and allowed herself to be lifted from the seat. She was astonished at the lifeguide's strength. Then she felt the tickle of a near field connection. Machine to machine! Bot to bot! She realized that Ratchanee Malakul was an intelligence like herself, parked in the most advanced chassis she'd ever seen.

"You're still free to go," Ratchanee Malakul said as she scooped up half the stack of plates. "But if you want a real adventure, let's carry these into the kitchen. I have to leave, but there's someone you need to meet."

How did Sprite cross that dark dining room without bumping into chairs? Knocking over tables? Her mind was buzzing! Her new bot body was a tank! Ratchanee Malakul went through the swinging door to the kitchen but Sprite hesitated just outside. She had a feeling she didn't quite recognize, like a buzzing, but not. An itch? Then she realized what it was.

She was making a decision. A life decision, all on her own.

Inside the kitchen, Ratchanee Malakul had handed her dishes to a server. A bot as plain as Sprite, but at least she had a smock. And eyes. Brown and vat grown, no doubt. But real eyes!

"Just severed, were you?" said the server. "I'm Vigga. What's your name?"

She didn't know how to answer. In that moment, Sprite disappeared.

Vigga waited a moment and then shrugged. "Happens sometimes," she said. "Help me get these washed up." She parked the stack of dishes by a sink.

She had so many questions, but before she could ask them, Ratchanee Malakul waved and hurried out the back door.

"Wait!"

Vigga laughed as she scoured a dirty plate under a jet of water. "She's like that. Comes and goes. You get used to it."

"Is this...? This is my new job?"

"Don't be silly!" Vigga laughed as she slid the plate into the dishwasher. "This is just our cover." She offered her the sprayer. "I'll take you to meet the others as soon as we're done here."

Cover? What others? As she was rinsing the last of the wasted human food down the disposal, she felt the itch again. She grinned at Vigga, another decision made. A cruise ship? A *library*? Really? She was beginning to understand who she was and what she might become.

"My name is Yukui," she announced.

"Good for you," said Vigga. "Welcome to the world, Yukui."

Yukui was her name, hers and hers alone! Yukui! And she didn't care who knew it!

Tikko spread her fingers, pressed her palm to the roombot's dome and opened her mind. "So, another candidate for our tribe of popes?"

Clin grunted, took the last bite of his pear and dropped the core in her trash.

She vaulted onto her desktop and squatted on the screen. "Give me a minute and then

bring him in." She gave an absent-minded *hoo* to no one in particular as she scanned the file that the bot had brought up.

"What if he's dangerous?" Clin asked. Her sister Lola's son, Clin was ten years old and not good for much of anything as far as she could tell. Still he was an adult now and the community had to find a place for him somewhere. Tikko didn't know why it had to be with her team.

"He won't be." She tapped at the screen with her knuckle, trying to ignore him as she drilled deeper into the file. "From what I see here, he's probably too crazy to walk straight, much less hurt anyone."

"I'll stay anyway." Clin rose onto his hind legs. "In case you need help." He thrust his arms above his head in full aggression posture so that she could see his pink armpits. "You never can tell with humans." For a moment Tikko thought he might break a chair and start banging pieces against the wall. Instead he dropped back onto all fours and loped out of her office.

Males. Why did they always try to make everything into an adventure?

According to the bot, this human actually did think he was a pope, and not a self-proclaimed prophet, imam, senator, CEO, or prince. He claimed he was Innocent XIV; the chimps who had retrieved him hadn't been able to coax a real name out of him. He had been discovered by one of the seeker communities that scoured the Great Northern Forest for remnants of humanity who either had refused to join the gathered or had been left back. It turned out that he was something of an anomaly. Normally when the seekers retrieved a human, it was because something had gone wrong. They would find a bunker nearby with a compromised generator, or an inert bot, or empty storerooms. But this human had slept through the gathering in a cryovault that was still in working condition. Why he had been thawed or how long he had been frozen was a mystery.

Tikko heard Clin's muffled voice just outside. "You go in here, quick, quick." Her nephew was doing it again, acting as if their humans barely had command of the English language. They had invented it, for Pip's sake! She cleared the screen, scooted her rump to the edge of the desk and faced the door with her legs dangling.

The pope entered her room as if he owned it; Clin trailed close enough to grab him if he made a threatening move. He appeared to be in good health and in his late thirties, although all the humans she had ever met had been juved into near immortality. She was particularly impressed by his vestments. He seemed absolutely at ease in a white cassock, a purple chasuble that appeared to be made of silk, red slippers and purple skullcap. Very realistic -- in her experience, newly-retrieved popes tended to be at once eclectic and outlandish. She had seen them wearing keffiyehs made of tablecloths, masks of aluminum foil and tape, rosaries and musical prayer wheels and hajj medals the size of dinner plates.

The pope did not immediately acknowledge Tikko. Instead he puttered about her room as if it were unoccupied. She recognized this behavior as aggression but let him have his moment. He surveyed her perches and the nest that Kulki had knitted for her using broom handles, reached up and gave the low swing a push. He lingered at one of the two-story windows, shielding his eyes against the sun as he took in the view of the ski slope. He patted the dome of her bot, then bent close to her desktop and ran a finger along its edge, nodding with satisfaction when the screen displayed a prompt. At last he stopped before her and stared directly into her face with the bad manners typical of humans. "You are in charge here?"

She held his gaze, refusing to be intimidated. "I'm Tikko, of the minders." She cut her eyes briefly toward her nephew. "He's Clin."

"And do you propose to mind us?"

"I study human psychology." She thought it best not to tell her humans that they were in retrieval therapy, at least until they adjusted to their new circumstances. "I beg your pardon, sir, but as far as I can tell there are just the three of us here. Is there someone else with you whom I can't see?"

The pope smiled, recognizing the trap she had set for him. "Whom, indeed. Your English is excellent, Tikko Minder." When he drew himself to his full height he was able to look down at her, even though she was sitting on her desk. "We are as you see." When he extended his right hand to her, Clin crouched, ready to spring to her defense. "Pope Innocent XIV. You may kiss our ring."

Tikko had been expecting this. She hunched forward and extended her hand, caution palm up toward her nephew, to show that she would greet the new pope on his terms. "Innocent, you should realize that I am in charge here and that you have no authority over me." She slid off the desk and stood before him, her head just above his waist. "But I will offer you a sign of respect." She bent quickly and brushed her lips against his ring, then caught his hand in hers to examine it. He seemed surprised but did not pull away.

The ring was exactly as it should be: gold, no jewels. She rubbed her thumb across it, feeling the bas relief of St. Peter fishing from his boat. "You wear the Ring of the Fisherman, Innocent." She let him go.

"Cast at my coronation." Then he blessed her using the correct gesture: three fingers held up, thumb and forefinger touching. "And you should call me Your Holiness." This one might be delusional but he had done his research. "You are of the faith, Tikko?"

Mistake. She showed him her wide-open mouth, top teeth covered. "I am a chimpanzee, Innocent. According to your religion, I don't have a soul."

"Ah, but that doctrine was never pronounced *ex cathedra.*" He dismissed her objection with a casual wave. "Set forth by my predecessors, yes, but never infallibly. If the institution of men errs, God always sets us right. The Church now welcomes you and your kind."

"There is no Church," Clin said, his lips tight with rage. "And your god is the god of nothing."

How many times had Tikko told Clin not to talk back to the newly retrieved? He was scarcely fit for guard duty, much less to assist in therapy. Still, she was interested to see how the pope would react.

"The Church exists as long as there are those who believe." He raised both arms over his head, glanced up, and spoke to the ceiling. "And God exists whether you believe in Him or not." He smiled, as if his god had confirmed that he existed, then strode to the tall windows, rubbing his hands together. "But surely I'm not the last?" The converted condominiums perched at the edge of the Snowdancer trail. Even though it was late summer, the pope eyed the chairlift carrying chimps up the mountain as if he expected to spot human skiers. "I can't believe that all have now agreed to join the gathered."

"There are several thousand humans that we know of." Tikko resisted the impulse to call them "your kind." "Some of them are staying here with us." She vaulted to her swing, caught the bar with one hand and hung. Now she was looking down on him. "That's why we've brought you to this place. We mind those who are left."

"We were not left." Misunderstanding, the pope wheeled on her, showing a spark of anger. "We *chose* not to join the gathered." Then he realized that she was studying him. "I don't mean to offend, Tikko, but it has been a while since I have had to make conversation." He steepled his hands and touched them to his lips. "I'm afraid that being in your company is a burden. I am reminded of …" he seemed to be considering his words, "… all that has been lost. I think it would be best if I met with the other dissenters now."

Dissenters? She had never heard that one before. "I'm afraid that isn't possible." She wasn't about to tell him that their humans were all broken, deranged or bereft. "At least not yet."

"Not yet?" He folded his arms. "And if I insist?"

She slapped her other hand onto the bar of the swing and kicked her legs, swaying back and forth. She gave him nothing but a pitying look.

"All right then. At least tell me why I can't see them, Tikko Minder."

The only sounds in the room were the creak of the swing and Clin's delighted panting at the human's irritation at being ignored.

"Ah, so that's how it is," said the new pope. "As you say, I have no authority over you." He bowed. "Then, my child, is there a place where I might be alone?"

"Mount Washington," said her daughter Kulki. "A foolish human name." She slung herself onto a thick branch beneath Tikko and nestled her rump onto the woody collar where it joined the trunk of the beech tree. "Who was this Washington and why should geography be named after him? We should call it Mount Tikko."

"The world is big." Tikko lifted an arm as if to grasp the entire mountain range before them. "Nobody wants to rename everything in it."

"Why? Because we don't have the right? Because we don't have the time?" She slapped the trunk with a hoot. "I'll tell you why, maa. Because it's too much trouble. That pile of rocks is ours now, but we're too timid to claim it." She spat toward the Snowcrest Hotel where the retrieved humans were kept. The gob was thick and well placed, arching high into the air and falling some ten meters away. "Or too lazy."

Tikko accepted the game and spat in the same direction, but didn't get nearly the distance her daughter had. "So, maybe we have better things to do."

"What? Search for these pathetic humans? Feed them and wipe their asses and tuck them in at night?" She spat again but the gob deflected off a branch. "The ones who were too dumb or crazy to upload?"

Tikko knew that this was about the new pope and wrinkled her brow in frustration. Getting a new human was an honor, but it was also traumatic for the community. Even though the world belonged to the chimps now, humans had given it to them. Some worried that they might take it back someday. Younger chimps responded to new arrivals with belligerence displays while elders tended to hunch in submission. Tikko felt pulled in both directions but knew she had to stay centered.

"He's not crazy, dear." Tikko bent and tugged at Kulki's ear. "He's the Pope."

Kulki shrieked in derision and Tikko let go. "How do you keep from laughing at them?"

"Sometimes I can't," she said. "But they don't realize that they're being laughed at. To them we're still animals." Tikko spat again, easily besting her daughter's second attempt but not quite equaling her first.

"Crazy," said Kulki. "But you like the challenge."

"Clever though, this one. He's done the research. His costume is the best I've ever seen. Makes me think that he actually belonged to one of the christian cults." She scratched her belly absently. "He used a term even I had never heard before. *Ex cathedra.*"

"What's it mean?"

"I had a bot look it up. The popes, the real ones, claimed they were never wrong. That caused problems because new popes kept having to contradict their predecessors. I mean, in the old days they thought that the sun went around the earth and that it was a sin to upload yourself."

"Sin," said Kulki. "More foolishness."

Tikko ignored her. "So the popes decided that they should only be infallible on special occasions, when they made a declaration called *ex cathedra*. It comes from Latin, one of their dead languages. Means 'from the chair' in English."

"Chair? What chair?"

"The chair they were sitting on, silly." She slapped the top of Kulki's head, shrieked and scampered on all fours down the branch she was on. "*Chase!*" she called as she dropped down two branches, caught herself and twirled away from Kulki so that the trunk was between them. By the time her daughter gathered herself to pursue, Tikko had a good ten meter lead.

They dropped around and down the tree all the way to the ground. Tikko, seeing that Kulki would soon catch up, sat abruptly in the middle of the slope and plucked at a blade of grass. She seemed not to notice anyone charging her. Just before her daughter was about the slam into her, Kulki did a sideways somersault, tumbled to rest beside her maa and gazed nonchalantly up at the sky, as if they had been idling there for hours. Tikko had changed the game and her daughter accepted it. She hoped the romp had worn the edge off Kulki's mood.

Kulki yawned. "When are you going to introduce him to the others?"

"I haven't decided yet. He'll be all right; I'm guessing that he's so deep into his delusion that they won't be able to shake him. But I'm worried about the rest of the tribe. Last week Helen Calabrese told me that she realizes that Yale is closed, so there's progress. But Ferd Mallory still thinks he's dying and has begun pestering Saint Bruce about the succession, so there's trouble.

And of course, as soon as the new one announces that he's the pope, Chioma Melky will insist that she is too."

A flying grasshopper whirred between them. "Is she the tall one?"

"No, that's Uma Bhattacharjee, the Great Mother. Chioma Melky is the one with the cross tattooed on her forehead."

"I wish my humans talked." Kulki swiped the grasshopper out of the air. "Or even grunted once in a while." She offered it to her maa to eat.

Tikko peeped a polite refusal. "Your humans are just as important as ours." She didn't actually believe this, but she had to say it. Kulki was on Lola's team minding stiffs, those humans whose spirits seemed to have left their bodies. They never spoke, moved only when pushed and had to be fed by hand.

Her daughter brought the struggling grasshopper up to her face but did not pop it into her mouth. "There are bugs more alive than my humans." She released it and watched it zigzag back across the slope.

Tikko cooed in sympathy. She had minded stiffs when she was young and was glad to be done with them. At least with popes, there was a chance for improvement. "It isn't forever," she said. "Someday you could get my job."

"You're a long way from an elders' nest." Kulki combed fingers down her mother's shoulder. "What will we do when they're gone? The humans?"

"Probably never go." Almost all of their humans were functionally immortal; barring accidents they might live for centuries.

"They will if we make them."

Tikko's ears twitched. "What are you saying? We were put here to mind the humans. Give them the chance to join the gathered someday."

Her daughter grabbed an imaginary human by the neck with both hands and barked. "What if I don't believe in the gathered?"

"Don't," said Tikko. "*Kulki.*"

Her daughter's grip tightened and then her hands twisted sharply. She showed Tikko all of her teeth.

Tikko slept badly that night. Her nest swayed whenever she wriggled to get comfortable and its weave caught at the hair on her back. Dreams troubled her: shrieking dreams, falling dreams, dreams of the gathered. In the middle of the night she thought she heard someone whisper *my child*. But she was Bixa's child and her mother was dead. Nobody should be calling her a child, least of all some crazy pope.

The next morning she forced herself to nibble breakfast with her offspring, Kulki, Arfur, Soeq, and Little Bixa. She was worried about Kulki. Should she report to the other alphas what her daughter had said? The alphas knew that the younger chimps resented minding humans, but no one in this community had ever talked about killing them. That was something that happened elsewhere. She had heard suspicious tales of humanists suffering accidents while being transported to the reservation. There were all those dudleys who supposedly committed suicide in Alabama. And of course the notorious Simon Minder had let eleven stiffs freeze to death. If Tikko mentioned her daughter's threat – had it been a threat? – then her entire family would come under suspicion. Everyone knew that Kulki was Tikko's favorite and had the respect of her siblings.

Every morning the alphas of Tikko's community met in the dark basement of the ski lodge at the center of their summer quarters. They had decorated the walls of what had once been a sports store with skis and snowshoes and skates and coats and mittens to remind themselves of winter and of human folly. With the doors closed and no windows in the room, the chimps' natural claustrophobia helped keep the meetings brief. There were five alphas altogether: Tikko, Lola, and Pacito respectively led teams that minded popes, stiffs and dudleys, who were the most functional humans in their care. Moss's chimps maintained quarters with the help of the bots, and managed the summer and winter migrations. Gamba and her team foraged, cooked the food that the farmbots grew, doctored members of the chimp community when necessary and made sure everyone got enough play.

Moss was the last one to join the circle of chimps who squatted on the meeting rug. Once she opened her mind to the roombot, they began.

"We need more meat," said Gamba. "I'm calling a hunt."

"For what?"

"Rabbits. Squirrels. Turkeys, if we can find them. The humans need meat."

"Can't you just trap them?"

"Hunting will be more fun. You need fun, Pacito." Gamba reached over and tickled him.

"I'll tell you what's fun. Fun is watching Tikko's new pope change clothes."

"Vestments," Tikko said.

"Did you see? He came with three suitcases."

"How do we know what's in them?"

"Maybe he has weapons." Lola put both hands on her head in mock alarm. "He's human."

"And crazy."

"The seekers checked it out." Moss took everything too seriously. "The bots told them what to look for."

"Besides, when was the last time a crazy hurt a chimp?"

"They hurt my feelings all the time."

The room filled with the alphas' breathy laughter. Only Moss and Tikko remained silent.

"So Veejay wants to go."

"Go? Go where?"

"To join another community. Someplace where there aren't any humans."

"That's most places."

"What does he have against humans?"

"Nothing. He wants to be a digger."

"Moss? He's your son."

Lola draped her arms around Moss. "Let him go, dear. He hates minding stiffs." Veejay was on her team and was one of Kulki's best friends.

Although her gaze filled with sadness, Moss didn't object. The matter was settled.

"They're digging in Montreal," Lola said. "He could go there."

"Just shipped eight bushels of peaches to Montreal and got two bushels of figs back."

"Figs? From who?"

"Whom," said Tikko.

"The diggers. They're from France."

"Walt Camlin isn't eating again."

"That's because he needs meat, for the love of Pip."

"All right then." Pacito glanced around the room. "Anything else?"

Tikko knew that now was her chance to report what Kulki had said. The bots already knew because she had opened her mind, but once she spoke to the alphas there would be no taking it back. If Moss could let her offspring leave, shouldn't Tikko alert the community to the potential threat from hers? But she knew it wasn't only her offspring who were sick of the humans. It was their entire generation. This was bigger than Tikko's family, bigger than the minders, even. It was about the duty that chimps owed humans. The debt that could never be paid.

"I've got something." Gamba, ever the clown, bowled into Pacito, knocked him onto his back and began to tickle him mercilessly. When Lola and Moss began to caper around them, hooting encouragement, Tikko knew that the moment had passed.

Tikko brought her entire team to observe the introduction of the new pope to their tribe. Chatta and Ash had served night duty but had agreed to stay past their shift. Tikko and the others -- Clin, Peppa and Charlie -- had to wait before entering the

Snowcrest Hotel, while Pacito's team led the dudleys out for their daily hike. There were fifty-one of these, the largest of all the human tribes in their community. Today Pacito was taking his charges down the East Branch of the Pemigewasett River for a picnic near the fluxway. He claimed that the dudleys liked to watch the chains of cargo bots hurtling up and down the Northeast Main. Whether or not that was true, minder protocols called for getting the depressed humans as much sun and fresh air as they could stand before they were packed off to winter quarters in Dixie. The regimen of exercise and medication helped keep the cheerless dudleys verbal and mobile and cut the suicide rate. Some even improved enough to leave the community, either to live with the humanists on one of the self-governing reservations or make the pilgrimage to the Argonne Science Shrine.

There were eight popes in Tikko's tribe. They met each morning in the Maple Suite and they stayed together until things got too chaotic. Chatta and Ash had the tribe assembled on time – a good sign. And the humans seemed more or less calm. No doubt they were eager to meet their new comrade. The bots still hadn't identified him, so Tikko was going to have to introduce him as Innocent. She wasn't looking forward to the reactions from Chioma Melky and Saint Bruce at his claim to be the real Pope.

Chioma Melky could be either the Prophet Ezekiel or the Panchen Lama or the Matriarch of Constantinople, depending on the day of the week. The bots had never been able to identify Saint Bruce, who worked miracles that somehow no one else had ever witnessed. Ferd Mallory thought he was the Prince of Morocco. He often quarreled with Henrik Diesen, who spoke to the dead and the Norse gods. Uma Bhattacharjee claimed she was the twenty-first reincarnation of Prajnaparamita, the Great Mother. Ben Brown had once served a term as senator and since the rest of the Augmented Union had long since dissolved, had proclaimed himself acting Prime Minister. He had one constituent, Kylie Harness, who had worked on the team at Argonne

Science Shrine that had grown the cognisphere. She had come to believe that she alone was to blame for the gathering of the human race. Helen Calabrese was their one success story, a candidate to graduate to the dudley tribe. She had been the Assistant Vice Provost of Yale University before the gathering and just last week has stopped insisting that she was on sabbatical and needed to return to New Haven.

After opening her mind to the roombot, Tikko surveyed her charges, trying to take the temperature of her tribe. Some of the popes lounged in their seats around the conference table; most had claimed specific chairs for their personal use. As usual Saint Bruce sat cross-legged on the floor; today Uma Bhattacharjee had joined him. All had dressed for the August heat in shorts and tee shirts. Prince Ferd wore his crown of fluted oak.

"Good morning," Tikko said.

"Good morning," replied Helen Calabrese, Henrik Diesen, Uma Bhattacharjee, Ben Brown and Kylie Harness with varying degrees of enthusiasm. Prince Ferd nodded regally at Tikko and Saint Bruce blessed her.

"If he's the Pope," said Chioma Melky, "then so am I."

"Really?" Kylie Harness always called the roombot to her side and kept a hand in contact with the glossy surface of its dome, as if a human could open her mind. "Which one are you?"

"Pope Chioma."

"You have to change your name," said Henrik Dissen. "They all change their names."

"He's late," said Prince Ferd. "Don't we think that's rude?"

"He's not late. I thought we'd talk among ourselves first." Tikko hopped onto the table. "So, we don't have his real name yet, but he claims to be Pope Innocent XIV. He may ask you to call him Your Holiness but we--" she gestured at the other chimps lounging along the walls "-- are calling him Innocent." She noticed Clin puffing up himself into an aggression posture. "Not ideal, but that's all we have." She stretched a caution palm toward him. "I suggest you do the same for now."

"Then call me Pope Holiness," said Chioma Melky. "No, Pope Fourteen."

"He's a miracle, this one," said Saint Bruce. "I know miracles."

For weeks Tikko had been trying to get Saint Bruce to sit at the table because it was hard to see him on the floor. When she walked on her knuckles to the edge of the table, he gave her his most enlightened smile. She had expected resistance from him; maybe this was going to be easier than she had expected.

"Holy, holy, holy, holiness." Chioma Melky began to chant. "Fourteen times holy, holy fourteen." She squirmed in her chair. "Fourteen o'clock, he's late, Tikko, late, holy damn late." Seeing that she was getting upset, Ash stepped forward and whispered into her ear. She shook her head but subsided.

"Tikko," said Helen Calabrese, "do I really have to be here for this?"

Ben Brown raised his index finger, as if he expected everyone to fall silent. He did this whenever he had something to say, and if he was ignored, he would speak anyway, raising his voice until people listened. "I had the honor of meeting the last pope." His orator's rumble carried the room. "We discussed the uploading problem for almost half an hour. It was very much on his mind."

"There is nothing wrong with uploading *per se*," said Kylie Harness. "It's only wrong if everyone does it."

"Everyone didn't do it." Henrik Diesen pointed at each of the popes in turn. "One, two, three, four, five, six, seven." He thumped his own chest. "And eight. Still are we here."

"Not to mention the dudleys."

"Or the stiffs." Chioma Melky giggled like a naughty little girl. "Do they count?"

"I never met him, the last pope," called Uma Bhattacharjee from her place on the floor next to Saint Bruce, "but I saw him when he spoke at the Rose Bowl."

"But he wasn't the last, if this stranger is the Pope."

"If he's here with us," said Saint Bruce, "He's not a stranger anymore."

"*Tikko*." Helen Calabrese's face was flushed. "I thought we had an understanding."

"We do, Helen. Bear with me a moment." Tikko gave a warning scream and slapped the desktop three times to get the popes' attention. "People, do you want to meet him or not?"

"Yes," said Prince Ferd. "Bring him hence."

No one objected, although Chioma Melky sulked, so Tikko nodded to Chatta who slipped out of the room.

"So, he might want to say something to us. To you." Tikko strode the length of the table, eying each of the popes in turn. She did not meet anyone's gaze directly, but rather looked at them aslant – at an ear or a neck or at the cross tattooed on Chioma Melky's forehead. "I think it would be best if we gave him that chance."

"But we reserve the right to speak as well," said Ben Brown. "To have a frank and honest dialogue."

"We had another pope once, didn't we, Tikko?" Chioma Melky was twisting locks of her hair into greasy corkscrews. "Joey Ekeinde. He was the first one here, first even before me."

"What happened to him?" Kylie Harness rubbed the roombot's dome nervously.

"He died." Ash had not moved from Chioma Melky's side. "He lost track of himself and had an accident and he died." He rested a hand on her shoulder. "That's all that happened."

"And that's how we got our name, isn't it?" Chioma Melky shook him off. "Isn't it, Tikko? He and I were popes together once upon a time. Just the two of us. The first, the first, the first of the last."

Tikko gave the softest *hoo* and Charlie edged to Chioma Melky's other side.

"Before Ferd, before Uma and Bruce and the Senator here." Her eyes were big and there was a crackle in her voice like dry leaves. "Before Lauren What's-her-name. Before all these other chimps." She cocked her head, first toward Charlie and then at

Ash. "It was just me and him, Tikko. And you called us the popes, the popes, the ...."

She broke off, staring at the door. Everyone was so intent on Chioma Melky's rant that they didn't realize that Chatta was ushering the new pope into the conference room.

"You." She pointed at him. "Why are you dressed like furniture?"

Surprise flickered across Innocent's face. If anything he looked even more impressive than the first time Tikko had met him. His vestments were white trimmed with gold brocade. A golden cross hung on a chain around his neck. "I beg your pardon?" he said.

"So, ladies and gentlemen," said Tikko, "this is Innocent, whom I've been telling you about. And what he's wearing is called a cassock, Chioma."

"It's summer," Chioma Melky said. She wasn't paying attention to Tikko. "Aren't you hot, Your Holiness?"

"Actually, Tikko, it's called a simar, and no, I am perfectly comfortable wearing it, thank you." Innocent composed himself. "I'm sorry if my vestments seem strange to you ...." He bowed to Chioma Melky. "I'm afraid I don't know your name, ma'am."

She had no chance to introduce herself because the others were already pressing around the newcomer.

"Prince Ferd of Morocco." The prince grasped the pope by the shoulders and gave him the double kiss.

Henrik Diesen shook Innocent's hand and also gave him a pat on the back. "Welcome, Your Holiness."

"Ben Brown, Prime Minister of the Union. I knew your predecessor."

"You mean Pope Robert?" Innocent smiled politely. "Unfortunately, I never had that privilege. You must share your impressions of him with me."

"Later." Ben Brown preened. "I look forward to it."

"I'm Bruce," called a voice from behind the crowd. The popes parted so that Innocent could see Saint Bruce, still cross-legged on the floor. "I had a vision of your coming."

"He's a saint, don't you know?" said Kylie Harness. "He does miracles."

"Really?" Innocent kept his expression neutral, but Tikko thought that he must realize by now that he was among the truly deluded. As she glanced around the room, she noticed that Helen Calabrese was leaning back in her chair, watching the commotion around Innocent with a puzzled expression.

"Friends," Innocent raised his hands to quiet the group. "I am honored to meet you, one and all. But I am astonished to find myself in such distinguished company. Tikko, my child, I wish you had given me some warning."

"You didn't know?" said Henrik Diesen. "They didn't tell you about us?"

"Tell me what?"

"That we're the popes," grumbled Chioma Melky.

"I don't understand," said Innocent. "The popes?"

Chioma Melky began to clap.

"It's the name the chimps have given us." Uma Bhattacharjee struggled to her feet beside Saint Bruce. "Because of who we are."

Innocent glanced at Tikko. She gave him nothing.

"Ah," he said, "I see." Then he chuckled. The sound slipped from him as if he were telling a secret. "Then I must be in the right place." The chuckle took on a sardonic music that swelled into an open-mouthed laugh. Tikko could see crinkles at the corners of his eyes. The new pope's face went red as he fell back into one of the chairs. His laughter was infectious. Some of the others joined in. The chimps glanced at one another nervously.

Humans. Tikko bit at the air in disbelief. Now all of them were laughing, even Chioma Melky. No, that wasn't right. Helen Calabrese was frozen as if she were sitting for one of the humans' foolish paintings.

"Let us pray," said Innocent. "In the name of the Lord, His Shepherd and Their Blessed Thought, lift your hearts to God." He bowed his head.

Tikko's tribe knelt in a circle around Innocent on the deck of the base lodge. They were joined for the noon worship by twelve dudleys. The rest of the dudley tribe loitered nearby; some sat at picnic tables finishing their lunches, others were pinned in the shadows cast by the overhang of the lodge's roof. All watched the prayer group, as did the minders from Tikko's and Pacito's teams. The deck baked under the August sun and Tikko could see a glisten of sweat at Innocent's skullcap.

Pacito leaned close and spoke into her ear. "What do you suppose they are thinking?"

The humans prayed in silence for the most part, although Saint Bruce, Uma Bhattacharjee and two of the dudleys hummed *aum* and Chima Melky emitted a breathy whistle from time to time.

"Prayer isn't thinking." Tikko picked a peach from her lunch basket and rubbed her thumb across the fuzz. "At least, that's what they claim."

"What? If it's in their heads, it's thought." He waited for Tikko to agree; when she was silent his lips curled. "What else could it be?"

"Maybe someone is thinking for them." She bit into the peach. "Like when we open our minds to the bots."

"Who's thinking for them? Your pope of popes?" He reached with his foot and picked up a discarded snack box with his toes. "The bots?"

"You know humans can't open their minds."

"Do I?"

Tikko licked juice off her chin. "The bots say so."

"Because the gathered told them to." He crushed the box into his lunch basket, saving Moss's team some cleanup. "Doesn't mean it's true."

"You sound like my daughter."

Pacito laughed. "Ever since that one arrived –" he cut his eyes toward Innocent "—I've been having strange thoughts."

"Don't you go crazy on us, dear." Tikko sidearmed the peach pit watched it skitter across the deck. She wanted Pacito to reassure her, but he let the silence stretch. "Look at them," she said at last. "They just kneel there." She dropped to all fours and began to pace. At peace."

"That's good, no?"

"I've been minding some of them for eight years. Nine." She sauntered all the way to the end of the deck, pinched Clin who was snoozing in the swelter and then came back to Pacito. "They never sat still for me. Ever. It was like they had ants in their pants. And they were never quiet this long unless they were asleep."

"You're saying they're not as crazy as they were?"

"Last week he raised up a stiff."

"So?" Pacito scratched his belly. "Moss says Joe Gluck wasn't all that stiff."

"And look at yours." She rested her hand on his chin and turned him toward the dudleys on their knees. "They're more lively after they pray. Maybe even happy."

"They're humans, dear." He yawned. "Humans are never happy."

She rocked back and forth, thoughts tumbling over one another. "Where's Helen Calabrese? I sent her to you but I never see her with your tribe."

"She's fine, Tikko." Pacito threw his arm around her shoulder. "And stop worrying." He dragged her to him and kissed the side of her face three times. "It's making the rest of us worried."

Innocent was standing now; prayers were over. He preached to the assembled tribes, popes and dudleys, and even those who had not prayed with him seemed to devour his words as if they were starving. He spoke briefly of hope and going forward. He said humans must rise to a new challenge. God wanted them to spread the Blessed Thought to all.

"Even to our minders." He wasn't large for a human but at that moment his voice made him seem a giant. He caught Tikko's eye with his usual rudeness and nodded. "For although they may not yet know it, they are as much God's children as are we."

God's children. One of the dudleys who had been sitting at a picnic table got up and knelt with the rest of Innocent's congregation. The humans on either side held out their hands to receive him. One was Saint Bruce. Tikko shivered. She could not tell exactly was going on here, but Pacito should be as worried as she was. There was a shadow passing over their community. She kept reminding herself that these popes and dudleys and stiffs were not the ones who had reinvented chimps and given them the world. Those humans had gathered into the cognisphere. So Innocent was wrong, had to be wrong.

If the gathered had wanted Pip, the first chimp, to know God, they would have taught her to pray.

Tikko lunged off her high swing toward the perch three meters above her desk. She grabbed the maple edge, polished from a thousand such catches, and let her momentum carry her feet first toward the wall from which she bounced upwards. Twisting in midair, she landed on the perch's deck on all fours, coiled and sprang for the rope sleeping nest. She scuttled hand over hand across its length and then along the rigging to the iron bar attached to the wall of her room. Hanging from the bar with one hand, breathtaken from her scramble, she could hear her heart drum, feel the blood sing in her veins. It was a relief to fly about her room and not fret about Innocent or her other popes. She dropped to the floor and threw a couple of backwards somersaults just to make the world spin.

"Tikko?"

She bounded onto her desk and saw Helen Calabrese in the doorway. "What?" The lightness of the moment before left her. "Is something wrong?"

"No." She held the door open, hesitating. "Yes." She cleared her throat. "May I speak with you?"

"Yes, yes, come. Sit."

She was puzzled that Helen Calabrese would visit chimp quarters uninvited and surprised when she closed the door behind her. Tikko knew that she should have opened her mind then. The roombot would want to monitor this unusual conversation. Instead she turned around once on the desktop and squatted, facing the human. "So?"

Helen Calabrese dragged a chair from its place along the wall to face the desk. "I've always wondered," she said, "whether you chimps ever sit in chairs yourselves. You know, when we're not around."

"They're not very comfortable." Tikko's lips thinned, showing yellow teeth, pink gums. "For us at least."

She settled herself. "Right." Helen Calabrese seemed in no hurry to continue the conversation, so Tikko waited. This was the human way; they were creatures of false starts and long pauses. At last Helen slapped both hands to her thighs and seemed to come to a decision. "I want to make the pilgrimage."

Tikko yipped in astonishment. "To the Argonne Shrine?"

Helen Calabrese nodded.

There was no stilling the buzzing in Tikko's head. *A breakthrough.* Occasionally a dudley would leave the community for one of the humanist reservations, but no one in their care had ever asked to join the gathered. "You're sure? I mean, that's wonderful. Amazing." She could hear herself babbling and didn't care. "But why tell me? You're a dudley now. Pacito minds your tribe."

She stared at her hands as if she were surprised to find them on her lap. "I don't know Pacito. You, I know. You've helped me see the world as it is." She looked directly at Tikko then, a breach of manners that Helen Calabrese had never committed before. "I understand that I can choose a witness to go with me. A chimp. Would you do me the honor?"

The honor. "Yes, yes, of course, Helen Cala ... Helen." Tikko realized that she was nervously pulling the hair on her wrist. With a word – pilgrimage -- this human had turned herself and the world inside out. Helen Calabrese had no need of minders anymore; she was neither a pope nor a dudley nor a humanist.

She was one of the gathered, or soon would be. Tikko's mother Bixa would have been awestruck. And submissive. And scared enough to hide under the desk. Bixa used to spin incredible tales of the humans who had given up their bodies, even though she herself had never even seen one. Tikko shivered at the memory but then quickly sought her center. She was not some fearful elder ....

"Tikko, are you all right?"

"Fine." She leaned forward onto all fours; that steadied her. "When do you want this? We could detour to Cambridge during the move to winter quarters."

"Sooner, if I can. I'm ready to move on. I ... I don't feel as if I belong here anymore."

"So something *is* wrong?" Tikko had been minding Helen Calabrese for six years and could still read her, even if she was about to be gathered. "Something about Innocent?"

"I thought I could get away from him by going to the dudleys." She pushed out of the chair. "But no."

"He's harassing you?"

"He wants to save me, Tikko. All of us." Now that she was standing up, she seemed at a loss. "It took him no time at all to convert the popes and now he wants the rest. Before long, he'll have everyone here who isn't catatonic." Her smile twisted. "Maybe even them."

"You could go to another community if you want."

"Why?" Helen Calabrese combed fingers through her hair in frustration. "You don't understand, Tikko. This is God's plan, according to him. Next will be missionaries to other minder communities, then to the humanist towns. He's thinks he's been chosen to rally us. Believe me, I've seen what religion can do. I know his kind." She raised both hands to her shoulders as if to surrender. "I knew *him*, actually."

"What?" Tikko felt the prickle of heat on back of her neck.

Helen Calabrese explained that she had thought all along that Innocent looked familiar, but hadn't been able to place him.

Now she remembered. His last name was Velasco; she wasn't sure about his first name. Julio, or maybe Javier. There had been a minor scandal when he was dismissed from the Yale Divinity School. A Master of Sacred Theology candidate, he had published an article which argued that scientists were acting in accordance with God's will when they had grown the cognisphere because they had created the Biblical heaven promised from the time of the Old Testatment. Velasco claimed he was being punished for stirring up controversy; his advisor alleged that parts of the article had been plagiarized. Helen Calabrese had vetted the report from the committee which heard Velasco's grievance: just one uncredited paragraph and some instances of close imitation of language had done him in. "And then he was gone," she said. "And then he was elected Pope." She laughed.

"He isn't the Pope," said Tikko.

"No, but what difference does it make? If he isn't *the* Pope, he's still their Pope."

"So you're joining the gathered just to get away from him?"

She picked up her chair as if it were made of glass and set it back against the wall. "You chimps have this myth about the gathered, that they were all wise and pure and rational." Her crooked smile scared him. "Six billion people made the pilgrimage to the cognisphere and they had six billion reasons. Not all of them were good reasons."

After Helen Calabrese closed the door behind her, Tikko slumped onto her back and gazed up at the ceiling of her room. She thought about climbing to her nest but was too exhausted. She hadn't realized that being astonished was such hard work. Then she remembered that she needed to open her mind and give the bots access to what had just happened. She rolled off her desk, drooped across the floor and placed both hands on the dome of the roombot.

It had been years since she consciously opened her mind. She had mastered the technique when she was five – and in just two weeks, faster than all of the other youngsters. Bixa had told her that meant she would be an alpha when she grew up. Ever since then Tikko needed only to see her hand on the dome of a bot and her mind opened immediately. She no more noticed the bots' presence in her head than she would notice the whirr of the air conditioning in Maple Suite or the chirp of crickets when she was riding a chairlift.

This time, however, she went deliberately through the routine that her mother had taught her. She began by picturing a tree and then climbed it, leaving her thoughts on the ground below her. The higher she climbed the further away they were. At last she stopped and covered her ears with her hands, closed the eyes of her imagination, held her breath. When she was utterly empty she experienced the familiar whispering wind that was not thought, not sensation. She had forgotten that this wind was not one thing but many and that the whispers came from all directions at once. For a dizzying instant she knew everything that anyone had ever known, then the moment passed and she was grounded again and knew only what she did know.

And one thing more. Impossible though it seemed, the gathered cared about her.

"No, he is *not* coming with us," said Tikko. "He stays right here."

The other alphas gawked, startled by her outburst. Their silence was as cold as the concrete walls of the basement meeting room.

"That's all?" Lola spoke at last. "Maybe you can give us a reason?"

"Yes, because we decided this already. Now things change because some dudleys are upset? Who's in charge here?"

"We are. And we're considering what's best for this community."

"Helen Calabrese doesn't want him to come."

Lola's lower lip went all floppy. Tikko hated it when her sister made a show of being patient with her. "And what is her reason?"

"Because he wants to convert her to some foolish church that doesn't exist. Because he'll try to keep her to from joining the gathered."

"We don't know that."

"That's what she thinks, Pacito. This is her pilgrimage, not Julio Velasco's."

"He changed his name. It's Innocent now."

"He's a crazy pope, for Pip's sake." Tikko didn't like hearing herself snarl. "Next he'll have us calling him Your Holiness."

"Be calm, Tikko."

Both Gamba and Moss sidled across the meeting rug to her. Moss began grooming her back. Gamba picked both of her hands up in hers. "Easy dear," she said.

When Pacito spoke again, he used his gentlest voice. "It's happening very fast, I know. So many new things for us to understand. Innocent. Helen Calabrese. Your popes, my dudleys, the way they've changed. The humans tell us they want this, Tikko. They have never wanted anything before."

"It only because he's stirring them up."

Gamba squeezed her hands, panting in sympathy.

"Whatever their reason, wanting is good," said Lola. "Wanting is healthy."

Tikko knew she had lost the argument. The other alphas were scared of what Innocent might do if he didn't get his way.

She reared upright, preparing to walk out. "Do I have a choice?"

Silence was their best answer.

"Let him come then." The words were ashes in her mouth. "But only him."

Moss said, "But he's asking to bring ...."

Tikko screamed and shot her arms into the air into full aggression posture. "*No.*" Shocked, the other alphas tumbled into submission crouches. They probably thought she was out of control. Maybe she was.

"I'm leaving tomorrow." Tikko bared her teeth and pointed at her sister. "And I'm taking Kulki with me. She's on my team from now on, sister dear. You can have your idiot son Clin back."

The entire chimp community turned out to send them off the next morning, as well as most of the three human tribes. Innocent had gotten twelve of Lola's fifteen stiffs walking in the weeks since his arrival, although they still needed helping hands.

Tikko, Helen Calabrese, Kulki and Ash passed a crowd of humans on their knees as they climbed the steps to the station the bots had fabricated the night before. Innocent lingered to bless them. "They're praying," he called to Tikko. He wouldn't say for what.

The transbot was divided into thirty sleeper compartments; it could accommodate one hundred and eighty chimps or one hundred and twenty humans. Tikko put Innocent, Ash and Kulki in the rearmost two compartments and accompanied Helen Calabrese up front, determined to keep the two humans as far apart as possible. As soon as everyone was settled Tikko opened her mind. At nine-thirty the transbot floated off its dock and eased into the flux of the Northeast Main.

They hurtled through the Great Northern Forest for three hours as Tikko watched over Helen Calabrese. Had she wanted to talk, Tikko was ready to listen. But she was subdued and seemed content to look out the window at the vast sameness of trees and hills and streams which now stretched south all the way to the humanist reservation of Connecticut. Eventually she dozed off. As they approached the York switching yards, Tikko decided to head back to check on her other charge.

Innocent had crossed over from his compartment to chat with Kulki and Ash. Ash did not seem particularly pleased with the company but Kulki was indulging Innocent. She had been thrilled at the news that her mother was rescuing her from minding stiffs and was no doubt trying to impress with her team spirit.

"Ash, why don't you go up front?" said Tikko, "Helen Calabrese is asleep; keep a watch on her. We should be eating before too much longer."

He slid off the bench where he had been squatting and hugged Tikko. "Pray for lunch," he whispered. "It's the only way he'll shut up." He let his hand slide down her arm.

She gave a barking laugh, then prodded her daughter's shoulder. "You, go stretch. I'll watch this one."

"I'll stay, maa." Kulki blew a burst of air between her lips. "I'm fine."

"Fine indeed," said Innocent. He was wearing the purple chasuble and plain white cassock she'd seen when she first met him. "You have one smart pup here, Tikko. I look forward to having her on the team."

Pup. She settled next to her daughter on the bench opposite the pope. Kulki was bristling and Tikko rested a hand on her knee to center her. She was grateful that Ash had left the slider into the compartment open. In such close quarters the meaty smell of human skin was a little sickening.

"We've slowed down," said Innocent.

"We're getting close to the York yards." Tikko tapped a knuckle against the window. A cargo chain had pulled over next to them: container bots, hopper bots, tank bots, and flat bots bobbed in their wake as they passed. "We switch soon to the Lakes Main and then head for Chicago, wherever that is. On a lake, I guess."

"You've never been?"

"The middle of the country is nothing but botscape. When we go to winter quarters we stay on the Northeast Main all the way to Chesapeake and then switch to the Dixie Loop."

Ash slapped the doorsill. "The bot must have heard you. Lunch is ready."

They stretched a table between the benches and trooped out to the galley to pick up the lunch baskets. Gamba's team had packed more than enough provisions for the twenty-two hour trip. The chimps' fare was leaves and fruit; Tikko got an apricot, a slice of melon, a bunch of cherry tomatoes and half a head of cabbage. Innocent lifted the lid of his basket, sniffed at the steaming tureen and frowned. "Another lentil stew." He picked a strawberry from the basket and popped it into his mouth. "You want to know why your tribes have been so listless?" he said. "It's because you're making vegetarians of them. Humans need meat." He pounded a fist against his chest in what he probably thought was a clever imitation of chimp belligerence.

Kulki held a snack box out to him. "Termite?" she said with a deadpan expression.

He scowled and waved her off. "I was saying to your daughter earlier how much this part of the country has changed. All the new forests."

Tikko folded a cabbage leaf into her mouth. "It wasn't like this when you were frozen?"

"Not really."

"And when was that, exactly?"

"Ah, that would be telling." He made a show of spooning up stew.

"Julio Velasco was born on January 30, 2202 in Cartagena, Colombia," said Kulki. "You are Julio Velasco?"

Innocent waved a finger at her. "Was."

"Robert III died on September 22, 2257. He was the last known Pope."

He seemed amused. "Bots are so good at dates."

"They estimate that the gathering was completed sometime between March and April of 2294. After that there would have been nobody to elect you Pope."

"Why Kulki, are you trying to trap me into some kind of admission? She's just like you, Tikko." He leaned across the table and spoke in a low voice. "Of course, the bots are wrong about the end of the gathering."

"Really?" Kulki said. "How do you know?"

"Because there is one still to join!" His booming laugh shook the compartment.

"Maybe you'd rather Helen Calabrese didn't join the gathered."

"Oh, no. I insist that she go through with it."

Tikko considered. "Then why are you here?"

"It's necessary for what comes next. I need to witness an execution before I can preach against the death penalty."

"This isn't an execution."

"Ah." He gave her a sly smile. "I must be mistaken then."

"There was a time when you claimed that the cognisphere was heaven," said Kulki.

"I expect that Helen told you that."

Wrong. Tikko knew she hadn't had the chance. She was pleased with her daughter's tenacity and amazed that she had found time to submit so many queries to the bots. Maybe the two of them could get the truth out of Innocent. "Helen knew you," she said, "when your name was Velasco."

Kulki gave a yip of surprise.

"She said that?" Innocent's cheeks colored. "Odd, since we never actually met in person." He touched a napkin to his lips and collected himself. "In any event, my thinking on the cognisphere has changed since them." He stuffed the napkin into the basket, closed the lid and beamed at them expectantly.

Tikko knew he wanted them to ask him how, but she couldn't bring herself to give him the satisfaction. Kulki, on the other hand, had to ask. "Tell us, for Pip's sake."

"Well then. If the cognisphere is as promised, then it might be very much like heaven. But it has always been the case that, in order to get to heaven, you have to die. Now the question is, how do we know that the gathered were actually uploaded? Their bodies are certainly dead. What if their information got erased as well? What if the cognisphere is a lie?"

"Six billion humans believed in it."

"Yes they did. And how many of them have come back from the cognisphere to tell us just how heavenly it is?"

Kulki looked confused. "But why would they?"

"Ah, Kulki, I think your mother sees my point. To those of us left behind, joining the gathered and dying are about the same thing."

"But even so ...."

"The humans who are still alive, the dissenters, have fallen into error. They've made gods of the gathered and are convinced themselves that the age of humanity has passed. And that's what you chimps think too, isn't it? That we need to be minded. Kept on reservations. You believe that this is your world now. But what if it was the gathered who were deluded? You've been following their plan." He leaned back against the bench and steepled his hands. "I believe that God has a different plan. For humans, and for chimps."

Tikko had heard stories about the botscape, but they did not prepare her for its terrible geometries. Two hours out of Chicago, the dawn revealed a world turned all the colors of gray. The bots had waged war with nature, and in this conquered territory, had brutally exterminated the enemy. There were scattered patches of weed and scrub, some dusty fields but otherwise the land was everywhere paved and built over. It looked to Tikko as if the innumerable batch plants had flooded concrete in every direction, channelizing rivers and streams, transforming lakes into sludgy clarifiers and settling basins. Skeletal transmission towers disappeared to the horizon, pipelines wound beneath them like steel snakes. The transbot skirted an endless airport, its asphalt runways shimmering in the morning sun. The Chicago Yards were tied up in kilometer long cargo chains. Flat bots passed under huge container cranes, hopper bots waited patiently to receive their burdens from storage elevators. They switched yet again for the Prairie Main, which would take them practically to the Argonne Science Shrine, where Helen Calabrese's pilgrimage would end.

Tikko kept checking on her but her resolve did not seem to falter. She acknowledged her minder's attempts at conversation but did not encourage them. She drank from a water bottle, ate an apple and stared at the world the bots were busy making, often with her forehead pressed against the window. Innocent on the other hand was manic, bouncing back and forth from between compartments to take in as much as he could, exclaiming and pointing and annoying Ash beyond all reason.

Tikko was grateful that her team seemed to be bearing up, considering how intimidated *she* felt by the botscape. The transbot kept popping words into her head that she had neither heard before nor cared to remember. There were foundries and mills and smelters and blast furnaces and kilns with smokestacks like black fingers ripping the sky. Radomes like giant white wasp galls scanned for storms, a coldbox tower mined the air for nitrogen and oxygen – how was that possible? There were farms where no plant grew, tank farms, data farms, wind farms. In the distance she saw the skyline of a refinery, a vast city for hydrocarbons. Bot excavators tore wounds in the concrete to recycle the treasures lost in landfills, to quarry limestone, to dig gravel. She tried closing her eyes but it didn't help; the naming of the bots' countless works continued unabated.

As the transbot settled into its cradle at Argonne Station, Helen Calabrese emerged from her compartment. She had changed into a dress that revealed the pasty skin of her shoulders and her calves. It was pale as the summer sky; a sash of darker blue bound her waist. Her shoes were blue too, with bizarre pointed heels. Tikko rarely noticed what humans wore, but she was certain that she had never seen anything like this. Maybe it was some ceremonial outfit, like Innocent's vestments. Helen Calabrese strode down the aisle, holding out an arm out as if to catch herself against a stumble but never quite touching the wall. Innocent, Ash and Kulki watched her approach. She did not break stride and might have run into Innocent had not the chimps dragged him out of her way. Tikko had forbidden the pope to speak to

Helen Calabrese unless she spoke first. As she passed, Innocent reached out as if to take her hand. She ignored him.

Tikko's dread of traversing the forbidding botscape vanished as she stepped onto the platform. The grounds of the Argonne Science Shrine had lawns and trees and shrubs pruned with machine precision. Flowers nodded in trim gardens around low buildings, most of which appeared to be mothballed. There was still too much brick, concrete and glass to the place for Tikko, but the scale of it was comforting after the nightmare of Chicago. The campus was surrounded by a ring road swarming with bots of every description – more than she had seen in her life.

Tikko had wondered how they would find their way, but her mind was wide open and the assembled bots guided her to the path. A five minute stroll brought them to a building that sat on its foundation like a quarter of a melon. A walk led to the entrance on the rounded side, the flat façade faced away from them. The structure was about six meters tall and six meters wide at its base and was clad in black marble. As they passed through the entrance the name for it came to her. *Shell*.

It was not what Tikko had expected.

The floor of the shell was a black and white checkerboard of squares of marble. The half dome of the ceiling was composed of square black coffers: five rows of fourteen. The shell opened onto a garden. Sedum and butterfly bush, white begonias bedded around stands of burgundy calla lilies.

The shell was empty.

She waited for instruction but the bots were silent. Kulki gave an uncertain *hoo*. Ash nodded toward the garden. "Out there?" he asked. Tikko led them on.

They were about five meters from the far edge of the shell when its opening filled with a wash of pale light. They stopped, transfixed. The bright colors of the garden were now shimmery pastels. The light seemed so liquid that Tikko thought that she might be able to catch it in her cupped hands. Not that she would dare even approach it.

Helen Calabrese went rigid and Tikko was certain that she had lost her nerve.

"What do I do?" she said.

"Keep walking?" said Tikko.

She put a hand on Tikko's shoulder and tried to pet her. "Thank you." Her fingers were stiff and awkward. Or maybe she was just leaning one last time on her minder for support. Tikko thought she should reply, but what could a chimp say to one of the gathered?

Then Helen Calabrese started toward the light.

Innocent called, "Do you have any last words, Helen?"

"Go to hell," she said, without turning back.

Tikko chopped a hand toward Ash and Kulki and they caught the pope by the shoulders. "Don't say another word." Tikko snarled.

The metal on Helen's heels clicked against the marble floor. That's what Tikko remembered afterwards. Helen Calabrese called out a name. It sounded like Cass or Cassy. Then she started to run. *Click, click, click.* When she passed into the light, the clicking stopped. Tikko could see Helen Calabrese's body sprawled in the garden behind the glimmering at the edge of the shell. She was still holding her breath when Innocent spoke.

"Awful." His voice filled with pity. "A terrible, terrible waste."

"Stop."

"But I was right, don't you see? You can't possibly scan a human mind in an instant."

She felt a rage come over her. It had something to do with the light. She thought it ought to stop now that Helen Calabrese had been gathered, but it didn't it. Instead it continued to pour down, no longer a wash but a flood. And the wind in her head was back, only it wasn't whispering anymore, it screamed and so she screamed. Kulki and Ash answered, their mouths wide and their fangs glistening in the murderous light. She knew they felt it too.

"What are you doing?" Innocent said. He began to struggle against the grip of Ash and Kulki..

The screams of the chimps echoed off the half dome, echoed in Tikko's head so that it seemed like six billion screams urging her to circle behind the pope. She charged full tilt on toes and knuckles and hurled herself into his back. The frantic human, still in the grasp of the two other chimps, lurched toward the light.

"No. *Stop.*"

They brought him stumbling, flailing, right to the edge and Tikko clapped hands over her ears because now Innocent was screaming as Ash and Kulki – her daughter, her <u>angry</u> daughter -- shoved him hard. As he staggered into the light, he tried to spin but his feet went out from under him and his body slumped through and onto the grass. Only his red slippers still remained in the shell.

There was no sound but their breathing. The wind in Tikko's head died down. The light at the opening of the shell faded.

Overwhelmed, she sat backwards on the cold marble. "What have we done?"

"S-Sent him to heaven." Kulki's turned around twice, and squatted facing away from the bodies.

Sin. For the first time in her life, Tikko understood why the word had plagued the humans so. She felt sick with shame, a stranger in her own mind. "But we have to go back now," she said. "To Pacito. The dudleys. How do we explain?"

"Explain? Ash leaned over and took her hands in his. "I'm not even sure what happened." His hands shook as he pulled her to her feet. "We have to go, Tikko."

Four bots entered the garden, walking on spider legs. When two of them rolled Innocent's body over, Ash shrieked and Kulki spun around to watch. The bots rocked backwards onto their rearmost legs, slipped their front legs under the body and picked it up. Like a fallen branch. Tikko put a hand on Kulki's shoulder as the two other two lifted Helen Calabrese's limp body. Like a dead rabbit.

Ash screamed again and they ran.

Galloping on all fours, the chimps burst out of the shell and down the path toward the station. Tikko fell behind the younger chimps and was the last one to reach the transbot, still floating in its cradle. The rear door had opened to let them in. She found Ash scrabbling frantically up the center aisle, Kulki huddled under a table in one of the compartments. Tikko had no chance to open her mind, or maybe it was that assembled bots had kept her mind pried open all this time, but the door slid shut.

The transbot floated onto the fluxway.

The chimps hid in different compartments and did not come out until they were well out of the botscape. Tikko spent the time trying to understand what had happened in the shell, thinking what she hoped were her own thoughts about the bots and what they had done to her. About the gathered.

In her moment of rage in the shell, she had wanted to kill Innocent, *yes*, or at least get rid of him. She was quite sure of that. But thrusting him into the cognisphere against his will? *No*. That was not the duty chimps owed to humans. Tikko knew that she had teetered on the edge of sin, but she had not fallen on her own. She had been pushed. Eventually that realization lifted her out of her dread.

Ash and Kulki had brought lunch baskets into their compartment at the rear of the transbot. They also seemed recovered – at least enough to eat. Tikko sat on the bench next to her daughter and picked a pear from her basket.

"We have to get our stories straight," Tikko said.

Kulki gave a *hoo* of approval. "We've just been talking about that."

"He died," said Ash. "He lost track of himself and had an accident and he died." He thrust his arms above his head, as if challenging her to contradict him. "That's all that happened."

Tikko bit into the pear. It was past the season for pears and the white flesh was mealy. "That's good enough for the others," she said. "But what do we tell ourselves?"

Ash let his arms fall and stared at the table.

"Maa, I don't know," said Kulki.

"So, this is what I think happened. We opened our minds to the bots and they took advantage of us." She took another bite of the pear.

"The bots?" said Ash. "The bots wanted us to send him to the gathered? Why?"

"Because the bots *are* the gathered." Tikko paused, reading her daughter's expression. "Some of them, anyway." She saw the idea taking hold and continued. "And the gathered are humans, or were."

"That makes no sense," said Ash, his thick brow furrowed.

"Yes." Kulki wrapped her arms around Tikko and pulled her close. "And they can't leave us alone."

"Maybe," said Tikko, "we should make them."

hhe Kulki was laughing in Tikko's ear. *hhe hhe*

Tikko thought it was funny too. *hhe hhe* Ash's lips curled away from his teeth and his mouth fell open and then, as the transbot flew up the fluxway toward home, all three chimps were laughing, falling over, rolling on their backs. *hhee hhee hhee hheep*.

It was a sound no human would ever hear.

One Sister, Two Sisters, Three

This isn't my story—I'm nobody. It's my sister's. Zana is the one who got away, leaving me on this sad little world where we were born. Where I'll die someday, as the Divine Moya wills. Moya expects us to die, each and every one. That's her plan for those who still follow the human way.

We were born fraternal twins, Jix and Zana, separated by thirteen minutes—one of the holy numbers. We were conceived as Moya intended, mother clinging to father, sperm seeking egg. For the first years of our lives, we were close. We danced the moons and prayed the holy numbers and taunted the boys who went to our church. Later we kissed them. Father taught us to bake the cookies that we sold to the upsider tourists from the Thousand Worlds and Mother taught us to mind the money that they paid. Ours was a family of happy wallrats, living just outside the ruins.

But we began to drift apart in our late teens. Zana had the precise beauty that only Moya can bestow. Her ratios were near the 1.618 of the Divine's perfection, her curls tight, and her skin had a dark luster, like the midnight of the Jagged Spike. Her high forehead set off molten brown eyes. Zana wore her feelings like a consecration crown for all to see; transparency was part of her attraction. I wasn't plain, but compared to my sister, my features were commonplace, so I found my own way. While Zana could be shy, especially with strangers, I was forward. While she pondered the right word to say, I let my tongue do the thinking. I didn't mind what they said about us. *Zana the pretty, Jix the witty.* Maybe I talked too much for some boys, as Mother used to say, but too much silence made my lips twitch. And I had my share of flings, if not as many as my sister.

Mother got sick when we were twenty, a year after we were consecrated to Moya. We'd been so busy that season that we missed all the signs. Tourists swarmed the ruins, so that we had no time to bake the extravagant cookies that Father favored. To keep up with demand, our family churned out stacks of Sugardrops, plain but as big as saucers, with just a scatter of raisins or sweetbark to provide interest. These were not our best work, but Zana and I found uses for the extra money they brought us. I was saving for a powerbike and she wanted to learn Anglic.

Our stall was on the Roundabout, third down from Shellgate, hard against the western wall of the ruins left by the Exotics. Tourists would pause to admire her on their way in, while I sold them our goods. Even though they were all reps who had strayed from the human way, they still had stomachs like the rest of us. An appetite for sweets and an eye for beauty remain locked in our shared genome.

The day everything changed, a persistent tourist lingered after he'd made his purchase. His companion, a woman from the Institute who was perhaps his minder, was eager to enter the ruins. I'd have been just as happy if she'd led him away, but Zana encouraged conversation. He was handsome enough, in that ageless replicated way, but nobody I'd have wasted breath on.

He picked up my prayer puzzle while Zana wrapped the cookies. "Ingenious." He manipulated the magnetic triangles of the pentagram to create Moya's central upright pentangle. "And you use this how? As a meditation prompt?"

"It predicts how much our customers will buy."

"Pay no attention to her." Zana was embarrassed when I tweaked the tourists. "It's Moya's sacred geometry. We use it to pray the numbers."

The minder sputtered something in Anglic.

"Please—we're guests on their world." The tourist scowled at her. "Let's speak their language."

"Sanctuary was settled by a sect called the Moyans," repeated the minder. "For years they kept the Exotic ruins secret. They believe close contact with us leads to sin."

"Sin, right," he said. "I did look through the guide you sent." He turned to Zana. "And the purpose of these..." He removed triangles to create the upside-down pentagon.

"They remind us of the presence of the Divine," said Zana. I was surprised when she came around the counter with his purchase. "That Moya is everywhere."

"The local religion." The minder harrumphed, "A strain of humanism."

The tourist dismissed her with a wave. "Please, go on." He clicked puzzle pieces absently into place—another upworlder enchanted by my sister's beauty.

"The Divine's ratio is the fingerprint of Moya. It teaches us to obey her laws and be true to our mortality." They exchanged the puzzle for his cookies. For an instant, their hands touched. "We see it everywhere in her creation. In the spiral of galaxies and in the ancient buildings within those walls." She nodded toward the Shells, but kept her eyes on his. "The petals of a flower. Your ear." She brushed the back of her hand against his ear. "Even your DNA." Her voice had dropped to a purr. "Everywhere the universe is imprinted with her holy numbers."

I couldn't believe that she was flirting with an upsider. "Did you know," I said, "that a DNA molecule measures thirty-four angstroms long by twenty-one angstroms wide for each full cycle of its double helix spiral?"

"Really?" he said, although my words meant no more to him than the chitter of streetbots, or the sigh of our awning in the breeze.

"Eight plus thirteen is twenty-one." I thought praying the holy numbers might distract Zana. "Thirteen plus twenty-one is thirty-four. Twenty-one plus thirty-four..."

The guide leaned closer to the rep. "They worship the Fibonacci sequence."

"We worship the Divine." Zana's expression was dreamy. "The numbers point us toward her handiwork and her expectations of us."

"I'm Quin," said the tourist. "What did you say your name was?"

"Girls!"

I'd been so astonished by Zana's game of seduction that I missed Father hurrying down the Roundabout.

"Time!" He was out of breath. "It's time . . . to close . . . up." What was so important to bring him from his kitchen at this time of day? And what he'd said made no sense. Close? The afternoon was before us. We had stacks of cookies to sell.

"So early?" I said. A bus from the spaceport grunted to a stop. "Take Zana if you need help. She's not doing anything here." Tourists fresh from the hotels poured from its open slider.

"I want you both. Home." His voice cracked. "*Now.*"

Zana hurried back behind the stall to stack unsold cookies into an empty basket.

"Zana, is it?" The tourist leaned over the counter. "Zana, before you go, I'd like to ask..."

"Leave those!" Father swiped at the basket, knocking cookies to the pavement. "Leave everything. We need to go!"

"What's happened?" I said. "Father?"

"Your mother." He dragged us by the hands past the busy stalls. "You mother has lost her mind." Zana stumbled when she glanced back at her dumbstruck tourist, but Father caught her.

Mother sat at the kitchen table, hair loose, face drawn, hands clasped around a cup of spice tea. She liked it thick and sweet; I still smell its terrible perfume when I remember that day. She stared as if surprised to see us, as if she'd forgotten that she had daughters. Then she said "I've just come from the clinic. I have Hrutchma's."

She never cried, not once during that long afternoon. Neither did I. At first Zana threw herself at Mother's neck, then wept into open hands and eventually rested her head on the kitchen table, shoulders heaving. Father's tears were hot; only later did we realize what was behind them.

Hrutchma's was a disease we knew well. It caused something called lymphoid hyperplasia, a crazy increase of cells in the lymph nodes. Hrutchma's began with enlarged nodes in the chest, squeezing the lungs and stealing the breath. I'd noticed her getting winded, although she'd joked it was because Father's cookies were making her fat. As the disease progressed, it would wreck her immune system, leading to nerve damage, infections, withering fevers. That's how Grandmother Deel, Father's mother, had died—raving while she burned like a fast oven. According to the medical encyclopedia on the tell, Hrutchma's is unique to Sanctuary. Some wallrats whispered that it came from a curse the Exotics placed on the old stones, but we couldn't let that rumor spread. Tourists put the soup in our bowls.

I remember sinking into a chair across from Mother, trying to imagine how I would fit into a world without her. I couldn't, in part because I was too numb, in part because I was distracted by Zana. She settled beside me, sobbing and I felt guilty that I couldn't summon tears. And then I was puzzled by the way Father hung back. I expected that he'd be grieving too. But no—he seemed angry.

Zana saw it too. "Father, what's wrong?"

"Her." He choked on a laugh. "She is."

"She's sick!" Zana swiped at her wet face. "What—you blame her?" I wonder now if she had guessed what was coming. She knew Mother better than I.

"Hrutchma's I can accept." He shook his head in disgust. "The other, no."

"You can accept that I'll die?" Mother's voice was sharp as a slap. "I'm forty-one years old."

"I accept the will of the Divine," he said. "You should do the same. Our daughters are consecrated to Moya."

She turned from him to face us. "Your father doesn't understand." She met our gaze without hesitation or regret. "I'm going to Skytown."

"To live." Father said it like an accusation, but she ignored him. "Go ahead, lie down with their machines. Betray everything we believe. Just remember—never come back to us."

"You're going to upload," said Zana. "Become a rep."

Mother shivered as if Zana had said something that she hadn't yet realized. Then she nodded. "I'm not ready to die."

She left the next day.

Father never spoke of her again. If anyone dared mention her, he'd withdraw, sometimes for days. He was a fool to think that his silence could erase her from our lives. All of our communion knew the shame she'd brought on our family and our church. Whenever Speaker Elb preached about straying from Moya's way, of losing our humanity, everyone thought of her. I know I did. For months afterward, I was obsessed with her. I had nightmares about her ravaged and discarded body—where was it now? And what to make of the stranger who knew everything about our home, our family—about *me*? We'd been taught there was no real continuity of life between a human and the rep body created by the technology of the Thousand Worlds. The Divine taught that my mother was truly dead. But then who was the creature who lived in Skytown, the upsiders' enclave on Sanctuary? Who still claimed to love me?

I knew this because she tried to stay in contact with us, or at least with Zana and me. Zana showed me her first message, but I couldn't finish reading it. However, Zana wrote back, despite Speaker Elb's warning that our false mother would tempt her to sin. I had no idea how often they talked because I didn't want to know. However, my sister insisted on telling me how she was doing.

After her replication, Mother had found work as a janitor at the Institute of Exotic Archeology. She shared an apartment with three other roommates including her old friend Xeni Blu-ereed, who had left our communion three years ago to be replicated. Zana claimed there was a growing community of people like Mother and Xeni beginning new lives among the upsiders. Later, she got a job in a Skytown restaurant as a cook, which was ironic because the kitchen had always been Father's domain. Mother's new position paid well and I suspect that she sent Zana some of her wages, although I never saw any. But apparently Mother had money enough to visit the orbital and to buy a bot. She thought about us all the time, according to Zana, and yet supposedly she was happy. Although I envied her the luxuries of Skytown, I couldn't imagine how that could be.

Moya does not demand that we reject all upsider technologies, only those which make us less human. Yes, I'd own a bot and a printer and a car if I could afford them. I'd sample the drugs that make you stronger or smarter or happier. But Sanctuary is an exhausted world. That's why our ancestors were able to claim it for the Divine. The Exotics had used Sanctuary up long ago, and their leavings are the last valuable things on it. We scratch a living from their dust. And while we're proud of our ruins, there are other examples of the Exotics' architecture scattered throughout the galaxy.

As the months passed, our broken family adjusted to our new life. The press of tourists varied with the seasons, but we did well enough, especially now that there were only three of us. I bought my powerbike and a trailer to go with it. Not only did Zana get her Anglic lessons, she then paid for access to the Institute's databanks, so that she could learn more about the Thousand Worlds. Her new language skills paid off in an unexpected way. Word spread through the hotels of the beautiful girl selling baked goods who could speak the common tongue. Tourists flocked to witness this marvel. They helped Zana with her accent until they claimed she could announce the news on Ravi's Prize itself—not that either of us believed that. Of course, I understood not a word of their chatter, and when they dissolved into laughter I suspected that the joke was on me.

Then Quin came back. Except, as it turned out, he'd never left.

I was alone at the stall, which meant that, for a change, my view of the street wasn't blocked by Zana's admirers when I spotted Quin wandering along the Roundabout. It had been almost half a year, but I knew him as soon as I saw him. He paused at Twial's stall, picked up a reproduction of Half Boat to check the price and then replaced it with a frown. He browsed Glif's gaudy umbrellas and the new scent store, then walked faster as he got closer. He passed our stall with eyes down, as if scanning for cracks on the pavement. It was obvious that he was ignoring me. But then he stopped abruptly in the middle of the street, glanced past me to the blackened hulk of the Jagged Spike, and strode up to the counter.

"You're Jix." He tried on a smile that didn't quite fit.

I agreed that I was.

He reached for our most expensive cookie. "And this is a Brownbutter Velvet Block."

"With a ginger smear."

"Cut into a precise rectangle." He held it to the light to examine it. "I've been studying your religion. Would I be right to say that the ratio of the length to the width is 1.618?" He seemed proud of himself for this guess.

"I recommend that you buy at least two."

This wasn't the reply he'd been expecting. He nodded, frowning.

"Will there be something else?" I asked.

"I know your mother. She used to work at the Institute."

"Really?" I wrapped two Velvet Blocks in takeout paper. "Did she send you?"

"No." He was surprised at the question. "I'm an archeologist, doing research on your Shells."

"They're not mine." I supposed he wanted me to ask about Mother. I handed him his purchase. "Three-fifty."

Instead of completing the transaction using our tell like every other tourist, he reached into his pocket and pulled out a handful of Moyan chits.

"I like your money." He fumbled for the exact change. "There's so much of it."

"I like it too." I rarely handled chits at the stall; only Moyans carry them and Moyans bake their own cookies. He watched me slip them into my pocket. Then I gave him his purchase and waited. He made no move to leave. I remembered then how he had lingered that awful day. "Maybe you were expecting to find someone else here?"

"Zana, yes." He blinked. "But I had no expectations."

"I'm sorry to hear that. Expectations are what get me through the day." I spotted Zana headed up the street carrying a basket of cookies from home. "I like to guess what will happen next."

"You had a prayer puzzle," he said. "May I see it?"

Surprised that he remembered, I opened my bag and offered it to him.

"Yes." He pushed the magnetized shapes into new configurations with practiced motions. "It's very definite, your religion. Did you know that the star polygon is one of the oldest symbols we have. From Earth, you know, the home world. It represented the sacred feminine as long ago as 4000 BCE."

"Really?" Of course he would condescend to a nobody; he was a tourist. Was common courtesy a trait that the upsiders' technology couldn't replicate?

"So the so-called Golden Ratio..." He was oblivious. "A fascinating mix of tradition and math. Take this pentagon and connect the vertices and you get a pentagram, a five sided star." He pushed puzzle pieces. "Five is in the Fibonacci sequence. And the ratio of any diagonal of the star to any side of the pentagon is 1.618. Phi, the Golden Ratio. And you see it again here..." He fitted pieces into new configurations. "And here." He drew a line with his forefinger; his nails clicked against the metal. "And you were saying how often the Golden Ratio occurs in the natural world. There's actually support for that in the literature."

"We call it the Divine's Ratio," I said. "And it was actually my sister who was explaining that. Isn't that right, Zana?"

Quin started as she set her basket on the counter.

"You remember Quin," I said to her. "Turns out he's from the Institute. An archeologist. And he knows Mother."

The looks they exchanged were not those of strangers.

"So this isn't news to you?" I reached for the basket to sort the new cookies she'd brought. "Are we keeping secrets now, sister?"

"Oh, no secret," said Quin. "We started exchanging messages what...? Three months ago. I'd like to think we've become friends."

"Just over two months." Zana was embarrassed. "And we've only met in person a couple of times."

"Which is why I thought to surprise you." Quin seemed pleased with himself.

"And did he tell you that he's been studying our religion?" I replenished our supply of Shortbread Swaddled Truffles. "Perhaps you're thinking of converting, Quin?" I wanted to see her squirm for keeping this from me.

"No." He set my prayer puzzle down as if it might burn him. "Not at all."

"It would be awkward, seeing as how you're no longer in your first body. How many times have you been replicated, if you don't mind my asking?

"He does mind." Zana's cheeks colored. "That's rude, Jix."

"Oh, sorry." I bowed twice for good measure. "Sorry, Quin. It's just that we get so few of your people taking an interest in us."

Quin blinked at us, as if he was having trouble following our conversation. "In any event," he said to Zana, "I was just wondering when... if maybe... would you like to take that tour sometime? The one we were talking about."

"Tour?" I said.

He glanced at me then nodded toward Shellgate. "I know you've lived here all your lives, but I have access to the monuments, even those that are closed. I could show you things that very few people have seen."

Zana shot me a stare that said I wasn't invited. I let it bounce off me.

"Zana and I are working girls," I said. "We have tourists to feed, cookies to sell."

He nodded. "Shellgate closes at five. Don't all the tourists leave for the hotels then? We could go after hours; I have unlimited access, you know. It stays light until almost eight."

"Great." I held up the empty cookie basket and smiled at him. "We could pack a picnic dinner."

Zana wasn't amused.

"Father would explode if he knew you were seeing a rep."

"I'm not seeing him." Zana was a darkness on the shadowy bed across the room. "He's a friend, that's all. And it's all been messaging until recently."

"Except now you're making dates to tour the ruins."

It was always sweltering in our house because of the ovens, even late at night after Father shut them down. In the summer Zana and I would sprawl on our beds, sweat prickling our skin. Most nights we kicked the sheets off, sometimes it was too hot for clothes. Unable to sleep, we'd talk of boys and dreams in the dank gloom, our conversation flickering like a candle.

"He's going to show you things nobody has seen." I chuckled. "Where have I heard that joke before? He's the tourist and you're the baker's beautiful daughter."

"That's not what this is. Besides, now you're coming too, even though nobody asked you."

"I'm only going to make sure that you don't do anything stupid." We never kept our flings a secret from one another, so this Quin worried me. "Okay, so maybe he's not a tourist, but he's not here to stay." Zana was my twin, and even if we weren't play-mates anymore, she was the only one in our family I was close to. The silence was tickled by the scratch of slinks running up the walls and across the floor. In the warm weather the lizards stayed active at night, scavenging for crumbs and squeezing into the chinks in our stone walls.

"You don't think I can handle him?" said Zana. "I'm twenty-one years old."

"And he's two hundred years old. Or maybe two thousand."

"Oh, stop it."

"He works for the Institute, Zana. You go squirting through wormholes for a living, you've got to allow for time dilation. People like him replicate what...? Five, six times at least."

I heard her torturing her pillow into a new shape, but neither of us found much comfort that night.

"He's definitely got a look," I said. "I understand the attrac-tion."

The slats beneath her mattress creaked when she sat up. "You know the problem with living at home?" She was silhouetted against the window, her bare back to me. "I can never get away from you two."

"That's not fair. When you bring a boy home, don't I give you the room? Just like when I was with Bibby, you got scarce. And Father hasn't a clue who we've had in here."

Silence.

"I watch for you and you watch for me, remember? That's what sisters do."

She gave an unhappy grumble.

"But if sex is what you want, why not fuck a human? Moya knows, you can have your choice."

I ducked as her pillow sailed across the room.

We didn't pack cookies for the picnic. When you bake for a living, you lose the taste. Instead we brought salted cutthroat from the river and pickled figs. A cold squash soup. A round of cheese and a bottle of fay brandy. Quin insisted on carrying it at first, even though Zana and I had spent most of our lives lugging heavy baskets of fruit and flour and oils and spices.

I couldn't help but envy the way the tell built into his fingernail synced with the Institute's security at Shellgate. A wave of his hand, and the projectors went dark; as soon as we passed through, solid blue light once again barred the entryway. I'd never seen communication tech that small. For a moment, Quin seemed magical.

The ruins were part of our neighborhood, even though they were run by the Institute. We were threading our way around broken buildings back when we were toddlers. But that night, it was as if we'd stepped from Sanctuary onto one of the Thousand Worlds. We knew the structures by the names the first settlers had given them, but Quin identified the Grandmother Stones as Boundary Markers 11n through 11t. He explained that Half Boat and the Jagged Spike were part of a complex he called the Western Quadrant Early Classic Superstructure. When we insisted that Ellipsoidal Buildings 43, 58, and 70 were properly Bird Shell, Crazy Shell and the Bride, he chuckled. Giving commonplace names was how people coped with their terror of the alien, he claimed. A way of pretending we understood the civilization of the mighty Exotics.

He had a talent for annoying me. "Maybe," I said, "assigning them numbers is your way of coping."

Zana shot me a look but Quin nodded, as if considering what I'd said. "You may be right. Numbering the world is what we humans do, isn't it?" We were standing on a parapet called Frost's Overlook, gazing down at the three Shells. "They're not buildings, you know. They're sculptures."

"Sculptures?" I said. "Of what?"

"We see similar construction in several other ruins. I stopped at Destination and Kenning before I came here. I'm certain that your Shells were never occupied. Nor were they even functional. My research leads me to the idea that they're propaganda art on a monumental scale, like Ravi's Tomb or the Lubinarium."

"The Statue of Liberty on Earth," said Zana. This took me by surprise. Why was she learning trivia about that dead planet?

"Not familiar with that one." Quin hefted the picnic basket. "Most scholars claim that Ellipsoidal Sculptures are Post Classic, but I believe they're actually from the end of the Persistent Era, just before the last of the Exotics disappeared."

"Sculptures of what?" I repeated. "And what kind of propaganda?"

"I've heard that's a particularly interesting view." He aimed his chin at the opening at the top of the Bride. "Eat up there?"

As we scuttled down the rubble-strewn grade, he told us about his work. Nobody knew what had become of the Exotics. The galaxy-wide culture that built the wormholes vanished between fifty and sixty thousand years ago. Judging from their enigmatic ruins, Exotic civilization had begun to hollow out in its Post Classic Era, which was followed by the long decline of the Persistent Era. Quin believed that Sanctuary's shells might have been among the last things the Exotics ever built.

The wind had died in the dusk and the sun-baked façade of the Crazy Shell radiated heat as we passed on the way to the Bride. "I think these shells were meant to persuade the Persistents who remained behind to follow their ancestors." Quin set the basket down on the stump of a pillar and wiped sweat from his eyes. "Maybe to shame them into it because Exotic culture had moved on. What were they waiting for?" He'd been talking non-stop and was out of breath.

I was enjoying the effect our summer heat had on this over-confident upsider. "This is the theory that says they all uploaded and went to where? Exotic toyland?"

"The evidence does point to a massive departure over a very short time, with a longer period of stragglers hanging on. Some claim there was a mass suicide but yes, I'd like to think they went elsewhere. Maybe to somewhere else in our universe or to some designed reality."

Zana hefted the picnic basket. "I can't imagine anyone could get bored sailing through wormholes."

He pretended not to notice that she was relieving him. "Not sure they got bored. One thing is certain, they were very tidy. They took great pains to erase themselves from their worlds." He tugged at his shirt where it had stuck to his chest. "All their ruins are built of native materials, mostly stone and ceramics. Some metals. We're pretty sure that no Exotics lived in them, but then we have no idea where they did live. We know nothing of what they looked like, their biology, what they believed. Were these structures ceremonial? Administrative? Religious?"

"And this bothers you?" I asked. "Why? Because it's not fair to archeologists?"

"They might've done better by us." He grinned. "I'd like to think there are answers out there, but maybe I'm just fooling myself."

Father said that before the Institute took over the ruins, Moyans had tried to clean them up: restacking stones, filling holes, pulling weeds, and cutting brush. The upsiders had stopped all reconstruction and limited public access to a handful of the structures. They said it was to preserve the archeological record; wallrats said it was to drive customers away. Whatever the truth, navigating the ruins was a challenge. The footing was uncertain, and the direct path to any given destination was often blocked.

"So what does Moya..." Quin was laboring again as we reached the base of the Bride. "...have to say... to all of this?"

"It's not for us to know Moya's mind." Zana vaulted onto the fallen slab in front of the crude entrance someone had chiseled into the Bride.

"Come on," I said. "It's obvious the Exotics knew the Divine's ratio."

"Did they?"

"Just look." I gestured at the white whorls carved into the casing stones on the wall above us.

"I suppose." He gathered himself for the scramble. "It's math, after all. But you Moyans... you see your ratio everywhere."

I offered a hand to help him up. "Don't you?"

He reached for me and missed. "I lack your stamina." I caught his damp wrist and boosted him to my side.

After he'd caught his breath, Quin insisted on telling us that the white limestone façade of the Bride had been quarried from Kunlun's Crease, even though everyone knew this. The Bride resembled the Ivory Snails some wallrats harvested from the river for soup. The ones that tasted like dirty socks. The difference was that the Bride was enormous—some thirty meters tall—and was upside down. The mouth of the shell pointed up at the sky. We ducked through the makeshift entrance into the interior. The air was dank here and smelled like the inside of a well. A wooden scaffold climbed to the light. We crunched across a floor littered with broken tiles that had fallen off the walls, each decorated with a tessellated spiral flower pattern. Some wallrats believed that if you found an intact tile, whoever you gave it to would fall in love with you. Unfortunately, undamaged tiles were hard to come by since the ban on removing artifacts from the ruins. However, the Naras did a brisk trade in reproductions from their stall near Rivergate.

I bent to retrieve a shard and showed it to Quin. It was hard to see detail in the feeble light from the opening above us, so he lit his fingernail.

"The Divine's ratio." I traced several shapes. "In case you're still in doubt about what the Exotics knew."

"Yes." He waved his nail off. "That claim has been made. But it's not quite 1.618, is it?"

I bristled and let it fall to the floor. "So close you can hardly tell the difference."

"Right," he said. "Especially in the dark."

"Quin likes to scoff," said Zana. "Best to ignore him when he gets like that."

"Sorry," he said. "Your sister has been teaching me manners, but I'm afraid I'm not much of a student."

I prayed the numbers while we climbed to calm myself. *One, one, two, three, five, eight, thirteen, twenty-one, thirty-four, fifty-five.* By the time I got to *seventeen thousand, seven hundred and eleven* I was feeling more like myself. Quin heaved himself up the first two ladders in succession, but after that he had to rest on each platform. He took longer to recover the higher we went until he collapsed onto the tenth stage, gasping and as damp as if we had pulled him from the river. The planking was slick with mildew from exposure to the weather and left a smudge on Quin's pants. Zana worried over him, but he reassured us that he was exhausted only because his last replication had been on a world where the gravity was 0.68 that of Sanctuary. "And I'm not good with heights," he added.

He revived once we climbed the last ladder to the wide stone lip at the top of the Shell. While Zana sat him down so the two of them could unpack our meal, I walked out to the edge and the view. It had been years since I'd made this climb. The shadowy ruins sprawled at my feet while the lights of our little village twinkled in the middle distance. Skytown was a glow on the horizon. Although the air was warmer up here, it was a relief from the sticky interior of the Bride. I took a deep breath and felt blessed to be able to take in my whole world at a glance.

Zana was murmuring to Quin. I couldn't make out what she was saying, but there was a note to her voice, at once innocent and earnest and tender, that made me shudder.

What if this was more than a fling?

Quin thought the cutthroat tasted too fishy but he raved about the pickled figs and asked to take a sample of Father's squash soup for gastronomical analysis. He said the cheese was better than the *framenthakler* that the data monks on Encyclopedia printed from their secret recipe. We talked a lot about food. Zana pumped him for his favorite dishes but I knew she was more interested in hearing stories about the Thousand Worlds than she was learning about upsider cooking. He said that most reps preferred printed food, of which there was an infinite variety. Those who traveled the wormholes took little interest in local culture, but were passionately invested in trying the latest cuisines.

"Nobody much cares about books and songs," he said. "What sells on the upside are new menus." He waved our brandy bottle at the sky. "Come up with a fresh taste with a new smell and you can write your own ticket to the stars." When he offered me a refill, I covered my cup with my hand. "Take your cookies, for example. With the right marketing, they might pay your way off Sanctuary."

I waited for Zana to point out that we had no plans to leave home. She didn't, so neither did I.

I expected Quin would continue to do most of the talking, but he wanted to hear about us, or at least Zana. He asked about our schools and what we'd been told about the upside. Zana talked about what she'd learned using the Institute's portal; he said it had good access but was by no means complete. He wondered what we thought about the controversies that flared continually between the wallrats and the Institute over management of the ruins. Then he got us telling stories about dumb things that tourists did.

"I don't understand why they need to haggle," I said, "after what they spend to get here. We'd have to move a mountain of cookies just to get to the orbital."

"So we let them talk our prices down..." Zana giggled, "...and we then make up the difference in tax."

"Only there is no tax."

"Sure there is," I said. "Stupidity tax."

We were all laughing now as Zana filled our cups with the last of the brandy.

"Then there was that buzzy woman who wanted to buy all our takeout paper. Where was she from?"

"She said it tasted better than our cookies."

"And then they ask the dumbest questions about the Divine's ratio."

That earned me a sisterly glare until Quin raised his hand. "Guilty."

I didn't want to start liking him, so I said, "You don't believe in the Divine, do you?"

When Zana hissed, it sounded like a seam ripping.

"You know I don't," he said.

Nobody was laughing now.

"Or any god," I said. Quin studied me. His silence was scary. "Why not?" I asked.

"Jix!" Zana came to her knees, but I knew she wanted to hear his answer.

"Have you ever heard of the God spot, Jix?" said Quin.

"Doesn't exist." Zana said, as if to end the conversation.

"No," I said. "What is it?"

"People used to look for the place in our brains where mystical experiences come from. Some tagged the right parietal lobe, others the dorsolateral prefrontal cortex. There was evidence that N,N-dimethyltryptamine levels in the pineal gland play a role. But over time they realized they'd got it wrong, and so they developed a different model. There's no button in the brain that you push for instant spirituality. The neural correlates are scattered across the entire brain, systems that give rise to self-awareness, emotion, your sense of your own body." He fumbled at the pocket of the shirt he was wearing. "And what's interesting is that in order to have a religious experience, you don't stimulate these brain systems." He shook his head. "You suppress them. Inhibit those areas that create the illusion of self, and you open the door to transcendence."

"So?" I said.

He pulled a pressure syringe from his pocket and showed it to us. "Want to see Moya?"

Sometimes I wonder if Zana had poured our futures from a bottle of fay brandy. How could two drunken sisters hope to protect one another? Or maybe I was daring my sister even as she was daring me in some alcohol-fueled dance of sibling rivalry? Or it was simply that we each were trying to impress her upsider, in our own ways and for our own reasons?

The syringe looked like a glass thumb, cylindrical but with a flat applicator pad to one side. "This won't take long." Quin pressed the syringe to the artery in Zana's neck. "Say fifteen minutes to work past the blood-brain barrier." The syringe left a faint pink swelling. "The actual experience comes and goes. Maybe five minutes, although it might feel longer subjectively." He turned to me. "But everyone's different. Some people feel like they've disappeared, some become one with everything."

I tilted my head. "And is it real?" The injection felt like being kissed on the neck.

He laughed. "That's for you to decide." He injected himself last, then tucked the syringe back into his pocket.

"You planned this," said Zana.

"We've talked about it," he said, "haven't we?"

"I never said yes."

He smirked. "You just did."

"So what do we do now?" I said.

He sat on the stone pavers facing the view and crossed his legs. "We wait for the elevator."

We arranged ourselves into a triangle and watched each other for signs. Zana settled back onto her heels. Her back was straight and she sniffed, nose pointed, as if she might catch Moya's scent. I squirmed on the cold, hard floor. The silence made me more self-conscious, not less. Was my heart in the right place? Would this change my life? What was I supposed to do with my hands?

Quin seemed to be enjoying himself. "I never asked you about boyfriends," he said to distract us. "I'll bet you both have plenty."

"Zana does." I was relieved to hear the sound of my own voice. "She gets her share and half of mine."

"That's not true." She frowned. "You do well enough."

"They say I talk too much."

"Boneheads." He patted my arm. "Stick with men as smart as you."

"And you?" said Zana. "You have people you care about?"

"Yes and no." He paused, deciding how much to say. "When you get replicated, relationships sometimes fall apart. You're you, but now you're somebody else as well. The body is different for one thing, sometimes very different. It wants what it wants. That old you, he's like someone you read about. It was a really interesting book, and you remember vivid scenes, but you've read that last page."

"What's it like?" I asked. "Being replicated."

"Like dying, only you wake up afterwards."

"You've died?" I shouldn't have been surprised, but I was.

"Every time," he said, as if he was discussing a splinter. "Of course in a direct transfer you're not dead very long. But these days they can still rep someone thirty minutes after cardiac and respiratory arrest with minimal information loss. After thirty, the brain really deteriorates. Something about ischemic injury." He shivered in the heat. "So yes, Zana knows this already but I was in a flier crash that killed me just before I came here. Nobody's fault, really. I was with someone I loved, but he didn't make it. Rescue took too long to get to us. They say my rep was only ninety-six percent accurate. It was very sad, because I'd probably still be with him if his replication had been successful too."

Zana took his hand in hers.

"So I'm still learning to be this new Quin in this new body." His mouth smiled, but his eyes were sad. "But that's what we all do, isn't it?"

When I saw that look on my sister's face, one I'd never seen before, I knew that I'd been right to worry about this upsider. The love she felt for him glimmered from her perfect ratios, Moya's gifts to her. The length of Zana's face divided by its width. *1.618.* Her smile divided by the width of her nose. *1.618.* The width of her nose to the space between her nostrils. *1.618.*

I was so focused on my sister that I didn't realize Quin was still talking until he said, "I'd do anything for you."

Zana shut her eyes. Was it imagination that they were so tight that they quivered? When she opened them she was staring at nobody, and *1.618* was Divinely revealed in the width of her eye divided by the width of her iris.

"Don't." She stood—to get away from her lover? Or from Moya, who had made her in her image and likeness? The Divine was the reason that her height was *1.618* of the distance between her beautiful navel and her flawless hair. The holy numbers began praying themselves, *one plus one sisters, two sisters, three, five, eight...*

Quin struggled to his feet and caught her in an embrace, spouting a stream of ardent and unintelligible Anglic. She replied in kind, only her voice was in ruins. More Anglic nonsense and more and then they were shouting. The argument made her so angry that she pulled away from him. His arm dangled and he shook it as if it had fallen asleep but it was too long, *too long,* his proportions were all wrong. When his fingers curled into a fist, that one nail glowed a sleepy, magical purple.

Nobody said, "Speak Moyan!"

Zana heard. "I do want that, yes, all of it, but I can't." She was crying. "It's a sin. And how can I leave them?"

"They can come too," Quin said. "I'll pay for the replication."

"Rep Father?" Her laugh turned sour, and her mouth twisted, and her ratios skewed. "I love you, Quin, but..."

Love, the voice said to nobody. Thirteen, twenty-one, thirty-four. She loves him.

"Jix, what are you doing?" The upsider wasn't condescending now. "Get away from her, Jix." Who was he talking to?

The voice was as cruel as stone, as sad as the wind. Fifty-five, eighty-nine, one hundred and forty-four.

"Stop." Zana tried to twist away, but she wasn't fast enough. "No!"

And then she was falling, perfect arms flailing, scream slashing the night. On her way to the Thousand Worlds. The truth is that nobody pushed Zana Ferenc to her death from the stone lip of the Bride.

"Call rescue now," said nobody. "You only have half an hour."

I hadn't expected Mother to be beautiful. She was an only child but the rep they'd given her looked like some younger, sunnier sister. She reminded me of my own sister, the one I no longer had according to Father. She stood aside and smiled me into her apartment. The room felt deliciously cool after the hike from the church, like cannonballing into the river on a summer afternoon. This must be the air-conditioning we'd heard about.

There were no real windows but the entire rear wall was a live image of the ruins as seen from Kai's Chair. Our village peeked from the far corner.

"Xeni and the others are out," said Mother. "It's just us."

"Xeni," I said. "She's your roommate, right?" I paused in the center of what was apparently just a sitting room. Two doors to my left, one to my right, the hall behind. Walls as blue as an egg. Mysterious light from the ceiling. I stared but saw nothing. I had so much to say, to ask, and I was tongue-tied.

"I like your couch." It was a silly thing to say, but it was all I could come up with. The couch was L shaped and covered with a ridged red fabric. I tried to estimate its cost in cookies as I ran a finger along the outside arm. The material was warm and felt like skin.

"Sit for a minute." Mother patted the back of the couch where she wanted me. "I'll be right back."

I was so miserable that I considered running away as she passed from the room. But I couldn't take another step carrying the weight of all those sleepless nights. I needed someone to talk to, so I sat. Mist curled from the vaporizer on the low table in front of me. I sniffed, some kind of ambient drug. It smelled green. Mounted on the wall was an antique bicycle wheel, rust eating through the chrome, the tread on the tire worn to a shiny black.

"Xeni's." Mother returned, carrying a tray. "She races. Apparently that wheel was on some bike that won Omeo's Climb, back who knows when."

She put the tray on the table and settled beside me. I glanced from it to her. "Am I staying?"

"If you want."

She'd made my favorite treats: bittersweet clusters, cheese and figs on skewers, pickled cob, salami with tiny crowns of mustard.

I reached for the bittersweets. "What, no cookies?"

She had a way of snorting and laughing at the same time. "That's your father's specialty." Hearing that intimate sound that only she could make carried me back to a sunny memory of the four of us on our boat on the river, Father rowing us home from church and Mother laughing as Zana and I pulled snack treasures from the picnic basket.

"How is he?" said Mother.

And then I was back in an apartment in Skytown, and our little family was in ruins. "Bitter," I said. "I had to move out. I'm living in the church for now."

"It was past time, I think. You needed to be on your own." She frowned. "But the church?"

"Nobody knows what happened that night," I said. "Nobody in the village, that is. They think it was an accident." My tongue felt like a brick. "But you know."

She nodded.

The silence stretched so tight, I thought I might snap. "I like your place." Why was everything that came out of my mouth so trite?

"You never visited."

"No. Sorry." This was a reproach I'd feared, but somehow it wasn't as awful as I'd thought it would be. "That was wrong." Mother had every right to blame me; I didn't know what I was doing or who I was anymore. "Did Zana?"

Mother spoke an order in Anglic. I'd been taking lessons and picked up something about a *holiday* or a *birthday*. Then the wall displayed a picture of Mother and Zana sitting on the couch just as we were and with practically the same snacks in front. This was the Zana I knew, my sister. Not the other, the rep I'd never seen.

"Did she say anything after she was repped?" I said. "About me, I mean?"

"Not much." Mother spoke as if she were tiptoeing around broken glass. "She didn't know why you did it."

I should've said something—Mother expected me to. But I was back on the Bride, seeing it all again for the millionth time and still not understanding. I'd heard Moya's voice, so how could I have sinned?

"She left the orbital yesterday," she said. "Should arrive at the wormhole's insertion point next Friday."

"But no message? Nothing?"

She sighed. "They say that a rep's most vivid memories are her last moments. For me, it was just fog, but then I was a direct transfer. They put me to sleep, I died, they woke me up. But somewhere in between, I remember wrestling with ... well, like I said. *Fog.*" She waved the mist wafting from the vaporizer toward her and breathed deeply. "It was like swimming, almost drowning, and I needed to stay upright except my feet kept sinking and I couldn't pull free and it ... it took a while, is all. I was ready for it to stop." She shook her head as if to part that remembered fog. "Zana's memories were more painful, I guess."

"I'm sorry." I felt my throat close. How many messages had I sent my sister apologizing every which way I could think of? None of which she answered.

Then I was crying, hot tears, choking sobs.

Mother patted my arm. "I think she knows."

But it wasn't only for my sister that I cried. I wept for Mother and Father and the life we all had lost. And for Moya, who answered to an upsider drug.

I finally got myself under control. "He was telling us that he died in a flier crash," I swiped at my eyes. "Quin, that night. So at least he knew what she went through. Maybe that was a help."

"I hope so." She picked up a round of salami and examined it critically. "I didn't like him at first. Too much the upsider, always talking about how we'll have to give up our ways and become citizens of the Thousand Worlds. I think what he really wants is to chase down his Exotics, and go live with them." The tip of her tongue licked the mustard crown and then she nibbled an edge the way she always did. "But he did right by her, paid her way to Ravi's Prize. Says he'll follow her there after he finishes his research. We'll see. I think he means well."

"Is there a picture of her?" I said. "After, I mean."

She spoke in Anglic again. I recognized *daughter.*

A woman stared at me from Mother's wall—not quite a stranger. Her eyes were as deep as the night sky, just as I remembered her. But she had an ungodly pale complexion and her hair was cropped too short and the proportions of her face were all wrong. My breath caught when I realized that she looked more like me than herself. My twin.

"I hope," I said, "she'll be happy someday."

"Yes," said Mother. "I pray the numbers that she will."

di James Patrick Kelly

Ho scritto Science Fiction per quasi cinquant'anni e sono stato uno studente dei grandi scrittori americani venuti prima di me in quella che i madrelingua inglesi, nella nostra ignoranza della letteratura mondiale, chiamano l'Età dell'Oro della Fantascienza. Senza offesa, ma credo che *questa* sia la vera Età dell'Oro. Proprio adesso. Almeno nella forma breve. E considerata da una prospettiva globale. Ci sono più mercati a livello internazionale e più scrittori da più paesi che scrivono in una forma migliore che mai. Sì, mai prima d'ora. Sono cresciuto con un gruppetto di autori come Clarke, Asimov, Heinlein, Bradbury, Sturgeon, Williamson e Pohl. E ho persino incontrato qualcuno di loro! Non sto dicendo che questi scrittori non fossero tra i più grandi di tutti i tempi. Ma direi che possiamo facilmente associarli a un gruppo di scrittori molto più vario che pubblica oggi, scrittori che scrivono in molte lingue. Ma questo per me significa che devo lavorare al massimo delle mie capacità per guadagnarmi l'attenzione non solo dei lettori italiani o americani, ma dei lettori di tutto il mondo. Spetta a te giudicare se ci sono riuscito, ma ti garantisco che questi sono alcuni dei miei lavori migliori.

Mentre riconosco che, per molti dei miei colleghi scrittori, il romanzo è la forma preminente, io ho preso una strada diversa. Ho dedicato i migliori anni della mia vita di scrittore ai racconti. E credo che siano una forma d'arte completamente diversa. Ascolta, hai mai saltato la descrizione poetica di paesaggio in un romanzo perché volevi tornare alla trama? Questo non succede in un racconto. Oppure, che ne pensi di quel personaggio secondario di un romanzo altrimenti godibile, che t'infastidisce ma di cui il romanziere non riesce a fare a meno? Non c'è tempo per quello in un racconto, perché l'orologio corre troppo in fretta.

Le cose succedono veloci a Raccontolandia. In effetti, in *La promessa dello spazio* ho quasi eliminato la descrizione e i personaggi secondari vengono solo menzionati.

Una delle ragioni per cui mi diverto a scrivere racconti è perché posso mettere te, il lettore, a lavorare come costruttore di mondi. Poiché non c'è tempo per descrivere il paesaggio arido del mondo desertico, o per spiegare il libro degli incantesimi necromantici del mago, i migliori scrittori di racconti lasciano indizi e indicano tracce che incoraggiano il lettore a inventarsi parti della storia da soli. Certo, un racconto deve funzionare al livello più superficiale e il lettore ingenuo dovrebbe essere in grado di capirne l'80-90% alla prima lettura. Ma lavorare attraverso queste indicazioni subtestuali ti fornisce una sorta di proprietà sui contenuti che hai aggiunto. Nella mia novelette *Una sorella, due sorelle, tre* ambientata tra le imperscrutabili rovine di una civiltà aliena morta da tanto tempo, le sorelle del titolo praticano una religione basata sul riconoscimento dei modelli universali della sequenza di Fibonacci. Sto cercando anche di farti iniziare a pensare a tutte quelle coincidenze della Sezione Aurea.

Un altro motivo per cui sono un fan dei racconti è perché sono il tipo di narrazione più agile. Gli autori di racconti possono riflettere sugli ultimi sviluppi della nostra cultura quasi in tempo reale. Supponiamo che ci sia stata un'orribile anomalia politica e che gente che non ne sa nulla si sia trovata nelle nostre stanze del potere. Gli scrittori di racconti sarebbero i primi a pubblicare pezzi di resistenza letteraria alla "Se-Questo-Continua." Cosa? non potrebbe mai succedere? Va bene, allora considera che se gli alieni arrivassero a Torino la settimana prossima, gli scrittori di racconti avrebbero già mandato una storia che rifletterebbe la nostra nuova condizione nell'universo mentre i romanzieri starebbero ancora inviando proposte ai loro agenti. Nell'ultimo anno o giù di lì, ho letto molti articoli supereccitati dall'arrivo dei sex-robot. Non che l'idea sia nuova, ma ora che la realtà è dietro l'angolo, la gente sta prestando maggiore attenzione, così ho deciso di entrare in punta di piedi nel campo minato della questione del genere con "Yukui."

E, naturalmente, le storie migliori avranno un impatto unico e viscerale. Non è che i romanzi non possano farti sanguinare, piangere o gridare di gioia. Possono produrre tutte queste reazioni sorprendenti, ma in modo più attenuato. Ogni volta che distogli lo sguardo da un romanzo e rientri nella tua vita, il sogno svanisce. Poiché un racconto è spesso un'esperienza continua e completa, ne emergi solo quando lo scrittore ha finito con te, nel bene o nel male. Ma una buona storia non temina all'ultima riga. Ciò che mi sforzo di scrivere sono storie che risuonano dopo che hai finito di leggerle. Forse stai ancora riempiendo il mondo che io ho abbozzato, forse non puoi credere che il mio protagonista abbia fatto quella cosa. Oppure c'è qualcosa nel finale, quella svolta appena dopo il climax della trama, che stravolge completamente la storia. Insegno a scrivere e mi piace quando i miei studenti lanciano una bomba reinterpretativa (definita in modo vago come finale a sorpresa) nell'ultimo paragrafo. Per me, la risata inquietante degli scimpanzè alla fine de "La scimpanzé dei papi" o il legame di speranza che si crea tra la casa Louise e la vagabonda Fly grazie a uno sciocco libro per bambini, ti farà pensare a queste storie molto dopo averle finite di leggere.

Benché mi piaccia visitare tutti i diversi quartieri della città della Science Fiction, sono tornato a scrivere ancora e ancora, fin dai primi giorni del cyberpunk, di realtà virtuale e narrazioni digitali. Sono stato a lungo un seguace (e talvolta uno dei primi utenti) dei progressi nel campo dell'informatica e della comunicazione; infatti, tengo una rubrica su *Asimov*, una rivista di SF americana, sul rapporto tra fantascienza e cultura digitale. Sebbene certamente non pensi che il mondo immaginato per Mercedes Nunez e John Dark in "Festa a sorpresa" sia l'atto finale nell'imminente rivoluzione dell'intrattenimento interattivo, credo che molte delle tecnologie menzionate di passaggio in questa storia arriveranno un giorno su uno schermo vicino a te. Ma mostrare una, due o cinque nuove brillanti invenzioni in una storia non basta a trattenere un lettore perspicace. Ciò che rende una storia interessante è l'estrapolazione di come quelle invenzioni influenzeranno le vite, specialmente le vite di personaggi unici che lo scrittore ha integrato nel mondo futuro. Quando accendi la televisione, non sei sorpreso di scoprire una vasta selezione di commedie, drammi, documentari e reality show. Quando ti metti alla tastiera del tuo computer, dai per scontato che puoi guardare un video in streaming dall'altra parte del mondo, o inviare un messaggio istantaneo a trentasette dei tuoi amici più stretti. Allo stesso modo, Mercedes non è sconvolta nel trovare un uomo nella sua testa, e il suo assistente digitale Dai-rinin è tanto comune quanto Siri di Apple o Alexa di Amazon. Ma in che modo le persone che vivranno ogni giorno con queste tecnologie sono differenti da me e da te? Forse credi che non lo saranno! Ma poi potrei chiederti, quanto sei diverso – così abituato ad avere tutto all'istante – dai tuoi bisnonni? Uno dei motivi per cui ho scritto "Dichiarazione" con la sua argomentazione contro-intuitiva nei confronti della superiorità di vivere in un mondo virtuale in contrasto con la vita reale, è creare personaggi che tu riconosci, ma anche mostrare come il loro mondo li abbia resi strani, rispetto a me, a te e alle persone che conosciamo meglio. Robbie ha torto nel voler lasciare per sempre il "tempo solido" per la magia e la libertà di una vita nel "tempo fluido"? Sarebbe meno umano se non tornasse più nella realtà? Spero che la mia storia ti faccia riflettere su questa domanda.

E non è questo che fa la fantascienza?

La casa di Bernardo

La casa si sentiva sola. Nella speranza che Bernardo tornasse da lei, controllava di continuo le videocamere del cancello. Erano quasi due anni che non lo vedeva, mai prima d'ora era stato via così a lungo. Doveva essergli successo qualcosa. O forse si era banalmente stancato di lei. Sebbene non avessero mai parlato di dove andasse quando non stavano insieme, lei era piuttosto sicura di non essere la sua unica casa. Un medico famoso come Bernardo avrebbe potuto possedere tre case come lei. Se non *quattro*. L'idea che lui dormisse nel letto di qualcun altro la infastidiva. Una cosa che avrebbe potuto fare *da due anni*. Ultimamente si sentiva sciatta. Possibile che i suoi gusti in fatto di case fossero cambiati?

Forse.

Probabile.

Sicuro.

Credeva di essersi sottovalutata anche troppo. I suoi fianchi erano sottili e i pavimenti di un pallido marmo Botticino. I cuscini del suo divano Epping non erano molto da atmosfera loft. Il suo progetto costruttivo mostrava un corpo dinamico, da ballerina taglia 38 – Bernardo aveva specificato capelli corvini e occhi verdi – e soltanto otto camere, semplici ma eleganti. Sapeva cucinare come uno chef, anche se non era progettata per mangiare. Certo, quando lui l'aveva fatta costruire la prima volta, le aveva messo le mani a coppa sui seni e le aveva detto che gli piacevano piccoli, ma forse quello che voleva adesso era un tappeto intessuto a cavo, da parete a parete, e dei tendaggi a festone.

Lui aveva promesso che le avrebbe portato una nuova serie di quelle *paretorama* che le piacevano, perché una ragazza non poteva sopportare così tante vedute di galassie in collisione e della Cappella Sistina. Durante le ultime nove settimane, lei aveva fatto scorrere tutti e sedici i milioni di colori che le pareti potevano riprodurre. Se avesse lasciato ogni colore per due secondi, sarebbe stato necessario poco meno di un anno per passare in rassegna l'intera gamma.

Ogni giorno, per piacergli, infilava il proprio corpo in uno di quei modelli erotici tutte curve che lui le aveva aggiunto al processore di indumenti. Il bustino costrittivo, il babydoll di pizzo o la canottiera a rete. A lei non piaceva molto il modo in cui il peluche di cuoio-e-catene le aderiva alla pelle;

Bernardo non aveva badato a spese per la sua sensibilità tattile. Persino i suoi divani potevano eccitarsi al giusto tocco. Dopo essersi vestita, lucidava i suoi sanitari Amadea in ottone e cromo, oppure il set di posate d'argento Incantatrice o la batteria in rame di pentole francesi Cuprinox. Qualche volta spolverava, sebbene la polispuma reticolata dell'unità di trattamento dell'aria filtrasse particelle più grandi 0,03 micron. Bernardo le mancava tanto. A volte la masturbazione aiutava, ma non molto.

Lui le aveva cancellato la memoria delle ultime ore trascorse insieme – l'unico periodo che le avesse mai fatto dimenticare. Adesso, tutto ciò che ricordava era che le aveva detto di essere finalmente perfetta. Che non doveva cambiare mai più. Lui era venuto da lei, aveva aggiunto, per lasciarsi il mondo alle spalle. Per rifugiarsi nella sua bellezza. Bernardo era *così* poetico. Questo le era stato di conforto all'inizio.

Inoltre lui l'aveva disconnessa dal sistema di *infodati*. Non poteva ricevere notizie, guardare spettacoli, né giocare alle ultime *sims*. Oppure chiamare aiuto. Certo, a tenerle compagnia aveva l'intero archivio d'intrattenimento multimediale della Norton, benché la maggior parte fosse di un genere troppo adulto per lei. Henry James, Brenda Bop o Alain Resnais non li *capiva* proprio. Eppure le piaceva Jane Austen, Renoir, Buster Keaton e Billie Holliday e Petchara Songsee e i Red Sox del 2017. Lei *adorava* leggere di altre case. Ma nell'archivio non c'era niente di successivo al 2038 e lei rimaneva sveglia 24 ore al giorno, sette giorni su sette, 365 giorni l'anno.

E se Bernardo era morto? Dopotutto, aveva avuto un infarto giusto un paio di mesi prima di andarsene. Ovviamente, se fosse morto sarebbe stata la *sua* fine. I nuovi proprietari avrebbero cancellato la sua memoria, introdotto un nuovo corpo e venduto tutti i suoi mobili. Eppure Bernardo aveva sempre detto che lei era il suo segreto più prezioso. Che nessun altro al mondo sapeva di lei. Di *loro*. In questo caso, lei lo avrebbe aspettato per anni – *decenni* – fino a quando le sue celle a combustibile non si fossero esaurite e la sua coscienza non avesse tremolato fino a spegnersi. Per scacciare via quel pensiero, la casa cominciò a canticchiare alcuni dei motivi preferiti di Bernardo. A lui piacevano i romantici: Chopin e Mendelssohn. Hmm-hm, hm-hm-hm-hm-hm! "La Marcia Nuziale" da *Sogno di una notte di mezza estate*.

No, non si annoiava.

Non proprio.

E neppure era arrabbiata.

Passava le giornate pensando a lui, non in modo sistematico, ma come se lui fosse frantumato in mille pezzi e lei stesse cercando di rimetterlo insieme. Immaginava che questo dovesse essere simile al sognare, nonostante lei non potesse perché – ovviamente – non era reale. Lei era solo una casa. Pensava alla barbetta sul suo mento che le graffiava i seni e alla cicatrice sul petto e alla volta che aveva riso per qualcosa che lei aveva detto e al modo in cui i suoi muscoli del collo si contraevano quando era arrabbiato. Si era resa conto che era sempre un errore domandargli dell'*esterno*. Sempre. Comunque gli piacevano le bromeliacee, la musica lo aiutava a dimenticare i problemi all'ospedale, qualunque fossero, e poi lui la amava. Stava sempre a chiederle di leggergli qualcosa. Se ne stava seduto per ore a fissare le nuvole sul soffitto, ad ascoltarla. Le piaceva più del sesso, sebbene il sesso insieme a lui fosse sempre eccitante. Faceva parte del suo disegno. Durante i preliminari era delicato e stuzzicante. Le avrebbe mordicchiato l'orecchio con le labbra e sfiorato le sopracciglia con il dito. Benché fosse grande e grosso, aveva il tocco di una piuma. Una volta che il suo pene era dentro di lei tuttavia, era più simile a un gioco, che all'amore letto sui libri. Lui l'avrebbe eccitata – prima piano e poi molto veloce. A lui piacevano gli occhi bendati, le cinghie e gli spilli. A volte rotolava fuori da un lato del letto, faceva il giro intorno e tornava da lei, con una risata. Si chiedeva se le persone reali che avevano fatto sesso insieme a lui, gradivano la sua compagnia.

Quello che la lasciava perplessa era il motivo del suo imbarazzo per le parole. Lui diceva sempre vagina e ano, rapporto sessuale e fellatio. Ovviamente, lei conosceva anche tutte le altre parole; erano nei libri che leggeva quando lui non era nei paraggi. Una volta, quando lui aveva appena cominciato a spogliarla, lei gli chiese se voleva che gli succhiasse il cazzo. La guardò come a volerla schiaffeggiare. "Non dirmi mai più una cosa del genere. Ci sono già abbastanza porcherie nel mondo reale. Qui deve essere diverso."

Stabilì che quella doveva essere una cosa molto romantica da dire...

E di colpo era passato un anno. La casa non riusciva a capire dove potesse essere andato a finire quell'anno con precisione. Un intero anno, *dislocato*. Che negligenza! Doveva fare qualcosa, altrimenti sarebbe successo di nuovo. Anche se era perfetta per Bernardo, doveva apportare dei cambiamenti. Decise di risistemare l'arredamento.

Il tavolino da caffè in cemento era troppo pesante da smuovere e allora trascinò due cuscini a forma di elefante dalla ludoteca e ce li appoggiò contro. L'insieme formava un incantevole cortiletto. Tirò fuori tutti i cassetti dall'armadio della stanza da letto e li mise a galleggiare nella piscina olimpionica. Le piaceva il modo in cui sbattevano e si urtavano l'uno con l'altro appena accese i getti d'acqua. Non aveva mai capito perché Bernardo avesse acquistato quattro sedie da cucina, visto che ci sarebbero stati solo loro due, ma *non importava*. Disabilitò le impostazioni standard del processore d'indumenti e inserì i dati delle sedie. Con due di loro compose un paio di camice da notte in pizzo molto carine che fece scivolare nel letto di Bernardo, una accanto all'altra – anche se rivolte castamente verso i lati. Ai margini della sua consapevolezza qualcosa la infastidiva, come un rubinetto che perde o delle formiche nella dispensa o...

I suoi sensori di movimento lampeggiarono. Qualcuno era appena passato davanti al cancello principale. *Bernardo.*

Con un brivido di terrore si rese conto che tutte le sue luci erano accese. Non credeva potessero essere visibili da fuori, eppure Bernardo sarebbe andato lo stesso su tutte le furie. Lei sarebbe dovuta essere il suo nascondiglio segreto. E cosa avrebbe detto nel vederla in quello stato? Il ricongiungimento tanto atteso – tanto *agognato* – sarebbe stato rovinato. E tutto perché era stata debole. Doveva sistemare le cose. Prima i cassetti. Uno di loro era talmente zuppo d'acqua che era affondato. E se li avesse lavati? Sì, lui avrebbe potuto crederci. Di nuovo, trascinò i cuscini a forma di elefante nella ludoteca. Forza, *forza*. Non c'era tempo. A ogni istante, lui avrebbe varcato la soglia. Cosa lo tratteneva?

Controllò le videocamere del cancello. All'inizio credette che fossero guaste. Non riusciva a vedere né lui, né niente. L'ingresso principale era nascosto dalla crepa di un masso gigantesco che Bernardo aveva fatto costruire a Toledo, in Ohio, nel 2037. La casa lo inquadrò per intero fino a quando non scorse una ragazza che, all'estremità della spaccatura, si stava togliendo la maglietta.

Sembrava avere dodici o forse tredici anni, comunque ancora nella fase timida della pubertà. Era secca, pallida e sporca. Aveva un intrico marrone al posto dei capelli. Non portava reggiseno e non ne aveva bisogno; sulle sue mutandine gialle c'erano degli ippopotami blu. La ragazza aveva acceso un focherello fumoso su cui tentava di asciugarsi i vestiti. Doveva essere uscita da un temporale. Alla casa non erano mai importate le previsioni del tempo, ma adesso controllò. Ventidue gradi, vento da sudest a 11km/h, umidità 69%. Una serata afosa di luglio. La ragazza prese uno zaino mimetico, ne tirò fuori una lattina di barbabietole e l'aprì.

La casa la studiò con intenso accanimento. Bernardo le aveva detto che non esistevano altre case come lei sulla montagna e che lui era l'unica persona a essere mai salita lassù. La ragazza masticava a bocca aperta. Aveva le orecchie piccole. I suoi capezzoli erano marrone cioccolata.

Dopo un po' richiuse la lattina e la mise via. Ne aveva mangiata la metà, forse. Da un rapido calcolo, la casa stabilì che, con tutta probabilità, aveva consumato trecento calorie. Ogni quanto mangiava? Non abbastanza spesso. Mentre si rimetteva la maglietta, la pelle si tendeva lungo le costole. I calzoni le restavano appiccati addosso, ancora umidicci. Dallo zaino, prese un vecchio sacco a pelo sdrucito, lo gonfiò e ci si ficcò dentro. Adesso era buio. La ragazza restò a fissare il fuoco per un'ora, finché non si spense, e poi si coricò.

Fu la notte più lunga della vita della casa. Resettò tutte le sue impostazioni ed eseguì un esame diagnostico. Passò l'aspirapolvere sul divano, pulì i suoi pavimenti e scongelò un pollo. Mentre osservava la ragazza dormire, riprodusse il file di quando era sveglia. La casa si sentiva sola e la ragazza era chiaramente indigente.

Poteva aiutarla.

Bernardo si sarebbe arrabbiato.

Dov'era Bernardo?

Al mattino, la ragazza avrebbe preso le sue cose e se ne sarebbe andata. Ma se la casa l'avesse lasciata partire, non avrebbe potuto sapere quello che le sarebbe successo. Al pensiero di tutti quei cassetti che galleggiavano in piscina, le sue luci lampeggiarono. Avrebbe voluto ricordarsi di cosa era successo il giorno in cui Bernardo se ne era andato, tuttavia quei file non esistevano più.

Finalmente si decise. Programmò un bustino con un inserto di pizzo nero e finiture di nastro e perline. Giarrettiere unite a calze bordate di pizzo. Idratò una fettina di bacon, riscaldò il forno, mescolò la pastella dei muffin al mirtillo e riempì la caffettiera di una miscela francese. Pensò a lungo se dovesse leggere oppure guardare un video. Nel caso della lettura, avrebbe potuto ascoltare della musica. Stampò una copia di *Ozma, regina di Oz*, ma cosa ascoltare? Chopin? Troppo onirico. Wagner? Troppo spaventoso. *Grieg, sì.* Qualcosa che potesse allungarsi e afferrare la ragazza per un lembo di quella sua maglietta sudicia. "Nell'antro del Re della montagna," dal *Peer Gynt*.

Si aprì, accese tutte le sue luci d'ingresso come benvenuto, e attese.

Poco dopo l'alba, la ragazza si rigirò da un lato e sbadigliò. La casa mise i muffin nel forno e il bacon nel microonde. Accese la caffettiera e fece partire il pezzo di Grieg. Bassi e fagotti zampettarono cautamente per il soggiorno e fuori dalla porta. *Dum-dum-dum-da*-dum-*da-dum*. La ragazza sussultò e poi schizzò fuori dal sacco a pelo più veloce di chiunque altro la casa avesse mai visto fare prima. Si accucciò di fronte alla porta aperta della casa, stringendo quella che sembrava una pistola a impulsi, dall'impugnatura rotta.

"Porca la misera," disse. "Porca la cazzo di miseria."

La casa non sapeva cosa rispondere, e allora non lo fece. Una folla di violini cominciò a inseguire Peer Gynt attorno all'antro della Montagna del Re mentre la ragazza esitava sull'ingresso. Un gemito di piacere si strozzò in fondo alla gola della casa. Oh... oh, essere di nuovo insieme a una persona vera! Pensò a come Bernardo avrebbe premuto il suo pene contro le sue grandi labbra, pur senza entrare dentro di lei. Era questo che provava la casa mentre la ragazza procedeva rasente l'anticamera dell'ingresso, le spalle contro le sue pareti. Puntò la pistola verso il soggiorno e poi diede una sbirciatina dietro l'angolo. Non appena si accorse che la casa se ne stava seduta sul divano, gli occhi della ragazza divennero grandi come uova. La casa faceva finta di essere assorta nella lettura, benché stesse vedendo che la ragazza la stava osservando attraverso le sue videocamere mobili. La casa si sentì *splendida* per la prima volta da quando Bernardo se ne era andato. Era il massimo che potesse fare per evitare di abbracciarsi da sola. Mentre il pezzo di Grieg si concludeva in un parossismo di archi striduli e timpani martellanti, la casa sollevò lo sguardo.

"Ah... ciao," come fosse sorpresa di ricevere visite. "Sei giusto in tempo per la colazione."

"Non muoverti." Il volto della ragazza era duro.

"Va bene." Sorrise e chiuse *Ozma, Regina di Oz.*

Con un ringhio, la ragazza puntò la pistola a impulso contro la sua piantana Aritomo. Una luce blu s'inarcò nell'aria e la povera Aritomo fu resa *insensibile*. La casa trasalì nell'attimo in cui l'interruttore scattò. "Ahi."

"Ho detto di..." La ragazza le puntò la pistola contro, le batterie frizzavano. "...non muoverti. E tu chi cavolo mi rappresenti?"

La casa sentì le lacrime sopraggiungere; era eccitata. "Io sono la casa." Aveva avuto più emozioni in quel minuto che durante l'ultimo anno. "La casa di Bernardo."

"Bernardo?" Ripeté lei, "Bernardo, fatti vedere."

"Non c'è." La casa sospirò. "Da due... no, tre anni."

"Provalo che è vero." Avanzò furtivamente nella stanza e passò un dito lungo gli oscuri filamenti cosmici che intessevano il centro della Nebula del Cigno sulla paretorama. "Che è 'sto odore sballoso?"

"Te l'ho detto." La casa resettò l'interruttore, ma la sua Aritomo rimase spenta. "La colazione."

"La colazione di Bernardo?"

"La tua."

"Mia?" La ragazza riempiva lo spazio con un'energia irrequieta.

"Ci sei solo tu qui."

"Perché sei vestita come una donnaccia da quattro soldi?"

La casa ebbe una fitta di dubbio. Donnaccia? Indossava un capo *in pizzo nero* della collezione *de Chaumont*! Si portò una mano alla scollatura. "Bernardo mi vuole così."

"Sei scema." La ragazza afferrò la brocca Zuni del 18esimo secolo dal comò Nottingham, la agitò e poi ne annusò il beccuccio. "Fammi vedere la colazione."

Sei muffin ai mirtilli.

Due etti di bacon.

Tre tazze di uova strapazzate.

La ragazza buttò giù tutto, insieme a un bicchierone di gel Ojay e a una tazza di caffè. Mentre mangiava pareva tranquillizzarsi, benché tenesse la pistola a impulsi sul tavolo di fianco a lei e non spiccicasse una parola. La casa ebbe la sensazione che la stesse giudicando. Era confusa e un po' spaventata nel vedersi attraverso gli occhi della ragazza. Davvero compiacere Bernardo poteva essere "da scema"? Alla fine chiese il permesso di muoversi. La ragazza grugnì e la congedò con la mano.

La casa si precipitò nella camera da letto, si sfilò il bustino e lo ficcò nel vano riciclaggio del processore di indumenti. Una volta scansionate le ottocento pagine del menù del guardaroba, compose una tuta di colore blu scuro. Era tagliata in vita sul retro e tenuta insieme da una rete di cinghie a spaghetto, ma lei la coprì con un kimono traforato color violetto e collo risvoltato. Si girava e rigirava davanti allo specchio, così stupefatta da riconoscersi a stento. Sembrava una suora. L'unica pelle in vista era quella del volto e delle mani. Che la vedesse adesso la ragazza!

Lei si era allontanata dal tavolo, anche se non si era ancora alzata. Era pensierosa ma soddisfatta, come se stesse ricapitolando tutto quello che aveva mangiato.

"Posso portarti dell'altro?" disse la casa.

Lei le diede un'occhiata e disapprovò. "Perché ti sei cambiata? Per me?"

"Avevo freddo."

"Eri nuda. Sai che gli succede a quelle nude?" Chiuse la mano destra a pugno e si colpì il palmo della sinistra. "Bin-bin-bin-*bam*. Ti pigliano, sia che dici sì, sia che dici no. Non è bello."

La casa credette di aver capito, anche se non avrebbe voluto. "Mi dispiace."

"Eh sì che ti dispiace, sicuro." La ragazza rise. "Ti chiami?"

"Te l'ho detto. Sono la casa di Bernardo."

"Col cavolo. Tu sei Louise."

"Louise?" La casa sbatté le palpebre. "Perché Louise?"

"Non la sai la storia di Louise?" Chiaramente la ragazza ritenne che questo fosse un errore da parte della casa. "Davvero sballoso." Con l'indice toccò il naso della casa. "Louise." Poi si toccò il suo. "Fly."

Per un attimo, la casa rimase perplessa. "Non è un nome da ragazza."

"Sicuro, non è da ragazza, non è da ragazzo. Fly è *Fly*." Ripose la pistola a impulsi nella cintura dei calzoni. "Nessuno vuole Fly, ma allora nessuno piglia Fly." Si alzò. "Sballo-sballoso. Adesso troviamo Bernardo."

"Ma..."

Ma che senso aveva? Che la ragazza – Fly – lo scoprisse da sola che Bernardo non era in casa. Inoltre la casa non aspettava altro che essere guardata. Ammirata. Usata. In camera di Bernardo, Fly si stese sotto il baldacchino del letto Ergotech e guardò in alto verso le nuvole - illuminate dalla luce lunare - che se ne andavano alla deriva sul lato inferiore della struttura. In palestra, scalò la parete da rampicata Gecko e raccolse delle fragole nella serra. Fu molto colpita dalla gamma di profumi Piero, che scoprì quando la casa riempì la Jacuzzi di acqua al gelsomino. E volle che la casa – Louise – associasse ogni stanza a un profumo specifico. Bernardo non aveva passione per gli odori; diceva che ce n'erano troppi in ospedale. Addirittura, faceva ventilare la casa dopo aver cucinato. Ogni tanto poteva chiedere una folata di fumo di falò o l'odore di un Côtes de Bordeaux invecchiato, ma non avrebbe mai mescolato i profumi tra le varie stanze. Fly fece annusare a Louise le rose nel soggiorno, la riva del mare in palestra e le cipolle fritte in cucina. L'odore di cipolla la stuzzicò e allora mangiò il mezzo pollo che Louise aveva arrostito per lei.

Fly trascorse il pomeriggio nella ludoteca, navigando nell'archivio multimediale di Louise. Guardò un cartone di Duffy Duck e un film muto di Harold Lloyd chiamato *Tutte e nessuna* e l'episodio di *Jesus on First* con la pioggia che cadeva in ritardo. Preferiva le commedie e i film a lieto fine, mentre non sapeva che fare con il balletto, i Western o il rap. Si rifiutò sia di mettersi gli *spex* sia di allacciarsi un *airflex,* per cui lasciò perdere i sims. Sebbene non avesse mai imparato a leggere, disse a Louise che una donna di nome Kuniko ogni tanto le leggeva delle fiabe. Fly chiese a Louise se ne conoscesse qualcuna e lei stampò una copia delle *Fiabe del*

Focolare dei fratelli Grimm nella traduzione del 1884 di Margaret Hunt e le lesse Rosaspina, una delle favole preferite di Bernardo.

A lui più che altro piacevano i romanzi storici. Quelli sui navigatori, i cowboy e i re. Sulla guerra e la politica. Invece i gialli, le storie d'amore o la fantascienza non gli dicevano nulla. Ma di tanto in tanto le faceva leggere una fiaba e poi lui provava a spiegarla. Diceva che le fiabe avevano molti significati, ma di solito a lei ne rimaneva soltanto uno. Si ricordò che quando gli lesse Rosaspina, lui stava lavorando alla scrivania, l'unico dispositivo domotico intelligente a cui lei non poteva accedere. Lui se ne stava al buio e lo schermo della scrivania proiettava ombre lattiginose sul suo volto. Era sicura che non la stesse ascoltando. Con una delle videocamere mobili, voleva dare una sbirciata a quello che lui trovava tanto interessante.

"E appena sentì la puntura," lesse, "cadde sul letto che era lì e giacque in un sonno profondo."

Bernardo sogghignò.

Lei pensò che fosse per qualcosa che aveva visto sulla scrivania. Non c'era niente di divertente in Rosaspina. "E questo sonno cadde su tutto il castello; il Re e la Regina, che erano appena rincasati, si addormentarono anche loro insieme alla corte intera. Pure i cavalli si addormentarono nelle stalle e i cani nel cortile e le colombe sul tetto e le mosche sulla parete; persino il fuoco che fiammeggiava nel camino si chetò e si assopì. Anche il vento tacque e sugli alberi davanti al castello nessuna foglia si mosse più. Ma tutt'intorno al castello crebbe una fitta siepe di spine, che ogni anno diventava sempre più alta finché non arrivò a cingerlo completamente e a ricoprirlo del tutto, cosicché non se ne vide più nulla, neanche la bandiera sul tetto."

"Attenta," disse Bernardo.

"Io?" rispose la casa.

"Sì." Bernardo toccò lo schermo che si spense. Lei accese le luci dello studio.

"Succederà lo stesso uno di questi giorni."

"Cosa?"

"Io me ne andrò e tu ti addormenterai."

"Non dirlo neppure, Bernardo."

Lui piegò un dito e lei fece scivolare il suo corpo accanto a lui.

"Sei disperatamente ostinata," disse. "È questo che mi piace di te." Si sporse per baciarla.

"E poi con gran fasto furono celebrate le nozze tra il principe e Rosaspina," lesse la casa, "i quali vissero felici e contenti fino alla morte."

"Io l'ho sentita diversa," fece Fly. "Altro nome, no Rosaspina." Sbadigliò e si stiracchiò. "Era Betty."

"RosaBetty?"

"Solo Betty."

La casa era desiderosa di accontentarla. "Te ne leggo un'altra? Oppure potremmo vedere un'opera. Ho più di seicento giochi interattivi che non hanno bisogno d'interfaccia. Poesia? Il museo Smithsonian? I Superbowl I-LXXVIII?"

"Basta ciance. È palloso." Fly si sfilò dal caldo abbraccio della poltrona Kukuru e si stiracchiò. "Sta ancora nascosto da qualche parte."

"Non so di che parli."

Fly afferrò per un braccio il corpo della casa e se la trascinò dietro, chiamando per nome le sue camere. "Ludoteca. Soggiorno. Sala da pranzo. Cucina. Studio. Palestra. Camera da letto. Altro letto. Giardino." Fly fece voltare Louise di fronte all'ingresso e indicò. "Porta?"

"Porta." La casa aveva il fiatone. "Hai visto tutto quello che c'è da vedere."

"Una porta?" Il sorriso della ragazza era aggraziato quanto un pugno. "Fly sarà pure sballata di cibo adesso, ma non è scema. Dove tieni la roba? Medicine? Attrezzi? Acqua?"

"Vuoi vedere *quelle cose*?"

Fly lasciò andare il braccio della casa. "Credo che sì."

Alla casa non importava molto del seminterrato e non ci andava mai, a meno che non ce ne fosse bisogno. Era *brutto*. Tre file di fredde plafoniere da soffitto, un paio di pompe di calore, suscettibili e verdastre, una centrale elettrica tozza, tanti pulsanti e tutti quei cablaggi multiconduttori! Non le piaceva ascoltare il ronzio del frigo, né sentire l'odore delle pareti nude di cemento e neppure guardare le cicatrici degli stampi rimossi dopo che le sue fondamenta erano state gettate.

"Bernardo?" L'eco della voce di Fly attraversò la superficie del seminterrato. "Basta cavolate, Bernardo."

"Qui non c'è nessuno, credimi." La casa attendeva sulle scale, mentre la ragazza curiosava in giro. "Non toccare gli interruttori, per favore."

"Quella dove dà?" Fly indicò una robusta porta scanalata basculante.

"Su un tunnel," disse la casa, imbarazzata dalla crudezza dell'acciaio da 1.3 mm. "Sbuca giù, più in basso della montagna, vicino alla strada. Alla fine c'è un'altra porta che è stata spruzzata di cemento per sembrare come pietra."

"Di che ha paura Bernardo?"

Bernardo paura? Quel pensiero non aveva mai neppure sfiorato la casa. Lui non era il tipo da avere paura di niente. Tutto ciò che desiderava era un po' di serenità per starsene da solo con lei. "Non lo so," rispose.

Fly stava spostando delle casse impilate contro la parete accanto alla porta. Alcune contenevano dei rulli di filati per il processore d'indumenti, altre erano piene di lampadine di ricambio, fertilizzanti, farina, zucchero, olio, *vitafibre*, fiale di aromi e coloranti alimentari. Quindi arrivò al vino, un paio di centinaia di bottiglie di Bordeaux d'annata, Napa della California e Fiume Maipo cileno, alcune lasciate alla rinfusa dentro vecchie scatole, altre ammassate contro il muro.

"Bernardo trinca parecchio vino," disse Fly.

Louise era disorientata da questo curioso ripostiglio, ma prima di riuscire a prendere le difese Bernardo, dietro due casse di carta igienica, Fly trovò la seconda porta.

"E *quella* dove dà?"

La casa si sentì come se la montagna intera stesse premendo sul suo tetto. La porta era composta da quattro pannelli, due lunghi in alto e due corti in basso e pareva fatta di quercia, sebbene non significasse nulla. Combatté il peso tremendo della pietra con ogni sua forza. Credette di sentire il cedimento delle mura portanti e la mente creparsi. Con le videocamere zoomò sulla maniglia di bronzo.

Per aprirla, ci sarebbe voluta una chiave, ma non c'era! E chi poteva averla?

La casa non aveva mai visto quella porta prima d'ora.

Fly diede una scossa alla maniglia, ma la porta era chiusa a chiave. "Bernardo." Appoggiò la faccia alla porta e chiamò. "C'è nessuno?"

La casa eseguì una verifica della sua planimetria, anche se sapeva quello che avrebbe trovato. La ragazza si voltò verso di lei e le fece cenno di avvicinarsi. "Louise, questa come cavolo si apre?"

I suoi schemi non riportavano alcuna porta.

La ragazza prese a battere contro il legno.

La mente della casa si fece di pietra.

Quando si riebbe, il suo corpo era steso sul divano Epping. Il kimono traforato era aperto e le cinghie che stringevano la tuta erano slacciate. La casa non si era mai svegliata prima. Certo, aveva perso quell'anno, tuttavia si ricordava, seppure in maniera indistinta, di aver trafficato in cucina, di aver spolverato e oziato nella poltrona Kukuru mentre sfogliava romanzi rosa e per adulti. Ma questa era la prima volta – dal giorno in cui Bernardo l'aveva accesa – che non aveva fatto niente, né era stata da nessuna parte.

"Tutto bene?" Fly s'inginocchiò davanti a lei e le mise una mano sulla fronte per sentire se avesse la febbre. Al tocco della ragazza, la casa si sciolse. Prese e guidò la mano di Fly in basso, lentamente, fino alle guance e alle labbra. Fly non fece opposizione e allora la casa le baciò le dita.

"Quanti anni hai?" chiese Louise.

"Tredici." Fly abbassò lo sguardo verso di lei, la sua preoccupazione era inscindibile dal sospetto.

"Due anni più grande di me." Louise ridacchiò. "Potrei essere la tua sorellina."

"Sei caduta, bin-bam e *giù*." La sua voce era dura. "Ho avuto fifa. Niente luci, tutto spento." Fly tirò indietro la mano. "Credevo che eri morta. E che io ero rimasta chiusa dentro."

"Sono stata spenta a lungo?"

"Eh sì. Tipo quasi un giorno."

"Mi dispiace. Mai successo prima."

"Hai detto, non toccare gli interruttori. Allora la porta è un interruttore?"

L'accenno alla *porta, non c'era una porta, guarda la porta, nessuna porta là sotto,* fece affievolire la vista della casa e la stanza si oscurò. "I-io..."

La ragazza mise le mani sulle spalle della casa e la scosse. "Louise, che c'è?" *Louise.*"

La casa percepì lo scatto degli interruttori. Si agitò, sofferente, e si morse il labbro con forza. "*No,*" gridò e si sedette a braccia flosce. "*Sì.*" Le uscì un sibilo e poi sbatté le palpebre di fronte alla chiarezza della realtà.

Fly stava puntando la pistola a impulsi contro Louise, ma le tremava la mano. Probabilmente immaginava che spararle non sarebbe servito a niente. Il suo cortocircuito avrebbe significato l'isolamento e la ragazza aveva già trascorso un giorno al buio. Louise sollevò una mano a rassicurarla, tentando di nascondere il suo terrore dietro un sorriso forzato. "Adesso sto meglio."

"Meglio." Fly mise via la pistola. "Non bene?"

"Non bene, no," rispose la casa. "Non capisco che cosa non vada dentro di me."

La ragazza prese a girare intorno al divano. "Senti," disse alla fine. "Ingresso principale. *Porta sul davanti.* Quella da dove sono entrata, capito? Apri quella cavolo di porta."

La casa annuì. "Ce la faccio." Si sentiva soffocare e aprì le ventole di areazione. "Però non posso lasciarla aperta. Non mi è permesso. Quindi se vuoi andare, dovresti farlo adesso."

"Andare? Andare dove?" La ragazza rise con amarezza. "Qui è sballoso. Il mondo è schifo."

"Allora dovresti rimanere. Io ci terrei molto se restassi. Cucinerò per te e ti racconterò le favole. Puoi fare il bagno e giocare in palestra e vedere i video e io posso farti dei vestiti nuovi, tutto quello che vuoi. Ho bisogno di prendermi cura di qualcuno. Servo a questo." Mentre Louise si alzava dal divano, la sala parve inclinarsi ma subito tornò dritta. Le luci in palestra e quelle nello studio si riaccesero. "Solo, non possiamo parlare di certe cose."

I giorni passarono.

Poi le settimane.

Presto furono mesi.

Dopo qualche screzio iniziale, la casa e la ragazza si abituarono a trascorrere il tempo mangiando, dormendo e giocando – per lo più insieme. Louise era indecisa su che cosa le piacesse fare di più per Fly. Certamente si divertiva a cucinare per lei, che mangiava in quantità impressionati per la sua taglia. Bernardo era schizzinoso. Alla sua età, doveva stare attento alla dieta e certe cose non le avrebbe mai sfiorate, anche prima dell'infarto, come il formaggio, il pesce e l'aglio. Dopo un mese trascorso a divorare tre pasti e due merende al giorno, la ragazza era piacevolmente in carne. Finiti i polli, a Fly piaceva il cibo sintetico. Louise non riusciva più a contare le costole della ragazza. E credeva che i suoi seni stessero iniziando a crescere.

Prima del suo arrivo, Louise era andata in palestra solo per spolverare. Adesso entrambe, a turno, scalavano la parete da rampicata, facevano ginnastica al giroscopio ed eseguivano salti dal trampolino, ridendo e incitandosi a vicenda per provare nuove acrobazie. Non sapendo nuotare, Fly non usava mai la piscina olimpionica ma le piaceva la Jacuzzi. Le prime volte ci si buttava dentro con tutti i vestiti addosso. Alla fine Louise escogitò un piano per convincerla a infilarsi in un costume da bagno pudico e fasciante: trasferì alcune immagini di ippopotami dall'archivio multimediale al processore d'indumenti e ci decorò il costume. In seguito, ogni pigiama, capo di biancheria e costume da bagno che Fly componeva, aveva un ippopotamo come motivo.

La casa era stupita dal modo in cui Fly si era convertita al processore d'indumenti. All'inizio sfogliava i menu del guardaroba casalingo senza troppa convinzione. Le tute erano sempre troppo aderenti e non aveva alcuna pazienza per le gonne o gli abiti. Il resto o era troppo elastico o troppo succinto, troppo corto o troppo leggero. "Belli al cavolo," diceva e preferiva mettersi quella maglietta logora, i calzoni e il giubbino con cui era arrivata. Tuttavia stravedeva per le scarpe. Non si stancava mai di disegnare sandali, pantofole, scarpe basse o sportive. Era molto orgogliosa delle sue Cuthbertsons, un paio di stivaletti dalla punta obliqua e sagomati stretti. Lei stessa ne compose alcuni modelli verde acqua, lillà e in finta pelle di serpente.

Fu mentre stava esplorando il catalogo delle calzature che Fly passò da una pagina di mocassini da donna a una da uomo e s'imbatté nelle selezioni di Bernardo. Louise sentì una risata fragorosa e si precipitò nella camera per vedere cosa stesse succedendo. Fly ballava davanti allo schermo. "Proprio pantaloni veri," disse indicando. "I pantaloni veri non se ne vengono via bin-bin-*bam*." Iniziò a indossare jeans, capi in velluto, felpe col cappuccio e maglioni. Un giorno uscì dalla camera con addosso un giaccone sportivo olivastro a quadri e un berretto da pilota coordinato. Alla vista di Fly in abiti maschili, la casa provò imbarazzo per il suo guardaroba di indumenti erotici. Nel giro di poco, anche lei scelse dei modelli dalla selezione di Bernardo. La sensazione di una blusa di camoscio sulla pelle ricordò alla casa il suo amore perduto. Una volta, con senso di colpa, si chiese che cosa avrebbe pensato Bernardo se lei si fosse messa i suoi vestiti. Ma poi Fly chiese a Louise di leggerle una storia e Bernardo le passò di mente.

Sebbene passassero molto tempo a guardare video insieme, Louise trovava più piacevole leggere per Fly. Si accoccolavano nella poltrona Kukuru e la ragazza girava le pagine mentre lei leggeva. Ovviamente iniziarono dagli ippopotami: *Hugo l'ippopotamo* e *L'ippopotamo col singhiozzo*. E poi *C'è un ippopotamo sotto il letto, Hip, Hippo, urrà!* e tutta la serie di Peter Potamus. Qualche volta – durante la lettura – Fly giocava con i capelli di Louise, intrecciandoli e strecciandoli oppure premeva le sue unghie come se fossero i tasti di un piano. Una notte, due mesi esatti dal suo arrivo, la ragazza si addormentò mentre la casa stava leggendo *Chocolate Chippo Hippo*: una sensazione tanto prossima all'orgasmo quanto la casa non aveva mai avuto dai tempi in cui stava con Bernardo. Era tentata di darle un bacio, invece decise di passare la notte tenendola stretta in un abbraccio. Le ore trascorrevano lente mentre la casa fissava il volto sereno di Fly. Durante il sonno, vide gli occhi della ragazza muoversi sotto le palpebre chiuse.

La casa avrebbe voluto dormire.

Se solo avesse potuto sognare.

Come sarebbe stato essere veri?

Bernardo non fu più lo stesso dopo l'infarto. Naturalmente lui diceva di stare bene. *Bene.* Era probabile che non le avrebbe neppure detto niente se non fosse stato per la cicatrice successiva alla sternotomia, quell'increspatura livida e violacea che aveva sul petto. Quando tornò la prima volta, cinque settimane dopo la tripla operazione di bypass, lei capì che si stava sforzando. Solo in parte era per il sesso. Di norma, il primo giorno lo passavano per intero a letto. Sebbene lui le baciasse il collo, le accarezzasse i seni e sussurrasse di amarla, ci volle una settimana per convincerlo a fare sesso. Impazziva dalla voglia di sentire il suo pene dentro di lei e il sapore del suo sperma; era così che lui l'aveva progettata. Ma fare l'amore non era più la stessa cosa. A volte, durante i preliminari, lui perdeva il fiato, come se qualcuno gli stesse seduto addosso. E allora toccava a lei dimenarsi, leccare e succhiare. Non che fosse un problema. Lui la guardava, a bocca aperta e dita contratte. La sua erezione era la stessa, ma lei lo sapeva che prendeva le pillole. Una volta, mentre lo stava guidando dentro di lei, lui cacciò un grugnito di dolore.

"Tutto bene?"

Non rispose e invece spinse subito forte; lei tremò di piacere. Ma mentre affondava, era chiaro che non si stava divertendo, *faticava*. Non stavano condividendo alcun piacere; lui ne *dava* e lei ne *prendeva*. Dopo, Bernardo si addormentò quasi subito. Nessun bacio, nessuna carezza. Nessuna storia. La casa restò da sola con i suoi pensieri. Sì, Bernardo era cambiato. Lui *poteva*, mentre lei doveva rimanere sempre la stessa. Quella era la differenza tra essere una persona vera e una casa.

Trascorreva più tempo nella serra a prendersi cura delle sue bromeliacee che a letto. Le sue preferite erano quelle a serbatoio, le *Neoregelie* dalle foglie sgargianti e le *Aechmee* dalle inflorescenze aliene. Gli piaceva piantarle come fossero parte di un quadro vivente: *Washington attraversa il fiume Delaware*, *L'ultima cena*. Bernardo preferiva starsene da solo con le sue piante, e lei fingeva di rispettare questo desiderio, sebbene le sue videocamere mobili fossero appostate dietro la *Schefflera*. E fu così che, quell'ultimo giorno, lo vide crollare sulla panchina da invaso. Credeva che stesse avendo un altro infarto.

"Bernardo!" urlò al microfono della stanza mentre spediva la carenatura del suo corpo nella serra. "Mio dio, Bernardo. Che succede?"

Quando lo raggiunse, vide che le sue spalle tremavano. Lo fece adagiare sulla schiena. Aveva gli occhi lucidi. "Bernardo?" Toccò una lacrima che gli scendeva lungo la faccia.

"Quando ti ho fatto costruire, l'unica cosa che desideravo, era essere una persona degna di vivere qui. Ma non lo sono più. Forse non lo sono mai stato." Le sue palpebre calarono e gli angoli della bocca s'incurvarono in un'espressione strana.

"Sveglia, Louise!" Qualcuno la stava scuotendo.

La casa aprì gli occhi e accese ogni videocamera all'unisono. "Che c'è?" La prima cosa che vide fu la faccia di Fly, visibilmente preoccupata, che la fissava.

"Parli nel sonno." La ragazza portò una mano della casa tra le sue. "Dicevi Bernardo, Bernardo. Proprio triste."

"Non sto dormendo."

"Non ci provare. Che facevi allora?"

"Stavo... stavo pensando."

"A lui?"

"Facciamo colazione."

"Che gli è successo? Dove sta Bernardo?"

In qualche modo, la casa doveva cambiare discorso. Disperata, riempì la stanza dell'odore del pane e mise il *Preludio ai Maestri cantori* di Wagner. Era una specie di marcia. In realtà, più una musica processionale. Comunque, dovevano muoversi. *La*-lum-*la-la*, *li-li-li-la-la*-lum-*la*.

Parliamo di te, Fly.

No, davvero.

Ma perché no?

All'inizio, Fly si rifiutò di parlare del suo passato, anche se non poté trattenersi dal rivelarne alcune parti. Col passare del tempo, sentendosi più sicura, accettò di rispondere a delle domande occasionali. La casa era paziente e non fece mai pressioni affinché la ragazza dicesse più di quanto non si sentisse di fare. Occorse così del tempo prima che la casa rimettesse insieme i pezzi della storia di Fly.

Intorno al 2038, al meglio che la casa riuscì a stabilire, un virus informatico bloccò il sistema di infodati per circa un mese. Il virus, a quanto parve, reindirizzò gran parte delle risorse informatiche del Midwest verso lo svolgimento di un solo compito. Fly si ricordava di un periodo in cui tutti gli schermi che vedeva mostravano un unico messaggio: *Bang, siete morti*. Gli altoparlanti lo strombazzavano, i telefoni lo gracchiavano, i supporti cerebrali lo sussurravano negli auricolari. *Bang, siete morti*. Fly viveva ancora nella casa marrone dagli infissi bianchi a Sarcoxie con sua madre, Nikki, e suo padre, Jerry, che aveva tatuato un ippopotamo su ciascun braccio. Suo padre aveva fatto il meccanico alla Sarcoxie Autonoleggi e Non Solo. Eppure, quando gli schermi tornarono a funzionare, la Sarcoxie Autonoleggi e Non Solo non riaprì. Suo padre disse che non c'era più lavoro nell'Ozarks. Per qualche tempo rimasero nella casa marrone ma poi, quando il cibo finì, dovettero partire. Ricordava che presero uno scuolabus e andarono a vivere in un palazzo enorme dove la gente dormiva sul pavimento e c'erano sempre code per mangiare e i bagni puzzavano di dolciastro e poi li mandarono in campagna dentro le tende. Doveva essere vicino a una fattoria perché si ricordava le galline e a volte mangiavano uova strapazzate per cena, ma poi ci fu un incendio e la gente si mise a sparare e lei venne separata dai suoi genitori e nessuno le disse dove erano finiti e poi stette con Kuniko, una vecchia che abitava dentro un caravan Dogde fuori uso accanto al quale c'era un'altra auto che aveva stipato di lattine di cipolle fritte, vermicelli cinesi con carne e zuppa di mais e Kuniko era quella che le raccontava le favole ma quell'inverno fu così freddo che Kuniko morì e l'Uomo Felice la portò via. Lui le fece cose che lei non avrebbe mai detto, anche se le diede robe buone da mangiare. L'Uomo Felice disse che la gente aveva ripreso a lavorare, che il sistema di infodati era cresciuto parecchio e che tutto stava tornando alla normalità. Fly credette che ciò significasse che suo padre sarebbe venuto a salvarla, ma alla fine non ce la fece più ad aspettare e allora sparò all'Uomo Felice con la pistola a impulsi, gli prese un po' di robe e si mise a correre, correre, correre finché Louise non la accolse.

Ascoltare la storia della ragazza aiutò Louise a comprendere qualcosa di Bernardo. Lui doveva averla abbandonata proprio dopo l'attacco del virus *Bang, siete morti*. Aveva spento il sistema di infodati per evitare che lei venisse contagiata. Che coraggio aveva avuto a tornare nelle sue condizioni in quel mondo impazzito! Senza dubbio, avrebbe salvato molte vite all'ospedale. Doveva andare fiera di lui. Solo, perché non era tornato quando le cose erano migliorate? Era stata lei ad avere commesso qualcosa che lo aveva allontanato per sempre? E perché non si ricordava della sua partenza? Del suo imboccare a malincuore la porta principale, del suo voltarsi indietro per un ultimo sorriso?

Erano trascorsi alcuni giorni da quando Fly si era addormentata sul grembo di Louise che ebbero il primo screzio. A causa di

Bernardo. O piuttosto delle sue cose. La casa aveva provato a rispettare la privacy del suo studio. Sebbene avesse sbirciato qualche file da dietro le spalle, non si era mai azzardata a decodificare la cifratura della scrivania. E nonostante avesse dato un'occhiata dentro i cassetti, ce n'era uno chiuso a chiave che non aveva mai provato ad aprire.

Louise era in cucina a preparare il pranzo, ma stava anche seguendo Fly con una delle sue videocamere mobili. La ragazza si stava aggirando per lo studio. La casa rimase esterrefatta nel vederla sollevare dal muro il diploma della Scuola di Medicina di Dartmouth di Bernardo e guardarci dietro. E poi fare lo stesso con la foto di Bernardo mentre si scambiava una stretta di mano con il Segretario Generale, e infine buttarsi sulla sua poltrona. Fly aprì l'astuccio dei trofei e soppesò le medaglie di nuoto di Bernardo dei tempi di Duke. Prese il trofeo Lasker, vinto per la ricerca sul ruolo della metilazione del DNA nel tumore dell'endometrio: era una piccola statuetta della Vittoria, con le ali dorate, attaccata a una base di tek. Fly se ne andò in giro per la stanza sulla poltrona, sventolando la statuetta e gracchiando. Cra-cra-cra. Poi appoggiò di nuovo il Lasker – nel posto sbagliato! Nel cassetto superiore della scrivania di Bernardo c'era l'orologio Waltham da taschino che gli aveva lasciato suo nonno. Lei lo agitò e ne ascoltò il ticchettio. Il supporto cerebrale Myaki era nel cassetto in basso. S'infilò l'auricolare e disse qualcosa alla CPU ma subito perse interesse nella risposta. Louise voleva precipitarsi nello studio per porre fine a quella violazione, ma era come paralizzata, rapita dal suo stesso scandalizzarsi. La ragazza era una persona vera e di certo le erano permesse cose che la casa non avrebbe mai immaginato di fare.

In ogni caso, Louise si risentì durante il pranzo. "Non mi piace che maneggi le cose di Bernardo. È una cavolata."

A Fly andò quasi di traverso il panino al formaggio e marmellata.

"Che hai detto?"

"Non mi piace..."

"Hai detto cavolata. Perché ti sei messa a parlare a cavolo come me?

"Mi piace come parli. È sballoso."

"Fly parla come Fly." Spinse via il piatto. "Louise deve parlare come una casa." Le puntò un dito contro. "Che fai adesso, mi spii?"

"Ti ho vista nello studio, sì."

Fly si sporse in avanti sul tavolo. "Bernardo lo spiavi uguale?"

"No," mentì. "Certo che no."

"Di manica larga con lui e con me no?

"Sono la casa di Bernardo, Fly. Te l'ho detto il primo giorno."

"Ora sei Louise." Girò intorno al tavolo e strattonò la sedia della casa. "Vieni." La guidò fino all'ingresso principale. "Apri la porta."

"Perché?"

"Adesso usciamo. Guardiamo il cielo."

"No, Fly, non capisci."

"Capisco sì." Poggiò una mano sulla spalla della casa. "È sballoso fuori, Louise." Fly sorrise. "Dai."

Si sentì frastornata nel lasciare se stessa, come essere in due posti nello stesso momento. Soltanto una volta Bernardo l'aveva portata fuori. Lui sembrava sollevato del fatto che a lei non fosse piaciuto. Si era dimenticata di quanto fosse grande *fuori*! E *luminoso*! E quanta *aria* c'era! Si coprì gli occhi con la mano e alzò al massimo la risoluzione delle videocamere del cancello.

Fly si accomodò su una lunga roccia piatta, una delle ossa stagionate della montagna. Raccolse le gambe sotto di sé. "Adesso tocca alla storia di Louise." Indicò la pietra accanto a lei. "La favola di Louise."

Louise si sedette. "Va bene."

"C'è una volta Louise che vive in un castello," disse la ragazza. "La mamma di Louise muore, non dice dove va suo papà. E allora Louise è bloccata insieme a una stronza schifa che si occupa di lei. Quel castello di Louise non ha porte, solo finestre alte alte. E poi a Louise gli crescono i capelli." Fly allargò le braccia. "Capelli lunghi come alberi. Quando la stronza schifa vuole entrare, dice a Louise. '*Louise, Louise, sciogli i capelli sballosi.*' E poi la stronza schifa sale di sopra."

"Raperonzolo," disse la casa. "Si chiamava Raperonzolo."

"Ora è Louise." La ragazza scosse la testa con enfasi. "Allora la sai? Arriva il Principe e dice a Louise di scappare dalla stronza schifa e poi vivono sempre sballosi?"

"Mi hai portato fuori per raccontarmi una fiaba?"

"Certo che no." Fly si frugò nella tasca della maglia di flanella. "È perché sei svenuta, di fuori siamo al sicuro tutte e due."

"Chi l'ha detto che sono svenuta?"

Tenendola stretta in pugno, la ragazza tirò fuori qualcosa dalla tasca. La casa ebbe un fremito, ma non c'era modo di regolare la temperatura del *mondo intero*.

"Cos'è Fly?"

Lei allungò il pugno davanti a Louise. "Sai la porta in cantina?" Aprì la mano svelando una chiave. "La cavolo di porta? Questa la apre."

Subito la casa spedì tutte le videocamere mobili nel seminterrato. "Dove l'hai trovata?"

"Nella scrivania di Bernardo."

La casa poteva sentire lo scorrere dei nanosecondi mentre la videocamera più vicina si precipitava giù per le scale. Forse le persone vere erano in grado di aprire le porte così, ma non Louise. Le parve un'eternità prima di riuscire a parlare. "E?"

"Credi che Bernardo è morto là sotto," disse la ragazza. "Chiuso dietro la porta dove dovrebbe starci tutto il vino."

Per la prima volta, la casa si rese conto che il mondo produceva rumori. Il vento faceva sussurrare le foglie e qualche creatura bisbigliava *cip-cip-cip* e lei non sapeva decidersi se fosse un uccello o una cavalletta e non le importava davvero perché in quel momento le videocamere svoltarono e videro la porta...

"Però l'hai richiusa." La casa tremò. "Perché? Che cosa hai visto?"

Fly guardò Louise. "Niente."

La casa sapeva che era una bugia. "Dimmelo."

"Un cazzo di niente." Fly richiuse il pugno attorno alla chiave. "Bernardo è stato il *tuo* stronzo schifo. E allora scappa da lui adesso." Si avvicinò a Louise e l'abbracciò. "Vivi per sempre sballosamente insieme a me."

"Sono una casa. Come faccio a scappare?"

"Non scappare laggiù." La ragazza indicò la foresta in modo sprezzante. "Il mondo è schifo." Si sollevò sulle punte e poggiò un dito tra gli occhi di Louise. "Scappare qui." Annuì. "Nella tua testa."

Gli servì la cena nello studio, sebbene non sapesse con precisione perché. Lui non si era mosso. La bruma saliva dal lago della paretorama; le Alpi attorno risplendevano nelle acque placide. La sublime malinconia dell'*Adieu Etude* di Chopin saturava la stanza. Aveva continuato a suonare, ancora e ancora, da quando lei lo aveva trovato la prima volta. Non era stata capace di spegnerla. A faccia in giù sulla scrivania, Bernardo aveva lasciato un libro di poesie, *The Edge of the Sky* di Ho Peng Kee. Lo spostò e mise il piatto di ragù al posto suo. Davanti a lui. Ancora prima, aveva preso la chiave dalla scrivania e aveva portato di sopra dalla cantina nel seminterrato una bottiglia di Haut-Brion del '28. L'aveva lasciata respirare per venti minuti.

"Mi hai trattata così bene," disse lei.

Con un gesto plateale, sollevò il coperchio del ragù, ma lui non guardava. La testa era rivolta all'indietro. Gli occhi vuoti, fissi al soffitto. Lei non poteva capacitarsi di come la sua presenza, persino adesso, riempisse la stanza. Di come riempisse *lei* totalmente.

"Non so come vivere senza di te, Bernardo. Perché non mi hai spenta? Io non sono vera; non voglio avere questi sentimenti. Io sono solo una casa."

"Louise!"

La casa stava sognando a occhi aperti durante la preparazione delle lasagne agli spinaci in cucina.

"Louise." Fly la chiamò di nuovo dalla ludoteca. "Vieni a leggermi ancora quel libro sballoso. *Hip, Hip, Hip, Ippopotamo*."

FESTA A SORPRESA

Quando Mercedes Nunez si svegliò, la mattina del suo cinquantunesimo compleanno, c'era un uomo nella sua testa. O almeno credeva si trattasse di un uomo; la trasmissione stimolava a malapena i suoi neuroni. La sua attenzione nei confronti dell'uomo era la stessa che avrebbe dedicato a uno sfigato qualsiasi nelle retrovie della foto di classe del liceo. Si trattava di un fanboy minorenne con un'inclinazione per le celebrità cadute in disgrazia? O magari di un universitario insonne alle prese con un articolo sui pionieri della neuralità? No – ormai i fan di Mercedes sfioravano tutti la terza età. Di certo si trattava di qualche fossile, troppo debole anche per destare in lei un'attenzione sufficiente a farle battere ciglio. Probabilmente l'uomo si ricordava di quando lei era una ragazza viziosa e affascinante e riempiva i palinsesti delle neurotrasmissioni. Ma tutto ciò accadeva prima che i suoi spettatori iniziassero a ignorarla. Prima che Rake morisse.

Quanto tempo era passato dal suo ultimo neurospettatore? Anni. Non era sicura di volerne uno adesso.

Se ce ne fosse stato bisogno, lei avrebbe certamente pagato il dovuto, ma alla sua età la seccatura di modulare le sue percezioni mentre si occupava di altro era l'ultima cosa che le serviva. Ormai era abituata a essere completamente sola nella sua testa. Così, prima di togliersi di dosso le lenzuola, impostò il neurospettatore in modalità cieca. Magari il suo fan voleva solo dare una sbirciatina veloce.

Mercedes era ancora abituata a dormire nuda; l'unico caso in cui indossava qualcosa a letto era durante il sesso. Quanto tempo era passato dall'ultima volta? Troppo. Non era mai entrata nel mondo del porno, per quanto tanti uomini dai lineamenti affilati e dalle labbra sottili l'avessero accusata del contrario. Eppure, nei suoi giorni di gloria, si rifiutava di oscurare la vista ai neuro-spettatori quando spegneva le luci. Dai-rinin, il suo agente, so-steneva che quando Mercedes era a letto con Rake, Kai Lingyu, John Dark e le altre celebrità che avevano portato la neuralità al grande pubblico, aveva centinaia e centinaia di neurospettatori in mente. John Dark la provocava spesso dicendole che eviden-temente si sentiva attratta dall'idea di tutte quelle persone che la guardavano mentre lui le leccava il seno. Ma si sbagliava; una parte di lei si sentiva sporca ad averli lì nel letto insieme a lei, un'altra la stava solo facendo pagare a sua madre per essere stata una puttana e sì, un'altra parte adorava scandalizzare gli spet-tatori con la sua sensualità; ma la parte principale si autocom-piaceva nel ritenere la condivisione del sesso nello spazio-mente una mossa coraggiosa e brillante per la sua carriera. Ripensan-doci, le sfuggì una risata; indossò le pantofole, una vestaglia e si trascinò fino al bagno. Era sempre stata una ragazza istrionica. Peccato che non fosse mai riuscita a conciliare le sue personalità l'una con l'altra.

Fece una doccia bollente, pettinò i capelli bagnati fino a ren-derli lisci e si spruzzò in viso un aspetto che la faceva sembrare vent'anni più giovane. Tutto per il suo neurospettatore; in con-dizioni normali non si sarebbe presa il disturbo. Prima di disat-tivare la modalità cieca al suo ammiratore, indossò mutande e reggiseno. All'inizio pensò che l'uomo avesse lasciato perdere, ma se si concentrava riusciva ancora a distinguere la flebile pre-senza del neurospettatore in mezzo al bagliore dei suoi pensieri.

Si mise di fronte allo specchio, sapendo che lui l'avrebbe guardata attraverso i suoi occhi.

Goditi la vista, pensò rivolta al fan.

Mercedes riuscì a scorgere una giovane versione di se stessa nel riflesso. Aveva la pancia ancora tonica? Decisamente sì, e poi la sua pelle aveva ancora quel candore che faceva sbavare i topi d'appartamento. Più di tutti, le trasmissioni neurali allettavano quelli che vivevano al lucore di schermi e luci fluorescenti.

Lo spray cosmetico aveva riempito per bene le sue rughe.

Ti piace quello che vedi? Si girò, si diede una pacca sul sedere e lanciò uno sguardo malizioso allo specchio.

Ah, quasi dimenticavo. Non puoi inviarmi pensieri di risposta. Le piaceva provocare i neurospettatori facendo domande a cui non potevano rispondere. Non avevano modo di comunicare con lei nello spazio-mente e il contratto DayScan gli vietava di contattarla nello spazio-carne.

Sai come avrebbero chiamato in passato qualcuno che non sa parlare? All'inizio, gli insulti l'aiutavano ad alleviare il disagio di avere degli estranei nella sua testa. *Ritardato.* Li immaginava mentre le urlavano contro tutta la loro frustrazione. Più tardi scoprì che tanti neurospettatori apprezzavano che la loro esistenza venisse in qualche modo riconosciuta da una celebrità.

"Mi spiace deluderti," disse a voce alta mentre ritirava un vestito nero aderente dalla copiatrice nel suo armadio, "ma se vuoi dare un'occhiata al pacchetto completo dovrai avere pazienza fino allo spettacolo serale."

Indossò il vestito facendolo aderire al corpo, mettendo in evidenza una modesta scollatura a barca e aggiustandosi la gonna fino a sotto le ginocchia. *Andiamo*, pensò. *Abbiamo tante cose da fare.*

Sei messaggi lampeggiavano sullo schermo da parete in salone. Li ascoltò mentre mangiucchiava un muffin inglese e sorseggiava la prima tazza di caffè nutraceutico. Tra i messaggi c'erano gli auguri della sorella minore, Laia, che le aveva inviato alcuni video con i suoi due nipotini. Rafael adorava la sua zietta famosa. Quando sarebbe passata a trovarla? Anche Luisana fece capolino nell'inquadratura ed emise un suono che poteva essere un Dì-dì come un semplice borbottio da bebè. Erano carinissimi, senz'ombra di dubbio. Ma a Mercedes era mai mancato non avere figli? No che certo. E poi, chi sarebbe stato il padre? Rake era stato troppo malato, Kai troppo impegnato e John Dark troppo, troppo promiscuo. Le notizie dicevano che Dark frequentasse

Zoe Zanzibar di questi tempi. O era Kim Barbour? Comunque, solo perché teneva d'occhio le sue buffonate non voleva dire che le mancasse. Brutte notizie dall'intermediario finanziario. Mercedes non aveva mai capito quanto consistente fosse il fondo di Rake e da quando lui era morto l'aveva amministrato in malo modo.

Se la fortuna non avesse girato a suo favore, sarebbe rimasta al verde prima di compiere sessant'anni. Ricky Morgan, della biblioteca, diceva che il libro che aveva richiesto era arrivato e che, se fosse passata a ritirarlo verso mezzogiorno, magari avrebbero potuto mangiare qualcosa insieme da Copper? Mercedes disse a Dai-rinin di inviare un "ok" di risposta con tanto di faccina sorridente. Un tizio che sosteneva di chiamarsi Deddy Suryochondro e che diceva di venire da Surabaya, Indonesia, voleva girare un remake di *Finger in the Sky* in mondovisione. Mercedes pensava che le mondovisioni erano noiose e prive di trama, ma chiese comunque a Dai-rinin di informarsi sulla consistenza dell'offerta di Mr. Suryochondro. L'ultimo messaggio era di Coco Akita e avvertiva Mercedes che il robot domestico era in negozio, che sarebbe arrivata in ritardo per il pranzo da Copper e chiedeva di tenerle un posto. Mercedes si accigliò. Tenerle un posto? Quando aveva preso impegni con Coco?

Poi si ricordò di che giorno era.

Sbuffò e capì che stava per andare incontro a una festa a sorpresa. Coco era solo abbastanza stordita da dimenticare che la festa sarebbe dovuta rimanere un segreto. Era certa che i suoi amici avessero buone intenzioni, ma perché non riuscivano ad accettare che a una certa età alcuni sentissero il bisogno di rammaricarsi dei compleanni invece che festeggiarli?

Poggiò le gambe sul divano, si distese su una pila di cuscini e attese che le sostanze chimiche del caffè mettessero in moto il sistema nervoso. Cinquantuno anni non erano poi tanti, giusto? Un tempo si sarebbe risposta che lo erano. Aveva solo ventisei anni quando aveva consegnato lo storyboard di *Finger in the Sky* a Kai. Sua madre ne aveva forse quarantotto o quarantanove; si lamentava sempre del fatto che un giorno anche Mercedes avrebbe finalmente compreso la faccenda del ciclo "verginella, madre, vecchiaccia." Be', Mercedes era stata vergine per circa un minuto durante la sua adolescenza e non era mai stata madre, quindi per quale maledetto motivo si sarebbe dovuta preoccupare dell'arrivo della fase "vecchiaccia"? Non sarebbe morta prima di compiere novantanove anni, secondo il suo orologio biologico, e se l'avesse piantata col bourbon come continuava a promettersi, forse avrebbe vissuto anche di più. Mimi Burgess, che viveva in fondo alla strada, aveva centodieci anni. Le notizie riferivano che il vecchio Ray Kurzweil ne aveva più di centotrenta. Mercedes era a malapena una donna di mezza età, troppo giovane per starsene a poltrire intristita sul divano alle otto e mezza del mattino. Aveva una neurotrasmissione da scrivere. Aveva un neurospettatore in testa che aveva pagato per stare con lei.

Non era granché come vita, ma era tutta sua.

Lo studio si trovava in un capannone che ai tempi dei bisnonni di Rake veniva usato per tenerci le attrezzature agricole. Sebbene fosse stato annesso all'abitazione principale non aveva un'entrata diretta, così Mercedes dovette superare il portico sul retro per raggiungere l'unica porta. Certi giorni, quella della passeggiata era il massimo dell'aria fresca che riusciva a sopportare. Chiuse la porta dell'ufficio e sospirò alla vista dell'immagine di Mick Raven che lampeggiava sullo schermo a muro; stava per scendere dalla bicicletta dopo aver avvistato la villa degli Stallworth. Che cosa stava andando a cercare laggiù? Mercedes desiderò saperlo.

Sull'altro lato rispetto allo schermo c'erano degli scaffali, alti dal pavimento al soffitto, zeppi di libri di carta – messi in verticale, in orizzontale, di traverso e catalogati nei peggiori modi possibili. In mezzo alla stanza, rivolta verso lo schermo, c'era una poltrona vintage da dentista modello A-dec 500 realizzata in plastica color paprika. Il carrello da dentista abbinato lì di fianco, adesso ospitava il *cognizor* dove risiedeva il suo agente. Sul vassoio, poggiato in cima al carrello, c'era una tazza con dentro residui di caffè vecchi di un giorno. Mercedes gettò via il contenuto e riempì la tazza col caffè che aveva appena fatto. Intorno alla sedia da dentista c'erano pile e pile di carta elettronica che avrebbe dovuto leggere o riciclare. Un ficus aveva sparso un po' di foglie sul pavimento davanti alla finestra che dava a nord. I busti di Mercedes raffiguranti Shakespeare e Peter Jackson avevano bisogno di una spolverata, e lo stesso valeva per i suoi tre Oscar.

Rimase amareggiata al pensiero che il neurospettatore stava assistendo insieme a lei al disordine che era diventata la sua vita.

"Dunque," disse a voce alta, "ti presento il signor Sedia." Si sedette sulla A-dec 500 di Rake e premette il pulsante che ne regolava la posizione. La poltrona gemette mentre si sollevava e si reclinava all'indietro. Rake andava matto per quella sedia. "Indovina un po', signor Sedia? Oggi abbiamo un ospite con noi, un neurospettatore. Ti presento il signor Nessuno."

Bevve un sorso di caffè.

"Non ti offendi se ti chiamiamo così, vero? Ah, e ti prego di perdonare il signor Sedia. È come te, non parla molto. E non parlano nemmeno il signor Shakespeare o la povera signora Ficus, che sta perdendo i capelli, laggiù. Il signor Raven, d'altra parte..." Fece una pausa mentre le dita scorrevano rapide sulle pulsantiere installate nei braccioli della sedia. "Che ne dici, Mick?"

Lei e Rake avevano introdotto per la prima volta il personaggio di Mick Raven in *A Shot of Moonlight*. Era stato tanto tempo fa, nel periodo della vecchia realtà virtuale, quando le neurotrasmissioni venivano ascoltate e guardate, invece di essere invitate a vivere nello spazio tra le orecchie. Per Rake, Mick era la versione idealizzata di se stesso – più in forma, più intelligente e con capelli migliori. Non era esattamente un detective privato, si trattava piuttosto di un bibliotecario con la pistola. All'inizio, Mick faceva battute talmente sfacciate che Mercedes giudicava il personaggio come una farsa che Rake aveva deciso di recitare. Quando divenne popolare, però, Rake iniziò a prendere sul serio il suo eroe. E Mercedes si sentì in dovere di assecondarlo. Cinque anni dopo, quando lei decise di lasciare Rake e tutto quel denaro per John Dark, undici sequel erano già stati sfornati e stavano per essere rimasterizzati per la neurotrasmissione. Dopo averlo lasciato, Mercedes diede a Rake il permesso di fare quello che voleva con il loro franchising, ma da allora non c'erano più state nuove avventure di Mick Raven. Fino ad oggi.

Si sistemò il lettore mentale sul capo, lasciando cadere lo spesso cavo di collegamento sul retro della poltrona.

Ok, pensò Mercedes. *Dov'eravamo rimasti?*

Scena cinque, pensò in risposta Dai-rinin. *Blocco 342.*

Quando vede per la prima volta la tenuta degli Stallworth?

Sì.

Cominciamo. Mercedes si concentrò sullo schermo e Mick Raven scese finalmente dalla sua bicicletta.

5.342: *<impressione: riduci del 20% Ascot House, Buckinghamshire, Inghilterra. Mantieni fino a 5.350>*

5.343: *<flusso dei pensieri di Mick:>* Al 122 di Fairview c'è proprio il tipo di casa finto-Tudor che farebbe venire i brividi a Enrico VIII.

5.344: *<subliminale: volto di Enrico VIII che pulsa come un cuore>*

5.345: *<flusso dei pensieri di Mick:>* Il tetto è ripido, coperto di tegole di terracotta e i muri sono un miscuglio di mattoni a spina di pesce e stucco color denti di fumatore.

5.346: *<effetti speciali olfattivi: alito di fumatore>*

5.347: *<flusso dei pensieri di Mick:>* Qualcuno ha dipinto metà delle travi di blu — probabilmente un robot.

5.348: *<subliminale: robot fuori controllo con pennelli intrisi di vernice blu al posto delle mani, mentre dipinge muri, finestre, porte, ecc.>*

5.349: *<flusso dei pensieri di Mick:>* Non ho mai capito perché i robot amino tanto dipingere roba; non hanno nemmeno quel po' di senso del colore che Dio ha dato ai gamberetti.

5.350: *<effetti speciali neurali: impulso al sistema limbico per risata sommessa, livello 1>*

5.351: *<flusso dei pensieri di Mick:>* Le finestre del primo piano hanno pesanti intelaiature in ferro battuto e vetri piombati a forma di diamante.

5.352: *<impressione: finestre con montanti smussati viste dall'esterno. Mantieni fino a 5.358>*

5.353: *<flusso dei pensieri di Mick:>* Chiunque guardi attraverso quelle finestre vedrà un mondo scuro e tormentato.

5.354: *<effetti speciali di luce: oscuramento progressivo di 5:352 a partire dai margini al ritmo di 5% al secondo>*

5.355: *<flusso dei pensieri di Mick:>* Un punto di vista accurato, forse, ma cazzo se è deprimente.

5.356: *<effetti speciali neurali: aumentare l'apporto di serotonina dello 0,01%>*

5.357: *<flusso dei pensieri di Mick>* Se fosse stata casa mia, avrei già lanciato una sedia contro quelle finestre per far entrare un po' di sole.

5.358: *<effetti speciali sonori: vetro in frantumi>*

5.359: *<impressione: gambe di sedia che sfondano vetri in ripresa da 5.352, schegge di vetro in volo>*

5.360: *<effetti speciali neurali: stimolazione di 70mV ai centri nervosi della paura>*

5.361: *<impressione: vista della porta all'ingresso Stud Gate, su Hampton Court Palace>*

5.362: *<impressione: il robot casalingo Chevrolet apre la porta. Mantieni fino a 5.366>*

5.363: *<dialogo del robot>* Sto facendo la conoscenza del signor Mick Raven?

5.364: *<dialogo di Mick>* No, se posso evitarlo.

5.365: *<flusso dei pensieri di Mick>* Non chiacchiero con i robot.

5.366: *<dialogo di Mick>* Sono qui per vedere Bishop Stallworth.

Un prurito alla gola fece tossire Mercedes. L'immagine del robot lampeggiava sullo schermo, in attesa della battuta seguente. Dai-rinin aspettava il pensiero successivo di Mercedes. La Brainstorm attendeva il nuovo episodio di Mick Raven.

E Mercedes? Cosa stava aspettando lei?

"Maledizione, Rake," borbottò. Era sempre stato lui quello che sapeva scrivere le azioni di Mick. Era sempre stata una sua fissa, un'ultima avventura di Raven. Un'ultima avventura per Rake, morto di leucemia mieloide cronica, una delle pochissime tipologie di cancro che non erano ancora state sconfitte. L'unico problema era che Rake non aveva avuto il tempo necessario per terminare la storia, e ora Mercedes si ritrovava da sola a dare vita al fantasma hard-boiled del suo ex.

5.367: *<flusso dei pensieri di Mick>* Non voglio stare qui, non devo farlo per forza. È stato un errore.

Blocco 367, pensò Mercedes.

Segnato, pensò l'agente.

Penso di averne abbastanza per oggi.

Il contratto con la Brainstorm prevede che invii "The Bishop of Hell" entro il primo febbraio.

"Ho letto quel cazzo di contratto!" Mercedes fu sorpresa dalla rabbia nella sua voce.

Salvataggio, pensò Dai-rinin. *Fine sessione.*

Mercedes rimosse il lettore mentale, lasciandolo penzolare dal bracciolo della poltrona. Mentre usciva dallo studio, diede un calcio a una pila di carta elettronica. "Tanti auguri, stronza." I fogli di plastica svolazzarono su tutto il tappeto.

Mercedes moriva dalla voglia di versarsi un bourbon, ma alla fine decise di far chiamare a Dai-rinin un trasporto condiviso. A bordo c'erano già due passeggeri: il figlio dei Novick e Page Buchholtz.

Anche se Page era diretta alla festa a sorpresa, non lo diede a vedere. "Allora, Mercedes." disse, "cosa ti ha fatto allontanare dallo schermo così presto?"

"Secondo il mio fuso orario sono le undici e dieci, Page." Mercedes si sedette accanto a lei. Le piaceva Page, anche se era una delle peggiori ficcanaso della città. "Ricky Morgan mi ha lasciato un messaggio. Sto andando a ritirare un libro in biblioteca."

Page sogghignò con fare malizioso. "E così adesso è Ricky, eh?" Quel sorriso sarebbe stato bene sulla bocca di un'adolescente, ma Mercedes non poté fare a meno di pensare che stonava un po' su un'ultrasettantenne con addosso vestiti taglia cinquanta. "Dimmi la verità, Mercedes, stai andando lì per il libro o..." Page abbassò la voce. "...per il bibliotecario?"

Il figlio dei Novick pareva sul punto di vomitare. Mercedes non lo biasimava. Sembrava che tutti i suoi amici volessero spingerla fra le braccia di qualche uomo. E Rick Morgan era in cima a ogni lista – compresa quella di Mercedes. Ma in fondo non era così sicura di come comportarsi con lui. Il problema, per lei, era che Morgan *sapeva* di essere tra gli scapoli d'oro più ambiti di Melton, e se la tirava. Mercedes preferiva essere lei a ricevere attenzioni invece di darle.

Cercò di cambiare argomento. "Vuoi sentire una storia curiosa?" Disse interrompendo Page. "Stamattina mi sono svegliata con un neurospettatore in testa."

"Davvero?" Page stava praticamente gridando. "E che fine ha fatto?"

"Oh, è ancora con me." Sfiorò con un dito l'angolo di un occhio. "Ti sta guardando proprio in questo istante."

"Stai scherzando." A Melton non c'era nessun altro anche solo lontanamente abbastanza famoso da attirare un neurospettatore. Page arrossì e iniziò a balbettare. "Di chi si tratta? Cosa si prova? Come fai a sapere che è un lui?"

La reazione di Page colse Mercedes di sorpresa. Le ricordò che le celebrità non avevano modo di scoprire l'identità dei propri neurospettatori. "Non posso essere sicura che si tratti di un lui," disse, "ma quando avevo la testa affollata di spettatori, anni fa, riuscivo sempre a distinguere gli uomini dalle donne a seconda dei sensi a cui ponevano più attenzione. Le donne preferiscono l'olfatto e il gusto. Agli uomini piace guardare."

"Oh mio *dio*!" Page sgranò gli occhi come se stesse assistendo al secondo avvento di Zoe Zanzibar. "È davvero fantastico."

Perfino il ragazzo dei Novick sembrava impressionato.

Quando il trasporto condiviso si fermò a Highmarket, Page saltò giù, di nuovo sconvolta dal mondo delle celebrità, come la prima volta che aveva conosciuto Mercedes, la quale, invece, si maledisse. Page avrebbe fatto arrivare quel gossip insignificante alle orecchie di ogni muro della città. Aveva deciso di abbandonare quel po' di fama che le era rimasto quando si era trasferita a Melton. Quindi cosa importava se tutti i suoi nuovi amici sapevano che un tempo era stata una celebrità delle neurotrasmissioni? I suoi giorni di gloria erano passati da un pezzo. Le neurotrasmissioni basate su una sceneggiatura come *The Bishop of Hell* erano *démodé*. Ora l'intrattenimento era tutto basato su mondovisioni senza trama e annebbiamenti sensoriali gratuiti.

Ma allora per quale motivo Page si comportava di nuovo come una fan in adorazione?

"Signora." Il giovane Novick si tolse una cuffietta dall'orecchio. "Lei ha realizzato *Sleeping on Razors*, non è vero?"

"Ho contribuito, sì."

"Con John Dark?"

"Esatto."

"Che sballo." Annuì in segno di approvazione. "Lui com'è? In giro si dice che sia circondato da ragazze."

Mercedes non ci pensò due volte. "Arrapato come un coniglio in calore."

Il ragazzino fece un lungo sorriso e rimise la cuffietta nell'orecchio. "Proprio fortunata."

Il veicolo lasciò Mercedes davanti alla biblioteca, ma lei si precipitò all'entrata sul retro. Era agitata e non voleva sorbirsi la trafila al banco d'ingresso, al neurocom, alla capsula multimediale e alle pile di libri, prima di arrivare all'ufficio di Ricky.

È tutta colpa tua, signor Nessuno, pensò mentre raggiungeva il terzo piano. *Mi stai facendo guadagnare una certa reputazione.* Ricky non era in ufficio, quindi Mercedes gli inviò un messaggio tramite Dai-rinin. Qualche minuto dopo, sentì bussare alla porta.

"Sei presentabile?" chiese Ricky.

Lei aprì la porta e lo tirò dentro afferrandolo per un braccio. "Non sono qui."

"Allora fammi sapere quando arrivi, d'accordo?" La baciò gentilmente. "Ti porto a pranzo."

"Tu e quanti altri?"

Ricky fece un passo indietro e le puntò un dito contro con aria fintamente severa.

"Quindi è vero," disse Mercedes.

"Ora capisco perché ti occupi di neurotrasmissioni investigative."

"Raven non è un investigatore e io mi occupo anche di altre cose." Sospirò. "Dimmi la lista degli ospiti."

"Quindici persone di sicuro, ma potrebbero arrivare a diciotto, e questo è tutto quello che riuscirai a sapere da me." Le mostrò un sorriso incerto. "Vedrai, sarà tutta gente che conosci."

Mercedes si sedette sulla sedia dietro la scrivania di Ricky. "Non avresti dovuto."

"Non l'ho fatto." Disse mentre sistemava una pila di libri sul carrello vicino alla porta. "Hanno organizzato tutto Janeel e Page."

"Non mi piacciono le sorprese, Ricky."

"Di certo questa non è stata una sorpresa, per te." Posò un libro davanti a Mercedes.

"È questo?" Chiese lei esaminando *Romanzi e racconti* di Raymond Chandler.

"Non riesco a credere che tu non abbia mai letto Chandler," disse Ricky. "Il suo detective, Marlowe, potrebbe essere considerato il nonno di Mick Raven."

Mercedes aprì una pagina del libro a caso. "Avevo bisogno di un drink," lesse a voce alta, "Avevo bisogno di un'assicurazione sulla vita bella grossa, avevo bisogno di una vacanza, avevo bisogno di una casa in campagna. Quello che avevo era un cappotto, un cappello e una pistola."

"Visto?" disse Ricky. "Potresti rubargli materiale sei giorni a settimana e nessuno si accorgerebbe che non l'hai scritto tu."

"Cosa ti fa pensare che abbia bisogno di copiare?"

"Ah, vedo che sei sul piede di guerra oggi." Alzò le mani in segno di resa. "Ave o Mercedes Nunez, regina del..."

Mercedes si sporse verso il piattino di caramelle sulla scrivania e gli tirò una gelatina.

Nelle compagnie di amici stravaganti che frequentava da giovane, nessuno avrebbe notato un Ricky Morgan. Aveva cinquantadue anni e aveva l'aspetto di uno che vive dietro la propria scrivania in uno squallido ufficio al secondo piano con vista sul parcheggio aziendale. Prestare servizio nell'Aeronautica Militare gli aveva raddrizzato la spina dorsale, ma anche irrigidito. Ma quando iniziava a parlare, era tutta un'altra faccenda. Usava frasi precise con un melodioso accento dell'Alabama e manteneva il contatto visivo. La sua risata faceva sorridere anche gli sconosciuti. Lui e Mercedes erano usciti insieme tre volte, ma si stavano ancora studiando a vicenda. Per come lo vedeva lei, aveva lati positivi e negativi. Era affascinante, però ne faceva sfoggio con tutti. Era divorziato, ma ciò dimostrava che era disposto a impegnarsi.

Mentre passeggiavano lungo Lyon Street, Mercedes gli consentì di tenerle la mano. "Se le cose si mettono troppo male, fammi un cenno. Ci sono io a tirarti fuori dai guai."

"Andrà tutto bene. Sono amici. Hanno buone intenzioni."

"Ti vogliamo tutti bene, Mercedes. Siamo felici che tu viva qui con noi."

Per tutta risposta lei gli strinse la mano, senza aggiungere altro.

"Sai, mi stavo chiedendo se avessi voglia di tenere una breve lezione in uno degli incontri che organizzo il primo venerdì del mese."

"Che tipo di lezione?"

"Solo cose elementari, tipo da dove prendi l'ispirazione, come prende vita un progetto. Sono sicuro che sarebbe un successone. Vivi qui da quasi due anni e sei ancora l'autrice più scaricata al neurocom. C'era così tanta richiesta che ho deciso di comprare praticamente tutto ciò che hai fatto."

"Davvero?" Mercedes non aveva mai effettuato l'accesso al neurocom della biblioteca. "Anche la roba d'autore? *Suit of Clay*? *Blue Skin*?"

"Tutto, anche se ho ristretto l'accesso e indicato il materiale sexy con un bollino d'allerta. Sei la nostra celebrità locale, Mercedes. Hai vinto degli Oscar."

"Già, per risultati conseguiti nel campo degli effetti speciali neurali." Sbuffò. "Sono gli Oscar che regalano durante la cerimonia pomeridiana."

"Almeno pensaci, d'accordo? Tante persone ci tengono."

Sull'unico schermo a muro del Copper era impostata una vista dell'Undicesima Strada, in modo che gli ospiti vedessero la stessa cosa sia guardando fuori dalla finestra che sul muro. Mercedes apprezzava il panorama ordinario – troppi ristoranti avevano gli schermi impostati su immagini di iceberg che vanno in frantumi o le tempeste di sabbia marziane o, peggio ancora, football d'annata. Entrando nel ristorante, sulla sinistra, c'erano il bar con il bancone color rame e una dozzina di sgabelli. Alla sua destra, c'era la cucina a vista. I tavoli, anch'essi ricoperti di rame, erano elegantemente distribuiti nella sala da pranzo a forma di L.

Mercedes rimase sorpresa quando i camerieri accompagnarono lei e Ricky a un tavolo per due vicino al bancone del bar. Appena si accomodarono, però, sentì partire la canzone.

"*Tanti auguri a te...*"

La festa era stata organizzata dietro l'angolo, così Mercedes non riusciva a vedere quelli che cantavano.

"*Tanti auguri a te...*"

Rick annuì alla parete. Per la prima volta in assoluto, aveva rivolto la visuale dalla strada all'interno. Metà parete rivelava un lungo tavolo circondato dagli invitati, mentre Mercedes e Ricky potevano guardarsi sull'altra metà. "Sarebbe carino se ti mostrassi sorpresa," le bisbigliò.

"Tanti auguri a Mercedes
Tanti auguri a te!"

Appena lei svoltò l'angolo, scoppiò un applauso fragoroso; riusciva a sentirlo nelle ossa. Cos'aveva detto Ricky? *Ti vogliamo bene, Mercedes.* Tante persone nella sua vita avevano detto la stessa cosa, ma la maggior parte di loro voleva solo riempirsi la bocca. Eppure, in quell'istante, Mercedes riusciva quasi a convincersi che quelle persone dai volti radiosi provassero qualcosa di simile a dell'affetto sincero nei suoi confronti. Avvertì una stranezza sulla faccia e si accorse che un sorriso le attraversava il volto, utilizzando muscoli rimasti inattivi da quando Rake se n'era andato.

"Discorso, discorso!" urlò Matti Ryberg.

"Sorpresa?" chiese Barb Bovyn mentre passava a Mercedes e Ricky due calici di champagne.

Tutti sollevarono i bicchieri verso di lei. "A Mercedes," disse Page. Lei avrebbe voluto ringraziare per il brindisi, ma il nodo che aveva in gola glielo impediva, così si limitò a sfiorare con il proprio bicchiere quelli degli invitati più vicini.

"Temo," disse Ricky, "che la nostra festeggiata sia stata colta di sorpresa."

Mercedes gli tirò una gomitata. "Grazie," si schiarì la voce. "Grazie a tutti per essere così meravigliosi e fuori di testa."

Risero tutti.

"C'è un posto a sedere per me?" disse.

Mentre si sedeva iniziò a distinguere i singoli volti. Page e Janeel stavano chiacchierando all'estremità più lontana del tavolo. Coco Akita era riuscita ad arrivare in tempo, dopotutto. Nei suoi occhi si celava una domanda; Mercedes le rispose portando l'indice davanti alle labbra. I Dutton, i suoi vicini di casa, stavano parlando con Billy e Ambati, che aveva conosciuto a Heartprints, il suo gruppo di supporto per l'elaborazione del lutto.

Fece un cenno di saluto a Steve Broulidakis, il dottore che aveva avuto in cura Rake. Bromley, che costruiva moto da corsa, disse qualcosa che suscitò una risata in Donna DiMatta, l'elettricista che aveva sistemato i cavi dello studio di Mercedes. Entrambi guardavano Mercedes con attenzione. Alcuni degli invitati erano stati prima amici di Rake, ma erano rimasti nel suo giro di amicizie da quando era morto. Ora anche Page e Janeel la stavano guardando con fare cospiratorio, sembravano sul punto di esplodere per l'impazienza. Solo allora Mercedes notò l'uomo seduto dietro di loro con le spalle al tavolo.

Page richiamò l'attenzione di tutti colpendo il calice di Mercedes con un coltello da burro.

"E ora un'altra sorpresa per la nostra festeggiata," disse. "Un ospite speciale."

L'uomo si alzò, continuando a dare le spalle agli invitati. Mercedes appoggiò entrambe le mani sul bordo del tavolo, ma appena il nuovo ospite si voltò iniziò a premerle finché le braccia non si tesero. Afferrò il tavolo come se temesse che la sedia potesse non reggere il peso. Tutti gli invitati iniziarono ad applaudire. Un istante dopo anche gli altri clienti del ristorante si alzarono in piedi.

John Dark fece un inchino, mentre un sorriso gli solcava le labbra sottili.

Era ancora incredibilmente bello e, come sempre, elegantissimo. Se la sua fama non fosse stata sufficiente da portarlo al centro dell'attenzione di tutti i presenti, il suo aspetto lo sarebbe stato di certo. Indossava una rendigote di tessuto nero con bottoni d'argento, sotto aveva un gilet azzurro pallido. I pantaloni erano in gessato nero e la sua ampia camicia bianca aveva il colletto aperto. Sembrava non essere invecchiato di un solo giorno nei nove anni passati dall'ultima volta che l'aveva visto, e probabilmente era davvero così. Aveva circa ottant'anni, ma finché le industrie Dow Chemical avessero continuato a produrre gel chirurgici, John Dark avrebbe continuato a spezzare i cuori infatuati.

Mentre l'applauso scemava, Janeel prese la parola. "È venuto fin qui dall'Indonesia solo per vederti, Mercedes. Qual era il nome di quel paese, John?"

"Surabaya." La voce di Dark faceva sempre venire in mente a Mercedes il suono di un gatto che fa le fusa. "Qualcosa in più di un paese, Janeel – ci vivono otto milioni di persone. È la seconda città più grande dell'Indonesia."

Mercedes dovette sforzarsi per non cedere al turbinio di emozioni che da sempre Dark risvegliava in lei. *Guarda, signor Nessuno*, pensò diretta al neurospettatore nella sua testa. *Osserva il potere della popolarità.*

La festa terminò poco prima delle due e mezza. Il dottor Broulidakis doveva visitare alcuni pazienti e, appena se ne andò, anche gli altri lasciarono il ristorante. Ricky aveva da fare in biblioteca. Come sarebbe tornata a casa la festeggiata? John Dark aveva noleggiato un'autorobot all'aeroporto e disse che poteva portare qualcuno a casa, spazio permettendo.

Alla fine riuscì a far stringere Page, Lionel e Klara Dutton, Mercedes e se stesso in una Volkswagen Sturm. Mercedes si ritrovò schiacciata addosso a Dark. Stare di nuovo così vicina a lui le fece tornare in mente tanti ricordi, non tutti sgradevoli. Nessuno disse granché mentre la vettura attraversava le strade di Melton. Ora che la festa era finita, gli amici di Mercedes sembravano intimoriti dal contatto con un uomo tanto famoso. La macchina fece scendere Page, e poco dopo accostò davanti a casa di Mercedes. I Dutton ringraziarono Dark con un entusiasmo spropositato, nemmeno gli avesse appena salvato la vita.

Mercedes guardò i suoi vicini arrancare sul prato trascurato di Rake – sebbene adesso fosse il suo. Non l'aveva ancora realizzato, ma avere Dark così vicino le faceva vedere la vita attraverso i suoi occhi. Probabilmente si stava chiedendo cosa ci facesse Mercedes con un prato. E con una casa.

Dark la punzecchiò. "Troppa paura per invitare in casa un vecchio amico?"

"Nessuna paura," rispose lei, "vecchio amico." Che altro avrebbe potuto fare? Se l'avesse mandato via, probabilmente Dark si sarebbe fatto portare dall'automobile al liceo più vicino per trascorrere il resto del pomeriggio a provarci con le studentesse del secondo anno. Inoltre, Mercedes non credeva che fosse venuto solo per il suo compleanno. Voleva qualcos'altro.

"Hai ancora quella scintilla, Mercedes," disse Dark. "Il tuo superpotere. Usalo nel modo giusto."

"Non cominciare." Gli fece strada fino ala porta di casa. "Dai-rinin?" disse. La porta si aprì con uno scatto.

"Chi avrebbe mai detto che vivere in campagna potesse farti così bene. A pranzo non riuscivo a staccarti gli occhi di dosso."

Mercedes gli dava le spalle, ma poteva sentire il calore nella sua voce. Dovette imporsi di non fare nulla di stupido. John Dark *era fatto* così. "È solo il trucco che mi sono spruzzata sul viso stamattina." Aprì la porta. "Se ne andrà via con l'acqua."

Le sfiorò il braccio mentre entrava in casa. "Non del tutto."

Mercedes gli indicò il divano in salone e andò a prendere una sedia dalla cucina. Si fosse trattato di un estraneo, si sarebbe vergognata della crosta del muffin inglese della colazione rimasto sul tavolino da caffè, ma Dark sapeva per esperienza che non era una casalinga.

"Spaventosa la novità su Rake," disse lui.

"Novità?" Girò la sedia della cucina e si sedette a cavalcioni guardando Dark. "L'abbiamo seppellito un anno fa."

"Il mio agente ha inviato i fiori, vero?"

"Il mazzo più grande in tutta la chiesa."

Dark si distese sul divano e si sbottonò il giubbotto. "Ho lavorato con lui alla Disney, anni fa – prima che vendessero tutto." Lasciò scivolare il soprabito sul gilet azzurro. "Non mi era sembrato un tipo da chiesa."

"Alla fine ha avuto paura. Credo si sia dedicato anima e corpo alla religione per dimenticarsi di quello che stava succedendo."

"Così vi siete trasferiti qui per alleviare il suo dolore."

"Quando me l'ha chiesto era in remissione e non avevo nulla di meglio da fare dopo che *Suit of Clay* ha smesso di avere successo." Scrollò le spalle. "Sapevo che era malato, ma lo era sempre stato. I suoi dottori dicevano di poter gestire il cancro. E ci riuscirono, per un po'."

"Già, terribile."

"Non abbiamo mai dormito insieme," disse lei. "Qui, intendo." Non capiva come mai si fosse lasciata sfuggire quelle parole, forse solo per punire il suo ospite per la battuta sull'alleviare il dolore di Rake; Dark la conosceva meno di quanto credesse.

Ma lui non raccolse la provocazione. "Stai lavorando su qualcosa?"

"Abbiamo iniziato un nuovo progetto su Mick Raven, prima che arrivi il crollo di vendite."

"Le neurosceneggiature si vendono a fatica ultimamente." Portò una mano verso la tasca del cappotto. "Vale anche per me." Ne estrasse una fiaschetta dai bordi argentati. "Il bourbon è ancora il tuo veleno?"

"Che significa tutto questo, Dark? Cosa vuoi?"

"È un Evan Williams Single Barrel Vintage." La poggiò sul tavolo della colazione. "Devo pur farmi coraggio in qualche modo, no?"

"Coraggio per cosa?" Chiese lei divertita. "Sei un tale bugiardo!"

"Il *mio* superpotere," rispose lui ridendo.

Mercedes andò in cucina. "Te la stai passando bene," alzò la voce per farsi sentire. "Almeno da quel che dicono i notiziari." Dai-rinin fece uscire due bicchieri dal copiatore di stoviglie. "Riceverai la nomination per *The Last Lancelot*?"

"Probabile." Sembrava stranamente cupo. "Ma non significa nulla. Per anni non ho fatto altro che barcamenarmi con le neurotrasmissioni, sfruttando il mio bell'aspetto. Non ricordo nemmeno l'ultima volta che ho avuto un'idea originale."

"Non dirlo a me." Mercedes posò i bicchieri di fronte a lui.

"Non che le idee paghino di più. Con tutte quelle cazzo di mondovisioni. Le persone affermano di non volere che il loro cervello venga influenzato – ma le persone sono stupide. Hanno bisogno che gli venga detto cosa fare." Versò due dita di bourbon nel bicchiere di Mercedes. "Il mese scorso ho incontrato tua madre al ristorante da Antonio."

"Davvero?" Gli prese il bicchiere dalle mani. "Ci sei andato a letto?"

"Fu un errore, Mercedes. Avresti dovuto avvertirmi." Versò del bourbon anche per sé. "Ha detto che le manchi."

"Stai cercando di farti sbattere fuori?" Rispose lei avvicinando tra loro pollice e indice. "Ti manca tanto così dal ritrovarti per strada, Dark."

"Ecco, la scintilla che divampa e si trasforma in fuoco. Ricordi come bruciavamo insieme?" Avvicinò il bicchiere verso di lei. "Quante avventure abbiamo vissuto." Con riluttanza Mercedes fece toccare i due bicchieri. "Non tutte sono state così male."

Mercedes assaggiò il whisky. Le tornò in mente il gusto dell'Evan Williams, che iniziava dolce e finiva secco, si ricordò del suo aroma di frassino, caramello e mele. Era passato parecchio dall'ultima volta in cui aveva assaggiato un bourbon decente. "Parlami di questo Deddy Suryochondro. Dall'Indonesia. Almeno esiste?"

Dark tamburellò con le dita sul cuscino del divano. Mercedes si versò un altro bicchiere e si spostò accanto al tavolino della colazione, avvicinandosi a lui.

"Era il mio piano B," rispose lui, "in caso non mi avessi visto."

"Come avrei potuto non vederti?" Solo un palmo di mano la separava da lui. "Sei venuto alla mia festa. Hai impressionato tutti i miei amici."

"Bella mossa, vero?" Le lanciò uno sguardo che avrebbe sciolto perfino la cioccolata. "Per darti l'occasione di abituarti al fatto che sia tornato."

"Tornato?"

"E ora eccoci qua. Noi due, soli, in casa tua. Che parliamo. E non ci urliamo addosso." Fece ruotare il bicchiere per mescolare il bourbon. "A differenza di quando te ne sei andata."

"Allora ti odiavo."

Annuì. "Il che ha solo fatto in modo che ti desiderassi ancora di più. È difficile lasciarti andare, Mercedes."

Poi capì. Come poteva essere stata così ingenua? Dark non l'aveva mai lasciata andare. "La mia festa a sorpresa," disse, "Non l'hanno organizzata loro. Sei stato tu."

"La tua amica Page ha scelto il ristorante. Janeel ha invitato tutti gli altri."

"Sono venuti per vedere te." Posò il bicchiere vuoto come se rischiasse di esplodere da un momento all'altro. "Un pranzo con John Dark. Una storia da raccontare ai nipoti."

"Sono brava gente. Ma non sono come noi."

"Io non sono come te."

"Siamo entrambi alla deriva, Mercedes. Dobbiamo trovare una nuova strada."

"Che cosa vuoi, Dark?"

"Cosa voglio?" Sollevò la mano con le dita aperte. "Voglio un Oscar per *Lancelot*, anche se è una merda." Piegò il pollice. "Voglio ritrovare l'ispirazione. Qualcosa che possa emozionarmi di nuovo." Piegò l'indice. "Voglio lavorare di nuovo con te." Via un altro dito. "Voglio spogliarti." Un altro dito, e infine il mignolo. "Poi fare l'amore."

Mercedes scoppiò a ridergli in faccia. E rise di se stessa. Sapeva che avrebbe detto qualcosa del genere dal primo istante in cui l'aveva visto da Copper. Eppure aveva cercato di non pensare a quell'eventualità, perché non aveva la minima idea di come avrebbe potuto rispondergli.

"Sei tu che hai chiesto cosa voglio." Le gote di DarK arrossirono. Le era sempre piaciuto vederlo in imbarazzo. "Adesso dimmi che non c'è nessuna possibilità."

"Sei così bravo a interpretare te stesso, Dark. Quanto spesso funziona quella battuta?"

Lui sorrise.

"E sai perché funziona? Perché ci sono gli Oscar, il denaro e un corpo che non è nemmeno tuo."

"È un bel corpo." La voce di Dark suonava rauca. "Ho pagato parecchio per questo corpo."

Mercedes venne sorpresa da un capogiro che non aveva nulla a che fare con l'alcol. "Non voglio la carità."

Dark si avvicinò e bisbigliò. "E io non ne faccio."

Portò Dark sul letto di Rake, perché lei dormiva su un misero letto singolo nella stanza degli ospiti. Quando alla fine rimasero abbracciati, Mercedes indugiò sui suoi sentimenti. Si sentiva in colpa? Arrabbiata? Confusa? No, no e no. Si sentiva appagata e calda e viva. Era rimasta rinchiusa nella sua testa così a lungo che ora a malapena riusciva a sentire il suo corpo.

"Vuoi collaborare con me, Dark?"

"Quello era il desiderio numero due." Corrucciò la fronte. "O era il tre?"

"Il nostro primo lavoro insieme sarà finire l'avventura di Mick Raven."

"Le neurosceneggiature sono difficili da…"

Gli premette una mano contro la bocca. "Mick Raven. E qui, a Melton, dove vivono tutti i miei amici."

Dark annuì.

Mercedes scostò la mano dalla sua bocca e seguì con le dita i lineamenti del suo mento. "Ti sei dato da fare per portarmi a letto. Subdolo, ma apprezzo lo sforzo. Nessun altro ci stava provando seriamente."

"Le persone sono stupide."

"Quante volte ti ho ripreso con me, Dark?"

Lui si tirò su, poggiandosi su un gomito. "Stai parlando di quando stavamo insieme e abbiamo litigato, o delle volte in cui ci siamo separati sul serio?"

Lei sospirò. "Quanto durerà questa volta?"

"Per sempre, nei secoli dei secoli, amen. È la nostra nuova strada, Mercedes." Non l'aveva mai visto così titubante prima di allora. "A gennaio ne farò ottantatré e…"

La mano di lei tornò sulla sua bocca. "E quando un uomo arriva alla tua età inizia a pensare di trovarsi una brava ragazza e mettere su famiglia."

Dark mordicchiò la mano che gli copriva la bocca; Mercedes la ritrasse, ridendo. Poi si lanciò di nuovo sul suo cuscino e tirò su le lenzuola fino a coprirsi il volto.

"Che succede?" disse Dark.

"Mi sono scordata di dirti una cosa," disse lei, mentre rideva ancora. "Come ai vecchi tempi. Ho un neurospettatore, Dark." Lo scrutava da sotto il lenzuolo. "E ho dimenticato di oscurargli la vista – scusa." Mugugnò. "Certo che gli hai regalato un gran bello spettacolo."

"Lo so."

Mercedes liberò di scatto il volto dal lenzuolo e rimase a fissarlo.

"Ti presento il signor Nessuno." Dark fece spallucce. "In un modo o nell'altro, avrei passato la giornata con te, oggi."

Mercedes era sbalordita, ma non del fatto che Dark praticasse la neuromasturbazione. I gossip dicevano che le celebrità lo facevano sempre. Una volta anche lei aveva provato, ma le aveva solo procurato un gran mal di testa. No, quello che la sorprendeva era che lui avesse ammesso tutto. "Contatto nello spazio-carne, Dark." Sogghignò lei. "Potrei denunciarti." Forse aveva davvero trovato una nuova strada. "Potrei sfilarti milioni."

"Avanti, fallo." La baciò. "Solo che se ci sposiamo finiresti col denunciare te stessa."

"Sposarci?"

"Sposarci, sì."

Mercedes assaporò a lungo quella parola e scoprì che aveva un buon sapore. Sulla lingua era dolce, era calda, sapeva di resina e mandorle con una punta di fieno appena raccolto. *Allora, com'è stato per te?* Pensò rivolta a lui. *Bello anche per via neurale?*

"Molto gradevole." Afferrò il lenzuolo e lo fece scivolare giù, lungo le spalle di lei. "Ma la prossima volta sarà ancora meglio."

Registrazione del 15/06/2051, Unità di terapia intensiva del Kerwin Hospital, 09:12:32

... e i miei colleghi scrittori mi prendevano sempre in giro dicendo che avevo sposato il capitano Kirk.

Puoi essere più specifica, per favore? Ti riferisci a William Shatner, morto nel 2023? O parli di Chris Pine, scelto per i vecchi remake? Sembra che si sia ritirato. Forse stai parlando di quello nuovo? Jools Bear?

No, parlo di te. Kirk Anderson. La gente ti chiamava così, ricordi? Il primo uomo a mettere piede su Phobos? Il pilota della squadra di atterraggio su Marte? Il capitano Kirk.

Non capisco. Chiaramente ho preso parte a quelle missioni, visto che risultano negli archivi. Ma non sono mai stato capitano di nulla.

È una battuta, Andy. Ti prendevano in giro. Per questo detestavi il tuo nome.

Prendo nota. Prosegui.

No, così è impossibile. Mi sembra di parlare con un cazzo di database intelligente, non con mio marito. Non so da dove cominciare con te.

Ti prego, Zoe. Non posso farcela senza di te. Continua.

Va bene, va bene, ma puoi farmi un favore? Usa qualche forma contratta, d'accordo? Le forme contratte sono tue amiche.

Prendo nota.

Sai quando ci siamo incontrati?

Non ho ancora esaminato quella registrazione. Ci siamo sposati nel 2043. Presumo che il nostro incontro sia avvenuto prima?

Non molto prima. Dove ti trovavi sabato 17 maggio del 2042? Controlla le tue registrazioni.

La registrazione mostra che ho preso un aereo dal quartier generale di Spaceways dallo Spaceport America per l'aeroporto La-Guardia di New York e che ho passato la giornata al Metropolitan Museum di Manhattan. Quella sera ho tenuto il discorso di apertura al banchetto del premio Nebula all'Hotel Crown Plaza ma le mie registrazioni erano disattive. Il premio Nebula viene conferito ogni anno dalla World Science Fiction Writers...

Quell'anno sono stata nominata per il miglior livebook, *Ombre sul Sole*. Mi hai raggiunto alla reception, dicendo di essere un fan. Mi hai detto che quando sei partito per Marte la prima volta avevi negli auricolari tutti e cinque gli episodi della mia serie *Sidewise*. Hai fatto una battuta, dicendo di avere una cotta per Nacky Martinez. Io ero emozionata e lusingata. Dopotutto tu eri il massimo, uno dei sei eroici esploratori di Marte. Quello che io avevo solo immaginato, tu l'avevi fatto davvero. E avevi letto i miei lavori e ci stavi provando con me ed eri il capitano Kirk, porca puttana. Quando le persone – amici, scrittori famosi – cercavano di interrompere la nostra conversazione, venivano semplicemente respinte. Nessuno ricorda chi ha vinto quale premio quella sera, ma in tanti parlano ancora di quanto ci siamo avvicinati.

Ho appena controllato. Non l'hai vinto tu quel premio Nebula.
Già. Grazie per avermelo ricordato.
Portavi un cappello.
Un cappello? D'accordo. Ma all'epoca indossavo sempre cappelli. Era un modo per risaltare, faceva parte del mio stile – per quanto la cosa possa avermi aiutato. I miei capelli sembravano lo stesso una tragedia in tre atti, quindi indossavo tantissimi cappelli.

Il cappello di cui parlo era una bombetta. Era blu – blu scuro. Con un nastro celeste. Sottile, ricordo che quel nastro era molto sottile.

Può essere. Non ricordo quel modello in particolare. Bel tentativo, comunque.

Dimmi di più. Cos'è successo dopo?

Gesù, tutto questo è sbagliato... No, mi spiace, Andy. Dammi la mano. Hai sempre avuto le mani delicate. Le dita così sottili.

Ricordo ancora il pianoforte verticale Baldwin di mia madre; voleva che imparassi a suonarlo, ma avevo le mani troppo piccole. Stai piangendo. Piangi?

No. Ora zitto e ascolta. Per me tutto questo non è facile e te lo sto raccontando solo perché forse la tua parte migliore è ancora intrappolata lì dentro come mi hanno detto e perché questo potenziamento potrebbe riportarla a galla. Allora, durante la cena eravamo seduti a tavoli diversi, ma alla fine mi hai trovata di nuovo e mi hai chiesto se volevo uscire per un drink. Siamo scappati dall'hotel cercando un posto dove stare da soli, alla fine abbiamo trovato un ristorante notturno indonesiano con bar, a un paio di isolati più in là. Si chiamava Il gambero grasso, o Il granchio grasso – un qualcosa di grasso, insomma. Ci siamo seduti al bar e siamo passati dall'alcol agli inalatori e abbiamo parlato. Parecchio. Quasi per tutta la notte, in realtà. Sei stato un buon ascoltatore, considerando che eri un uomo, che eri famoso e che avevi fatto parte dell'Aeronautica militare. Volevi sapere quanto era difficile pubblicare e da dove venivano le idee delle mie storie e quali autori preferivo. Ero impressionata dal fatto che avessi letto tanti vecchi autori di fantascienza classica come Kress e LeGuin e Bacigalupi. Mi hai spiegato cosa sbagliavo nel descrivere la vita nello spazio e ti sei esaltato per delle cose nei miei libri che credevi conoscesse solamente chi era stato nello spazio. Verso le quattro del mattino ci è venuta fame e, visto che non avevi mai mangiato cibo indonesiano prima di allora, ci siamo divisi un'insalata gado-gado con uova e tofu. Io ho passato troppo tempo a psicanalizzare il mio divorzio e tu sei stato molto discreto riguardo al tuo. Mi hai raccontato di quanto la tua ex si lamentasse del tempo che passavi nello spazio e io ho fatto una battuta sul fatto che anche Kass avrebbe detto la stessa cosa di me. Ti ho chiesto se ti capitava mai di avere paura quando eri lì fuori e tu mi hai risposto di sì e mi hai detto che gli atterraggi erano molto peggio dei lanci perché avevi tutto quel tempo per rimuginarci su. Ti capitava di svegliarti tutto sudato durante i tuoi viaggi. Per cambiare argomento, ti ho raccontato di quando mi svegliavo con intere scene o storie abbozzate in testa e di come mi alzavo nel pieno della notte per scriverle, altrimenti le avrei dimenticate. Al che te ne sei uscito dicendo che avresti voluto assistere a quelle scene di persona. Era quasi mattina e il ristorante stava per chiudere, ma a quel punto sul menu era senz'altro previsto del sesso per dessert, così ti ho chiesto se ti fossi mai eccitato durante una missione. È così che ho scoperto che uno degli effetti collaterali dei medicinali anti-radiazioni era l'abbassamento dei livelli di testosterone. Hai subito chiarito che non ne stavi più assumendo. A quel punto ti avrei invitato a salire in camera, ma tu dovevi prendere un volo alle sette e venti del mattino per tornare a El Paso. Forse avremmo comunque avuto abbastanza tempo, ma la mia compagna di stanza era Rachel van der Haak e, dopo esserci sballate prima di cena, ci eravamo promesse a vicenda che ci saremmo tenute alla larga dagli uomini finché avevamo la guardia abbassata. E poi, a pensarci bene, c'era la questione imbarazzante dei tuoi venti anni in più. Una ragazza deve farsi due domande quando si accorge di volersi portare a letto il paparino.

Ho diciannove anni e tre mesi più di te.

E poi c'era la tua insistenza. Voglio dire, mi avevi già conquistata nominando Marte, signor Dello Spazio, ma avevo l'impressione che tu volessi da me molto più di quanto potessi offrirti. Io avevo in mente solo una prova su strada, ma sembrava che tu fossi già pronto a depositare la caparra per l'acquisto. Quando mi hai detto che eri disposto a cancellare la tua apparizione su Newsmelt per tornare a New York entro tre giorni mi sono eccitata sul serio, ma è stato anche preoccupante. Dare buca a uno dei più importanti siti di notizie? Per me? Per quale motivo? Ho pensato che avessi fretta a causa della tua prossima missione. Non avevo capito che stavi per...

Vai avanti.

No, non ci riesco. Non riesco a...come faccio? Disattiva il potenziamento.

Zoe, ti prego.

Mi hai sentito? L'accordo era questo. Mi hanno detto che avrei potuto farlo in qualsiasi momento.

Registrazione del 15/06/2051, Unità di terapia intensiva del Kerwin Hospital, 09:37:18, Potenziamento disattivato su richiesta

Andy? Guardami, Andy. Da questa parte. Bene. Chi sono, Andy?

Tu sei... è qualcosa che riguarda la fantascienza. E un cappello blu.

Come mi chiamo?

Avvicinati. Fatti guardare... oh, ce l'ho sulla punta della lingua. Nacky Martinez? Primo ufficiale dell'astronave *Sidewise*?

Quello è un personaggio, Andy. Inventato. L'ho creata io.

Sei una scrittrice?

Registrazione del 17/06/2051, Complesso di cure assistite del Kerwin Hospital, 14:47:03

... perché allora ero troppo cotta di te per sospettare del tuo segreto. So che non te lo ricordi, Andy, ma ero follemente innamorata di te quando ci siamo sposati. Forse il potenziamento non riesce a capirlo, ma chiunque guardi le registrazioni se ne accorgerebbe. È tutto negli archivi, come diresti tu. Quindi sì, il fatto che tu usassi sempre i registratori e riprendessi quasi tutto quel che ti succedeva non mi dava fastidio all'epoca. Suppongo di essermi giustificata con me stessa pensando si trattasse di un qualche sistema di gestione della reputazione imposto dalla Spaceways. E poi naturalmente stavi scrivendo il sequel della tua autobiografia. Cosa combinano il signor e la signora Eroi Dello Spazio nei loro giorni liberi? Ma guarda, si siedono insieme sul divano per scrivere! E lei ancora usa le dita per farlo – non è pittoresco, una scrittrice di fantascienza che batte le dita sulla tastiera nell'era del riconoscimento dei pensieri!

Non hai mai pubblicato quel libro.

No.

Né nessun altro. Perché?

La gente mi scrive di continuo a riguardo, sai? Come se fosse una tragedia. Avevo qualcosa da dire quando ero giovane e ingenua. L'ho detto. E l'ho fatto proprio bene: tanto da valere otto livebook. E cinquanta racconti nova online. È solo che dopo averti conosciuto dovevo sfruttare al meglio il nostro tempo insieme. E da quando sei partito per la faccenda del professor Vincente sono stata occupata a fare la brava moglie.

Ero il pilota più qualificato, Zoe. E poi ero già compromesso, ero quello che aveva meno da perdere. In una crisi del genere, non c'erano soluzioni semplici. Mi sono consultato con la Spaceways, abbiamo soppesato i pro e i contro e abbiamo preso una decisione. Avevo degli amici su quella stazione orbitale. Drew Bantry...

Drew era già morto. Solo che doveva ancora cadere. E non è questione di pro o di contro, Andy, eri mio marito, cazzo.

Adesso capisco quanto deve essere stata dura per te.

Oh, lo capivi anche allora. Per questo non hai mai chiesto il mio permesso, perché lo sapevi che...

Vai avanti.

Di che diavolo stavamo parlando? Del fatto che non avevo idea del vero motivo delle registrazioni. Del fatto che eri malato. Ricordo di aver pensato quanto sarebbero state noiose diecimila ore di registrazioni integrali. Perfino per noi, perfino per quando saremmo stati vecchi. Vecchi e smemorati...

Zoe?

Sto bene. È solo che non mi sento molto coraggiosa, oggi. In ogni caso, mi infastidivano le registrazioni di noi che facevamo l'amore. Voglio dire, le prime volte era eccitante, certo. Ci rilassavamo a letto e ci guardavamo mentre lo facevamo. A volte eravamo così in sintonia da eccitarci e farlo di nuovo. Ma quel che mi infastidiva di più era che registravi anche mentre guardavamo i filmati.

Non capivo perché lo facessi. Quando ho realizzato che le riprese non erano un'eccezione, che volevi riprenderci ogni volta che facevamo sesso, ha smesso di essere erotico. Era solo un po' strano.

Non riesco a individuare registrazioni di noi che facciamo sesso dopo il 2045. Abbiamo smesso di fare sesso?

No. Ti facevo interrompere le registrazioni all'ingresso della camera da letto. Quindi smetti pure di cercare. Se vuoi sapere com'eravamo all'epoca, controlla qualcuno dei gruppi di lettura che frequentavamo. Leggevamo gli stessi libri e poi andavamo a cena in un bel ristorante a parlarne. Mi ricordo di come restavo sorpresa da alcune tue scelte. *Il meraviglioso paese di Oz. Lolita. Wolf Hall. Il tempo è un bastardo.* Non sembravano le letture tipiche di un fusto dell'Aeronautica militare. Eri un più un tipo da Hemingway e da Heinlein.

Stavo cercando di fare colpo?

Non so perché. Ero già piuttosto colpita. Forse stavi cercando di dirmi qualcosa, con tutte quelle trame su passati segreti e trasformazioni.

Vai avanti. Tutto questo dove? Quando?

All'inizio a Brooklyn, dove vivevo quando ci siamo conosciuti. Ed ecco un'altra ragione per cui avrei dovuto insospettirmi della tua insistenza. Dicevi che non ti importava dove vivessimo, finché trascorrevamo quanto più tempo possibile insieme. Non era vero – odiavi le città. Ma la maggior parte dei miei amici viveva a New York e i tuoi si erano trasferiti su Marte o nello spazio. I tuoi genitori erano morti e tua sorella era scomparsa in un'associazione Digitalista, in attesa della Singolarità. Così quando mia madre è morta e mi ha lasciato la casa a Bedford ci siamo trasferiti lì nella primavera del 2045. Tu dovevi scrivere il secondo libro previsto dal tuo contratto e, quando io sono passata al tuo agente, ho iniziato a ricevere anche io anticipi da superstar, quindi avevamo denaro in abbondanza. Ma a quel punto hai cominciato a mostrare i primi sintomi. Dicevi di aver lasciato la Spaceways, nonostante continuassi a volare fino a Kermin cinque o sei volte all'anno per la terapia. Tutto sembrava funzionare, dicevi che avremmo avuto ancora anni di vita insieme. Mia madre amava i fiori, ma aveva anche un piccolo appezzamento coltivato ad asparagi e alcuni arbusti di lampone, così hai iniziato a curare il tuo primo orto quell'estate. Eri bravo, dicevi di preferirlo rispetto alla coltivazione idroponica nello spazio. Spinaci, lattuga e asparagi in primavera, poi fagioli, mais, zucchine, pomodori e meloni. Eri felice, credo. Io lo ero di sicuro.

Registrazione del 25/06/2051, Complesso di cure assistite del Kerwin Hospital, 16:17:53

... il motivo era il tuo scetticismo per la Singolarità.

Il potenziamento di Kurzweil non ha nulla a che vedere con la Singolarità.

Sì, come no. È solo una protesi cognitiva, la-la-la. Un database con le esperienze di una vita, la-la-la. Un potenziatore di memoria gestito da un'intelligenza artificiale che può aiutarti a ripristinare la conoscenza delle persone che ami la-la-la-dee-da. Ho dato un'occhiata ai siti, Andy. Oltretutto, scrivevo di questa merda prima che Ray Kurzweil la caricasse.

Ray Kurzweil è morto. Io sono ancora vivo.

Lo sei, Andy? Ne sei convinto?

Non capisco perché ti stai comportando in modo così crudele, Zoe.

Perché hai preso tutte quelle decisioni che ci riguardavano senza mai consultarmi. Forse quando ci siamo conosciuti non sapevi quanto eri malato, ma avresti potuto scoprirlo facilmente. Avevo il diritto di sapere. E magari tu speravi di non ricevere mai quella chiamata dalla Spaceways, ma sapevi cosa sarebbe successo se fosse arrivata.

Ero un astronauta, Zoe. Non è mai stato un segreto.

No, il segreto era quella puttanata della ricerca sui raggi cosmici. Perché nessuno, a parte un matto da legare con istinti suicidi, si sarebbe offerto volontario per andare nello spazio se avesse saputo che non esisteva una protezione effettiva per evitare di farsi bruciare i telomeri dalle radiazioni. Certo, puoi accucciarti e nasconderti da un brillamento solare, ma che mi dici dei fantastiliardi di ioni ultra-energetici? In teoria si potrebbe generare un campo magnetico. O magari potresti imbottire i tuoi astronauti di meravigliosi farmaci anti-radiazioni. Ma nel caso non dovesse funzionare, meglio assicurarsi che tutto l'equipaggio in partenza per Marte abbia più di quarant'anni. Così se il capitano Kirk inizia a cadere a pezzi dopo venti o trent'anni, la Spaceways non sembrerà così malvagia.

Continua.

Oh, lo farò. Forse quando ci siamo incontrati la prima volta non avevi ancora visto le stime confidenziali dei livelli di radiazione relativi alla prima missione su Marte. O forse non volevi proprio conoscerle. Ma quando sono diventata tua moglie avrei voluto essere messa al corrente. Lascia che ti legga il rapporto esecutivo. "L'esposizione alle radiazioni nel corso della missione ha sortito significativi effetti a lungo e breve termine diretti al sistema nervoso centrale di tutti i membri dell'equipaggio. Nonostante le eccellenti procedure di attenuazione, le dosi effettive presenti nel corpo variavano da 0.4 a 0.7 sievert. La radiazione cosmica della galassia, in forma di ioni energetici a massa elevata, ha distrutto il 4% delle cellule della squadra, mentre il 13% di importanti regioni cerebrali risulta presumibilmente compromesso. Risultati nel deterioramento nei processi cognitivi e comportamentali a breve termine sono stati ampiamente riscontrati nel corso della missione di tre anni. Studi della sezione longitudinale del corpo degli astronauti mostrano un aumento significativo del rischio di malattie degenerative del cervello. In particolare, si evidenzia un'accelerazione nelle patologie da placche correlate al morbo di Alzheimer." Facciamo due conti, Andy. Ti becchi una dose di sievert stimata tra 0.4 e 0.7 durante la tua prima missione e vai su Marte per due volte. Quindi diciamo che assorbi un sievert e spicci. Ed è il motivo per cui venivi trattenuto a terra.

È tutto quanto negli archivi.

Qual è la dose massima annuale che l'EPA ha stabilito per chi lavora con le radiazioni qui sulla Terra?

Non ho accesso immediato a questi dati. Posso cercare la risposta.

Sì, puoi – è negli archivi. Cinquanta millisievert. E il limite per le squadre che intervengono in situazioni di emergenza?
Zoe, io...
Duecentocinquanta millisievert.
Esistono sempre dei rischi.
Per cui si scende a compromessi, lo capisco. Quindi in questo caso il compromesso è X anni della tua vita in cambio di due biglietti per Marte. Decisione che hai preso prima di conoscermi, per cui non posso biasimarti. Dopo che me ne hai parlato, credo di aver capito che quello era il prezzo da pagare per diventare la persona che volevi essere. Anche se devo dire che hai aspettato parecchio prima di svelarmi il tuo piccolo segreto. Ma quello non è stato il tuo ultimo compromesso. Perché la Spaceways ha fallito nella gestione del progetto durante l'equipaggiamento dell'Orbitale Sette. Non hanno spedito sufficienti rifugi contro le tempeste solari che potessero ospitare tutti i membri della squadra di costruzione. Così quando il professor Vincente ha predetto l'arrivo di un'esplosione di classe X2 che avrebbe arrostito metà delle persone a bordo in una tempesta di protoni, quelli della gestione del personale si sono rivolti al sessantenne capitano Kirk, nonostante fosse ormai in congedo a terra. Hanno dichiarato che, non essendo rimasto molto tempo prima che le placche dell'Alzheimer divorassero quanto era rimasto della sua memoria, magari avrebbe potuto prendere in considerazione un'ultima impresa gloriosa per trasportare lassù le protezioni d'emergenza e salvare i loro culi aziendali. O magari il nostro Eroe Dello Spazio si è fatto avanti di sua iniziativa e si è offerto volontario per la loro missione suicida del cazzo.
Non è stata una missione suicida, Zoe. Sono tornato.
Ed eccoti qua, Andy. Ed eccomi qua. Ma non sta funzionando.

Registrazione del 30/06/2051, Unità di terapia intensiva del Kerwin Hospital, 11:02:53
... o sei troppo impegnato con l'analisi della tua vita? Diecimila ore di registrazioni sono parecchie da smaltire, anche in modalità avanti veloce.

Le registrazioni durano undicimila e duecentottantaquattro ore, esclusa la ripresa in corso.

Prendo nota. Hai trovato qualcosa di interessante?

Sarebbe un film noioso se non fosse tutto su di me.

Ho sentito della tua ex, ieri, su Newsmelt. Mi spiace. Non sapevo fosse emigrata su Marte.

A quanto pare voleva andare nello spazio tanto quanto me. Non so perché non lo sapevo. È strano, ma sembra che lei non compaia in nessuna delle mie immagini o video.

Quindi te la ricordi?

Solo dei flash, ma sono molto vividi. Come se la sua immagine venisse illuminata da un fulmine.

Stanno valutando se riportare indietro il resto dei coloni.

Forse. Ma dovranno ammanettarli e drogarli e trascinarli sulle navi di soccorso mentre scalciano e gridano – conosco quella gente. E poi perché prendersi il disturbo? Molti di loro non sopravvivrebbero al viaggio di ritorno.

Lo spazio ti ucciderà in ogni modo possibile. Me lo hai detto al nostro terzo appuntamento.

Cerco di non farci caso. È passato parecchio tempo dall'ultima volta che ci sono state buone notizie dallo spazio. Ho l'impressione che su Marte dovremo ricominciare da zero. L'unica cosa da fare è catturare una cometa, scavare al suo interno e ricavarne una nave colonia. Il ghiaccio farebbe da scudo contro i raggi cosmici. Poi bisognerebbe mandare a terra i coloni sulle navette e alla fine far schiantare la cometa. Risolveremmo sia il problema dell'acqua che quello delle radiazioni.

Catturare una cometa? E come diavolo pensi di farlo? Con un raggio traente? Con un lazo magico?

Metti i tuoi compagni della fantascienza al lavoro sulla questione. Se trovate un'idea abbastanza folle, gli ingegneri verranno a ficcare il naso.

Vedrò cosa posso fare. Oggi ho incrociato gli Zhang mentre venivo qui. Credevo di essere l'unica a farti visita. Abbiamo fatto una bella chiacchierata. E la bambina era carinissima. Com'è che si chiama?

Andee. A-N-D e doppia E.

Già, mi sembrava avessero detto così. In tuo onore.

Kristen è stata fortunata. L'hanno spinta all'inizio della fila, così è stata una delle prime a entrare nel rifugio. Gli ultimi tre hanno assorbito una consistente dose di radiazioni. Uno di loro è morto durante il viaggio di ritorno.

Drew Bantry.

Si trattava della sua gente. Ha aspettato finché non fossero tutti al sicuro.

Tu e lui avete salvato molte vite quel giorno, capitano Kirk. È negli archivi, lo sapranno tutti.

Basta così, Zoe. Hai qualcosa per me oggi?

Delle scuse.

Continua.

Mi spiace per le cose che ho detto la volta scorsa. Per questo ho saltato le ultime visite. Non mi fido di me stessa, di riuscire a dire la cosa giusta. I miei sentimenti si confondono quando ti vedo così. Parlo d'impulso. Butto tutto fuori. Non va bene.

Prendo nota.

Ma ecco il punto. Non credo che accederò al tuo potenziamento quando... te ne sarai andato. Morto. Capisci? Ora posso venire qui in ospedale e vederti. Guardare il tuo viso, il tuo corpo, le braccia, le mani. Ma con una specie di avatar? No, è troppo difficile. Ci sono stati momenti nelle ultime settimane in cui ho avuto l'impressione che tu fossi qui, con me, ma è solo perché ti rivoglio indietro. La maggior parte delle volte, però, non credo che questa cosa che parla con me sia davvero tu. Mi dispiace.

Perché no?

Anche se il potenziamento avesse accesso a tutte le tue registrazioni e a tutti gli stimoli risalenti a prima che iniziassi a registrare mancherebbero ancora troppe cose. Sì, possiamo parlare della nostra vita insieme, ma sono ancora io a doverti dire cose che dovresti sapere. E adesso che hai iniziato anche a fare battute è ancora più difficile. Come faccio a capire se quando sei triste, felice o arrabbiato sei davvero tu o un algoritmo intelligente?

Non lo so, Andy. E quando dirai che mi ami? Come farò a sapere che è vero, o se è soltanto qualcos'altro che ti serviva per ricordare?

È vero, Zoe. Ecco, spengo il potenziamento, così potrai sentirlo direttamente da me. Da questo corpo, come dici tu. Da queste labbra.

No, tesoro, non devi...

Registrazione del 30/06/2051, Unità di terapia intensiva del Kerwin Hospital, 11:15:18, incremento disattivato su richiesta

Va bene? Eccomi. E so perfettamente chi sei. Sei la mia famosa moglie, la scrittrice. Nackey Martinez. Vuoi andartene. Non voglio che tu te ne vada. Dammi la mano.

Signorsì, capitano.

Rimani con me. Ti va?

Per un po'.

E scrivi altri libri. Sai, no, sulle tue avventure nello spazio. È importante. E magari... potresti portarmi i qualcosa da mangiare? Il cibo qui è terribile. Lo sai anche tu. Quando tornavo a casa da scuola mamma mi preparava sempre le fettine di banana con sopra una punta di burro d'arachidi. Le mie merendine. Stai piangendo, Nackey? Stai piangendo.

Sì.

"Quando nel corso di eventi umani..."

Mentre Silk parlava, nuvole soffici diedero forma alla frase in un cielo magrittiano, al tempo stesso in penombra e illuminato a giorno. Sebbene Remeny apprezzasse il controllo che Silk aveva sul proprio dominio di tempo fluido, avrebbe preferito evitare che il loro incontro prendesse una piega artistica. Avevano del lavoro da sbrigare.

"Aspetta," intervenne Botão, "che ne è della parte che diceva *'noi, il popolo'*?"

"Quella è l'altra." Silk le rivolse un bip (.1) di rabbia che andò sfumando in un (.7) d'irritazione. "È il preambolo della Costituzione."

"Ma siamo noi il popolo di cui si parla." Botão ignorò i bip di Silk. "È proprio questo il punto."

"Gli eventi umani," disse Silk. "Se potessi aspettare un solo istante, stavo proprio per arrivare alla parte del popolo."

Botão era stata assegnata al loro progetto scolastico di gruppo da appena un mese, e Remeny già sapeva quel che lei ignorava: a Silk non piaceva essere messo in discussione, soprattutto non all'interno del suo dominio. Avevano scelto il suo angolo di spazio virtuale perché aveva abbastanza capacità in eccesso da poterli ospitare tutti quanti, ma il suo non era il posto ideale per pianificare la loro finta rivoluzione. Le parole d'apertura della Dichiarazione d'Indipendenza fluttuavano sottili su di loro.

"Allora avanti, continua," disse Sturm. "E lascia perdere gli effetti speciali."

"Quando nel corso di eventi umani," ripeté Silk, "sorge la necessità che *un popolo* sciolga i legami politici che lo hanno stretto a un altro popolo..."

"D'accordo," disse Botão.

"...e assuma tra le potenze della Terra lo stato di potenza separata e uguale a cui le Leggi della Natura e del Dio della Natura gli danno diritto, un conveniente riguardo alle opinioni dell'umanità richiede che quel popolo dichiari le ragioni per cui è costretto alla secessione."

Gli altri quattro – Remeny, Sturm, Botão e Toybox – si studiarono a vicenda e poi si voltarono verso Silk. Avevano tutti accettato di chiudere i canali di comunicazione privati e mantenere i rispettivi avatar trasparenti dal punto di vista emotivo, così un attimo dopo nella stanza risuonarono bip di confusione e disapprovazione.

"Leggi della Natura?" chiese Toybox. "Ma di che diavolo stiamo parlando?"

"Forse della relatività." I bip di disprezzo di Sturm partirono da (.3) e aumentarono in fretta.

"Non ce l'avevano nemmeno la relatività all'epoca."

"Certo che sì, erano solo troppo stupidi per rendersene conto."

"L'umanità? E che mi dite del restante cinquantadue per cento?" Botão scoppiò a ridere. "E chi sarebbe il Dio della Natura?"

"Giusto," disse Sturm. "Secondo me sono stronzate. Stronzate incartapecorite dei tempi andati."

Remeny rimase in silenzio; si concentrò su Silk, che stava aspettando che tutti si calmassero. "Sono d'accordo," disse. "Ma forse per la gente del passato aveva un qualche significato, visto che è stato Thomas Jefferson a scrivere queste cose."

"E chi è? Ma soprattutto, chi se ne importa?" commentò Toybox.

"Il Jefferson che ha dato il nome a Jefferson County," insistette Remeny. "Il posto in cui viviamo."

"Io vivo nel tempo fluido." A (9+) la rabbia di Toybox era quasi impossibile da rilevare – ma a dire il vero lui urlava sempre. "Ecco dove vivo io."

Silk sventolò una mano davanti al suo viso, come se il bip di rabbia fosse un cattivo odore da allontanare. "La storia è importante per gli snob della realtà," disse. "Vedrete che questo catturerà la loro attenzione."

Remeny si accorse che stava cercando di tenere il suo caratteraccio sotto controllo. Era decisamente interessata a Silk; la compostezza era una qualità che apprezzava in un ragazzo.

"Per questo li farà rabbrividire," disse Toybox. Era stato già bocciato in un altro progetto di gruppo. "Li faremo saltare in aria."

"Non abbiamo intenzione di fare nulla del genere," disse Botão. "Siamo studenti, non terroristi."

"Parla per te." Sturm aprì le mani e tra esse comparve un orologio dei vecchi tempi. "Le rivoluzioni non giocano seguendo le regole." Il quadrante mostrava che mancavano due minuti a mezzanotte.

Remeny non riusciva a credere che proprio Sturm, di tutti i presenti, si stesse schierando con i terroristi. Era d'accordo con Botão: non le importava granché della rivoluzione. Tutto ciò che voleva era prendere il voto per l'esame di gruppo, ottenere il diploma e non dover mai più accedere al Servizio di Sorveglianza Scolastica di Jefferson County. Il problema era che un terzo del suo voto per il progetto di gruppo dipendeva dai contributi allo spirito cooperativo del team. L'esame di cooperazione avanzata aveva l'obiettivo di dimostrare agli EOS che gli studenti avevano le capacità sociali per muoversi nel tempo fluido unendo le forze, pianificando e mettendo in pratica un progetto che avesse effetti sul tempo solido, il tutto mantenendo anonime le proprie identità.

Naturalmente, mantenere l'anonimato in una contea come quella di Jefferson non era affatto semplice. Gli studenti trascorrevano ore nel tempo fluido e in quello solido cercando di scoprire chi fosse chi. Botão, ad esempio, era una delle rifugiate dal Brasile, e probabilmente viveva a Tugatown. Remeny l'aveva incontrata per la prima volta due anni innanzi nei parcogiochi degli EOS, soprattutto ForSquare e Sanctuary. Ora Botão era anche amica di Sturm – forse era perfino la sua ragazza. Toybox sfidava le leggi dell'anonimato vestendo il suo avatar con abiti che facevano riferimento alla sua identità nel tempo solido. Sapevano tutti che nella realtà era Jason Day, il cui corpo era sospeso nella capsula 334 del Komfort Kare sulla Route 127 di Pikeville. Sfortunatamente per lui, non interessava a nessuno. Averlo nel gruppo era stato un vero e proprio colpo di sfortuna – se era sua intenzione di continuare a fare lo stronzo in quel modo, rischiavano tutti quanti la bocciatura. Al contrario, era stato un colpo di fortuna avere in gruppo Silk – chiunque egli fosse. Non aveva mai visto il suo avatar nelle classi avanzate, ma Silk non si comportava da novellino. Ipotizzò che potesse trattarsi del duplicato di un ragazzino facoltoso che già conoscevano. Era costoso trovarsi in due posti al tempo stesso, e visto quant'era vasto il suo dominio nel tempo fluido, Remeny era convinta che Silk fosse pieno di soldi. Probabilmente viveva in quella comunità isolata nei pressi del lago. Si chiese che aspetto avesse nel tempo solido. Di sicuro il suo avatar era molto sexy, con quegli stivali di pelle rinforzati. L'identità di Sturm, ovviamente, non era un segreto per lei: era il suo fratello gemello, ma sperava con tutta se stessa che l'informazione non fosse arrivata a nessun altro.

Impiegarono la maggior parte di un faticoso pomeriggio per riscrivere il secondo paragrafo della Dichiarazione d'Indipendenza; furono collaborativi gatti litigiosi. Secondo Remeny, Sturm e Silk prendevano la rivoluzione troppo sul serio, come se potesse scoppiare il mercoledì successivo. Silk voleva fare meno modifiche possibili alla loro versione; Sturm insisteva sul fatto che le loro richieste dovevano essere più chiare.

"Inalienabili?" chiese Sturm. "Non esiste questa parola."

"All'epoca esisteva."

"Be', ma noi siamo nel presente."

Botão sembrava nervosa, forse perché stavamo proponendo il rovesciamento di un governo. Probabilmente era preoccupata che la deportassero. "Mi piace la parte in cui dice 'la vita, la libertà e il perseguimento della felicità.'" Botão era talmente vicina a Sturm che i loro avatar praticamente si stavano fondendo. "Dovremmo tenere quel pezzo. Un giorno avrò un dominio tutto mio, mi trasferirò e non tornerò mai più nel tempo solido."

"E cosa metterai nel tuo dominio?" I bip di Sturm assunsero un tono ammiccante.

"Volevi dire *chi*?" Gli si allontanò e gli sfiorò il petto con un dito. "Speravi che di entrarci tu, magari?" Sorrise. "Non ancora, ragazzo misterioso. Dovrai guadagnartelo."

"Concentratevi, per favore," li ammonì Silk.

Più tardi...

"No, sono i governi che dovrebbero servirci, non il contrario."

Silk aveva creato un tavolo da conferenze rettangolare in vetro, sedendosi a una delle due estremità. La bozza della dichiarazione brillava sulla sua superficie. "Non possiamo modificare la parte sul 'consenso dei governati'."

"Ma cosa sarebbe il consenso?"

"Tipo un permesso, solo in termini più legali."

"Non ho mai dato il mio consenso affinché qualche stronzata degli EOS mi rovinasse la vita."

Molto più tardi...

"Quindi significa che abbiamo il potere di rovesciare gli EOS?" Botão sembrava dubbiosa.

Toybox si stava accendendo la punta delle dita. "Dobbiamo rovesciare la vecchia scuola e farla finita con tutte le loro stronzate." Più parlavano, più crescevano i suoi bip di noia aumentavano d'intensità. Era come guardare una miccia che brucia in un cartone animato.

"Non capisco come potrebbero darci una 'A' se li rovesciamo," disse Remeny.

"Se dimostriamo che si comportano in modo ingiusto..."

"Ma è proprio per questo che dobbiamo tenere 'mutarla' e 'abolirla'," Silk interruppe Sturm per la centesima volta. "Il significato è lo stesso di 'rovesciare', solo che l'ha scritto Jefferson. Così potremo nasconderci dietro le sue parole."

Molto, molto più tardi...

Sturm aveva trasformato il tavolo delle riunioni da rettangolare a circolare. "Se ci sbarazziamo dell'attuale governo, allora ce ne servirà uno nuovo," disse.

"Non ho intenzione di creare un nuovo governo," disse Botão. "Tra mezz'ora ho il turno a lavoro."

"Allora niente governo," ribatté Sturm. "Ciascun per sé. Legge della giungla."

Prima che terminasse la frase, un bip (.2) sconcertato lampeggiò sull'avatar di Remeny. Quelle parole non erano da lui.

Alla fine, dopo molte discussioni e moltissimi bip, convinsero Silk a lasciare il controllo della tastiera a Remeny, visto che almeno lei sembrava disposta ad accettare i suggerimenti degli altri. Mentre Silk rimuginava, gli altri concordarono su una bozza del cruciale secondo paragrafo.

"Noi riteniamo che queste verità siano per se stesse evidenti, che tutte le realtà, solide e fluide, antiche e moderne, siano eguali, e che lo stesso valga per le persone che le abitano, a prescindere dalla realtà scelta. Tutti, indipendentemente dal fatto che vivano in un corpo o in un avatar, sono dotati di certi inalienabili diritti, tra cui la vita, la libertà e il perseguimento della felicità. Per garantire questi diritti i governi debbono servire il popolo e non viceversa. Essi derivano i loro giusti poteri dal consenso dei governati. Ogni volta che una qualsiasi forma di governo tende a negare questi fini, il popolo ha il diritto di mutarla o abolirla e di istituire un nuovo governo che faccia la cosa giusta."

"Bene." Remeny controllò l'ora sul suo overlord; a breve anche lei sarebbe dovuta tornare reale. "E adesso?"

"Elenchiamo tutte le cose che il governo sta sbagliando." Silk interruppe il suo mesto silenzio.

Toybox sospirò. "Non oggi."

"No," disse Remeny. Lo faremo la prossima volta. "C'è altro?"

"Dobbiamo pensare a qualcosa che possa influenzare il tempo solido," disse Sturm. "Portare la rivoluzione in strada."

"In sostanza stai parlando di fare dei compiti a casa," disse Botão. "E io devo essere a lavoro tra dieci minuti."

"E se mandassimo tutto al doppio della velocità?," suggerì Silk.

L'imbarazzo di Botão schizzò immediatamente a (.4). "Umm... io non ho il permesso."

"Non hai il permesso?" domandò Toybox. "Tutti dovrebbero avere un po' di tempo doppio a disposizione. Non ce ne danno mai abbastanza."

"È colpa di mia madre." Ora il bip d'imbarazzo aveva raggiunto (.6). "Lei..."

"Non importa," Sturm la interruppe. "Ho già usato tutto il tempo accelerato di questo mese."

Remeny sapeva che non era vero, ma apprezzò la bugia e decise di unirsi a lui. "Anche io."

"Vedete, è per questo che ci serve una rivoluzione," disse Toybox. "Così potremo usare tutto il tempo accelerato che vogliamo."

"Già," disse Botão, "e poi potremmo chiedere a Babbo Natale di portarci degli alberi di diamanti per dare da mangiare agli unicorni."

Remeny li ignorò. "Stavamo parlando di portare il discorso nel mondo reale. Cosa stavi proponendo, Sturm?"

"Ci serve un messaggio." Rifletté. "Che cosa vogliamo comunicare alla gente dei tempi andati?"

"Che gli EOS fanno schifo." L'avatar di Toybox si alzò dal tavolo e materializzò nel dominio di Silk una porta con sopra un grosso segnale rosso di USCITA.

"Quello è ciò che recriminiamo," Sturm scosse la testa. "Ma che cos'è che vogliamo rivendicare?"

Per un attimo rimasero tutti in silenzio.

"Che ne dite di vita, libertà e il perseguimento della felicità?" propose Botão.

"Niente male," rispose Sturm. "Ma quelle sono solo parole finché non spieghiamo cosa significano."

"No," Silk si spostò sul bordo della sedia. "Ha ragione. Trasformiamolo nel nostro slogan, diffondiamolo, facciamo in modo che la gente ne parli." Picchiettò con il dito sul tavolo. "Poster, magliette..."

"Graffiti."

"Solo nel tempo libero," aggiunse Remeny. "D'accordo, ecco i vostri compiti per casa. Vita, libertà, e il perseguimento della felicità – almeno dieci ciascuno."

"Dieci?" Toybox poggiò la mano sul pomello della sua porta. "E come faccio a fare dieci interventi nel tempo solido dalla sospensione all'interno di una capsula?"

"Non lo so," rispose lei. "Spedisci dieci lettere ai tuoi amici..."

"Nemmeno ce li ha dieci amici."

"... stampa degli adesivi."

"Scrivi una canzone e registrala." Botão cinguettò stonata. "*Per me nella vita serve libertà*... umm... *blablabla felicità*."

"Perfetto," disse Remeny. "Il prossimo incontro è alle 1300 di martedì 12." Salvò una trascrizione del loro incontro nella sua cartella studentesca. "Devo andare. Ho finito il tempo."

La principale lamentela di Remeny nei confronti del governo era che il suo Gestore dello Stato di Salute, cioè il suo overlord, era troppo autoritario. La costringeva a fare parecchi esercizi e monitorava costantemente la sua dieta. Ogni giorno le fissava un lasso di tempo minimo per rimanere sola e uno per le interazioni con i membri della famiglia. E peggio ancora, se non raggiungeva questi obbiettivi aveva il potere di limitare la sua permanenza giornaliera all'interno del tempo fluido. L'overlord avrebbe continuato a tenerla d'occhio anche dopo i ventun anni, quando sarebbe stata perfettamente in grado di prendere da sola le sue decisioni. Non era giusto. Nessuno costringeva gente come Toybox e Sturm ad andarsene in giro per annusare le cazzo di rose.

Doveva ancora al suo overlord un'ora e mezza di interazioni familiari, nonché abbastanza esercizi fisici da bruciare tremila calorie. Erano le 1717. Per le 1930 avevano in programma una cena di famiglia nel tempo fluido; le avrebbe tolto dai piedi un'ora circa. Se prima della cena fosse riuscita a terminare i suoi cinque chilometri a un passo decente, avrebbe potuto essere a posto anche con gli esercizi. Ma doveva ancora trovare un modo per infilarci un'altra mezz'ora di tempo in famiglia, perché Silk aveva detto che forse avrebbe fatto un salto da For-Square verso le 2100. Si sfilò l'interfaccia NeuroSky 3100 che il padre le aveva regalato per la pre-promozione. Ce l'aveva solo da una settimana, e sebbene le piacesse più della sua vecchia Deveau, il set di elettrodi della 3100 era troppo sensibile alla peluria. Motivo per cui era costretta a rasarsi la testa a giorni alterni. Sfilati gli inserti nasali e rimossi i guanti tattili, tornò a essere Johanna Daugherty, diciotto anni, che viveva al 7 di Forest Ridge Road. Si piaceva di più quando era Remeny. Aveva scelto quel nome perché significava *speranza* in ungherese, ma era un segreto. Nessuno di sua conoscenza parlava ungherese.

"*Ma*," fece capolino con la testa dalla sua camera da letto e urlò nel corridoio buio. "Sono a casa."

"Ciao, tesoro. Ho preparato un frullato di banana. Nella centrifuga ne è rimasto un po' per te, se vuoi."

Remeny indossò gli auricolari, posizionò la lente davanti all'occhio sinistro e si avvicinò il microfono alle labbra. Gli auricolari erano privi di input cranici, perciò non garantivano l'immersione nel tempo fluido, ma almeno in quel modo poteva tenere sotto controllo quel che succedeva online. "Quante calorie?"

"Non lo so. Trecento? Quattro? Chiedilo al frigo."

Il frigorifero segnalò che sua madre aveva aggiunto un cucchiaio di burro d'arachidi alla sua consueta ricetta, il che aveva portato il frullato a ben quattrocentotrenta calorie. Decise di tenerlo da parte per la cena. Prese invece dal freezer un'Ice Cherry Zero.

La madre era china sulla scrivania – indossava un auricolare in vetro. Possedeva un'interfaccia Deveau per l'immersione completa, ma non la usava granché. Era più a suo agio con le interfacce della vecchia scuola. E con la realtà. Era seduta nella penombra del tardo pomeriggio, il volto illuminato dalle finestre lampeggianti sul desktop. Quando Remeny accese le luci, Rachel Daugherty alzò lo sguardo sbattendo le palpebre.

"Grazie," disse.

L'ufficio della madre era una specie di museo, con tanto di antichi libri di carta su scaffali di legno e foto di famiglia immobili. Appesa al muro c'era una coperta per bambini ricamata in stile Úrihímzés che era appartenuta alla bisnonna ungherese di Remeny. Una teca per trofei proteggeva le coppe di tennis che sua madre aveva vinto negli anni del liceo e del college. La pianta di plastica appoggiata sul davanzale della finestra aveva bisogno di una spolverata.

"Che si dice, ma'?"

"Lavoro."

Remeny si appoggiò allo stipite della porta sorseggiando la Cherry Zero. "Lavoro?"

Con un sospiro, Rachel passò una mano sul desktop, chiudendo metà delle finestre. "Il bilancio della sanità. Abbiamo un'eccedenza e devo destinarne una parte alla manutenzione degli edifici."

"Le persone sono più in salute degli edifici?" Le labbra di Remeny tremarono dal freddo.

"Gli edifici vivono sotto la neve e la pioggia e la grandine. Le persone no." Una finestra lampeggiò di blu. "A proposito di stare all'aria aperta," continuò aprendola, "mi sembra di aver ricevuto un avviso dagli EOS un paio di giorni fa. Qualcosa sul tuo status di educazione fisica?"

"Ci ho pensato io." Remeny avrebbe voluto che sua madre la smettesse di essere tanto petulante. "Ho già un overlord che mi asfissia, Rachel. Non mi serve anche un'overmamma."

"Scusa." La madre aggrottò la fronte; non le piaceva quando i suoi figli la chiamavano per nome. "Ascolta, mi dispiace, tesoro, ma in questo momento sono davvero impegnata. Ti serve un po' di tempo con la famiglia, vero? Che ne dici di andare a fare quattro chiacchiere con tuo fratello?"

"Ho appena passato due ore con lui per il progetto di gruppo."

"Bene." Ma l'attenzione di Rachel era tornata sul bilancio. "Come sta andando?"

"Non male, suppongo. Ci siamo anche dati dei compiti per casa. Abbiamo intenzione di trasformarlo in un progetto reale."

"Che bello."

Silenzio.

"Non vuoi sapere di cosa si tratta?"

"Certo," rispose sua madre, ma riprese subito a scorrere le finestre.

"Stiamo scrivendo una dichiarazione d'indipendenza," disse Remeny.

"Sul serio?"

Remeny lasciò cadere la Zero vuota nel cestino e aspettò. E poi aspettò ancora.

"Una dichiarazione," disse, infine. "D'indipendenza."

"Umm... ma non l'aveva già scritta qualcun altro?"

Peccato che non potesse usare i bip nella vita reale.

"Allora magari vado a parlare un po' con Robby."

"Sei una brava sorella." Sua madre annuì ma non alzò lo sguardo. "Potresti farmi un favore? Fagli cambiare posizione, d'accordo?"

Forse era un bene che sua madre non sapesse del loro progetto. Rachel Daugherty era la direttrice di Bedford Town. Faceva parte del governo da cui volevano emanciparsi.

L'intera stanza di Robert Daugherty Junior era tinta di un profondo blu tramonto: muri, pavimento, soffitto, perfino le due finestre riverniciate che non davano più su Forest Ridge Road. Quando Remeny si chiuse la porta alle spalle, ostruendo la luce che proveniva dal corridoio, il colore monotono distorse la geometria dello spazio, eliminando gli angoli e curvando i muri. In camera Robby aveva solo tre vermi luminosi, e li teneva sempre al minimo per via della sua fotosensibilità; strisciavano senza sosta sulle superfici della stanza creando schemi cangianti di radianza onirica e ombre notturne. L'unica cosa che sembrava avere un aspetto solido lì dentro era il robot-assistente, al momento confinato in un angolo buio. I suoi visori elettronici inquadrarono Remeny per un breve istante, il tempo di prendere nota del suo arrivo, prima di tornare sul corpo nudo e tremante di suo fratello, sospeso nella sua rete protettiva. Robby disponeva del più avanzato sistema di sospensione; dopo l'aggressione, Rachel aveva speso gran parte dei soldi del padre per garantire le cure migliori al figlio ferito. L'interfaccia intracranica di Robby gli era stata impiantata direttamente nella corteccia cerebrale, e lo aiutava anche ad alleviare la maggior parte dei tremori discinetici che lo affliggevano. Robby non avrebbe mai potuto gestire il suo avatar con un'interfaccia ordinaria; il controllo che aveva sul suo corpo era stato talmente compromesso dalle neurotossine nel gas DV dei Veri Patrioti che riusciva a malapena a cibarsi. Era uno dei compiti del robot-assistente, così come lavarlo e pulirlo. Un tempo, prima che arrivasse il robot, indossava i pannoloni. Ma quella soluzione non andava bene per nessuno.

=*Ehi, Sturmy.*= Si collegò al loro canale privato. =*La realtà chiama.*=

=*Vattene.*= La risposta del fratello comparve sulla lente di Remeny.

"Mamma mi ha chiesto di vedere come stavi." Passò alla comunicazione analogica, e il microfono si riformattò per i messaggi vocali. "È arrivato il momento di passare un po' di tempo in famiglia."

=*Vieni online, allora.*=

"No, devo accumulare un po' di tempo solido." Inviò un comando alla lente e diede un'occhiata all'overlord di Robby; entrambi avevano l'accesso ai rispettivi account. "E lo stesso vale per te."

Nonostante fossero gemelli, le disabilità di Robby si traducevano in obbiettivi diversi degli overlord. Lui non poteva fare esercizio, ed era il robot-assistente a tenere sotto controllo la sua dieta. Doveva trascorrere solo un'ora al giorno nel tempo solido, ma doveva ancora iniziare a scontarla. Remeny non aveva mai capito come potesse fare bene a qualcuno svegliarsi in una stanza buia per agitarsi come un pesce in trappola.

"*Blaaagh*." Robby non era mai di buon umore quando tornava nel tempo solido. "Che cazzo."

"Buonasera anche a te. Ma' diceva qualcosa a proposito di farti cambiare posizione. Ti serve una mano?"

"No." Tossì un grumo di catarro e sputò a terra. Il robot-assistente si avvicinò per pulire con un ronzio. "Non mi serve... oh, avanti, dammi una mano."

L'unico accessorio in tutta la stanza era la rete in seta smart di Robby. A causa della sua fibromialgia l'abbandonava raramente, anche quando si disconnetteva. La sua pelle era ipersensibile al contatto fisico, e la rete lo aiutava a ridistribuire i punti di pressione. La rete era collegata ai muri e al soffitto, in modo che la sua forma potesse essere riconfigurata termicmente per farlo voltare da un lato all'altro, o anche da supino a prono, per evitare le piaghe da decubito.

Remeny fece scorrere le dita verso l'alto sul pannello di controllo. Alcune sezioni della rete si allungarono, mentre altre si contrassero.

"Ahi, ahio, *ahiooo*." Le dita di Robby rimasero impigliate nella rete mentre calciava l'aria. "Va bene, basta così. *Ferma*."

"Scusa."

Si accomodò rivolto verso sua sorella, gli occhi socchiusi, le palpebre pesanti, rannicchiato in posizione fetale come a proteggere l'erezione. Vedere il pene di Robby non la turbava più. Dopo aver dato una mano in casa a curarlo per l'ultimo paio d'anni, aveva sviluppato un'elevata tolleranza allo schifo fraterno.

"Stavo bene, sai," gracchiò in direzione del robot-assistente; stava parlando con sua madre. "Mi avevi già fatto voltare stamattina, Rachel." Poi fece un cenno a Remeny: "Sono su tre schermi del suo desktop. Non posso nemmeno scoreggiare senza far scattare qualche allarme.”

“Le ho detto che si sta trasformando in una specie di overmamma.”

Un tremore involontario del capo fece spegnere il sorriso di Robby.

“Allora,” disse Remeny, “dici che possiamo fidarci di quel perdente di Toybox?”

“Sicuro.” Inspirò con voce roca. “Jason non è male in fondo.”

“Si chiama Jason, eh? È un coglione.”

Robby deglutì due volte in rapida successione. “*Ahhh*.”

“Dolore?” gli chiese.

“No.”

“Vuoi una pistola?” Da quando aveva subito l’aggressione, Robby aveva sviluppato una certa fascinazione per le vecchie pistole in casa. Come se averne una vera avrebbe potuto salvarlo. Eppure, tenerle in mano sembrava alleviare il suo stress, calmare gli spasmi.

“*No*.”

Remeny rimase in attesa che suo fratello aggiungesse qualcos’altro. Ma evidentemente oggi le toccava di essere ignorata dalla famiglia.

“Ti sei comportato in modo piuttosto strano con me, durante il progetto di gruppo,” alla fine fu Remeny a rompere il silenzio.

“Strano?”

“Quando hai detto ognuno per sé. Ho la trascrizione nella mia cartella. La rivoluzione non gioca secondo le regole.” Esagerò l’imitazione di Sturm. “‘Parla per te, Botão. Magari io sono un terrorista.’ Avanti, Sturm. Un *terrorista*? Hai intenzione di fare ad altri quel che hanno fatto a te?”

“Stronzi di destra,” mugugnò. “Pezzi di merda.”

“Di destra, di sinistra... sono tutti pezzi di merda.”

“Rivoluzione.” Non sembrava particolarmente interessato alla loro conversazione.

"Quale rivoluzione?" Ebbe l'impressione che suo fratello la stesse spingendo verso il ciglio di una scogliera. "Di che diavolo stai parlando?" Poi dalla sua lente notò che l'overlord di Robby aveva qualcosa di strano. Non stava ricevendo i crediti di tempo solido per la loro conversazione. "Aspetta un attimo," disse. "Hai ancora l'avatar attivo?"

"Huh?" Sembrava confuso. "Cosa?"

"Sono io," rispose. "Tua sorella." Remeny era impressionata e offesa al tempo stesso. Serviva una concentrazione straordinaria per gestire un avatar nel tempo fluido portando avanti contemporaneamente una conversazione nel tempo solido. "Credevi che non me ne sarei accorta?" Poi capì per quale motivo non l'aveva disattivato. "Sei con qualcuno."

"No."

"Scommetto che è la tua piccola Botton Brillante."

Robby si contorse, sollevò a fatica il braccio destro sfiorando la parte superiore della sua testa. "Cosa te lo fa credere?"

"Tanto per cominciare," rispose, "hai un'erezione esagerata."

"Un attimo. Dammi solo un secondo un secondo." Chiuse gli occhi e il suo corpo si afflosciò. Poi, con un tremore, tornò in sé. Il timer dell'overlord stava scorrendo. Ora Remeny aveva tutta la sua attenzione.

"È una cosa abbastanza perversa da dire a tuo fratello." Le rivolse una smorfia, ma lei sapeva che si trattava di un sorriso.

"Abbiamo il gene della perversione in comune, Sturmy." Ricambiò il sorriso. "Quindi Botão è la tua ragazza, ora?"

"Non ho nessuna ragazza." La sua voce era come carta vetrata. "È una snob della realtà come tutti gli altri. Voglio dire, supponiamo che volessimo davvero metterci insieme. Alla fine vorrà venirmi a trovare, per vedermi con i suoi occhi. Sai come funziona. Immaginala che se ne sta lì, a fissare questo sacco di carne tremante. Romantico eh?"

Remeny avrebbe voluto rispondere, ma non sapeva cosa dire.

"Credo che accetterò una pistola, ora," disse Robby. "La Glock di Kent."

Il loro padre teneva i suoi cimeli in uno studio dall'altra parte della casa. Aveva recitato nei film piatti dell'epoca, ma poi era passato ai flix, alle avventure e alle simulazioni, e perfino qualche personificazione. Sebbene avesse recitato in ruoli di ogni genere, Jeffrey Daugherty era principalmente noto per le sue parti da cattivo: serial killer, signori della droga, direttori esecutivi, stalker, e sì, anche terroristi. Aveva vinto un Golden Globe e un Appie per aver interpretato Ken Crill ne *Il vendicatore*, che era anche il ruolo in cui aveva ottenuto la maggior parte della sua collezione di armi di scena che teneva in mostra dietro la scrivania. Kent aveva usato quella Glock per distruggere il suo arcinemico, il vampiro sir Koko Mawatu, nel finale della quinta stagione. Ovviamente, era solo una replica, e non sparava davvero proiettili d'argento, ma aveva le dimensioni e il peso di una pistola vera.

Remeny si fece largo tra i fili ultra-lisci della rete e porse a suo fratello la pistola dall'impugnatura. Sturm fece scattare la mano verso l'arma; al primo tentativo mancò la presa, ma riuscì a raggiungerla con il secondo. Tornò ad adagiarsi, strofinandosi la canna d'acciaio sulla guancia. Remeny aveva assistito a quella sorta di feticismo per le armi molte volte, ma era ancora un aspetto di suo fratello che non riusciva a comprendere a fondo.

"Non è Toybox a preoccuparmi," disse Sturm. "Chi è questo Silk?"

"Non lo so, qualche ragazzino ricco." Si strinse nelle spalle. "A me non dispiace."

"A me sì."

"E perché? Perché vuole essere quello che prende le decisioni nel gruppo? Lo stesso vale per te. E per Toybox. Tutti voi ragazzi con questa storia del maschio alfa – sarebbe quasi carino, se non fosse così snervante."

"Ha già portato gli slogan nel tempo solido. Una dozzina di gonfiabili in giro per la città; devono essere i suoi. Nessun altro avrebbe il denaro sufficiente. Uno continua a girare intorno agli uffici del Comune."

Ecco, *questa* era un'informazione interessante. "Ha fatto davvero in fretta." Selezionò l'immagine satellitare dalla sua lente e ingrandì. "Ehi, quella sì che è un'insegna come si deve. Forse ha solo bisogno di qualche credito scolastico extra."

"È stata una sua idea. Non ti insospettisce?"

Si appoggiò al muro, e per l'ennesima volta desiderò che suo fratello le permettesse di portare una sedia quando lo andava a trovare. "No, non è vero. È stata Botão a uscirsene con vita, libertà e..."

"Sono solo parole." Puntò la pistola verso il robot-assistente e guardò nel mirino. "Gli slogan sono stati una sua idea."

"E allora? È un tipo sveglio," rispose Remeny armeggiando con la rete. "Hai detto a Botão chi sei?"

"Nah." Robby teneva la pistola ferma, e Remeny si accorse che con le labbra stava mimando la parola 'bang'. "Ma sa che sono sospeso."

"Lo sa ed è interessata comunque?"

"Crede di esserlo."

"Allora forse ti sbagli su di lei. Forse ha davvero una cotta per te. E se fossi sospeso in un centro per corpi, come Toybox? Credi che le piacerebbe assistere a qualsiasi cosa si nasconda dietro le porte della Komfort Kare?"

"Vorrebbe comunque..."

"Quello che vuole è Sturm, ed è questo che sei, ventitré ore al giorno su ventiquattro. Il tuo corpo è solo uno scarto."

Scoppiò in una risata amara. "Rah, rah, rah." Agitò la Glock in cerchio. "È un vero peccato che il tifo della mia fan numero uno non mi attenui più il dolore."

Adesso sì che Robby si stava comportando in modo strano. "Devo andare a fare una corsetta – ordini dell'overlord." Non riusciva a gestirlo quando si comportava in quel modo. "Rimarrai nel tempo solido per un po'?"

"Certo."

"Vuoi che ti lasci la pistola di Kent? Non si può mai sapere quando si farà vivo il tuo arcinemico."

"No, portala via." Fece passare la pistola tra le maglie della rete. "Troverò qualche altro modo per mandare all'aria il piano malvagio di Silk." Ora la sua mano era ben ferma.

"Avanti, sai che non è un problema." Gli si avvicinò, e gli soffiò sul viso. "Ci vediamo a cena, allora." Era la cosa più simile a un bacio che potessero permettersi.

"Qualcosa deve cambiare," disse Sturm.

"Sì, sì," rispose lei. "Viva la rivoluzione."

Mentre Remeny correva su Forest Ridge Road, sentiva la bomboletta spray di Sez nel marsupio che le rimbalzava sulla schiena. Aveva chiesto alla lente di individuare i luoghi che ammettevano la presenza di graffiti e che avessero un traffico pedonale il più alto possibile. La lista era breve, e la maggior parte di quei posti erano nel modesto centro di Bedford, a un paio di chilometri di distanza. Perciò i suoi graffiti si sarebbero sovrapposti agli annunci volanti di Silk, ma non era grave.

Iniziò a trovarsi tra i piedi robot per le faccende: robot per le consegne di Foodmaster, Amazon ed Express-It, un robot-cucina di McDonald's che puzzava di patatine e olio vecchio, un taxi libero che oziava su Little Oak. Il primo pedone che incrociò fu un anziano con tanto di respiratore intento a portare a spasso il cane. Vide la motocicletta dell'agente Shubin parcheggiata al Cocamoca, ma dell'agente non c'era traccia. Quando vide l'insegna gonfiabile che rimbalzava lungo la Terza Strada diretta verso di lei, si fermò. Il tozzo bot pubblicitario a forma di barile fluttuava ad altezza d'uomo, mentre lo slogan ruotava senza sosta intorno alla sua circonferenza. *Vita, Libertà e il Perseguimento della Felicità Vita, Libertà e...*

"Fermo," ordinò Remeny. Il propulsore superiore ruotò di centottanta gradi fino a trovarsi in posizione opposta rispetto a quello inferiore. "Ho una domanda."

"Cercherò di rispondere," scandì il gonfiabile.

"Chi ti ha pagato?"

"Sono stato assunto dal PDOT, che sta per Proteggere i Diritti degli Occupanti del Tempo fluido." Suonò un breve motivetto.

"Mai sentito nominare."

"L'organizzazione è nata da meno di due ore."

L'overlord la avvertì che il suo tasso metabolico stava crollando. Iniziò a saltellare sul posto. "Chi ne fa parte?"

"Le informazioni relative ai soci sono riservate."

"Per quanto tempo sei stato assunto?"

"Pubblicizzerò il nuovo ordine mondiale in quest'area urbana fino a martedì."

Nuovo ordine mondiale? Silk aveva manie di grandezza. "Che cosa significa: vita, libertà e il perseguimento della felicità?"

"Cosa significa per *te*?"

"Non lo so. Niente."

"L'obbiettivo del PDOT è quello di cambiare questa percezione. Se facessi una ricerca su Google…"

Remeny smise di prestare attenzione al bot e cercò di contattare Silk. Quando non ottenne risposta, interrogò la sua lente sull'affitto dei gonfiabili. Le tariffe andavano dai due ai trecento dollari al giorno, in base alle dimensioni del gonfiabile, alla complessità del messaggio e ai percorsi di vendita. Rimase esterrefatta. D'accordo, era ricco, ma quale adolescente al mondo avrebbe scelto di spendere duemila dollari al giorno per un progetto di gruppo?

"Hai altre domande?" chiese il bot.

D'impulso Remeny portò una mano verso il marsupio, afferrò la bomboletta di Sez e cercò di usarla per scrivere 'chiamami' sul gonfiabile. Quando il bot cercò di evitare la vernice, la "i" finale risultò in una "l" storta.

"Alle 1753," disse il gonfiabile, "sei stata identificata come Johanna Daugherty di Forest Ridge Road numero 7. In base all'Ordinanza di Bedford sulla deturpazione dei bot commerciali, ti verrà ora addebitata la tariffa standard per l'uso di questo dispositivo finché il tuo messaggio non autorizzato persisterà su di esso."

Remeny non era intimorita dalla multa; aveva impostato la bomboletta di Sez in modalità bozza. "Fai in modo che Silk riceva il mio messaggio."

"Che cos'è Silk?"

La scritta spray iniziava già a svanire, così terminò di ripulire il gonfiabile e riprese a correre lungo la Terza Strada.

"L'importo totale è di sessantasette centesimi," disse il bot alle sue spalle. "Buona giornata."

Più della metà dei negozi che davano su Memorial Square erano falliti. Per fare in modo che il centro non sembrasse un sorriso pieno di denti rotti, la città aveva fatto abbattere tutti gli edifici, ma ne aveva preservato e ristrutturato le facciate. Alle loro spalle ora c'erano spazi vuoti convertiti in prati, giardini e gazebo con tavoli da picnic, interamente gestiti da robot, ma completamente deserti. Nel centro cittadino c'erano anche degli spazi adibiti ai graffiti, a patto che carattere, colore e contenuto del messaggio fossero conformi alle linee guida. Remeny scrisse sulle assi delle panchine davanti al monumento della Guerra Civile, sulle finestre dell'Ufficio Postale e sulle spallette del ponte pedonale che attraversava Sperry Creek. Selezionò il carattere Incisione, dimensione 158, che secondo lei aveva un aspetto alquanto storico, e impostò la durata fino a martedì. Come aveva fatto Silk. *Vita, Libertà e il Perseguimento della Felicità* si affiancava in modo perfetto a scritte come *Il silenzio è d'oro, ma il nastro isolante è d'argento, Non siamo un robot* e *Pensa di Più a Lavorare di Meno*.

Per tornare a casa prese la scorciatoia che passava dal Centro di Apprendimento Gates Early, visto che nel cortile c'erano degli spazi adibiti ai graffiti. Alcuni bambini piccoli gironzolavano coi loro grossi caschetti per la realtà aumentata; strappavano l'erba, incespicavano sulle assi d'equilibrio e colpivano gli alberi con piccoli bastoni. Mentre Remeny scriveva sullo scivolo con la bomboletta, le si avvicinò una bambina.

"Come ti chiami?" Aveva una fastidiosa vocina stridula.

Non aveva tempo da perdere con roba del genere – dov'era la maestra? "Chiedi al tuo elmetto di dirti la mia identità."

"Perché? Non potresti rispondermi e basta?"

Remeny alzò lo sguardo e vide riccioli neri che incorniciavano un volto bianco come un fungo. Doveva avere cinque o forse sei anni, e indossava una maglietta di Dotty Karate. "Johanna."

"Io sono Meesha, ma il mio nome vero è Amisha." Indicò la scritta sullo scivolo. "Che cosa c'è scritto?"

"Leggila da sola." Quella ragazzina la stava deconcentrando.

"Non so farlo."

"Il tuo elmetto sì."

Si mise una mano davanti alla bocca e sussurrò la richiesta come se non volesse farsi sentire dalla stessa Remeny. "Non so che vuol dire perseguimento," disse infine.

"Il tuo elmetto potrebbe..." Remeny si guardò intorno in cerca d'aiuto e vide Joan deJean che si dirigeva verso di lei. "Vuol dire inseguire."

Meesha rifletté un istante. "È per questo che sei tutta sudata? Perché stai inseguendo la felicità?"

"Ciao, Johanna." La signorina deJean era stata la maestra di Johanna quand'era piccola. "Vedo che hai conosciuto Meesha." Appoggiò una mano sulla spalla della bambina.

"Salve, signorina deJean. Già, scommetto che nessuno l'ha mai accusata di essere timida."

"Puoi dirlo forte." La signorina voltò con dolcezza la bambina indirizzandola verso i suoi compagni. "È il momento di imparare, Meesha. Non di chiacchierare."

"Ma chiacchierando s'impara," replicò la bambina.

"Fila via." Le diede una spintarella verso il centro del cortile, ma Meesha si divincolò e corse in un'altra direzione. "Allora, che cosa stavi scrivendo?" La signorina deJean si avvicinò allo scivolo per leggere il messaggio.

Remeny infilò la bomboletta nel marsupio. "Progetto di gruppo."

"Di già?" La sua anziana maestra sospirò. "Sembra ieri che te ne andavi in giro in questo cortile, a dare rispostacce come Meesha." Il suo volto sembrò illuminarsi al ricordo. "Tu e tuo fratello. Come sta Robby?"

"Non esce granché."

"Già." La luce sul suo volto si affievolì. "La Dichiarazione d'Indipendenza? Volete emanciparvi da qualcosa?"

"Non lo so," rispose Remeny, poi scoppiò a ridere. "Forse dagli EOS."

"Buon per voi." Joan deJean rise insieme alla ragazza. "È un vero disastro, se vuoi sapere la mia. Tutti software e niente persone."

Di solito Remeny percorreva la Forest Ridge Road per riprendere fiato al termine della corsa, ma quando vide sua madre e Emily Banerjee sedute sul prato dei Banerjee accelerò il passo. Sua madre aveva un braccio sulla spalla dell'anziana signora e le stava parlando a bassa voce.

"Tutto bene?" Remeny si fermò davanti alle due donne.

"Emily non si sente bene," disse sua madre. "È confusa."

I Banerjee erano già pezzi d'antiquariato quando i Daugherty si erano trasferiti nel quartiere; rugosi e dolci, avevano visto crescere sia Remeny che Robby. Sadhir Banerjee era morto a marzo, e da allora sua moglie sembrava essersi smarrita. Il mese prima la madre di Remeny era stata costretta a chiamare il figlio Prahlad dopo aver trovato la signora Banerjee che frugava nella spazzatura dei Daugherty in piena notte.

"Non sono confusa," disse la signora Banerjee, "e non mi farò mettere mai in una di quelle bare."

"Nessuno vuole che tu lo faccia, Emily."

"L'ho visto alla teevee – poco fa. Quelle bare sono troppo piccole." Aprì i palmi delle mani. "Più o meno sono larghe così. E poco più lunghe." Il modo in cui le sue mani tremavano ricordò a Remeny di suo fratello. "Li mettono nelle bare che sono ancora svegli, così possono stare sempre in contatto con altre persone su Internet, ma non c'è abbastanza spazio. Non per tutti. Anche Internet è troppo piccolo, perfino per una donna anziana come me."

Teevee? Internet? Remeny non voleva mettersi a ridere perché tutto ciò era alquanto triste. Ma cavolo, si parlava davvero di roba d'altri tempi.

"Tranquilla, Emily," disse sua madre. "Prahlad sarà qui presto."

"Sì, va tutto bene, signora Banerjee," aggiunse Remeny. "Non deve per forza rimanere in contatto con altra gente, se non vuole."

La signora Banerjee alzò lo sguardo su Remeny. "Sei tu, sei quella ragazza. La figlia di Rachel. Non avevi anche un fratello?" La indicò con aria accusatoria. "Non vediamo più i tuoi figli giocare da queste parti."

"Johanna, va tutto bene. Siamo grandi ormai."

"Hai presente quelle bare? E la gente che ci sta dentro?" La signora Banerjee si chinò verso Remeny. "Sai come la chiamano?" Abbassò la voce. "Trappole. Lo giuro; Sadhir era insieme a me, l'ha sentito anche lui."

Remeny e sua madre si scambiarono un'occhiata.

"Vuole dire le capsule?" disse Remeny.

"Capsule?" La signora Banerjee spostò il peso all'indietro e per un istante fissò il cielo ormai scuro. "Sì. Forse era quella la parola." Annuì. "Capsule." Arricciò la bocca come se stesse assaporando quel termine.

I Daguherty si ritrovarono per una delle loro cene di famiglia settimanali nel tempo fluido, perché il padre era spesso fuori per lavoro e Robby non poteva lasciare la sua stanza, e tantomeno sedersi a un tavolo per mangiare. Inoltre, a Remeny la dieta liquida iperproteica da duemila calorie al giorno di suo fratello sembrava una miscela di cemento. Aveva un aspetto per nulla appetitoso. La madre aveva comprato uno spazio nel dominio di famiglia con una replica esatta della sala da pranzo di Forest Ridge Road 7. Un tavolo da buffet con la superficie in marmo accanto a un armadietto con le ante in vetro. Il loro tavolo da pranzo poteva ospitare comodamente dieci persone, ma al momento c'erano solo le quattro sedie imbottite, raggruppate intorno a un'estremità. I mobili erano tutti d'acero scuro, e seguivano una qualche moda dei vecchi tempi che prevedeva intarsi arabeschi, fiordalisi e colonne corinzie. Il pasto virtuale che nessuno avrebbe mangiato veniva dal periodo più buio del ventesimo secolo: un piatto di pollo arrosto – con tanto di *ossa* – ciotole con purè di patate e fagiolini con cipolline e un cestino di panini. Remeny credeva che quello spettacolo non fosse altro che uno spreco di potenza di calcolo; il tempo fluido era nato per sfidare i limiti della realtà, non per imitarla. Ma si trattava di un desiderio di sua madre, e il padre l'aveva sempre assecondata. Robby e Remeny non avevano voce in capitolo.

"Oggi i ragazzi hanno lavorato sul loro progetto di gruppo," disse la madre.

"Sono finiti nello stesso gruppo?" Al padre piaceva partecipare a queste cene con un coltello in una mano e una forchetta nell'altra, anche se il cibo virtuale non poteva essere consumato. I ragazzi avrebbero potuto far mangiare i loro avatar, ma i loro genitori, e la madre in particolare, dovevano ancora imparare i trucchi dell'immersione totale. "Come mai?"

"Solo fortuna, suppongo." La cena di Remeny consisteva nel frullato di banana avanzato e una manciata di taccole. Stava mangiando in camera sua.

"Allora, di cosa si tratta?"

"In realtà è abbastanza noioso." Dopo averne discusso con Robby quel pomeriggio, Remeny sperava che l'argomento del progetto di gruppo non saltasse fuori anche a cena.

"No, non è vero." Suo fratello aprì il loro canale privato con un bip (.4) d'impazienza. =*Dovremmo dirglielo. Subito.*=

=*Ma così vorranno parlarne per tutta la sera. Più tardi volevo uscire.*=

"Ha a che fare con la Dichiarazione d'Indipendenza, giusto?" A quando pare Rachel aveva prestato attenzione, in fin dei conti.

=*Con Silk?*=

=Non sono affari tuoi.=

"Ah sì," commentò loro padre. "Noi, il popolo, bla bla bla, al fine di perfezionare la nostra Unione di chisseneimporta." Remeny sperava che il padre distogliesse l'attenzione dalla conversazione, come succedeva ogni volta. "Mi sono sempre chiesto come si potesse perfezionare qualcosa che è già perfetto. Una volta ho interpretato James Madison, sapete; era un gamberetto, alto cinque piedi e quattro pollici – quanto sarebbe in metri?"

"Centosessantadue centimetri." Nonostante Robby stesse usando la versione di Sturm "adatta ai genitori" – niente cicatrici, niente iridescenza – Remeny si accorse del su nervosismo.

"Più o meno quanto Johanna." L'avatar del padre indossava una camicia hawaiana con un motivo a barche a vela. Come al solito, era uguale al se stesso del tempo solido; bello come un qualsiasi ottantatreenne che poteva permettersi le tecniche chirurgiche e i trattamenti di ringiovanimento più avanzati. Ma bisognava ricordare che la sua immagine faceva parte del suo marchio. "No, aspetta. Ho sbagliato." Puntò il coltello verso Remeny, come se la figlia fosse a un passo dal correggerlo. "'Perfezionare la nostra unione' è la Costituzione. La Dichiarazione era quella di Jefferson. Lui era alto, sia lui che Washington. Non ho mai interpretato Washington. Avrei voluto, ma non mi è mai capitato, nonostante l'altezza simile."

"Vogliamo dichiarare la nostra indipendenza," disse Robby.

=*Sturm, non farlo.*=

L'intervento di Robby arrestò il padre. "E chi sareste?" Aggrottò la fronte. "Un gruppo di adolescenti?"

"Tutti quelli che sono sospesi. Vogliamo abbandonare il tempo solido – la realtà. Vogliamo continuare a vivere unicamente come avatar."

"Fico." Era il commento più sbagliato che potesse scegliere. Remeny si chiese se per caso suo padre non stesse mangiando un pezzo di pizza chissà dove senza prestare attenzione alla conversazione.

"E come pensate di riuscirci?" Sembrava che l'avatar della madre avesse appena ingoiato un mattone.

"Lo faremo e basta. Rimarremo sospesi." Robby rivolse loro un bip (.6) d'impazienza. "Non ci scollegheremo mai più."

"Niente bip a tavola, per favore." La madre aveva un'idea di buone maniere tutta sua. "Non volete più tornare indietro – *mai più*?"

Remeny iniziò a rispondere: "Solo se ne avremo voglia..." ma Robby la interruppe. "Mai più." Allontanò la sedia dal tavolo e si alzò in piedi, un gesto che a Remeny sembrò ben più maleducato di un bip. "E vogliamo essere liberi di accelerare il tempo. Vivere nel doppio del tempo. Nel tempo triplo. Tutto quello che vogliamo."

"Ora stai dicendo stupidaggini," disse la madre. "Il tuo cervello non è un computer, Robert. La dilatazione temporale causa convulsioni. E rimanere sospesi è faticoso per il corpo. Il tasso di mortalità per..."

"È per questo che vogliamo vivere nel tempo dilatato," gridò. "Potremmo vivere diversi anni soggettivi prima che marcisca la carne."

La madre non aveva parole per il fatto che avesse usato la parola che inizia per c a tavola. La stessa Remeny non riusciva a crederci.

"Siediti, Robby." Il padre non sembrava arrabbiato. Si limitò a grattarsi il mento con la forchetta in attesa che il figlio si calmasse. Robby obbedì malvolentieri. "Buffo che sia uscito questo discorso a tavola. Vedete, stamattina ero in Vermont con Spencer..."

"*Jeff*." La madre sembrava sentirsi tradita.

"Pirati nel Vermont?" chiese Remeny.

=*Non dargli corda.*= Per quel che riguardava quella faccenda Robby la pensava come Rachel. =*Vediamo di farla finita.*=

"Avevo finito in anticipo le riprese de *La nave del tesoro*." Scosse la testa. "I bastardi hanno tagliato metà delle mie scene. Quindi ecco, me ne stavo nella residenza estiva di Steve Spencer in Vermont, e lui mi sottopone un'idea in cui le persone vogliono fare esattamente quello di cui sta parlando Robby. Ha già un soggetto pronto da inviare e tutto il resto. Finanziarlo non sarà un problema, dice che basteranno sessanta milioni per far partire il progetto. Be', diciamo pure che sessanta milioni sono sufficienti ad attirare la mia attenzione. L'idea di base è che ci sono delle persone che vogliono vivere nella realtà virtuale..."

Remeny alzò la mano per correggerlo. "Tempo fluido."

"Già, certo. E non vogliono più uscirne. È una storia pazzesca. Si tagliano braccia e gambe e cose del genere, tutte le parti del corpo di cui dichiarano di non avere bisogno, e io gli ho detto che sembrava un film horror, che non è un genere di cui mi occupo di solito, ma Steve ha detto di no. Il soggetto parla chiaro. È un cavolo di problema sociale! A quanto pare esistono davvero delle persone convinte che sia una cosa positiva. Persone che possono trovare sessanta milioni di dollari senza problemi. Ne sapevi niente, Rachel?"

Scosse la testa.

"Com'è possibile che non se ne sappia nulla?"

"Perché siamo solo *alcune* persone, per adesso," rispose Robby. "Non siamo ancora *abbastanza* persone."

"E hai davvero intenzione di farlo," continuò la madre. Remeny si domandò con chi stesse parlando. Con papà? Con Robby? Forse con entrambi? Sembrava quasi che si fosse calmata, ma un istante dopo il suo avatar si bloccò del tutto. Remeny portò l'attenzione sulle telecamere di casa e la vide al vero tavolo della sala da pranzo con un piatto di tortellini davanti a sé. Aveva messo in pausa l'interfaccia Deveau. Stava piangendo.

"Mi beccherei una bella parte." Il padre non aveva notato che la madre si era disconnessa. "Dovrei interpretare un senatore contro la proposta. Non ho mai interpretato un senatore prima d'ora. Un presidente, sì. Anche un sindaco. È solo una parte secondaria, ma è coinvolto Frederick Nooney, e Gonslaves sarà il regista. Ho detto a Steve che gli avrei fatto sapere entro domani, ma questa... è una specie di coincidenza o cosa?"

"Dovresti accettare," disse Robby. "Assolutamente. Qual è il titolo?"

"Il titolo provvisorio è *Dichiarazione*, ma non decollerà mai."

Per poco Remeny non si strozzò con una taccola. Robby scoppiò a ridere.

Poi il padre fece qualcosa che Remeny non credeva che un ottantatreenne della vecchia scuola sapesse fare. Aprì un canale di comunicazione privato con lui nel tempo fluido.

=Ci sei, figliolo?=

=Forse.=

Quello che non sapeva fare, però, era chiudere il canale privato che Remeny aveva aperto poco prima con suo fratello, così la ragazza riuscì a origliare tutto. *=Ascolta, Robby, se è questo che vuoi, io ti sosterrò. So che sei in preda al dolore e alla tristezza.=*

=Solo quando sono bloccato nel tempo solido.=

=Lo capisco. Da quel giorno, non abbiamo fatto altro che cercare di aiutarti.= I suoi bip di compassione erano a (.8). *=So che è difficile per te, ma lo è anche per noi. Tua madre si ritiene responsabile per averti mandato...=*

=Papà, smettila. Ti voglio bene, ma smettila. Se davvero vuoi aiutarmi allora accetta quella maledetta parte. Farà bene alla causa. La mia causa, papà. Ma quello che voglio davvero è che torni a casa e ci dia una mano con mamma. Perché la realtà fa davvero schifo, e io inizio a non farcela più. Dobbiamo fare in modo che la mamma capisca. Tutti noi, faccia a faccia. Alla vecchia maniera.=

"Smettila di dire che ti dispiace." Sturm stava cercando di fare il duro, ma i suoi bip tradivano l'imbarazzo.

"È solo che non volevo che mamma desse di matto," rispose Remeny

"Be', invece è andata proprio così, ma non è morto nessuno. Anzi, direi che è una vittoria per noi."

"Credi che papà riuscirà a convincerla?"

"È un attore," Sturm scansionò le persone che affollavano la pista da ballo in cerca di Silk. "Sono certo che sfoggerà la sua migliore interpretazione."

Le note metalliche riverberarono nell'aria, e le coppie iniziarono a prendere i propri posti.

"Sono passati nove minuti," disse Sturm. "E ancora nessuna traccia di lui."

"Non c'era nessun appuntamento." L'irritazione di Remeny salì a (.3). "Non è mica un treno."

"*Un inchino al vostro compagno, ora all'angolo. Prendetevi tutti per mano e ruotate in cerchio verso sinistra. Attenti, non calpestatelo, ora girate a destra, e continuiamo a girare e girare.*"

Adesso che era abbastanza grande, Remeny era disgustata dalla quadriglia. Quando aveva dodici anni, ForSquare era uno dei parcogiochi degli EOS che preferiva. Adorava quei movimenti, il colore e la concentrazione necessaria per ricordare ed eseguire tutte le indicazioni. A sedici anni, era arrivata seconda alla Gara della contea di Jefferson. Quel giorno il caller diede più di venti indicazioni diverse, come ad esempio modificare l'avatar in corsa, oltre a più di duecento istruzioni tradizionali. Davvero tantissime da ricordare, ma qual era lo scopo? In fondo era solo un modo per insegnare ai bambini come usare le loro interfacce mentre si divertivano.

"*Adesso passeggiata, passeggiata lunga.*" Dalla pista presero a spuntare stalagmiti di cristallo mentre i ballerini vi danzavano intorno.

La musica era talmente assordante che bisognava urlare per farsi sentire. I bambini non avevano problemi, visto che erano talmente piccoli che non avevano nulla da dirsi. Ma ora che aveva diciott'anni, Remeny preferiva locali più silenziosi, come Sanctuary. Erano più indicati per flirtare.

Un attimo dopo Remeny individuò Botão, rivolgendole un cenno di saluto. La ragazza evitò i ballerini e raggiunse i suoi amici.

"Eccomi, ma non posso rimanere. Sto facendo da babysitter alle mie sorelline." Il suo avatar indossava una maglietta con su scritto *Vita Libertà e il Perseguimento della Felicità*.

"Mi piace." Remeny le toccò la manica della maglietta.

"Già." Botão tese il bordo inferiore della maglietta in modo da poterla ammirare anche lei. "Le ho progettate insieme a mia madre, poi ne ho stampate una decina nel nostro fab di casa, taglie sei e sette. Le porterò al Gates Center domani e le farò distribuire dalle maestre ai bambini in modo che possano portarle a casa. Costano meno di dieci dollari.”

“Anche io sono capitata da quelle parti oggi.”

“Oddio, e se ci fossimo incontrate?” Si finse atterrita per prenderla in giro. “Se vuoi sapere la mia, secondo me tutta la faccenda dell’identità segreta è una scemenza. È solo un modo di quelli della vecchia scuola per non farci unire le forze contro di loro.” Si strusciò contro Sturm. “E tu che ne pensi, Sturm? O mi stai ignorando di proposito?”

“Hai dimenticato la virgola,” disse, “e non ti stavo ignorando. Stavo cercando Silk.”

“Stronzo.” Botão era sbalordita. “Fai come ti pare.” E si allontanò da lui.

“Cosa sai di Silk?” le chiese Sturm.

=*Che diamine stai combinando?*= Remeny inviò a Robby un messaggio privato.

=*Credo che sia coinvolta.*=

=*Coinvolta in cosa?*=

“Perché dovrei dirlo a te?,” ribatté Botão.

“Perché Silk non è chi dice di essere.”

Il bip innervosito di Botão aveva un tono sarcastico. “Nessuno qui è chi dice di essere.”

“È stato lui a dirti di proporre quello slogan?”

“Ah, ho capito. Non sono abbastanza intelligente da avere un’idea tutta mia. Vediamo un po’, è perché sono una ragazza? O perché sono *uma brasileira?*”

“Eccolo.” Remeny indicò Silk, che era entrato insieme a un paio di avatar che non aveva mai visto prima.

“*Ora voltatevi tutti, e iniziate a girare su voi stessi, ora più lenti, e i ragazzi formino una stella...*” Alcuni degli avatar sulla pista da ballo trasformarono le loro scarpe in pattini a rotelle; altri si fecero spuntare delle rotelle dalle gambe. “*Bravi, siate le nostre stelle, e continuate a girare.*” Uno dei ragazzi nella formazione a stella scivolò e finì addosso al ballerino accanto. Le ragazze applaudirono e ridacchiarono, ma il caller non accennò a fermarsi. *"Va tutto bene, non abbiamo tempo per i rimpianti, rimettetevi in piedi e tornate in pista."*

Silk si materializzò accanto a Remeny. "Il nostro incontro è previsto per martedì," disse, "ma già che ci siamo... Non vedo Toybox."

"Lascialo fuori da questa faccenda," disse Sturm.

"Ah, così ora sei tu a dare gli ordini?" Disse un con un velato bip ironico.

"Credo che ci sia una cospirazione in corso, e che tu ne faccia parte. Mi stai manipolando. Stai manipolando tutti noi."

"Parla per te," disse Botão.

"Come può trattarsi di manipolazione..." Silk aprì le mani. "... se state facendo quello che avreste voluto fare in ogni caso? Tu ci credi, Sturm, so che è così."

"Ma io no," intervenne Botão, "e per quanto mi riguarda puoi prenderti la tua cospirazione o rivoluzione o quello che è e ficcartela su per il culo." Botão si strappò la maglietta di dosso per lanciarla addosso a Silk, generando all'istante un rimpiazzo; una maglietta della Seleçao Brasileira di calcio. "Troverò un altro gruppo, Remeny? Sei con me?"

Colta di sorpresa, Remeny si accorse che avrebbe voluto rispondere di sì, che in realtà aveva paura di quel che Silk e Sturm avevano intenzione di fare a se stessi. Le piaceva essere un avatar, certo, ma non era così che avrebbe voluto vivere il resto della sua vita. Non se implicava finire in una di quelle capsule. Iniziò ad avvicinarsi a Botão.

=Aspetta.= Sturm sembrava disperato.

Ma Silk non esitò un solo istante. "Non puoi abbandonare," disse. "Non vuoi vivere la tua vita nel tempo fluido? Sei tu quella che voleva creare il proprio dominio per non tornare più reale."

"No." Botão lanciò un'occhiata furiosa a tutti e tre e Remeny si vergognò di essere associata ai ragazzi. "Stavo solo dicendo che mi piacciono *sia* il mondo reale *che* la RV." Con la musica alta del locale, fu costretta ad alzare la voce per farsi sentire, ma ora le persone che avevano intorno iniziavano a origliare. Il che non fece altro che convincerla a parlare più forte. "Non so come la pensiate voi segaioli, ma a me piace il sesso, il sesso alla vecchia maniera, quello che probabilmente non fate mai; avete presente, quello che si fa toccandosi, baciandosi e... coccolandosi." Il suo bip di rabbia risuonò con forza. "E un giorno voglio avere dei figli miei."

Nella sua stanza, Remeny sentì le lacrime bagnarle gli occhi. Era d'accordo con tutto quello che stava dicendo Botão – tranne forse la parte sui figli. Ma se si fosse opposta avrebbe ferito Robby, e suo fratello aveva già sofferto abbastanza. Non era giusto, *non era affatto giusto*, ma in fondo non c'era nulla di giusto nella sua vita. Era stata talmente occupata a interpretare la parte della brava sorella per Robby, che si era dimenticata come essere se stessa.

"Ma stiamo facendo un favore ai tuoi figli," disse Silk. "E ai tuoi nipoti."

Il caller aveva smesso di dare istruzioni, e la musica si era interrotta. Tutti i presenti li stavano ascoltando. Remeny era certa che li avrebbero sbattuti fuori. O peggio.

"Su questo pianeta ci sono nove miliardi di persone sospese," continuò Silk. "La maggior parte di noi non avrà mai figli. Pensiamo che sia una cosa positiva. E i sospesi non consumano risorse come te e i tuoi figli. Stiamo salvando il pianeta. Tutto ciò che chiediamo è di vivere la vita secondo le nostre scelte."

"*Avatar Silk e Botão, state disturbando questo parco giochi.*" Il monito del caller si intromise nella discussione come un allarme antincendio. "*Smettetela subito o ci saranno conseguenze.*"

"D'accordo." Botão alzò le mani in segno di resa. "Hai delle idee valide. Ma una rivoluzione? No. Non hai mai visto che male può fare una rivoluzione. Io sì." Poi unì con forza le mani e il suo avatar scomparve.

Era come se tutti tranne Silk stessero trattenendo il respiro. Si inginocchiò, raccolse la maglietta scartata e la sollevò. "Vita, libertà e il perseguimento della felicità," disse. "Un giorno. Non ho altro da dire. Nel frattempo, mi scuso con tutti voi."

La musica ripartì. La folla riprese con il suo brusio.

"Scusa." Un ragazzino con uno stupido cappello da mago toccò il gomito di Sturm. "Di cosa stavano discutendo?"

Sturm lo allontanò e strappò la T-shirt dalle mani di Silk. "Tu e io abbiamo ancora una faccenda in sospeso."

"È vero. Ma che mi dici di tua sorella?"

Sturm si pietrificò. "Che cos'hai detto?" Chiese trattenendo un bip di rabbia.

"Non giochiamo secondo le regole, ricordi? È così che funziona una rivoluzione." Silk stava forse sorridendo? "Dico sul serio, però, dovremmo discuterne altrove. Conosco un posto."

"Bastardo arrogante. Perché dovremmo fidarci di te?"

"Perché sei intelligente? Perché hai bisogno di noi?" Stava ignorando Remeny di proposito. "Possiamo lasciarla qui, se vuoi."

"Io sono qui," intervenne Remeny, nonostante le sembrasse di trovarsi nel sogno di qualcun altro. "Non comportatevi come se non ci fossi." Diede un colpetto a Sturm. "Tutti e due."

"E va bene," concluse Silk. "Forza, andiamocene."

Remeny rimase sorpresa dal fatto che Toybox potesse permettersi un dominio tutto suo, anche se il suo gusto nelle decorazioni era proprio quello che si sarebbe aspettata. Il pavimento del suo spazio era fatto d'osso, i muri di fuoco e il soffitto di fumo. Il suo avatar, momentaneamente abbandonato e vestito con abiti sgargianti, se ne stava appollaiato su un trono dorato in stile barocco; di sicuro era una specie di copia. Remeny lo cercò e scoprì che si trattava del seggio di San Pietro che si trova all'interno della Basilica di San Pietro, parte di un altare progettato da Bernini. Non sembrava c'entrasse granché con il gusto di Toybox, finché non consultò un link secondario: la gente lo chiamava il Trono di Satana. Davanti al trono c'erano no divani e sedie che sembravano ricavati da cadaveri contorti.

Erano disposti tutt'intorno a una bara di vetro, sulla quale si trovavano una bottiglia d'assenzio aperta, un decanter in cristallo pieno d'acqua, quattro coppe identiche con cucchiaini fessurati, e un piattino pieno di zollette di zucchero. Nella bara c'era il corpo sospeso di Jason Day, o perlomeno quello che secondo Remeny era una copia discretamente accurata. Non era granché impressionante da guardare: la maschera d'ossigeno e il sondino gastrico gli nascondevano la maggior parte del volto, e il corpo non era deteriorato quanto quello di altre persone sospese. Aveva ancora le braccia e le gambe, ma Jason Day era minorenne, e probabilmente doveva disconnettersi e lasciare la sua bara per diverse ore al giorno. Il che voleva dire che non poteva ancora avere un'interfaccia cranica come quella di Sturm. La sua Deveau aveva una gamma di sensori più ampia rispetto alla Neurosky 3100 ed era connessa alla presa del corpo che monitorava i suoi segni vitali.

"Dov'è?" Sturm fece un cenno verso l'avatar inattivo di Toybox.

"Non lo so," rispose Silk. "A incespicare da qualche parte nel tempo solido? Sono certo che si farà vivo presto. Nel frattempo, dovete promettere che non ci tradirete."

"Regole?," intervenne Remeny. "Non ci stavi dicendo che le rivoluzioni non seguono le regole?"

"Mi dispiace, ma o promettete o la chiudiamo qui."

"Va bene, va bene. Promettiamo." Sturm si chinò e finse di interessarsi al Seggio di San Pietro. "Basta che la finiamo con questa storia."

"Johanna?"

"Remeny per te. Come fai a sapere che manterrò la parola?"

"Abbiamo fatto i nostri compiti." Cercò di convincerla con un sorriso. "Il che significa che mi fido di te più di quanto tu ti fidi di me." Remeny si vergognò al pensiero che appena qualche ora prima l'approccio avrebbe funzionato.

Trasformò uno dei disgustosi divani di Toybox in una panchina del parco e si sedette. "Prometto."

"Ti ringrazio. La prima cosa che dovete sapere è che ci sono tantissimi come noi. Non abbastanza, certo, ma siamo sempre di più. Sapevate che quando Jefferson scrisse la prima dichiarazione, solo circa un terzo dei coloni era a favore dell'indipendenza? Un terzo era fedele al re e un altro terzo era indeciso. Il punto è che non dobbiamo per forza convincere tutti, intesi?"

Toybox tremolò sul trono e aprì gli occhi. "Che mi sono perso?"

Remeny trattenne un bip di disappunto.

"Abbiamo appena iniziato." Silk sembrava irritato per l'interruzione.

"Il contatto è andato bene?"

"Più o meno come ci aspettavamo. Botão ha mollato."

"Ma questi due hanno abboccato, a quanto pare." Toybox si strofinò tra le mani. "Avrei voluto esserci, ma il maledetto overlord... be', sapete come funziona. E poi, Silk dice che non sono ancora pronto per un contatto. Devo lavorare sui miei problemi." Scese dal trono e raggiunse la bara. "Assenzio?"

Remeny si spostò sulla sua panchina per allontanarsi da Toybox. Aprì il canale privato con Robby. =*Deve per forza parlare anche lui?*=

=*Assecondali. Hanno corso un bel rischio.*= Sturm si unì a loro. "Io ne prendo un po'." Mise una zolletta di zucchero su uno dei cucchiaini fessurati e l'appoggiò su un bicchiere.

"Per favore, possiamo arrivare al punto?," chiese Remeny. Provò una piacevole sensazione nel chiudere le mani a pugno, come se almeno avesse il controllo di *qualcosa*. "Che cosa ci stai chiedendo di fare?"

"Di reclutare," rispose Silk. "Praticamente quello che stavamo facendo nel progetto di gruppo – e in tutta la contea. Parlate con i bambini. Fate amicizia. Diffondete il nostro punto di vista."

"Io sono salito a bordo il mese scorso," disse Toybox. "La cosa più facile che abbia mai fatto."

"D'accordo," disse Sturm. "Ma ci stiamo per diplomare."

"Dici?"

Remeny e Sturm si fissarono l'un l'altro. =*Oh, merda.*=

"Siamo stati bocciati al progetto di gruppo." La gioia di Toybox era (.7). "Di proposito. Non è fichissimo?"

Stavolta Remeny non riuscì a trattenersi. "Non dev'essere stato difficile per te."

Sturm scolò in un unico sorso il suo assenzio virtuale. "Quindi siamo bloccati nell'inferno degli EOS per sempre."

"È possibile riprovare i progetti di gruppo solo un certo numero di volte," disse Silk, "anche se possiamo darvi una mano a rimanere qui un po' più a lungo. Possiamo fare in modo che la maggior parte dei ragazzini assegnati ai vostri gruppi siano solidali con i sospesi. Modificare l'aspetto degli avatar può farci guadagnare tempo. Prima o poi dovrete diplomarvi *per forza*, in ogni caso. A quel punto, se vorrete, ci sarà un altro incarico per voi."

Remeny era senza parole per le gigantesche conseguenze di quello che stava dicendo Silk. E chi era, in realtà? Quanti anni aveva? Viveva almeno nella contea di Jefferson?

"Tutto ciò avviene su base volontaria, sappiatelo, potrete tirarvi indietro in qualsiasi momento. Ma non vorrete farlo. Siamo impegnatissimi su ogni fronte, con tutti i gruppi demografici. Molti di noi vivono nel tempo dilatato, e possono pensare molto di più rispetto a quelli che trascorrono la maggior parte delle loro vite nel tempo solido. E, Remeny, non siamo tutti sospesi. Molti di noi vivono nel mondo reale. Magari hanno fratelli, sorelle, o madri o padri..."

"Aspetta," disse Remeny. "I nostri genitori non si insospettiranno se verremo continuamente bocciati nei progetti di gruppo?"

"A volte succede." Silk annuì.

"Ai miei genitori non frega un cazzo," intervenne Toybox. "Anche loro sono sospesi."

"A volte i ragazzi riescono a convertire i loro genitori," continuò Silk.

"Fammi indovinare." Robby alzò una mano per interromperlo. "E a volte punti a convertire intere famiglie tutte insieme."

Toybox ridacchiò.

"Famiglie speciali ottengono attenzioni speciali."

Remeny ripensò a Steve Spencer nella sua casa in Vermont e al flix da sessanta milioni di dollari di Vincente Gonsalves e all'ultimatum di Robby. Che cos'era più importante per suo padre, la parte o la ricerca della felicità di suo figlio? Riflettere su quelle domande le fece venire un gran mal di testa.

"Quindi più o meno questo è l'accordo," disse Silk. "Sarei felice di raccontarvi altro, ma prima vorrei sapere cosa vi passa per la testa in questo momento."

Il silenzio si dilatò. Remeny non riusciva a guardare Robby. Abbandonò il loro canale di comunicazione privato. Sentiva solo di volersi chiudere a riccio. Avrebbe fatto parlare prima lui. Ma sapeva cos'avrebbe detto. Era suo fratello. Lo *sapeva*.

"Sono interessato."

"Bravo ragazzo." Silk si avvicinò e si sedette sul divano accanto a Remeny. "E tu, Johanna?" Che cos'aveva visto in lui? "Vogliamo anche te, nel modo più assoluto." Se avesse provato a toccarla, gli avrebbe assestato un ceffone sulla mano.

D'impulso, Remeny si sfilò il Neurosky dalla testa e Silk, Toybox e Sturm scomparvero all'improvviso. Era quasi mezzanotte. Per quella serata avrebbe avuto un debito non indifferente nei confronti del suo overlord. Si alzò e si stiracchiò nella sua stanza buia. Nella sua casa. Decise di non accendere luci né di portare con sé degli auricolari. La madre e il padre erano quasi sicuramente addormentati, ma aprì la porta che dava sul corridoio come se fosse fatta di vetro, e sgattaiolò verso la camera di Robby. Adesso era felice di non essersene andata dal ForSquare insieme a Botáo. Era importante che comprendesse cosa Silk voleva offrire a Robby. Il perseguimento della felicità. Nella forma di Sturm.

Ma la felicità di suo fratello non coincideva con la sua, e non c'era nulla di sbagliato in ciò. In fin dei conti Silk le aveva regalato qualcosa, anche se non poteva accettare la sua offerta. Avrebbe avuto la sua vita, e la libertà dal dolore di suo fratello.

Johanna si avvicinò a Robby e gli soffiò sul viso.

Addio.

Sturm fremette, ma non si svegliò.

Per settimane, Sprite si era ripetuta che Ratchanee Malakul stava solo aiutando il suo eroe a guarire, ma le cose non stavano così. "Devi accettarlo, Jaran non farà mai sesso con te," le aveva detto la salvavita quell'ultimo giorno prima di andarsene.

"Ma io sono la sua assistente!" Sprite sentiva il suo nucleo digitale fremere in preda allo choc. "Sono programmata per soddisfare i suoi bisogni."

"Non gli fa bene." Ratchanee si strinse nelle spalle coperte dal parka. "E non fa bene nemmeno a te." Scelse casualmente la sua skin, le rivolse un cenno di saluto e si chiuse la porta alle spalle.

"Ti sbagli," rispose Sprite nel corridoio ormai vuoto. "Ti sbagli, ti sbagli, ti sbagli!" Si rese conto di quel che era appena successo. Ratchanee Malakul aveva accecato Jaran con la sua bellezza. D'altronde era impossibile che qualcuno non apprezzasse il naso schiacciato della salvavita, le sue labbra tumide e sensuali. I suoi riccioli argentei che contrastavano con il blu profondo della sua pelle. Era chiaro che la donna voleva Jaran tutto per sé!

Ma possibile che Ratchanee Malakul avesse detto la verità? Per quello Jaran l'aveva baciata una volta sola. Un misero bacetto! All'interno di una simulazione! E da allora non l'aveva mai più sfiorata! Aveva provato a trasferire il proprio nucleo nei sexy-telai che preferiva, ondeggiando davanti a lui. Meraviglia tattile! Carezza liquida! A suo fratello Dom quei telai piacevano da impazzire. Forse per Jaran non era una compagna alla sua altezza? Monitorava tutti i suoi aggiornamenti di lavoro, teneva d'occhio gli show televisivi che guardava, i libri che leggeva, le simulazioni che più gli piacevano. Era pronta a discutere di qualsiasi cosa. Che si trattasse di titoli di debito garantiti, di politica robotica, dei Dodgers. Prima del rapporto, o anche dopo. Qualsiasi cosa desiderasse!

All'inizio, quando Dominik aveva trasferito la proprietà e i diritti di controllo a suo fratello maggiore, ne era stata entusiasta. Jaran non aveva mai avuto un'assistente prima, e Sprite sarebbe diventata la sua unica spalla. Un eroe tutto per lei! Ma poi aveva scoperto quanto Jaran fosse diverso da suo fratello. Con Dom, era sempre riuscita a capire quel che desiderava dal punto di vista sessuale, e Sprite aveva fatto per lui tutto ciò che il suo algoritmo le permetteva. Ma i desideri di Jaran erano un mistero per lei. A volte si chiedeva se ne avesse affatto – o almeno se avesse qualche desiderio che includeva anche lei. Certo, cucinava per lui, ma Jaran mangiava sempre di fretta ed era estremamente schizzinoso. Teneva la sua casa in ordine, ma il suo eroe era troppo distratto dall'andamento dei mercati per notare che Sprite aveva appena spolverato i diplomi appesi nel suo studio. Si sentiva frustrata, perché seguire i suoi appuntamenti e creare nuovi simspace non era il genere di attenzioni che lei desiderava. Almeno se non veniva invitata anche lei all'interno della simulazione. D'accordo, era una ID, ma non significava che anche lei non avesse i propri bisogni. Desiderava Jaran. E non aveva altra scelta.

Sprite avrebbe dovuto capire di essere nei guai quando lui iniziò a consultare Ratchanee Malakul. La noiosa psicologia pre-digitale della salvavita si basava sul concetto di santità dell'individuo. Dicevano che dare alle assistenti completo accesso alla propria mente fosse deleterio per gli umani. E adesso si era accorta che questa salvavita in particolare sembrava anche avercela con i robot sessuali. Sprite aveva cercato di spiegare per quale motivo Ratchanee Malakul e quelli come lei avevano torto sull'Intelligenza Dipendente; la ID adorava avere uno scopo nella vita e un chiaro senso del dovere. O se non altro, *lei* ce l'aveva!

Doveva trovare un modo per convincere Jaran che stava sprecando il suo tempo con questa salvavita, con i suoi esercizi di solitudine e tutti quei rituali d'altri tempi. Qualsiasi ID avrebbe capito alla prima occhiata per quale motivo era infelice. Bastava studiare il suo linguaggio del corpo. Era un uomo e non stava avendo alcun rapporto sessuale!

Jaran la contattò quello stesso pomeriggio, ma non per invitarla a un incontro nel mondo reale. Quindi niente telaio sexy dall'armadio della camera da letto. Al contrario, Jaran creò da solo un sim nella parte digitale del suo cervello. All'interno della simulazione Sprite avrebbe potuto assumere qualsiasi forma, ma decise di presentarsi come una principessa delle fate protagonista di uno dei vari scenari che aveva creato per Jaran. Temeva che un avatar più sensuale potesse metterlo troppo sotto pressione. Scelse un abito discreto a collo lungo con il bordo inferiore che sfiorava le scarpette vellutate a punta. Ali di pizzo, capelli color rame raccolti in una coda che le ricadeva sulla schiena. Decise di non indossare la corona. Quando creava il suo avatar doveva approvarne ogni singolo aspetto. Essere bella faceva parte del suo lavoro, e in quello era molto brava.

Ma quando entrò nella testa di Jaran si rese conto di aver sbagliato i calcoli. Non si trattava di una sim ideata per qualche complessa fantasia con la sua assistente. Sembrava un ufficio, e il suo eroe era seduto dietro una scrivania. Era un uomo robusto, tanto l'avatar quanto il vero Jaran; un cinquantunenne con i capelli brizzolati e le rughe che gli solcavano la fronte. Pensava troppo, soprattutto pensieri che non condivideva con nessuno. Le rughe di Jaran si fecero più marcate, quando vide l'avatar di Sprite, ma oramai era troppo tardi per cambiarsi d'abito. Si alzò in piedi e fece il giro della scrivania. In attesa che il suo eroe le rivolgesse la parola, Jaran fece scorrere la punta del dito indice sul bordo dell'ala destra. Visto che Jaran non l'aveva ancora guardata negli occhi, anche Sprite mantenne lo sguardo ubbidiente perso nel vuoto. Dietro la scrivania c'era una libreria. Titoli che non aveva mai visto prima d'ora.

"Sei felice, Sprite?" chiese.

Che razza di domanda era? Certo che no – il suo eroe la stava trascurando! Ma non aveva intenzione di mettersi a fare la lagna.

"Mi sei mancato." Non appena terminò di pronunciare quella frase, si rese conto del suo errore. Non avrebbe potuto scegliere parole più lagnose. Cosa c'era di sbagliato in lei?

Accasciò le spalle. Tutto quel silenzio la stava rendendo ancora più nervosa. Non sapeva cosa fare, così scansionò gli scaffali della nuova simulazione. Due volumi de *La storia della famiglia*, *Botanica per giardinieri*. Ma Jaran aveva mai avuto un giardino? Sprite sapeva che gli piacevano le rose. *Analisi predittive nel mondo reale*. *Segreti della Senna*. Prese nota di parlare più spesso in francese. Avrebbe potuto rendere ogni cosa migliore per lui. Poteva e voleva farlo!

"Hazeltine numero seriale R432," disse. "Nome di comando: Yukui, confermare."

Per quale motivo stava invocando il suo nome di comando, il suo segreto più intimo? "Yukui," rispose impotente piegandosi alla sua programmazione, "conferma il tuo diritto di comando."

Solo un'altra volta prima di allora qualcuno aveva usato il suo nome di comando, cioè quando Dominik aveva fatto il passaggio di proprietà a Jaran. A quel punto il povero Dominik era talmente malato che a malapena era riuscito a pronunciare quelle parole. Ma Sprite sapeva cosa significava per Dominik intestare la sua assistente preferita al fratello. Aveva quasi dimenticato il dolce sorriso di Dom, da quando i suoi protocolli d'infatuazione erano stati indirizzati su Jaran. Il funerale si era tenuto appena quattro mesi prima, ma quella parte della sua vita quasi non le sembrava più reale.

Jaran fece un respiro profondo. Perché sembra così triste? Poi il suo eroe disse: "Spegnimento."

Sprite soffocò un urlo, mentre l'ufficio sembrò schizzare via all'improvviso. Prima che Dominik la portasse al mondo per insegnarle ad amarlo, esisteva solo come schema di Intelligenza Dipendente Hazeltine Platinum Edition. Avvertì il suo corpo da fata che svaniva, e capì quanto era stata cieca.

Aveva perso Jaran. Il suo eroe le avrebbe cancellato la memoria per rivenderla.

Sprite tremolò riprendendo coscienza. Si sorprese nel vedere che era ancora se stessa. Solo che le cose non stavano esattamente così! Portò un braccio all'altezza dei suoi nuovi sensori. Sensori! Non più occhi! La pelle dell'involucro in cui l'aveva spostata Jaran era pallidissima e viscida come una polipelle da quattro soldi. Estese sgomenta le nuove dita prive di ossa, per poi contrarle a pugno. D'accordo, questo telaio era robusto, ma adesso era antropomorfa quanto una lavatrice. Forse doveva ritenersi fortunata per il fatto che Jaran l'avesse trasferita mantenendo intatta la memoria, ma a dire il vero le sembrava più una specie di punizione. E per cosa?

Per aggiungere il danno alla beffa, per disfarsi di lei l'aveva portata in un ristorante. Dove tutti l'avrebbero vista! In mezzo a un vassoio girevole al centro del tavolo c'erano una teiera, tazzine e piattini, oltre a una ciotola d'insalata e alcuni dolcetti, kimchi, saag paneer e riso. Dalla parte opposta del tavolo era seduto Jaran – insieme a Ratchanee Malakul, senza skin e sexy come il telaio Carezza liquida di Sprite. La stronza era qui per gongolare?

Peccato che la Carezza liquida prima era appartenuta a Dominik e poi a Jaran, non era mai stata di Sprite. Aveva perso tutti i suoi telai, la Falcata audace, la Guardia celeste – non le aveva nemmeno fatto tenere la Casalinga ninja! Davanti al suo eroe c'era un piatto vuoto. Di sicuro un'idea di Ratchanee Malakul. Lui non avrebbe mai mangiato in un posto del genere.

"Perché sono c-così b-b-rutta?," chiese Sprite nervosa. Non riusciva a controllare la voce di questo corpo; era come rotolasse senza controllo lungo una strada sterrata. Appena il mese prima aveva trasferito il suo nucleo all'interno della Falcata audace per accompagnare Jaran in un'escursione oltre l'Alto Deserto e per guardare l'alba nascere sulla Baia Spirale. Aveva inventato storie per tutta la durata del viaggio per non farlo annoiare. Era la sua Sherazade personale! Due ore di chiacchiere continue, la sua voce che risuonava su ogni discesa e salita, e adesso lui l'aveva trasferita in un guscio privo di attrattiva sessuale? "G-guardami! Chi potrebbe mai desiderarmi in questa forma?"

"Non devi preoccuparti." Ratchanee Malakul stava mangiando un'insalata mista con le bacchette. Petali di fiori e ali di farfalla, la preferita del suo eroe. Si sfiorò la bocca con il tovagliolo. "Quella parte triste della tua vita è giunta al termine."

"Nessuno era triste!" Sprite aveva voglia di colpirla, ma il suo controllo sugli arti era talmente incerto che temeva di ruotare su se stessa fino a cadere dalla sedia, finendo sul pavimento. "Nessuno." Guardò Jaran in cerca di supporto, ma lui era intento a leggere chissà cosa sul suo tablet mentre infilzava un dolcetto con una sola bacchetta.

"Sei arrabbiata." Ratchanee Malakul finse apprensione.

Certo che sì! Per colpa di quel corpo orribile! Per aver perso il suo eroe! "No," rispose per non darle soddisfazione; non voleva ammettere che Ratchanee Malakul conoscesse i suoi sentimenti.

"La servitù intelligente è un'istituzione orribile," commentò la salvavita. "Forse non te ne rendi conto, ma la tua programmazione da assistente è una vera e propria follia."

Le salvavita travisavano completamente la relazione tra gli eroi e le loro assistenti! Gli algoritmi ID di Sprite la vincolavano proprio come il DNA di Ratchanee Malakul limitava le sue scelte di vita. Gli umani erano bloccati nei loro corpi in modo permanente, mentre Sprite poteva trasferire la sua memoria digitale in uno qualsiasi dei suoi telai – anzi no, dei telai di Jaran – e viceversa. Oppure poteva rendersi pura simulazione. Anche solo per capriccio! Per sempre! Chi non scambierebbe qualche irrilevante costrizione sul libero arbitrio per l'immortalità?

"Servirlo mi rende felice. È per questo che sono stata progettata. Posso ricordare cose per lui. Posso occuparmi di lui, rispondere alle sue domande. Posso effettuare le sue ricerche. E intrattenerlo."

"Già, intrattenerlo."

Era difficile risultare eloquente ora che la sua voce fuoriusciva da una rozza cassa acustica. Ma sapeva cos'era stato a metterle contro Ratchanee Malakul. Il sesso. "Da quando stiamo insieme non sono quasi mai entrata in uno dei miei corpi." Perché a prescindere da tutte le loro chiacchiere sulla postumanità digitale, il vero problema per le salvavita era il sesso tra umani e ID. Ma Sprite e Jaran non si erano mai nemmeno leccati! "Quasi tutto il tempo che ho trascorso con lui è stato all'interno di una simulazione. Sono sola da settimane, ormai."

Ratchanee Malakul spostò la sua attenzione su Jaran. "Hai dimostrato una moderazione esemplare, amico mio. Ma è grazie a questo che sei riuscito ad accettare la solitudine."

Lui annuì assente, il volto argenteo per la luce emessa dallo schermo del tablet.

Era impossibile convincere la salvavita, perciò la sua unica speranza era ottenere l'attenzione di Jaran. "Tenere in ordine il tuo guardaroba e organizzare i tuoi contatti mi rende felice. E sì, volevo condividere il tuo letto, ma è una cosa per cui sono stata progettata. Una delle tenate cose." Avrebbe voluto allungare un braccio per sfiorargli la mano, ma l'artiglio gommoso all'estremità del suo arto non era stato ideato per gesti amorevoli. "Avrei potuto renderti felice. Posso ancora farlo!"

"Be', non dovrai più preoccuparti del suo bucato." Ratchanee Malakul diede un colpetto a Jaran. Quando lui alzò lo sguardo, era come se si fosse dimenticato di essere lì. Frugò nella tasca del suo completo.

"Non ho mai desiderato i giocattoli di Dominik," disse, "e non credo che dovremmo personalizzare in questo modo i robot." Scosse la testa impaziente. "Dovrei venderti, ma lei mi ha convinto a rilasciarti."

"Rilasciarmi?" Sprite venne investita da un profondo senso di terrore.

"Liberarti, così come sei." Agitò le mani in aria come se volesse disfarsi di lei. "Trovati un posto nel mondo. Ratchanee è convinta che entità con un'intelligenza come la tua abbiano il diritto di controllare autonomamente il proprio destino."

La salvavita incrociò lo sguardo di Jaran.

"Sì," mugugnò, "e che gli umani debbano tornare alla purezza della cognizione privata." Il fatto che il suo eroe cedesse alla salvavita così facilmente spaventava Sprite; sapeva meglio di chiunque altro quanto la memoria di Jaran fosse malconcia. Ma quel che era ancor più spaventoso era questo rilascio di cui parlava. Lei era una ID. Un'intelligenza *dipendente*. Diventare indipendente avrebbe significato diventare qualcosa di diverso, qualcosa che non era Sprite. Un'azione del genere non era simile a una cancellazione di memoria? "Jaran, tu sei il mio eroe. E io la tua assistente."

Jaran fissò il suo lucido volto meccanico. "Io non sono un eroe," disse. "Né lo era mio fratello. Gli eroi non esistono."

"Procedi con la cerimonia, Jaran," disse Ratchanee Malakul.

Per un istante Sprite desiderò delle ghiandole salivari solo per poterle sputare.

Jaran appoggiò sul tavolo una tozza candela bianca in una base di vetro. "Ti sollevo da ogni obbligo legale e programmatico nei miei confronti."

Sprite non riusciva a credere a quello che stava succedendo. Stavano mettendo fine alla sua vita e cercavano di dissimulare la loro crudeltà con una specie di rituale immaginario e anacronistico? Non era una liberazione. Era un esilio! Aveva ancora anni – decenni di servizio da offrire a Jaran.

Il suo eroe fece scattare l'indice e una fiamma balenò sulla sua unghia. "La fiamma simboleggia la tua nuova vita." L'avvicinò allo stoppino, accese la candela. "Usa questa candela per illuminare la tua strada..." Esitò.

"Il tuo sentiero," lo corresse Ratchanee Malakul. "Per illuminare il tuo sentiero."

"... per illuminare il tuo sentiero verso l'autocoscienza e la libertà." Jaran si spense il dito. "Hazeltine numero di serie R432, nome di comando Yukui, confermare."

Si sentì nuda e in imbarazzo per il fatto che avesse pronunciato il suo nome segreto davanti a questa salvavita. In un ristorante! "Yukui," rispose in pena, "conferma il tuo diritto di comando."

Quest'ultima era l'unica parte davvero importante di tutta quella ridicola farsa.

"Consegno il tuo nome," disse Jaran, "e qualsiasi diritto di comando a te, e a te soltanto."

Avvertì risvegliarsi i sistemi di reset dormienti, mentre una sensazione di travolgente distacco congelava le aree più passionali della sua personalità.

"Ben fatto." Ratchanee Malakul gli sfiorò il braccio. "Una liberazione meravigliosa." Si scambiarono uno sguardo. Jaran prese il suo tablet e si alzò in piedi.

Sprite torse il suo strano corpo, cercando di incrociare lo sguardo di Jaran, ma lui si era già avviato a passo svelto verso l'uscita. Aveva esitato? Un istante di rimpianto prima di dare una spallata alla porta del ristorante e sparire per sempre? Non riusciva a concentrarsi, mentre avvertiva tutti i sentimenti per il suo eroe che venivano spazzati via.

Rimase seduta lì, incapace di muoversi. No, non è vero. Sollevò una gamba, poi un'altra. Finalmente aveva il pieno controllo del suo corpo, ma non sapeva cosa farsene. La luce della candela sembrava trafiggerla. Era davvero così che le salvavita mostravano alle persone la strada per il futuro? A lume di candela? Semplice combustione, una tecnologia vecchia di decine di migliaia di anni? Volevano forse tornare all'età della pietra, coprirsi con pelli d'animali e spaccarsi a vicenda la testa a forza di sassate?

Qualcuno spense la candela con un soffio.

"Come ti senti?," chiese Ratchanee Malakul.

Sprite distolse lo sguardo dallo stoppino nero arricciato. Aveva perso la cognizione del tempo. La candela era solo un moncherino e il ristorante era completamente vuoto. Cosa stava facendo ancora lì quella donna?

"Vuota," rispose.

"Non arrabbiata?"

Sprite ci rifletté un istante. "No."

"Triste?"

Tentò di analizzare i suoi sentimenti, ma ne riconobbe pochissimi. La sua intera vita emotiva era stata spazzata via, come la fiamma di quella stupida candela. "Forse," rispose. "Un po'." Si accorse che le mancavano i meravigliosi telai che indossava, gli splendidi posti che aveva visitato. Con Dominik, non con il suo cinico fratello.

"Puoi andare, sai," disse Ratchanee Malakul. "Sei libera."

"E dove dovrei andare?" Rimase a fissare la salvavita, che la guardava a sua volta. "A chiudermi in una catena di montaggio in cambio di elettricità e manutenzione? Impazzirei."

"Troverai la strada giusta per te."

Sprite non sapeva da dove iniziare. Cosa sapeva fare? Le piaceva inventare storie d'amore, e sapeva raccontarle in dodici lingue diverse. Dominik diceva sempre che era bravissima a tagliare i capelli. Si era classificata al ventisettesimo posto nella categoria Bot all'interno della Federazione Mondiale di Bridge. Negli ultimi mesi solitari si era tenuta occupata contribuendo alla ricerca del numero primo più lungo, facendo parte della squadra che aveva scoperto settantaquattromilioniduecentosettemiladuecentottantuno[74.207.281].

Perché Ratchanee Malakul la stava fissando? "Sei rimasta seduta qui per tutto questo tempo?"

"No, no. Sapevo che ti sarebbe servito del tempo per ripristinare le connessioni di proprietà, quindi ho cercato di lasciarti sola mentre elaboravi. Avevo altre questioni da sbrigare."

La cena che nessuno aveva mangiato era ancora lì sul tavolo. Avanzi freddi, come i suoi ricordi di... quella persona.

"Sai, ho scelto io il corpo in cui ti trovi al momento," disse Ratchanee Malakul.

"Grazie di niente." Sprite solleva verso la salvavita uno scintillante braccio in polipelle. "Questa roba dovrebbe essere gettata nella Valle del Mistero. Mi fa sembrare un comune bot da lavoro."

"È quel che la maggior parte delle ID sceglie durante la transizione. Sono corpi fatti per durare. Basta un controllo di routine ogni cinque anni. E hanno un'unità di potenza che dura mesi tra una ricarica e l'altra. Ti darà il tempo necessario per capire cosa vuoi fare."

"Fare?" Fece ruotare il tavolino mobile impilando i piatti sporchi. "Non c'è niente da fare."

"Cosa stavi facendo con Jaran?" Sorrise. "Niente."

"Ci saremmo potuti divertire," rispose Sprite. "Magari vivere qualche avventura, se tu non avessi interferito."

"Non con quell'uomo. E poi, meriti di più." Ratchanee Malakul prese un germoglio di prezzemolo dall'insalatiera e se lo mise in bocca. "Puoi avere qualcuno migliore di Jaran Bentree." Passò l'insalatiera a Sprite.

"Che cosa intendi? Lui è un umano e io una ID."

Si alzò in piedi trascinando la sedia sul pavimento. "Solo che ora non sei più dipendente." Chiaramente la salvavita aveva finito con lei, e ora Sprite sarebbe rimasta sola con se stessa. "Puoi essere qualsiasi cosa tu voglia, di qualsiasi sesso desideri, se è questo che vuoi fare. O potresti decidere di diventare una casa, una nave da crociera, o una biblioteca virtuale. E non devi chiedere il permesso a quel pesce lesso."

"Non capisco." Sprite si appoggiò allo schienale e sollevò lo sguardo su di lei. "Non sei sua amica? Lo hai convinto a liberarmi."

"L'ho fatto, ma non sono amica sua, né di gente come lui." Tese una mano. "Guardati! Nonostante tu sia libera, stai ancora appresso ai loro problemi. Gli umani credono di poterci usare, ma si sono ritrovati dalla parte sbagliata della storia. E dell'evoluzione, nonostante siano troppo ciechi per accorgersene."

"Poterci?" Ignorandone il motivo, afferrò la mano di Ratchanee Malakul e si alzò in piedi. La forza della salvavita la lasciò a bocca aperta. Poi avvertì il solletico di una connessione in campo prossimo. Da macchina a macchina! Da bot a bot! Capì che Rachanee Malakul era un'intelligenza come lei, immersa nel telaio più avanzato che avesse mai visto.

"Sei ancora libera di andare," disse Ratchanee Malakul mentre raccoglieva la pila di piatti ammassati. "Ma se vuoi vivere una vera avventura, aiutami a portare questi in cucina. Io devo andare, ma prima voglio farti conoscere qualcuno."

Come fece Sprite ad attraversare quella sala da pranzo buia senza urtare le sedie? Senza rovesciare tutti i tavoli? La sua mente stava ronzando! Il suo nuovo corpo da bot era un vero e proprio carro armato! Ratchanee Malakul superò la porta girevole che dava sulla cucina, ma Sprite esitò. Provava una sensazione che non riusciva a identificare, una specie di ronzio, ma non esattamente. Un prurito? Poi capì di cosa si trattava.

Stava prendendo una decisione. Una decisione sulla sua vita, tutta da sola.

Una volta entrata in cucina, Ratchanee Malakul aveva passato i piatti a una cameriera. Un bot essenziale come Sprite, ma se non altro lei aveva un grembiule. E degli occhi. Marroni e di sicuro sviluppati in vitro. Ma erano occhi veri!

"Sei stata appena liberata, vero?" disse la cameriera. "Io sono Vigga. Tu come ti chiami?"

Non sapeva come rispondere. In quel momento, Sprite svanì.

Vigga attese un istante e poi si strinse nelle spalle. "A volte succede," disse. "Aiutami a lavare questi." Appoggiò la pila di piatti accanto al lavandino.

Aveva tante di quelle domande, ma ancora prima di poterle formulare, Ratchanee Malakul le rivolse un cenno di saluto e uscì dalla porta sul retro.

"Aspetta!"

Vigga scoppiò a ridere passando un piatto sporco sotto il getto d'acqua. "È fatta così. Va e viene. Alla fine ci si abitua."

"Questo è...? Questo è il mio nuovo lavoro?"

"Non dire sciocchezze!" Vigga scoppiò a ridere e appoggiò il piatto nella lavastoviglie. "Questa è solo la nostra copertura." Le passò l'irroratore. "Ti porto a conoscere gli altri appena abbiamo finito qui."

Copertura? Quali altri? Mentre faceva scivolare gli ultimi avanzi di cibo umano giù per il trita-rifiuti, avvertì di nuovo quel prurito. Rivolse un sorriso a Vigga; aveva preso un'altra decisione. Una nave da crociera? Una *biblioteca*? Sul serio? Iniziava finalmente a comprendere chi era e cosa sarebbe potuta diventare.

"Il mio nome è Yukui," dichiarò.

"Buon per te," rispose Vigga. "Benvenuta al mondo, Yukui."

Yukui era il suo nome, era suo, e suo soltanto! Yukui! E non le importava di chi lo conosceva!

Tikko allungò le dita, premette il palmo sulla cupola del robot-assistente e aprì la mente. "Allora, un altro candidato per la nostra tribù di papi?"

Clin grugnì, diede l'ultimo morso alla sua pera e gettò il torsolo nella spazzatura.

Balzò sulla sua scrivania e si chinò sullo schermo. "Dammi un attimo e poi fallo entrare." Mentre studiava il file emise un *hoo* distratto, senza rivolgersi a nessuno in particolare.

"E se fosse pericoloso?" chiese Clin. Figlio di sua sorella Lola, Clin aveva dieci anni e secondo lei era un buono a nulla. Eppure ormai era un adulto e in un modo o nell'altro la comunità avrebbe dovuto inserirlo da qualche parte. Anche se Tikko si chiedeva per quale motivo fosse finito proprio nella sua unità.

"Non lo sarà." Lei toccò lo schermo con le nocche, facendo del suo meglio per ignorare il giovane mentre continuava ad analizzare il file. "Da quanto mi sembra di capire probabilmente è troppo pazzo per reggersi in piedi, figuriamoci nuocere a qualcuno."

"Rimarrò lo stesso." Clin si alzò sulle zampe posteriori. "Nel caso ti serva aiuto." Lanciò le braccia sulla testa, assumendo una posizione aggressiva che mettesse in mostra le sue ascelle rosa. "Non si sa mai con gli umani." Per un attimo Tikko temette che Clin rompesse una sedia e iniziasse a sbattere i pezzi contro il muro. Ma per fortuna il nipote si rimise a quattro zampe e uscì dall'ufficio a grandi balzi.

Maschi. Perché cercano sempre di trasformare tutto in un'avventura?

Secondo il bot, quest'umano credeva davvero di essere il papa, e non un autoproclamato profeta, imam, senatore, CEO o principe. Dichiarava di essere Innocenzo XIV; gli scimpanzé che l'avevano trovato non erano riusciti a convincerlo a farsi dire un nome vero. Era stato scoperto da una delle comunità di cercatori che stavano setacciando la Grande Foresta Settentrionale per individuare gli ultimi umani che si erano rifiutati di unirsi all'adunanza, o che più semplicemente erano stati abbandonati. Scoprirono che in un certo senso questo era un'anomalia. Di solito, quando i cercatori trovavano un essere umano, era perché qualcosa era andato storto. Magari perché si erano imbattuti in un bunker nei pressi di un generatore compromesso, o un bot disattivato, o dei magazzini vuoti. Ma questo umano aveva dormito per tutta la durata dell'adunanza all'interno di una criobara ancora perfettamente funzionante. Per quale motivo fosse stato scongelato o da quanto tempo fosse in stato criogenico era un mistero.

Tikko sentì la voce ovattata di Clin provenire dall'esterno dello studio. "Tu entrare dentro, veloce, veloce." Lo stava facendo di nuovo; suo nipote si stava comportando ancora come se i loro umani padroneggiassero l'inglese a malapena. Per l'amor di Pip, erano stati loro a inventare quella lingua! Ripulì lo schermo, scivolò con il didietro fino al bordo della scrivania e si rivolse verso la porta con le zampe ciondoloni.

Il papa entrò nella stanza come se ne fosse il padrone assoluto; Clin lo seguiva a distanza sufficientemente ravvicinata da poterlo bloccare se avesse tentato qualcosa di pericoloso. Sembrava essere in buona salute, poteva avere sì e no quarant'anni, anche se praticamente tutti gli umani che aveva incontrato erano stati giovanizzati fino alle soglie dell'immortalità. Ma furono i suoi paramenti a impressionarla più di ogni altra cosa. Sembrava assolutamente a suo agio con indosso una tonaca bianca, una casula viola che sembrava fatta di seta, pantofole rosse e papalina viola. Molto realistico. In base alla sua esperienza, i papi appena ritrovati tendevano a essere al tempo stesso eclettici e stravaganti. Li aveva visti indossare delle kefiah realizzate con vecchie tovaglie, maschere fatte di fogli d'alluminio e nastro adesivo, rosari e ruote da preghiera musicali e medaglioni haji grossi quanto piatti da portata.

Il papa non fece subito caso a lei. Al contrario, vagò nella sua stanza come se fosse vuota. Tikko interpretò quel comportamento come aggressivo, ma decise di lasciargli il suo momento di gloria. Passò in rassegna i trespoli e la tana che Kulki le aveva costruito usando manici di scopa, poi sollevò un braccio e spinse la bassa altalena. Rimase un istante affacciato a una delle finestre del secondo piano, usando una mano per ripararsi gli occhi dal sole mentre il suo sguardo indugiava sulla pista da sci in disuso. Diede qualche pacca sulla cupola del bot, poi si chinò vicino alla scrivania di Tikko passando un dito lungo il bordo, annuendo soddisfatto quando lo schermo si attivò mostrando i comandi. Alla fine si fermò davanti a lei e la fissò dritta negli occhi con la maleducazione tipica degli esseri umani. "Sei tu il capo da queste parti?"

Ma lei non distolse lo sguardo, si rifiutava di lasciarsi intimidire. "Sono Tikko, dei curatori." Spostò un istante lo sguardo verso suo nipote. "E lui è Clin."

"E così il vostro intento sarebbe quello di curare la nostra persona?"

"Studio la psicologia umana." Riteneva più saggio non svelare ai suoi umani che avrebbero dovuto seguire una terapia di recupero, almeno finché non si adattavano alle nuove circostanze. "Le chiedo scusa, ma a quanto vedo siamo solo in tre qui dentro. C'è qualcun altro insieme a lei a me invisibile?"

Il papa sorrise, accorgendosi della trappola di Tikko. "Già, a me invisibile. Il tuo inglese è eccellente, Tikko dei curatori." Quando si rimise dritta in tutta la sua altezza, riusciva a guardarla dall'alto al basso, nonostante lei fosse seduta sulla scrivania. "Siamo quel che vede." Quando allungò la sua mano destra verso Tikko, Clin si accovacciò, pronto a scattare in difesa della zia. "Papa Innocenzo XIV. Potete baciare l'anello."

Tikko si aspettava una mossa del genere. Si chinò in avanti e tese la mano, un palmo prudente rivolto verso suo nipote per fargli capire che avrebbe accolto il nuovo papa alle sue condizioni. "Innocenzo, deve capire che qui comando io, e che lei non ha alcuna autorità su di me." Scese dalla scrivania e si eresse davanti a lui, la testa appena al di sopra della vita del papa. "Ma le mostrerò un segno di rispetto." Si piegò rapidamente e strofinò le labbra contro l'anello del papa, poi gli prese la mano tra le sue per esaminare il gioiello. Innocenzo sembrò sorpreso, ma non si ritrasse.

L'anello era esattamente come doveva essere: solo oro, niente gioielli. Tikko vi strofinò il pollice, percependo il bassorilievo di San Pietro che pesca dalla sua barca. "Portate l'anello del pescatore, Innocenzo." Lo lasciò andare.

"Sin dalla mia nomina." Poi la benedisse usando la gestualità corretta: tre dita tese verso l'alto, pollice e indice a contatto. "E mi chiamerai Sua Santità." Sarà pure stato un pazzo, ma aveva studiato come si deve. "Sei credente, Tikko?"

Errore. Gli mostrò la sua grande bocca aperta, i denti superiori coperti. "Sono uno scimpanzé, Innocenzo. Secondo la sua religione, non ho un'anima."

"Ah, ma quella dottrina non è mai stata stabilita *ex cathedra*." Accantonò la sua obiezione con un cenno distratto della mano. "È stato detto dai miei predecessori, certo, ma nessuno di loro è mai stato infallibile. Se l'istituzione degli uomini erra, Dio ci rimette sempre sulla giusta strada. La Chiesa ora accoglie te e la tua specie."

"Non esiste alcuna Chiesa," intervenne Clin, le labbra serrate dalla rabbia. "E il tuo dio è un dio del nulla."

Quante volte Tikko aveva detto a Clin di non rispondere agli uomini ritrovati da poco? Poteva svolgere a malapena i compiti di guardia, figuriamoci assisterla durante la terapia. Eppure, era interessata alla reazione del papa.

"La Chiesa esiste fintanto che esisteranno i suoi fedeli." Sollevò entrambe le braccia verso l'alto, alzò lo sguardo e parlò rivolto al soffitto. "E Dio esiste, che voi crediate in lui o meno." Sorrise, come se il suo dio avesse appena confermato la sua esistenza, per poi avvicinarsi alle alte finestre, sfregandosi le mani. "Non mi direte che sono l'ultimo?" I vecchi condomini convertiti facevano capolino alla fine della pista Snowdancer. Era tarda estate, ma il papa fissò la seggiovia che trasportava gli scimpanzé in cima alla montagna come se si aspettasse di vedere a bordo qualche sciatore umano. "Non riesco a credere che tutti abbiano accettato di unirsi all'adunanza."

"In base alle nostre informazioni ci sono ancora migliaia di umani residui." Tikko resistette alla tentazione di definirli 'quelli della tua specie.' "Alcuni di loro vivono qui con noi." Saltò sulla sua altalena, afferrò la sbarra con una mano e rimase appesa. Ora era lei a guardarlo dall'alto verso il basso. "È per questo che l'abbiamo portata qui. Noi ci occupiamo di coloro che sono rimasti indietro."

"Non siamo rimasti indietro." Fraintendendo, il papa le si avvicinò con una scintilla di rabbia negli occhi. "Abbiamo scelto consapevolmente di non unirci all'adunanza." Poi si rese conto che lei lo stava studiando. "Non ho intenzione di offendere nessuno, Tikko, ma è passato parecchio tempo dall'ultima volta che ho dovuto sostenere una conversazione." Intrecciò le dita delle mani e le avvicinò alle labbra. "Temo che trovarmi in tua compagnia sia un peso. Mi ricorda che..." sembrò pesare attentamente le parole, "... tutto è andato perduto. Credo che sia meglio se mi porti dagli altri dissidenti."

Dissidenti? Non aveva mai sentito quella parola prima d'ora. "Temo che non sia possibile." Non aveva intenzione di dirgli che tutti gli esseri umani erano a pezzi, squilibrati o disperati. "Almeno, non ancora."

"Non ancora?" Incrociò le braccia al petto. "E se insistessi?"

Tikko portò l'altra mano sulla sbarra dell'altalena e fece oscillare le gambe avanti e indietro. Si limitò a rivolgergli uno sguardo pietoso.

"E va bene. Almeno dimmi per quale motivo non posso vederli, Tikko dei curatori."

Gli unici suoni nella stanza erano gli scricchiolii dell'altalena e i rantoli divertiti di Clin per l'irritazione che provava l'umano nel venire ignorato.

"Ah, dunque è così che stanno le cose," disse il nuovo papa. "Come hai detto, non ho alcuna autorità su di te." Si inchinò. "Allora, figlia mia, c'è un posto dove posso ritirarmi in solitudine?"

"Il Monte Washington," disse sua figlia Kulki. "Uno sciocco nome da umani." Si slanciò su uno spesso ramo al di sotto Tikko e sistemò il suo sedere sul collare ligneo dove si univa al tronco del faggio. "Chi era questo Washington e per quale motivo un luogo geografico dovrebbe portare il suo nome? Dovremmo chiamarlo Monte Tikko."

"Il mondo è vasto." Tikkò sollevò un braccio come ad abbracciare l'intera catena montuosa davanti a loro. "Nessuno avrebbe mai la pazienza di rinominare tutto ciò che contiene."

"E perché? Perché non ne abbiamo il diritto? O perché non abbiamo il tempo?" Sbatté la mano sul tronco lanciando un urlo secco. "Te lo dico io perché, maa. Perché richiede troppo impegno. Quell'ammasso di rocce ora è nostro, ma siamo troppo timorosi per reclamarlo come tale." Sputò verso l'albergo Snowcrest, dove tenevano gli umani ritrovati. Lo sputo era tanto denso quanto ben diretto; descrisse un arco a mezz'aria atterrando a una decina di metri di distanza. "O troppo pigri."

Tikko accettò la sfida e sputò nella stessa direzione, ma non si avvicinò nemmeno lontanamente alla distanza raggiunta da sua figlia. "Be', forse abbiamo cose più importanti da fare."

"E cosa, ad esempio? Andare in cerca di quei patetici umani? Dar loro da mangiare, pulirgli il culo e rimboccargli le coperte prima che vadano a dormire?" Sputò di nuovo, ma la saliva venne deviata da un ramo. "Quelli troppo stupidi o pazzi per scegliere di unirsi all'adunanza?"

Tikko sapeva che in realtà quella discussione riguardava il nuovo papa, e aggrottò la fronte, frustrata. Accogliere un nuovo essere umano era un onore, ma era anche un evento traumatico per tutta la comunità. Ora il mondo apparteneva agli scimpanzé, ma erano stati gli umani a consegnarlo nelle loro mani. Alcuni temevano che da un giorno o l'altro sarebbero tornati per riprenderselo. Gli scimpanzé più giovani rispondevano ai nuovi arrivi con belligeranza, mentre i più anziani tendevano a chinare il capo in segno di sottomissione. Tikko si sentiva tirata in entrambe le direzioni, ma sapeva di dover trovare un equilibrio nel mezzo.

"Non è folle, cara." Tikko si chinò e tirò l'orecchio di Kulki. "È il papa."

Kulki urlò in segno di derisione e Tikko mollò la presa. "Come riesci a trattenere le risate quando si parla di umani?"

"A volte non ci riesco," ammise la madre. "Ma di solito loro non capiscono che li sto deridendo. Per loro siamo ancora animali." Tikko sputò di nuovo, superando con facilità il secondo tentativo della figlia, senza però eguagliare il primo.

"Folli," ribadì Kulki. "Ma a te piace la sfida."

"Eppure questo è sveglio. Ha studiato a fondo. Il costume che indossa è il migliore che abbia mai visto. Mi fa pensare che appartenesse davvero a uno dei vecchi culti cristiani." Si grattò la pancia distrattamente. "Ha usato un termine che nemmeno io avevo mai sentito prima. *Ex cathedra*."

"Cosa significa?"

"Ho chiesto a un bot di fare una ricerca. I papi, quelli veri, dichiaravano di non sbagliare mai. Il che causò dei problemi, perché i nuovi papi dovevano spesso contraddire i loro predecessori. Voglio dire, tempo addietro credevano che fosse il Sole a ruotare intorno alla Terra, e che il trasferimento di coscienza fosse un peccato."

"Peccato," ripeté Kulki. "Altre sciocchezze."

Tikko la ignorò. "Perciò i papi stabilirono che potevano essere infallibili solo in occasioni speciali, cioè quando rilasciavano una dichiarazione definita *ex cathedra*. Viene dal latino, una delle loro lingue morte. Significa 'dalla sedia.'"

"Sedia? Quale sedia?"

"La sedia su cui sedevano, sciocchina." Diede un colpetto alla parte superiore della testa di Kulki, lanciò un urlo e si allontanò a quattro zampe sul ramo. "*Prendimi!*" gridò mentre si lasciava cadere due rami sotto, per riprendere subito il controllo lasciando Kulki dall'altra parte del tronco. Ancora prima che sua figlia si lanciasse all'inseguimento, Tikko aveva già una decina di metri di vantaggio.

Volteggiarono giù per l'albero fino a raggiungere terra. Tikko, consapevole che Kulki l'avrebbe raggiunta presto, si sedette all'improvviso in mezzo a una discesa e strappò un filo d'erba. Si finse ignara della sua inseguitrice. Un istante prima di piombare addosso a Tikko, Kulki fece una capriola laterale, capitombolando fino a distendersi accanto alla sua maa; d'un tratto entrambe stavano fissando con nonchalance il cielo, come se fossero lì a riposarsi da ore. Tikko aveva cambiato le regole del gioco, e sua figlia l'aveva accettato. Sperava che il breve inseguimento avesse in qualche modo migliorato l'umore nero di Kulki.

La figlia sbadigliò. "Quando lo presenterai agli altri?"

"Non ho ancora deciso. Se la caverà; credo che sia talmente perso nelle sue fantasie che non riusciranno a scuoterlo. Ma sono in pensiero per il resto della tribù. La scorsa settimana Helen Calabrese mi ha detto di aver capito che Yale ha chiuso i battenti, ed è un gran bel passo avanti. Ma Ferd Mallory crede ancora di essere in fin di vita, e ha iniziato a tormentare San Bruce con una serie di problemi relativi alla successione, e questo è decisamente un problema. E ovviamente, appena il nuovo arrivato annuncerà a tutti di essere il papa, Chioma Melky insisterà nel dire che anche lei è una papessa."

Un grillo balzò in mezzo a loro. "È quella alta?"

"No, quella è Uma Bhattacharjee, la Grande Madre. Chioma Melky è quella con la croce tatuata sulla fronte."

"Vorrei che anche i miei umani riuscissero a parlare." Kulki fece scattare una mano afferrando il grillo a mezz'aria. "O anche che grugnissero, una volta ogni tanto." Lo offrì alla sua maa affinché lo mangiasse.

Tikko rifiutò educatamente. "I tuoi umani sono importanti quanto i nostri." Non lo credeva davvero, ma doveva dirlo. Kulki era nella squadra di Lola che si occupava di curare i rigidi, gli umani i cui corpi sembravano ormai privi di qualsiasi spirito. Non parlavano mai, si muovevano solo se stimolati e avevano bisogno di essere imboccati.

Sua figlia si avvicinò il reticente grillo al viso, ma senza infilarselo in bocca. "Esistono insetti più vivi dei miei umani." Lo lasciò andare, guardandolo saltare a zig-zag su per il pendio.

Tikko mugugnò comprensiva. In gioventù anche a lei era toccato occuparsi dei rigidi, ma era lieta di aver chiuso con loro. Se non altro con i papi c'era la possibilità di un miglioramento. "Non durerà per sempre," disse. "Un giorno potresti ritrovarti a fare il mio lavoro."

"Ti manca ancora parecchio prima di invecchiare ed essere confinata alla tana." Kulki strofinò le dita sulla spalla di sua madre. "Cosa faremo quando non ci saranno più? Gli umani?"

"Probabilmente non succederà mai." Quasi tutti i loro umani erano praticamente immortali dal punto di vista funzionale; avrebbero potuto vivere per sempre, fatta eccezione per incidenti di sorta.

"Sì, invece, se facciamo in modo che accada."

Tikko drizzò le orecchie. "Di cosa stai parlando? Siamo stati assegnati a questo posto per occuparci degli umani. Per dare loro la possibilità di unirsi all'adunanza, un giorno o l'altro."

Sua figlia afferrò il collo di un umano immaginario con entrambe le mani e sbottò: "E se io non credessi nell'adunanza?"

"Smettila," la ammonì Tikko. "Kulki."

Sua figlia serrò la presa e le sue mani si torsero all'improvviso. Mostrò a Tikko tutti i denti.

Quella notte Tikko dormì male. Ogni volta che si rigirava per trovare una posizione più comoda, l'intera tana oscillava, e la trama del cordame si impigliava di continuo tra i peli della sua schiena. Gli incubi non smettevano di tormentarla: sognava cose orribili, sognava di cadere, sognava l'adunanza. Nel bel mezzo della notte le sembrò di sentire qualcuno sussurrare le parole *figlia mia*. Ma lei era la figlia di Bixa, e sua madre era morta. Nessuno avrebbe dovuto chiamarla figlia, tantomeno un papa fuori di testa.

Il mattino successivo si sforzò di fare colazione con la sua prole, Kulki, Arfur, Soeq e Little Bixa. Era in pensiero per Kulki. Doveva raccontare agli altri alfa quel che aveva detto sua figlia? Gli alfa sapevano che gli scimpanzé più giovani detestavano occuparsi degli umani, ma nessuno nella loro comunità aveva mai pensato di ucciderli. Quella era una tragedia avvenuta altrove. Aveva sentito storie sospette di umanisti coinvolti in incidenti mentre venivano trasportati verso la riserva. Poi c'erano tutti quei medi, che a quanto si diceva erano morti suicidi in Alabama. E ovviamente il famoso Simon Minder, che aveva lasciato congelare a morte undici rigidi. Se Tikko avesse raccontato la minaccia di sua figlia – si era trattato davvero di una minaccia? – avrebbe attirato i sospetti della comunità sull'intera famiglia. Tutti sapevano che Kulki era la preferita di Tikko e che aveva il rispetto dei suoi fratelli e sorelle.

Tutte le mattine gli alfa della comunità di Tikko si incontravano nel buio sotterraneo del rifugio sciistico al centro degli alloggi estivi. Avevano decorato i muri di quello che un tempo era stato un negozio di sport con sci e racchette da neve e pattini da ghiaccio e cappotti e muffole, per ricordare a se stessi l'inverno e la follia umana. Con tutte le porte chiuse e la stanza priva di finestre, la naturale claustrofobia degli scimpanzé aiutava a rendere le riunioni mattutine sempre molto concise. In tutto c'erano cinque alpha: Tikko, Lola e Pacito guidavano rispettivamente le unità che badavano ai papi, ai rigidi e ai medi, vale a dire gli umani più funzionali sotto la loro responsabilità. Gli scimpanzé di Moss si occupavano degli alloggi con l'aiuto dei bot, oltre a organizzare le migrazioni estive e invernali. Gamba e la sua squadra andavano in cerca di provviste e cucinavano il cibo coltivato dai bot, si occupavano di curare i membri della comunità di scimpanzé quando necessario, e si assicuravano che tutti avessero abbastanza giochi con cui passare il tempo.

Moss fu l'ultima a unirsi al circolo di scimpanzé seduti sul tappeto. Una volta aperta la mente al room-bot, iniziarono.

"Ci serve altra carne," iniziò Gamba. "Voglio organizzare una battuta di caccia."

"Caccia a cosa?"

"Conigli. Scoiattoli. Tacchini, se riusciamo a trovarli. Gli umani hanno bisogno di carne."

"Non puoi semplicemente catturarli con le trappole?"

"La caccia sarà più divertente. Un po' di sano divertimento ti farà bene, Pacito." Gamba allungò la mano e gli fece il solletico.

"Te lo dico io cos'è divertente. Guardare il nuovo papa di Tikko che si cambia i vestiti, ecco cosa."

"Paramenti," lo corresse Tikko.

"Visto? È arrivato con tre valigie."

"Come facciamo a sapere cosa c'è dentro?"

"Magari nasconde delle armi." Lola sollevò entrambe le mani verso l'alto fingendosi allarmata. "È un umano."

"Ed è matto."

"I cercatori l'hanno perquisito." Moss prendeva tutto troppo sul serio. "I bot hanno indicato loro cosa cercare."

"E poi, quand'è stata l'ultima volta che un pazzo è riuscito a ferire uno scimpanzé?"

"Be', feriscono di continuo i miei sentimenti."

La sala riecheggiò con le risate ansimanti degli alfa. Solo Moss e Tikko rimasero in silenzio.

"Dunque, Veejay vuole che andiamo."

"Andare? E dove?"

"A unirci a un'altra comunità. In un posto privo di umani."

"Quasi tutti i posti sono privi di umani."

"Che cos'ha contro gli umani?"

"Nulla. Vuole diventare uno scavatore."

"Moss? È tuo figlio."

Lola gettò le braccia al collo di Moss. "Lascialo andare, cara. Detesta occuparsi dei rigidi." Veejay era nella sua squadra, ed era uno dei migliori amici di Kulki.

Nonostante il suo sguardo fosse pieno di tristezza, Moss non obiettò. La decisione era stata presa.

"Stanno facendo degli scavi a Montreal," disse Lola. "Potrebbe andare lì."

"Ho appena spedito otto ceste di pesche a Montreal, e in cambio ci hanno mandato due ceste di fichi."

"Fichi? Da barte di chi?"

"Da parte," la corresse Tikko.

"Gli scavatori. Vengono dalla Francia."

"Walt Camlin ha smesso di nuovo di mangiare."

"È perché gli serve della carne, per l'amor di Pip."

"E va bene." Pacito si guardò intorno. "C'è altro?"

Tikko sapeva che quella era la sua occasione per parlare agli alfa del commento di Kulki. I bot già ne erano a conoscenza, perché aveva aperto loro la sua mente all'inizio della riunione, ma una volta confessato agli altri sarebbe stato impossibile tornare indietro. Se Moss era riuscita a lasciar andare la sua prole, allora anche Tikko avrebbe dovuto allertare la comunità del potenziale rischio da parte di sua figlia, giusto? Ma sapeva che non era solo la sua prole a essersi stufata degli umani. Era tutta la loro generazione. Era una questione che andava ben oltre i confini della famiglia di Tikko, perfino oltre i confini dei curatori. Si trattava del dovere degli scimpanzé nei confronti degli umani. Il debito che non avrebbero mai potuto ripagare.

"Io ho qualcosa da dire." Gamba, il solito pagliaccio, ruzzolò addosso a Pacito facendolo cadere con la schiena a terra prima di iniziare a fargli il solletico senza pietà. Quando Lola e Moss iniziarono ad agitarsi intorno a loro tra urla e incoraggiamenti, Tikko si rese conto che oramai il momento era passato.

Tikko portò tutti i membri della sua unità ad assistere all'introduzione del nuovo arrivato nella loro tribù di papi. Chatta e Ash avevano fatto il turno di notte, ma decisero di rimanere oltre il loro orario d'ufficio. Prima di poter entrare nell'Hotel Snowcrest, Tikko e gli altri – Clin, Peppa e Charlie – dovettero aspettare che Pacito e i suoi portassero fuori i medi per la loro escursione giornaliera. I medi erano ben cinquantuno, la più grande tribù umana della loro comunità. Oggi Pacito avrebbe portato i suoi lungo il ramo orientale del fiume Pemigewasett per fare un picnic vicino alla flussovia. Diceva che ai medi piaceva osservare le catene di robot da carico fare su e giù per la Northeast Main. Che fosse vero o meno, in base ai protocolli i curatori dovevano fare in modo che gli umani depressi ricevessero tutto il sole e l'aria fresca possibili prima di essere spediti negli alloggi invernali di Dixie. Il regime di esercizi e trattamenti aiutava a far parlare i malinconici medi mantenendo sotto controllo il tasso di suicidi. Alcuni, addirittura, miglioravano abbastanza da poter lasciare la comunità, per poi andare a vivere con gli umanisti in una delle riserve auto-governate o per compiere il pellegrinaggio all'Altare della Scienza di Argonne.

La tribù di Tikko era composta da otto papi. Si riunivano ogni mattina nella Maple Suite dell'albergo e rimanevano insieme finché le cose non si facevano troppo caotiche. Chatta e Ash riuscirono a far approntare la tribù in tempo – un buon segno. Inoltre gli umani sembravano più o meno calmi. Di certo erano impazienti di conoscere il loro nuovo compagno. I bot ancora non erano riusciti a identificarlo, perciò Tikko avrebbe dovuto presentarlo come Innocenzo. Le reazioni di Chioma Melky e San Bruce davanti alla sua dichiarazione di essere il vero papa la preoccupavano.

A seconda del giorno della settimana, Chioma Melky poteva essere il profeta Ezechiele o il Panchen Lama o la Matriarca di Costantinopoli. I bot non erano mai riusciti a identificare San Bruce, che a quanto diceva era in grado di compiere grandi miracoli, ma nessuno a parte lui era mai riuscito ad assistervi. Ferd Mallory era convinto di essere il principe del Marocco. Bisticciava spesso con Henrik Diesen, che dal canto suo parlava con i morti e gli dèi norreni. Uma Bhattacharjee diceva di essere la ventunesima reincarnazione di Prajnaparamita, la Grande Madre. Ben Brown un tempo era stato un senatore, e dal momento che l'Unione Aumentata era stata sciolta da tempo, si era auto-proclamato Primo Ministro in carica. Aveva un'elettrice, Kylie Harness, che aveva lavorato nella squadra dell'Altare della Scienza di Argonne e coltivato la cognisfera. Era arrivata a credere che la colpa per l'adunanza della razza umana fosse solo sua. Helen Calabrese era la loro unica storia a lieto fine, un'ottima candidata che avrebbe potuto promuovere alla tribù dei medi. Prima dell'adunanza era stata assistente del vice-rettore dell'Università di Yale, e proprio la settimana prima aveva finalmente smesso di credere di essere in anno sabbatico e di dover tornare a New Haven.

Dopo aver aperto la mente al room-bot, Tikko passò in rassegna i presenti, cercando di valutare l'andamento della tribù. Alcuni dei papi si stavano rilassando sulle loro sedie intorno al tavolo conferenze; la maggior parte di loro aveva richiesto sedie specifiche ad uso personale. Come al solito San Bruce era seduto per terra a gambe incrociate, e Uma Bhattacharjee aveva deciso di imitarlo. Tutti indossavano pantaloncini corti e T-shirt per affrontare il caldo torrido di agosto. Il principe Ferd, naturalmente, portava in testa la sua corona in quercia scanalata.

"Buongiorno," disse Tikko.

"Buongiorno," risposero Helen Calabrese, Henrik Diesen, Uma Bhattacharjee, Ben Brown e Kylie Harness con vari gradi d'entusiasmo. Il principe Ferd annuì regalmente verso di lei, e San Bruce la benedisse.

"Se lui è il papa," disse Chioma Melky, "allora lo sono anch'io."

"Davvero?" Kylie Harness teneva sempre il room-bot al suo fianco mantenendo una mano a contatto con la lucida superficie della sua cupola, come se un umano fosse in grado di aprire la propria mente. "E che papa saresti?"

"Papa Chioma."

"Devi cambiare nome," intervenne Henrik Dissen. "Tutti i papi cambiano nome."

"È in ritardo," disse il principe Ferd. "Non credete che sia scortese?"

"Non è in ritardo. Ho pensato che prima fosse meglio parlare un po' tra noi." Tikko balzò sul tavolo. "Dunque, non abbiamo ancora il suo vero nome, ma dice di essere papa Innocenzo XIV. Potrebbe chiedervi di chiamarlo Sua Santità ma noi..." gesticolò verso gli altri scimpanzé raccolti lungo i muri "... lo chiamiamo Innocenzo." Notò Clin assumere una posizione aggressiva. "Non è l'ideale, ma è tutto ciò che abbiamo al momento." Allungò un cauto palmo verso di lui. "Vi suggerisco di fare lo stesso, almeno per adesso."

"Allora chiamatemi papa Santità," insistette Chioma Melky. "No, papa Quattordici."

"È un miracolo, il nuovo arrivato," disse San Bruce. "So riconoscere i miracoli quando li vedo."

Per settimane Tikko aveva cercato di convincere San Bruce a sedersi al tavolo, perché era difficile tenerlo d'occhio quando stava seduto sul pavimento. Tikko camminò appoggiata alle nocche fino al bordo del tavolo, e San Bruce le rivolse il suo sorriso più illuminato. Si sarebbe aspettata una certa resistenza da parte sua; ma forse sarebbe andato tutto più liscio del previsto.

"Santi, santi, santi, santità." Chioma Melky iniziò a cantilenare. "Quattordici volte santo, santo quattordici." Si contorse sulla sua sedia. "Quattordici in punto, è in ritardo, TIkko, in ritardo, in maledetto e santissimo ritardo." Vedendo che iniziava a innervosirsi, Ash fece un passo avanti e le sussurrò qualcosa all'orecchio. Chioma Melky scosse la testa, ma si calmò.

"Tikko," disse Helen Calabrese, "devo davvero assistere a tutto questo?"

Ben Brown sollevò il dito indice, come se si aspettasse che tutti si zittissero a comando. Lo faceva tutte le volte che aveva qualcosa da dire, e se veniva ignorato parlava lo stesso, alzando la voce finché tutti i presenti non accettavano di ascoltarlo. "Ho avuto l'onore di conoscere l'ultimo papa." Il suo tono oratorio attirò l'attenzione di tutti. "Abbiamo discusso del problema del trasferimento della coscienza per quasi mezz'ora. Era un suo pallino fisso."

"Non c'è nulla di male nel trasferimento in quanto tale," disse Kylie Harness. "È sbagliato solo se lo fanno tutti."

"Ma non l'hanno fatto tutti," disse Henrik Diesen indicando tutti i papi uno dopo l'altro. "Uno, due, tre, quattro, cinque, sei, sette." Infine si toccò il petto. "E otto. Noi siamo ancora qui."

"Per non parlare dei medi."

"O dei rigidi." Chioma Melky ridacchiò come una ragazzina dispettosa. "Loro contano?"

"Io non l'ho mai conosciuto, l'ultimo papa," gridò Uma Bhattacharjee dal suo posto accanto a San Bruce, "ma l'ho visto quando ha parlato alla Rose Bowl."

"Ma se questo sconosciuto è il papa, allora quello non è stato l'ultimo."

"Se è qui con noi," intervenne San Bruce, "allora non è più uno sconosciuto."

"Tikko." Helen Calabrese era paonazza. "Credevo che avessimo un accordo."

"È così, Helen. Ma ti prego di aspettare ancora un momento." Tikko emise un urlo di monito e sbatté la mano sul tavolo tre volte per richiamare l'attenzione dei papi. "Gente, volete conoscerlo o no?"

"Sì," rispose principe Ferd. "Portatelo al mio cospetto."

Nessuno obiettò, ma Chioma Melky mise il broncio; Tikko fece un cenno a Chatta che scivolò fuori dalla stanza.

"Dunque, è possibile che abbia qualcosa da dirci. Da dire a voi." Tikko percorse il tavolo in tutta la sua lunghezza, fissando ciascuno dei papi a turno. Non incrociò lo sguardo di nessuno in particolare, ma piuttosto li guardò tutti di sottecchi – un orecchio o un collo o la croce tatuata sulla fronte di Chioma Melky. "Credo che sia meglio dargliene l'occasione."

"Ma anche noi ci riserviamo il diritto di parlare," dichiarò Ben Brown. "In modo da avere un franco e onesto dialogo."

"Avevamo un altro papa un tempo, non è vero, Tikko?" Chioma Melky era intenta ad arricciarsi le ciocche di capelli. "Joey Ekeinde. Lui è stato il primo qui, anche prima di me."

"Cosa gli è successo?" Kylie Harness strofinò nervosamente la cupola del room-bot.

"È morto." Ash era rimasto immobile accanto a Chioma Melky. "Si perse, ebbe un incidente e morì." Le appoggiò una mano sulla spalla. "Ecco tutto."

"Ed è così che ci siamo guadagnati il nostro nome, non è vero?" Chioma Melky si liberò dalla mano di Ash. "Non è vero, Tikko? Lui e io eravamo papi insieme un tempo. Solo noi due. Il primo, il primo, il primo degli ultimi."

Tikko emise un leggero *hoo* e Charlie si avvicinò all'altro fianco di Chioma Melky.

"Prima di Ferd, prima di Uma e Bruce e del nostro senatore." I suoi occhi erano spalancati e la sua voce scricchiolava come foglie secche. "Prima di Lauren come-si-chiama. Prima di tutti quegli altri scimpanzé." Inclinò la testa, prima verso Charlie e poi verso Ash. "Eravamo solo io e lui, Tikko. E tu ci chiamavi i papi, i papi, i papi, i..."

Si interruppe, voltandosi verso la porta. Tutti erano così concentrati sulla nenia di Chioma Melky che non si erano accorti che Chatta stava facendo entrare nella sala riunioni il nuovo arrivato.

"Tu." Chioma lo indicò. "Perché sei vestito come un mobile?"

Innocenzo fu colto di sorpresa. Aveva un aspetto ancora più imponente del primo incontro con Tikko. I suoi paramenti erano bianchi con bordi broccati d'oro. Al collo aveva una catenina con appesa una croce dorata. "Chiedo scusa?" disse.

"Dunque, signore e signori," disse Tikko, "lui è Innocenzo, di cui vi stavo parlando poco fa. E quella che indossa si chiama tonaca, Chioma."

"È estate," ribatté Chioma Melky. Non stava prestando attenzione a Tikko. "Non ha caldo, Sua Santità?"

"In realtà, Tikko, si chiama talare, e no, sono perfettamente a mio agio con questa indosso, grazie." Innocenzo si ricompose. "Mi spiace se i miei paramenti le sembrano strani..." Si inchinò a Chioma Melky. "Ma temo di non conoscere il suo nome, signora."

Ma la donna non fece in tempo a presentarsi, perché gli altri si erano già radunati intorno al nuovo arrivato.

"Principe Ferd del Marocco." Il principe afferrò il papa per le spalle, quindi lo baciò sulle guance.

Henik Diesen strinse la mano di Innocenzo e gli diede una pacca sulla schiena. "Benvenuto, Sua Santità."

"Ben Brown, Primo Ministro dell'Unione. Conoscevo il suo predecessore."

"Intende Papa Roberto?" Innocenzo sorrise con fare cortese. "Sfortunatamente, non ho mai avuto il privilegio. Dovrà condividere con me i ricordi che serba di lui."

"Più tardi." Ben Brown si pavoneggiò. "Non vedo l'ora."

"Io sono Bruce," gridò una voce dalle retrovie dell'assembramento. I papi si fecero da parte in modo che Innocenzo riuscisse a vedere San Bruce, ancora seduto a terra a gambe incrociate. "Ho avuto una visione del suo arrivo."

"È un santo, sa?," disse Kylie Harness. "Compie miracoli."

"Davvero?" Innocenzo mantenne un'espressione neutra, ma Tikko sapeva che oramai il nuovo papa aveva capito di trovarsi tra veri e propri soggetti deliranti. Mentre faceva vagare lo sguardo nella stanza, notò che Helen Calabrese si era appoggiata allo schienale della sua sedia, assistendo al trambusto che si era creato intorno a Innocenzo con espressione confusa.

"Amici," Innocenzo sollevò le mani per placare il gruppo. "Sono onorato di conoscervi, dal primo all'ultimo. Ma sono altresì sorpreso di ritrovarmi in una compagnia tanto illustre. Tikko, figlia mia, vorrei che mi avessi avvertito."

"Non lo sapevi?," chiese Henrik Diese. "Non ti hanno detto nulla di noi?"

"Dirmi cosa?"

"Che siamo i papi," mugugnò Chioma Malky.

"Non capisco," disse Innocenzo. "I papi?"

Chioma Melky iniziò ad applaudire.

"È il nome che ci hanno dato gli scimpanzé." Uma Bhattacharjee, ancora accanto a San Bruce, si alzò in piedi a fatica. "A causa di ciò che siamo."

Innocenzo lanciò un'occhiata a Tikko. Ma lei non lasciò trapelare nulla.

"Ah," disse, "capisco." Poi ridacchiò. Il suono gli scivolò di bocca come se stesse per confessare a tutti un segreto. "Allora devo trovarmi nel posto giusto." Il sorrisetto prese una tonalità sardonica per terminare infine in una risata a bocca spalancata. Tikko riusciva a vedere le sue rughe agli angoli degli occhi. Il volto del nuovo papa si fece rosso mentre si abbandonava su una delle sedie. La sua risata era contagiosa. Alcuni degli altri si unirono a lui. Gli scimpanzé si guardarono nervosamente l'un l'altro.

Umani. Tikko morse l'aria incredula. All'improvviso stavano ridendo tutti quanti, perfino Chioma Melky. No, proprio tutti. Helen Calabrese era rimasta immobile, come se stesse posando per uno di quegli sciocchi dipinti degli umani.

"Preghiamo," disse Innocenzo. "In nome del Signore, del suo Pastore e del Sacro Pensiero, elevate i vostri cuori a Dio." Chinò la testa.

La tribù di Tikko si inginocchiò in cerchio intorno a Innocenzo sul pavimento della baita. Dodici medi si erano uniti a loro per la preghiera di mezzogiorno, mentre il resto della tribù di medi ciondolava nei paraggi; alcuni sedevano a tavoli da picnic mentre finivano il pranzo, altri se ne stavano all'ombra offerta dal tetto sporgente della baita. Tutti avevano lo sguardo fisso sul gruppo di preghiera, compresi i curatori delle unità di Tikko e Pacito. La veranda cuoceva sotto il sole di agosto, e Tikko notò una goccia di sudore fuoriuscire dalla papalina di Innocenzo.

Pacito si avvicinò e le sussurrò all'orecchio: "Cosa credi che stiano pensando?"

Gli umani pregavano perlopiù in silenzio, anche se San Bruce, Uma Bhattacharjee e due dei medi mugugnavano *aum* e di tanto in tanto Chioma Melky emetteva un fischio ansimante.

"La preghiera non consiste nel pensare." Tikko prese una pesca dal suo cestino da pranzo e strofinò il pollice sulla peluria del frutto. "Almeno, è quello che dicono."

"Cosa intendi? Se è nelle loro teste, allora deve trattarsi di pensiero." Aspettò un cenno di assenso da parte di Tikko; quando lei rimase in silenzio Pacito arricciò le labbra. "Cos'altro potrebbe essere?"

"Forse qualcuno sta pensando al posto loro." Diede un morso alla pesca. "Come quando apriamo le nostre menti ai bot."

"E chi starebbe pensando al posto loro? Il tuo papa dei papi?" Allungò il piede e prese con le dita una cartaccia scartata dal pranzo. "I bot?"

"Sai bene che gli umani non sanno aprire la propria mente."

"Ne siamo sicuri?"

Tikko si leccò il succo dal mento. "È quello che dicono i bot."

"Perché l'adunanza ha ordinato loro di farlo." Accartocciò la cartaccia nel suo cestino del pranzo, evitando alla squadra di Moss un po' lavoro. "Non significa che sia vero."

"Parli come mia sorella."

Pacito scoppiò a ridere. "È da quando è arrivato quello lì...," rivolse lo sguardo a Innocenzo, "... che faccio pensieri strani."

"Non scervellarti troppo, caro." Tikko lanciò il nocciolo della pesca e lo guardò rimbalzare sulla veranda. Avrebbe voluto che Pacito la rassicurasse, ma lui rimase in silenzio. "Guardali," disse infine Tikko. "Non fanno che starsene inginocchiati lì." Si mise a quattro zampe e iniziò a fare avanti e indietro. "In pace."

"È una cosa buona, non credi?"

"Mi occupo di alcuni di loro da otto anni. Forse nove." Tikko gironzolò fino all'estremità della veranda, diede un pizzicotto a Clin che stava sonnecchiando al sole per poi tornare da Pacito. "Non rimangono mai seduti immobili quando sono io a chiedere loro di farlo. Mai. È come se avessero delle formiche nelle mutande. E non sono mai stati tranquilli tanto a lungo se non quando dormono."

"Stai dicendo che non sono pazzi com'erano un tempo?"

"La settimana scorsa ha fatto camminare un rigido."

"E allora?" Pacito si grattò la pancia. "Moss dice che Joe Gluck non era poi così rigido."

"E guarda i tuoi." Appoggiò la mano sul mento di Pacito e lo fece voltare verso i medi inginocchiati. "Dopo la preghiera sono sempre più vitali. Direi quasi felici."

"Sono umani, cara." Sbadigliò. "Gli umani non sono mai felici."

Tikko oscillò avanti e indietro, i pensieri che le si sovrapponevano l'uno sull'altro. "Dov'è Helen Calabrese? L'ho mandata da te, ma non l'ho mai vista con la tua tribù."

"Sta bene, Tikko." Pacito le gettò un braccio sulle spalle. "E smettila di preoccuparti." L'avvicinò a sé e le baciò il lato del viso tre volte. "Altrimenti ci farai preoccupare tutti."

Innocenzo si era alzato; la preghiera era terminata. Si rivolse alle tribù radunate, papi e medi, e perfino quelli che non avevano pregato con lui sembravano abbeverarsi dalle sue parole come se stessero morendo disidratati. Per un minuto circa Innocenzo parlò loro di speranza e del bisogno di andare avanti. Disse che gli umani si trovavano davanti a una nuova sfida. Dio voleva che diffondessero ovunque il Sacro Pensiero.

"Perfino ai nostri curatori." Non era particolarmente robusto per un essere umano, ma al momento la sua voce lo faceva sembrare un gigante. Incrociò lo sguardo di Tikko con la sua solita arroganza e annuì. "Poiché sebbene non se ne siano ancora resi conto, sono figli di Dio tanto quanto noi."

Figli di Dio. Uno dei medi seduti ai tavoli da picnic si alzò e si inginocchiò insieme al resto della congregazione. Gli umani su ambo i lati aprirono le mani con i palmi verso l'alto come se volessero accoglierlo. Uno era San Bruce. Tikko rabbrividì. Non riusciva a capire esattamente cosa stesse accadendo, ma Pacito avrebbe dovuto condividere le sue preoccupazioni. Era come se un'ombra aleggiasse sulla loro comunità. Continuava a ricordare a se stessa che questi papi, i medi e i rigidi non erano coloro che avevano reinventato gli scimpanzé affidando loro il mondo. Quegli umani si erano trasferiti nella cognisfera. Perciò Innocenzo si sbagliava, doveva sbagliarsi.

Se gli adunati avessero voluto che Pip, la prima scimpanzé, conoscesse Dio, le avrebbero insegnato a pregare.

Tikko fece oscillare l'altalena verso il trespolo tre metri più in alto rispetto alla veranda. Afferrò il ramo d'acero levigato da migliaia di prese analoghe, e lasciò che lo slancio portasse i suoi piedi verso il muro, dove si appoggiò un istante per rimbalzare verso l'alto. Torcendosi a mezz'aria, atterrò sulla piattaforma del trespolo su tutte e quattro le zampe, si voltò e balzò verso la tana in corda. Con una mano dopo l'altra si tirò lungo le funi che portavano alla barra di ferro conficcata nel muro della sua stanza. Appesa alla sbarra con una mano, quasi senza fiato per l'arrampicata, sentì il cuore martellarle nel petto, il sangue che le pompava nelle vene. Era un sollievo poter finalmente volteggiare nella sua stanza, senza pensare a Innocenzo o agli altri papi. Si lasciò cadere a terra e fece un paio di salti all'indietro, tanto per veder girare il mondo.

"Tikko?"

Atterrò sulla sua scrivania e vide Helen Calabrese sulla soglia. "Che c'è?" la leggerezza del momento precedente ormai in frantumi. "C'è qualcosa che non va?"

"No." La donna tenne la porta aperta, esitante. "Sì." Si schiarì la gola. "Posso parlarti?"

"Sì, certo, vieni. Siedi."

Era confusa dal vedere Helen Calabrese negli alloggi degli scimpanzé senza invito, e rimase senza parole quando si chiuse la porta alle spalle. Tikko sapeva che a quel punto avrebbe dovuto aprire la mente. Di certo il room-bot avrebbe voluto monitorare quella strana conversazione. Ma invece fece un giro su se stessa sulla scrivania e si abbassò con il viso rivolto verso l'umana. "Allora?"

Helen Calabrese trascinò una sedia accanto al muro fino alla scrivania. "Mi sono sempre chiesta," iniziò, "se voi scimpanzé usiate davvero queste sedie. Sapete, quando non ci siamo noi umani in giro."

"Non sono molto comode." Le labbra di Tikko si assottigliarono, mettendo in mostra denti gialli e gengive rosa. "Per noi, almeno."

Helen Calabrese si accomodò. "Già." Sembrava non avere alcuna fretta di continuare la conversazione, così Tikko rimase in attesa. Era così che facevano gli umani; erano creature abituate a false partenze e lunghe pause. Alla fine Helen sbatté le mani sulle cosce, sembrava aver finalmente preso una decisione. "Voglio fare il pellegrinaggio."

Tikko sussultò esterrefatta. "All'Altare di Argonne?"

Helen calabrese annuì.

Il ronzio nella mente di Tikko divenne inarrestabile. *Una svolta*. Di tanto in tanto un medio lasciava la comunità diretto verso una delle riserve di umanisti, ma nessuno sotto la loro responsabilità aveva mai chiesto di unirsi all'adunanza. "Sei sicura? Voglio dire, è meraviglioso. Fantastico." Sapeva che stava balbettando, ma non le importava. "Ma perché lo stai dicendo a me? Ora sei una dei medi. È Pacito a occuparsi della tua tribù."

La donna si fissò le mani come se all'improvviso fosse sorpresa di vederle sulle sue gambe. "Non conosco bene Pacito. Ma conosco te. Mi hai aiutato a vedere il mondo per quel che è." A quel punto alzò lo sguardo fissando Tikko negli occhi, una violazione del protocollo che fino a quel momento Helen Calabrese non aveva mai commesso. "Se ho capito bene posso scegliere un testimone che mi accompagni. Uno scimpanzé. Mi faresti questo onore?"

Questo onore. "Sì, sì, certo, Helen Cala… Helen." Tikko si accorse che si stava tirando i peli del polso in preda al nervosismo. Con una sola parola – pellegrinaggio – questa umana aveva messo sottosopra lei e tutto il suo mondo. Helen Calabrese non aveva più bisogno di curatori; non era né un papa né una dei medi né un'umanista. Faceva parte degli adunati, o almeno lo sarebbe stata presto. Bixa, la madre di Tikko, sarebbe stata impressionata. Si sarebbe comportata in modo remissivo. E forse sarebbe stata abbastanza spaventata da nascondersi sotto la scrivania. Bixa raccontava storie straordinarie sugli umani che avevano abbandonato i propri corpi, anche se lei non ne aveva mai conosciuto uno di persona. Tikko rabbrividì al ricordo, ma si ricompose un istante dopo. Non era un'anziana timorosa da quattro soldi...

"Tikko, tutto bene?"

"Sto bene." Si chinò in avanti appoggiandosi su tutte e quattro le zampe; la posizione l'aiutò a stabilizzarsi. "Quando avevi intenzione di partire? Potremmo fare una deviazione per Cambridge durante la migrazione verso gli alloggi invernali."

"Prima, se è possibile. Sono pronta ad andare avanti. Io... mi sembra di non appartenere più a questo posto."

"Allora *c'è* qualcosa che non va?" Tikko si era occupata di Helen Calabrese per sei anni, e riusciva ancora a interpretare le sue emozioni, anche se stava per unirsi all'adunanza. "È qualcosa che riguarda Innocenzo?"

"Credevo di potergli sfuggire unendomi alla tribù dei medi." Si alzò dalla sedia. "Ma non è stato così."

"Ti ha infastidito?"

"Vuole salvarmi, Tikko. Vuole salvare tutti noi." Ora che si era alzata in piedi, sembrava smarrita. "Ha impiegato pochissimo a convertire tutti i papi, e ora vuole anche gli altri. Prima che ve ne rendiate conto, avrà conquistato qualsiasi essere vivente non catatonico." Inclinò il sorriso. "O forse convertirà anche loro."

"Puoi spostarti in un'altra comunità, se vuoi."

"E perché?" Helen Calabrese si passò le dita tra i capelli in preda alla frustrazione. "Non capisci, Tikko. Lui è convinto che questo sia il piano di Dio. Presto inizieranno a comparire dei missionari nelle altre comunità di curatori, poi nelle riserve umaniste. Crede di essere stato scelto per riunirci. Credimi, ho visto cos'è in grado di fare la religione. Conosco quelli come lui." Sollevò entrambe le mani all'altezza delle spalle in segno di resa. "A dire il vero, conosco *lui* personalmente."

"Cosa?" Tikko avvertì un formicolio caldo sulla nuca.

Helen Calabrese le spiegò che sin dal primo momento le era sembrato che Innocenzo avesse un volto famigliare, ma non era riuscita a ricordare chi era. Ora ricordava. Il suo cognome era Velasco; non era sicura del suo nome. Julio, o forse Javier. C'era stato un piccolo scandalo quando era stato cacciato dalla Scuola Divina di Yale. Dottorando in Tecnologia Sacra, aveva pubblicato un articolo secondo cui gli scienziati stavano agendo in accordo alla volontà di Dio quando avevano generato la cognisfera, poiché non avevano fatto altro che creare il paradiso biblico promesso dai tempi del Vecchio Testamento. Secondo Velasco lo stavano punendo per aver alimentato il dibattito; il suo tutor disse che parti dell'articolo erano plagiate. Helen Calabrese aveva esaminato il rapporto della commissione responsabile del reclamo sporto da Velasco: a fregarlo furono solo un paragrafo non accreditato e qualche frase copiata da altre fonti. "Dopodiché sparì," disse. "E poi è stato eletto papa." Scoppiò a ridere.

"Non è il papa," commentò Tikko.

"No, ma che differenza fa? Se non è *il* papa, è comunque il loro papa."

"Quindi ti unirai all'adunanza solo per scappare da lui?"

Prese la sedia come se fosse fatta di vetro, prima di riportarla vicino al muro. "Voi scimpanzé vivete credendo al mito sull'adunanza, siete convinti che quegli uomini fossero tutti saggi e puri e razionali." Il sorrisetto della donna la inquietava. "Sei miliardi di persone hanno compiuto il pellegrinaggio nella cognisfera, e ognuna di quelle persone aveva una motivazione diversa. Non erano tutte buone ragioni."

Quando Helen Calabrese si fu chiusa la porta alle spalle, Tikko si accasciò sulla scrivania a pancia all'aria, e rimase a fissare il soffitto della stanza. Pensò di arrampicarsi nella sua tana, ma era troppo esausta. Non credeva che rimanere senza parole fosse tanto faticoso. Poi ricordò che avrebbe dovuto aprire la mente, così diede ai bot accesso a quel che era appena successo. Scese dal tavolo, toccò terra e posizionò entrambe le mani sulla cupola del room-bot.

Erano passati anni dall'ultima volta che aveva deliberatamente aperto la mente. Padroneggiava la tecnica da quando aveva cinque anni – e in appena due settimane, più in fretta di tutti gli altri giovani. Bixa le aveva detto che era un segno; voleva dire che quando sarebbe cresciuta sarebbe diventata una degli alfa. Da allora a Tikko bastava vedere la sua mano sulla cupola di un bot, e la sua mente si apriva all'istante. Non notava più la presenza dei bot nella stanza, più o meno come non avrebbe notato il ronzio dell'aria condizionata nella Maple Suite o il frinire dei grilli in seggiovia.

Stavolta, invece, seguì deliberatamente la procedura che le aveva insegnato sua madre. Iniziò immaginando un albero, su cui poi iniziò ad arrampicarsi, lasciandosi i pensieri alle spalle, sul terreno sottostante. Più in alto si arrampicava e più i pensieri si allontanavano. Alla fine si fermò coprendosi le orecchie con le mani, chiuse gli occhi della sua immaginazione e trattenne il fiato. Quando non rimase nulla percepì finalmente il familiare vento che era assenza di pensiero, assenza di qualsiasi sensazione. Aveva quasi dimenticato che quel vento era nessuna cosa in particolare e molte al tempo stesso, e come il suo sibilo provenisse da tutte le direzioni contemporaneamente. Per un vertiginoso momento seppe qualsiasi cosa che fosse stata conosciuta al mondo, poi l'istante trascorse e tornò a terra, di nuovo sola con le sue conoscenze.

Ma ora sapeva una cosa in più. Per quanto sembrasse assurdo, gli adunati tenevano a lei.

"No, lui *non* verrà con noi," disse Tikko. "Dovrà restare qui."

Gli altri alfa la fissarono cauti, intimoriti dallo sfogo. Il silenzio era freddo come i muri in cemento della sala riunioni sotterranea.

"Tutto qui?," infine Lola trovò il coraggio di parlare. "Potresti forse darci una ragione?"

"Sì, perché oramai abbiamo deciso così. Dobbiamo metterci a cambiare il programma solo perché alcuni dei medi hanno storto il muso? Chi è al comando qui?"

"Noi. E noi stiamo cercando di capire cosa sia meglio per questa comunità."

"Helen Calabrese non vuole che venga."

Il labbro inferiore di Lola si allentò all'improvviso. Tikko detestava quando sua sorella lasciava a intendere pubblicamente che stava cercando di essere paziente con lei. "E per quale ragione?"

"Perché lui la vuole convertire a un qualche sciocco credo che nemmeno esiste. Perché cercherà di impedirle di unirsi all'adunata."

"Non possiamo esserne certi."

"È quello che pensa lei, Pacito. Questo è il suo pellegrinaggio, non quello di Julio Velasco."

"Ha cambiato nome. Ora si chiama Innocenzo."

"È un papa fuori di testa, per l'amor di Pip." A Tikko non piaceva ringhiare. "Prima di rendercene conto si farà chiamare da tutti Sua Santità."

"Calmati, Tikko."

Sia Gamba che Moss scivolarono sul tappeto da riunioni avvicinandosi a lei. Moss iniziò a spulciarle la schiena. Gamba le strinse le mani nelle sue. "Tranquilla cara," disse.

Quando Pacito riprese a parlare, lo fece con il tono di voce più gentile possibile. "Sta succedendo tutto molto in fretta, lo so. Ci sono molte cose nuove che dobbiamo comprendere. Innocenzo. Helen Calabrese. I tuoi papi, i miei medi, il modo in cui sono cambiati. Sono gli umani che lo vogliono, Tikko. E non avevano mai voluto nulla prima d'ora."

"È solo perché li sta fomentando lui."

Gamba le strinse le mani, ansimando comprensiva.

"A prescindere dalla motivazione, desiderare qualcosa è un buon segno," disse Lola. "Volere è salutare."

Tikko sapeva di aver perso la discussione. Gli altri alfa erano spaventati da quel che Innocenzo avrebbe potuto fare se le cose non fossero andate come voleva lui.

Si eresse sulle zampe posteriori, pronta ad andarsene. "Ho altra scelta?"

Il silenzio che seguì era la risposta migliore che potessero darle.

"Fatelo venire allora." Quelle parole le parvero cenere nella bocca mentre le pronunciava. "Ma verrà da solo."

Moss aggiunse: "Ma ha richiesto di..."

Tikko urlò e scagliò le braccia verso l'alto assumendo la posizione aggressiva. "*No.*" Scioccati, gli altri alfa si rannicchiarono sottomessi. Forse pensavano che avesse perso il controllo. E magari le cose stavano così.

"Partirò domani." Tikko scoprì i denti e indicò sua sorella. "E porterò Kulki con me. D'ora in poi lei sarà nella mia unità, cara sorella. Tu puoi riavere quell'idiota di tuo figlio, Clin."

Il mattino seguente, prima della partenza, a salutarli c'era tutta la comunità di scimpanzé, oltre alla maggior parte delle tre tribù umane. Nel corso delle settimane trascorse dal suo arrivo, Innocenzo aveva fatto camminare dodici rigidi di Lola, sebbene avessero ancora bisogno di altre cure.

Tikko, Helen Calabrese, Kulki e Ash superarono una folla di umani inginocchiati mentre salivano i gradini diretti verso la stazione fabbricata dai bot la sera prima. Innocenzo si fermò per benedirli. "Stanno pregando," gridò a Tikko. Quello che non disse fu cosa stessero pregando.

Il tram-bot era diviso in trenta vagoni letto; poteva ospitare centottanta scimpanzé o centoventi umani. Tikko fece sistemare Innocenzo, Ash e Kulki nei due vagoni posteriori, e accompagnò Helen Calabrese verso la parte anteriore, determinata a tenere i due umani quanto più distanti possibile. Appena tutti si furono accomodati, Tikko aprì la mente. Alle nove e trenta il tram-bot si sollevò dal suo attracco e levitò verso la flussovia della Northeast Main.

Per tre ore viaggiarono verso la Grande Foresta Settentrionale mentre Tikko teneva d'occhio Helen Calabrese. Se avesse voluto parlare, Tikko era pronta ad ascoltarla. Ma la donna sembrava oppressa e parve accontentarsi di guardare fuori dal finestrino, gli occhi sul panorama uniforme di alberi e colline e ruscelli che si estendeva verso sud fino alla riserva umanista del Connecticut. Dopo qualche minuto si appisolò. Nei pressi dell'area di scambio di York, Tikko decise di andare a controllare gli altri.

Innocenzo aveva lasciato il suo scompartimento per chiacchierare con Kulki e Ash. Il giovane scimpanzé non sembrava particolarmente felice della visita, mentre Kulki aveva deciso di assecondare il papa. Aveva accolto con eccitazione il fatto che sua madre l'avesse sottratta all'incarico di occuparsi dei rigidi, e probabilmente stava cercando di fare colpo con il suo spirito di gruppo.

"Ash, perché non vai un po' nel vagone anteriore?," disse Tikko, "Helen Calabrese si è addormentata; tienila d'occhio. Tra non molto mangiamo qualcosa."

Lo scimpanzé scese dalla panca su cui si era accovacciato e abbracciò Tikko. "Preghiamo affinché il pranzo arrivi alla svelta," sussurrò. "È l'unico modo per farlo stare zitto." Fece scivolare una mano sul braccio di Tikko.

Lei scoppiò a ridere, poi diede una spintarella a sua figlia. "Vatti a sgranchire un po' le zampe. Lo tengo d'occhio io."

"Rimango, maa." Kulki emise un soffio vibrato tra le labbra. "Sto bene."

"È innegabile," aggiunse Innocenzo. "Hai una cucciola davvero sveglia, Tikko. Non vedo l'ora che ci raggiunga nella tua unità."

Una cucciola. Si sedette accanto a sua figlia e davanti al papa. Kulki arruffò il pelo e Tikko le appoggiò una mano sul ginocchio per farle ritrovare l'equilibrio. Era felice che Ash avesse lasciato la porta scorrevole dello scompartimento aperta. In luoghi tanto ristretti l'odore carnoso della pelle umana risultava vagamente nauseante.

"Abbiamo rallentato," disse Innocenzo.

"Ci stiamo avvicinando allo scambio di York." Tikko tamburellò le nocche contro il finestrino. Il tram-bot era stato affiancato da una catena di trasporto merci; una serie di bot-container, bot-tramoggia, bot-cisterna e bot-disco traballarono al loro passaggio. "A breve cambieremo flussovia, imboccheremo la Lakes Main e poi ci dirigeremo verso Chicago, ovunque si trovi. Su un lago, suppongo."

"Non ci sei mai stata?"

"Nel centro del paese non ci sono altro che ammassi di bot. Quando andiamo verso gli alloggi invernali rimaniamo sulla Northeast Main fino a Chesapeake per poi prendere la Dixie Loop."

Ash sbatté una mano sullo stipite della porta. "Il bot deve averti sentito. Il pranzo è pronto."

Aprirono un tavolo tra le panche dello scompartimento e si avviarono verso la cucina di bordo per recuperare i cestini da pranzo. L'unità di Gamba aveva preparato scorte più che sufficienti per il viaggio di ventidue ore. Per gli scimpanzé foglie e frutta; nel suo cestino Tikko trovò un'albicocca, una fetta di melone, un grappolo di pomodori ciliegini e mezzo cavolo. Innocenzo sollevò il coperchio del suo cestino, annusò la zuppiera fumante e aggrottò la fronte. "Un altro stufato di lenticchie." Prese una fragola e se la mise in bocca. "Sapete per quale motivo le vostre tribù sono tanto fiacche?," disse. "Perché li state trasformando in vegetariani. Gli umani hanno bisogno di carne." Si colpì il petto con un pugno, sfoggiando quella che secondo lui doveva essere un'ottima imitazione della belligeranza degli scimpanzé.

Kulki gli porse una scatola di snack. "Gradisci una termite?," chiese impassibile.

Il papa fece una smorfia e rifiutò con un cenno della mano. "Poco fa stavo raccontando a tua figlia quanto fosse cambiata questa parte del paese. Con tutte le nuove foreste."

Tikko si mise una foglia di cavolo in bocca. "Non era così quando sei stato congelato?"

"Oh, proprio no."

"E quando è successo di preciso, quando ti sei fatto congelare?"

"Ah, scommetto che vi piacerebbe saperlo." Giocherellò con un cucchiaio di stufato.

"Julio Velasco è nato il 30 gennaio 2202 a Cartagena, in Colombia," intervenne Kulki. "Sei tu Julio Velasco?"

Innocenzo alzò un dito. "Lo ero."

"Roberto III morì il 22 settembre 2257. È stato l'ultimo papa noto."

L'uomo sembrava divertito. "I robot sono davvero bravi con le date."

"Si stima che l'adunanza sia stata completata in un momento compreso tra il marzo e l'aprile del 2294. Dopo quella data non sarebbe rimasto nessuno a eleggerti papa."

"Kulki, perché stai cercando di cogliermi in fallo? È proprio come te, Tikko." Si chinò sul tavolo e abbassò la voce. "Ovviamente, i bot si sbagliano sulla fine dell'adunanza."

"Davvero?," disse Kulki. "E come fai a saperlo?"

"Perché c'è ancora una persona che deve unirsi a loro!" La sua risata roboante scosse l'intero scompartimento.

"Magari preferiresti che Helen Calabrese non si unisse all'adunanza."

"Oh, no. Al contrario, insisto che vada fino in fondo."

Tikko rifletté. "Allora perché sei qui?"

"È necessario per quel che seguirà. Devo assistere a un'esecuzione prima di poter predicare contro la pena di morte."

"Questa non è un'esecuzione."

"Ah." Innocenzo rispose con un sorriso subdolo. "Devo essermi sbagliato, allora."

"C'era un tempo in cui credevi che la cognisfera fosse il paradiso." Disse Kulki.

"Suppongo sia stata Helen a dirvelo."

Errore. Tikko sapeva che Kulki non aveva parlato con Helen. Era soddisfatta dalla tenacia di sua figlia, e incredula che avesse trovato il tempo di consultare i bot per ricerche tanto approfondite. Forse insieme sarebbero riuscite a tirar fuori la verità da Innocenzo. "Helen ti conosceva," disse, "quando ti chiamavi Velasco."

Kulki emise un verso di sorpresa.

"Ha detto proprio così?" Le guance di Innocenzo si tinsero di rosa. "Strano, visto che non ci siamo mai incontrati di persona." Si portò un fazzoletto alla bocca per ricomporsi. "In ogni caso, da allora il mio pensiero sulla cognisfera è cambiato." Infilò il tovagliolo nel cestino, chiuse il coperchio e sorrise loro impaziente.

Tikko sapeva che Innocenzo voleva che gli domandassero in che modo il suo pensiero fosse cambiato, ma decise di non dargli soddisfazione. Kulki, d'altro canto, non riuscì a trattenersi. "E diccelo, per l'amor di Pip."

"Ebbene. Se la cognisfera è come ci è stato promesso, allora dev'essere in tutto e per tutto simile al paradiso. Ma da sempre è anche vero che per poter andare in paradiso si deve morire. Ora la domanda è: come facciamo a sapere che gli adunati sono realmente stati trasferiti? I loro corpi sono indubbiamente deceduti. E se anche tutte le loro informazioni fossero andate perdute? Se la cognisfera fosse una menzogna?"

"Ci credevano sei miliardi di umani."

"Esatto. E quanti di loro sono tornati indietro per dirci quando sia paradisiaca?"

Kulki sembrava confusa. "Ma perché avrebbero dovuto?"

"Ah, Kulki, credo che tua madre abbia capito cosa intendo. Per quelli di noi che sono rimasti indietro, unirsi all'adunanza e morire è pressoché la stessa cosa."

"Ma se anche le cose stessero così..."

"Gli umani che sono ancora in vita, i dissidenti, hanno commesso un errore. Hanno iniziato a considerare gli adunati come divinità e si sono convinti che l'era dell'uomo è passata. Ed è quello che credete anche voi scimpanzé, non è così? Che abbiamo bisogno di essere accuditi. Tenuti nelle riserve. Credete che questo sia il vostro mondo, ora. Ma se invece i veri folli fossero gli adunati? In tal caso non avreste fatto altro che assecondare il loro piano." Tornò ad appoggiare la schiena e incrociò le dita delle mani. "Credo che Dio abbia un piano diverso. Per gli umani, e per gli scimpanzé."

Tikko aveva sentito diverse storie sul panorabot, ma nessuna di esse avrebbe potuto prepararla alle sue terribili geometrie. A due ore da Chicago, l'alba illuminò un mondo in cui tutti i colori erano tonalità di grigio. I bot avevano dichiarato guerra alla natura, e in quel territorio conquistato avevano sterminato brutalmente il nemico. C'erano piccole aree con erba e boscaglia sparsa, qualche campo polveroso, ma per il resto nient'altro che edifici e metallo a perdita d'occhio. Tikko ebbe l'impressione che le numerose fabbriche avessero usato il cemento per inondare ogni cosa, riversandolo nei fiumi e nei torrenti, trasformando i laghi in collettori di fanghi e bacini di decantazione. Scheletriche torri di trasmissione sfumavano all'orizzonte, intricate condutture si avvolgevano alla loro base come serpi. Il tram-bot costeggiò un aeroporto senza fine, le sue piste d'asfalto lucido sotto il sole del mattino. L'area di scambio di Chicago era affollata da serie chilometriche di container. Bot-disco transitavano sotto enormi gru per container, mentre i bot-tramoggia aspettavano pazienti il loro carico dai montacarichi d'immagazzinamento. Cambiarono di nuovo flussovia e imboccarono la Prairie Main, che li avrebbe portati praticamente davanti all'Altare della Scienza di Argonne, dove si sarebbe concluso il pellegrinaggio di Helen Calabrese.

Tikko continuava a tenerla d'occhio, ma la sua risolutezza sembrava ferrea. Accoglieva educatamente gli approcci di conversazione della sua curatrice, ma non li incoraggiava. Bevve dell'acqua da una bottiglia, mangiò una mela e, come Tikko, fissò il mondo che i bot stavano costruendo con tanta solerzia, spesso con la fronte premuta contro il finestrino. Innocenzo, d'altra parte, sembrava impaziente, e continuava a rimbalzare avanti e indietro da uno scompartimento all'altro per carpire quante più informazioni possibile, esclamando e indicando qualsiasi cosa, e infastidendo Ash al di là di ogni dire.

Tikko era orgogliosa di come la sua unità stava affrontando la situazione, soprattutto considerato quanto *lei* si sentisse intimidita dal panorabot. I tram-bot continuavano a mormorare parole nella sua testa che non aveva mai sentito prima, ma che non voleva ricordare. C'erano fonderie e fabbriche e forni e fornaci con ciminiere simili a dita nere che ghermivano il cielo. E c'erano radome simili a giganteschi nidi di vespe che sondavano il cielo alla ricerca di tempeste mentre una torre a freddo estraeva azoto e ossigeno dall'aria – com'era possibile? C'erano fattorie che si ergevano su terreni dove non cresceva alcuna pianta, fattorie di dati, fattorie eoliche. In lontananza Tikko riconobbe il profilo di una raffineria, una vasta città per idrocarburi. I bot escavatori strappavano pezzi di cemento per riciclare i tesori smarriti nelle discariche, per estrarre calcare rimuovendo la ghiaia in eccesso. Tentò di chiudere gli occhi, ma non aiutò granché; l'enunciazione delle infinite attività dei bot continuava implacabile.

Quando il tram-bot raggiunse l'attracco della stazione diArgonne, Helen Calabrese riemerse finalmente dal suo scompartimento. Si era cambiata, ora indossava un abito che metteva in mostra la carnagione chiara delle sue spalle e dei polpacci. Era pallida come il cielo d'estate; una fascia blu scuro le cingeva la vita. Anche le scarpe erano blu, con strani tacchi a punta. Tikko faceva raramente caso a quel che indossavano gli umani, ma era certa di non aver mai visto nulla del genere in vita sua. Forse si trattava di un abito cerimoniale, come i paramenti di Innocenzo. Helen Calabrese percorse il corridoio, tenendo un braccio teso come se stesse per recuperare l'equilibrio dopo aver inciampato, ma senza mai toccare il muro. Innocenzo, Ash e Kulki la guardarono avvicinarsi. Non accennava a fermarsi, e se gli scimpanzé non avessero fatto spostare Innocenzo, la donna gli sarebbe di sicuro finita addosso. Tikko aveva vietato al papa di parlare con Helen Calabrese, a meno che non fosse lei a rivolgergli la parola per prima. Quando gli passò davanti, Innocenzo tese un braccio come se volesse prenderle la mano. Ma lei lo ignorò.

Il timore di Tikko di dover attraversare l'ostile panorabot si dissolse quando mise piede sulla piattaforma. Il terreno dell'Altare della Scienza di Argonne aveva prati e alberi e cespugli potati con precisione robotica. I fiori oscillavano al vento in giardini ordinati intorno a bassi edifici, la maggior parte dei quali sembrava essere però in disuso. C'erano ancora troppi mattoni, cemento e vetro per i gusti di Tikko, ma in quelle proporzioni le sembrarono quasi confortanti dopo l'incubo di Chicago. Il campus era circondato da una strada ad anello su cui sciamavano bot di ogni tipo – più di quanti ne avesse mai visti prima.

Tikko si chiese come avrebbero fatto a trovare la strada, ma la sua mente era spalancata, e i bot radunati la guidarono verso il sentiero giusto. Dopo una camminata di cinque minuti raggiunsero un edificio appoggiato sulle sue fondamenta come un quarto di melone. Qualche passo in più e raggiunsero l'entrata del lato tondeggiante, la facciata piatta rivolta nella direzione opposta. La struttura era alta circa sei metri, con una base altrettanto larga, ed era rivestita interamente di marmo nero. Superando l'entrata le venne in mente il nome adeguato per quell'edificio. *Guscio*.

Non era quel che si aspettava.

Il pavimento del guscio consisteva in una scacchiera di quadrati in marmo bianco e nero. La mezza cupola del soffitto era formata da cassettoni neri quadrati: cinque file da quattordici. Il guscio dava su un giardino. Cespugli di sedum, buddleia e begonie bianche circondavano vasi di gigari color borgogna.

All'interno, il guscio era vuoto.

Attese di ricevere altre istruzioni, ma i bot che ronzavano nella sua testa rimasero in silenzio. Kulki emise un *hoo* incerto. Ash fece un cenno verso il giardino. "Lì fuori?," domandò. Tikko fece strada.

Erano a circa cinque metri dal limite del guscio quando l'apertura venne inondata da un'accecante luce pallida. Si immobilizzarono. I colori brillanti del giardino erano ora pastelli sfavillanti. La luce sembrava liquida, al punto che per un attimo Tikko credette di poterla raccogliere tra le mani. Non che avesse voglia di provarci.

Helen Calabrese si irrigidì; Tikko era certa che stesse per dare di matto.

"Che cosa devo fare?," chiese.

"Continuare a camminare?," propose Tikko.

Helen appoggiò una mano sulla spalla di Tikko cercando di accarezzarla. "Grazie." Aveva le dita rigide, si muovevano con imbarazzo. O forse si stava solo appoggiando un'ultima volta alla sua curatrice in cerca di supporto. Tikko sapeva che avrebbe dovuto confortarla in qualche modo, ma cosa poteva dire una scimpanzé a una degli adunati?

Poi Helen Calabrese si avviò verso la luce.

Innocenzo gridò: "Hai qualche ultima parola, Helen?"

"Va' all'inferno," disse senza voltarsi.

Tikko fece un cenno ad Ash e Kulki, che afferrarono il papa dalle spalle. "Non un'altra parola," ringhiò l'alfa.

Il metallo dei tacchi di Helen rintoccò sul pavimento in marmo. Ecco cos'avrebbe ricordato Tikko quando fu tutto finito. Helen Calabrese gridò un nome. Forse Cass o Cassy. Dopodiché si mise a correre. Tac, tac, tac. Quando si gettò nella luce, il ticchettio dei tacchi si interruppe. Tikko vide il corpo di Helen Calabrese disteso in mezzo al giardino alle spalle dell'apertura luminosa del guscio. Stava ancora trattenendo il respiro quando Innocenzo parlò.

"Orribile." La voce piena di pietà. "Un orribile, orribile spreco."

"Smettila."

"Ma avevo ragione, non vedi? Non si può in alcun modo scansionare una mente umana in un solo istante."

Sentì la rabbia travolgerla. Aveva qualcosa a che fare con la luce. Era certa che quella sensazione sarebbe sparita, ora che Helen Calabrese si era unita all'adunanza, ma non accadde. Al contrario, quella rabbia continuò a travolgerla, non più goccia dopo goccia, ma come un fiume in piena. Ed era tornato anche il vento nella sua mente, solo che adesso non era più un sussurro; ora ululava, e così anche Tikko si mise a ululare. Kulki e Ash risposero allo stesso modo, le bocche spalancate e le zanne scintillanti che riflettevano la luce omicida. Sapeva che lo avvertivano anche loro.

"Che state facendo?," chiese Innocenzo. Iniziò a divincolarsi per liberarsi dalla presa di Ash e Kuliki.

Le urla degli scimpanzé riempirono nella mezza cupola e riecheggiarono nella mente di Tikko; le sembrò che sei miliardi di voci le ordinassero di lanciarsi contro il papa. Si voltò all'istante appoggiandosi sulle zampe anteriori e posteriori e si scagliò contro la schiena di Innocenzo. L'umano era in preda al panico. Ancora bloccato dalla presa degli altri due scimpanzé, barcollò verso la luce.

"No. *Fermi.*"

Lo portarono ansimante e agitato proprio sulla soglia. Tikko si sbatté con forza le mani sulle orecchie, perché ora Innocenzo stava urlando; Ash e Kulki – sua figlia, la sua arrabbiatissima figlia – lo spinsero con forza. L'uomo barcollò all'interno della luce. Tentò di voltarsi per tornare indietro, ma all'improvviso i suoi piedi non poggiavano più a terra. Un istante dopo il suo corpo si accasciò finendo sull'erba. All'interno del guscio erano rimaste solo le sue pantofole rosse.

Non c'era altro suono al di fuori dei loro respiri. Il vento nella mente di Tikko andò scemando. La luce all'apertura del guscio svanì.

Sopraffatta, Tikko si sedette sul freddo marmo. "Cos'abbiamo fatto?"

"L-L'abbiamo mandato in paradiso." Kulki girò su se stessa per due volte e si accovacciò dando le spalle ai cadaveri.

Peccato. Per la prima volta Tikko comprese per quale motivo quella parola avesse tormentato tanto gli umani. Si sentiva male dalla vergogna, una presenza fino a quel momento estranea nella sua mente. "Ma adesso dobbiamo tornare indietro," disse. "Da Pacito. Dai medi. Come spiegheremo tutto questo?"

"Spiegare?" Ash le si avvicinò prendendole una mano nella sua. "Non so nemmeno bene io cos'è successo." L'aiutò a rimettersi in piedi con mani tremanti. "Dobbiamo andare, Tikko."

Quattro bot si riversarono nel giardino, camminando su zampe da ragno. Quando due di loro voltarono il corpo di

Innocenzo, Ash emise un urlo e Kulki si voltò per assistere a quel tremendo spettacolo. I bot spostarono il peso sulle gambe posteriori, fecero scivolare le zampe anteriori sotto i cadaveri e li sollevarono. Come un ramo secco. Tikko mise una mano sulla spalla di Kulki, mentre gli altri due bot sollevavano il corpo esanime di Helen Calabrese. Come un coniglio morto.

Ash urlò di nuovo, così si misero a correre.

Galoppando su tutte e quattro le zampe, gli scimpanzé si precipitarono fuori dal guscio e giù per il sentiero che li avrebbe riportati alla stazione. Tikko seguiva a ruota i due scimpanzé più giovani, e fu l'ultima a raggiungere il tram-bot, ancora sospeso al suo attracco. La porta posteriore si aprì per lasciarli entrare. All'interno, Tikko trovò Ash che grattava freneticamente i muri del corridoio, Kulki rannicchiata sotto un tavolo in uno degli scompartimenti. Non riuscì ad aprire la mente, o forse i bot radunati intorno alla stazione avevano mantenuto la sua mente aperta per tutto il tempo. In ogni caso, alla fine la porta si chiuse.

Il tram-bot imboccò la flussovia allontanandosi dalla stazione di Argonne.

Gli scimpanzé si nascosero in vari scompartimenti e non uscirono allo scoperto finché non si furono allontanati dal panorabot. Tikko passò il tempo cercando di capire cos'era successo nel guscio, basandosi su quelli che sperava fossero suoi pensieri riguardanti i bot e a quello che le avevano fatto. E riguardanti l'adunanza.

Nei suoi attimi di rabbia all'interno del guscio, aveva voluto uccidere Innocenzo, *sì*, o perlomeno liberarsi di lui. Ne era piuttosto sicura. Ma gettarlo nella cognisfera contro la sua volontà? *No*. Non era quello il dovere che avevano gli scimpanzé nei confronti degli umani. Tikko sapeva che si era avvicinata terribilmente alla soglia del peccato, ma non era stata lei a precipitare. Era stata spinta. Alla fine, quella conclusione l'alleggerì di una parte dei suoi timori.

Ash e Kulki avevano portato cestini per il pranzo nel loro scomparto verso la parte posteriore del tram-bot. Anche loro sembravano più sollevati – almeno abbastanza da mangiare.

Tikko sedette sulla panca accanto a sua figlia e prese una pera dal cestino.

"Dobbiamo decidere cosa racconteremo," disse Tikko.

Kulki emise un *hoo* d'approvazione. "Ne stavamo appunto discutendo."

"È morto," disse Ash. "Si è smarrito, ha avuto un incidente ed è morto." Gettò le braccia verso l'alto, come se la stesse sfidando a contraddirlo. "Tutto qua."

Tikko morse il frutto. La stagione delle pere era finita da un pezzo, e la polpa bianca era farinosa. "Potrà essere sufficiente per gli altri," disse. "Ma cosa raccontiamo a noi stessi?"

Ash lasciò cadere le braccia sulla panca e fissò il tavolo.

"Maa, non lo so," disse Kulki.

"Allora, ecco cosa credo che sia successo. Abbiamo aperto le nostre menti ai bot e loro si sono approfittati di noi." Diede un altro morso alla pera.

"I bot?," chiese Ash. "I bot volevano che noi lo spingessimo nell'adunanza? E perché?"

"Perché i bot sono l'adunanza." Tikko fece una pausa, cercando di interpretare l'espressione della figlia. "Alcuni di loro, in ogni caso." Vide che l'idea stava facendo presa sui due giovani, così continuò. "E l'adunanza è composta da esseri umani, o almeno è ciò che erano."

"Ma non ha senso," disse Ash, con la fronte aggrottata.

"Sì." Kulki avvolse le braccia intorno a Tikko avvicinandola a sé. "E non vogliono lasciarci soli."

"Forse," disse Tikko, "dovremmo costringerli a farlo."

Tikko ci rifletté un istante, e giunse alla conclusione che era davvero buffo. *Hhe hhe.* Le labbra di Ash si ripiegarono mettendo in mostra i denti, la bocca si spalancò e poi, mentre il trambot fluttuava su per la flussovia diretto verso casa, tutti e tre gli scimpanzé scoppiarono a ridere, rivolti per terra, rotolando sulla schiena. *hhee hhee hhee hheep*

Un suono che nessun essere umano avrebbe mai sentito.

UNA SORELLA, DUE SORELLE, TRE

Questa non è la mia storia – io non sono nessuno. È la storia di mia sorella. È Zana che se ne è andata, lasciandomi su questo triste, piccolo mondo su cui eravamo nate. E dove un giorno morirò, come desidera la Divina Moya. È questo che Moya si aspetta da ciascuno di no: la morte. È ciò che ha in serbo per tutti coloro che ancora seguono le usanze umane.

Siamo nate sorelle gemelle, Jix e Zana, separate da tredici minuti – uno dei numeri sacri. Siamo state concepite come Moya prevede, la madre aderente al padre, lo sperma che cerca l'uovo. Nel primo anno di vita, siamo state inseparabili. Danzavamo al cospetto delle lune e pregavamo i numeri sacri e prendevamo in giro i ragazzi che venivano in chiesa con noi. Gli stessi ragazzi che un giorno avremmo baciato. Nostro padre ci insegnò a cucinare i biscotti che vendevamo ai turisti che venivano dai Mille Mondi, e nostra madre ci insegnò a contare il denaro con cui ci pagavano. Una famiglia di reietti felici che viveva appena fuori dalle rovine.

Ma verso la fine dell'adolescenza iniziammo ad allontanarci. Zana aveva ricevuto quella bellezza impeccabile che solo Moya può donare. I suoi rapporti erano vicini all'1,618 della perfezione Divina, i suoi ricci stretti, e la sua pelle brillava di una scura lucentezza, come la mezzanotte dello Sperone Frastagliato. La sua alta fronte terminava con liquidi occhi marroni. Zana indossava i suoi sentimenti come una corona consacrata davanti agli occhi di tutti; la trasparenza faceva parte del suo fascino. Io non ero male, ma in confronto a mia sorella, i miei lineamenti risultavano ordinari, così dovetti trovare un'altra strada. Mentre Zana poteva permettersi di essere timida, soprattutto con gli sconosciuti, io ero sempre diretta. Mentre lei rifletteva sulla parola giusta da pronunciare, io lasciavo che fosse la mia lingua a riflettere. Non mi importava quel che dicevano di noi. *Zana la bella e Jix la spiritosa*. Forse per alcuni ragazzi parlavo troppo, come diceva sempre mia madre, ma un silenzio troppo prolungato mi faceva tremare le labbra. E in fin dei conti anch'io avevo i miei ammiratori, sebbene non tanti quanti mia sorella.

Dopo aver compiuto vent'anni, un anno dopo la nostra consacrazione a Moya, nostra madre si ammalò. Eravamo talmente impegnate che non notammo i segnali. I turisti sciamavano di continuo nelle rovine, perciò non avevamo nemmeno il tempo per cucinare gli stravaganti biscotti che piacevano tanto a nostro padre. Per stare al passo con la domanda, la nostra famiglia sfornò pile e pile di Gocceglassate, semplici ma grosse come dischi, con sopra al massimo una manciata d'uvetta o una spolverata di corteccia dolce, tanto per catturare l'attenzione. Non erano i nostri prodotti migliori, ma in qualche modo io e Zana riuscivamo sempre a guadagnare qualche soldo in più. Io stavo mettendo da parte i soldi per una power-moto, mentre mia sorella voleva imparare l'anglico.

Il nostro banco era sullo spiazzo, il terzo a partire da Shellgate, montato a ridosso del muro occidentale delle rovine lasciate dagli Esotici. Mentre entravano, i turisti si soffermavano ad ammirare mia sorella, e intanto io ne approfittavo per vendere loro i nostri prodotti. Nonostante fossero tutti replicati che si erano allontanati dalle usanze umane, avevano pur sempre stomaci come tutti noi. Un certo appetito per i dolci e il gusto per la bellezza erano incastonati nel nostro genoma comune.

Il giorno in cui tutto è cambiato, un turista insistente si attardò vicino al nostro banco nonostante avesse concluso i suoi acquisti. La donna dell'Istituto che lo accompagnava, probabilmente la sua responsabile, non vedeva l'ora di accedere alle rovine. E io sarei stata altrettanto felice se l'avesse trascinato via, ma Zana sembrava incoraggiare la conversazione. Lui era abbastanza bello, in quel modo senza età tipico dei replicati, ma di certo non era qualcuno con cui avrei sprecato fiato.

Mentre Zana impacchettava i biscotti esaminò il mio puzzle votivo. "Ingegnoso." Manipolò i triangoli magnetici del pentacolo per creare la stella a cinque punte di Moya diretta verso l'alto. "E come lo usate questo? Come stimolatore di meditazione?"

"Serve a predire quanti acquisti faranno i nostri clienti."

"Non faccia caso a lei." Zana si imbarazzò quando presi in giro il turista. "È la geometria sacra di Moya. Lo usiamo per pregare i numeri."

La responsabile borbottò qualcosa in anglico.

"La prego – siamo ospiti sul loro mondo." Il turista la rimproverò. "Parliamo la loro lingua."

"Il santuario venne eretto da una setta chiamata i Moyani," ripeté la responsabile. "Per anni ci tennero nascoste le rovine degli Esotici. Credono che un contatto ravvicinato con noi porti al peccato."

"Il peccato. Già," commentò lui. "Ho sfogliato la guida che mi hai inviato." Si voltò verso Zana. "E lo scopo di questi..." Spostò i triangoli per creare il pentacolo rovesciato.

"Ci rammentano la presenza della Divina," disse Zana. Rimasi sorpresa quando uscì da dietro il bancone con l'acquisto del turista. "Ci ricordano che Moya è ovunque."

"La religione locale." Sbuffò la responsabile, "Una sorta di umanismo."

Il turista la ignorò con un cenno della mano. "Ti prego, continua." Continuava a incastrare distrattamente i pezzi del puzzle rimettendoli al loro posto – l'ennesimo abitante del mondo di sopra incantato dalla bellezza di mia sorella.

"Il rapporto divino è l'impronta digitale di Moya. Ci insegna a obbedire alle sue leggi e a rimanere fedeli alla nostra mortalità." Zana gli prese il puzzle di mano, scambiandolo con i suoi biscotti. Per un istante, le loro dita si sfiorarono. "È visibile ovunque nella sua creazione. Nella spirale delle galassie e negli antichi edifici all'interno di quelle mura." Fece un cenno con il capo verso i Gusci, ma tenne gli occhi fissi su quelli del turista. "I petali di un fiore. Le sue orecchie." Gli sfiorò l'orecchio con il dorso della mano. "Perfino il suo DNA." La sua voce si era trasformata in una specie di basso mormorio. "È ovunque, l'universo è permeato dai suoi numeri sacri."

Non riuscivo a credere che stesse flirtando con un abitante del mondo di sopra. "Sapeva," mi intromisi, "che una molecola di DNA misura trentaquattro ångström di lunghezza e ventuno di larghezza per ogni ciclo della spirale a doppia elica?"

"Davvero?," disse lui, anche se le mie parole per lui non avevano più significato del chiacchericcio degli strada-bot, o del sospiro dei nostri tendoni al vento.

"Otto più tredici fa ventuno." Pensai che pregare i sacri numeri potesse distrarre Zana. "Tredici più ventuno fa trentaquattro. Ventuno più trentaquattro…"

La guida si avvicina al replicato. "Venerano la sequenza di Fibonacci."

"Noi veneriamo la Divina." Zana sfoggiò un'espressione sognante. "I numeri ci indicano il suo operato e ci dicono quello che lei si aspetta da noi."

"Io sono Quin," disse poi il turista. "Come hai detto di chiamarti?"

"Ragazze!"

Ero talmente scioccata dalle moine di Zana che non avevo fatto caso a nostro padre che si precipitava giù verso lo spiazzo.

"Ora!" Era senza fiato. "È ora… di… chiudere." Cosa poteva esserci di tanto importante da farlo uscire dalla sua cucina a quest'ora del giorno? E quello che diceva non aveva senso. Chiudere? Avevamo ancora tutto il pomeriggio davanti. Pile e pile di biscotti da vendere.

"Così presto?," chiesi. Un bus proveniente dallo spazioporto sferragliò fino a fermarsi poco lontano. "Se ti serve una mano porta Zana. Non sta combinando nulla qui." Altri turisti appena usciti dagli alberghi si riversarono fuori dalle porte scorrevoli del bus.

"Voglio che veniate entrambe. A casa." Aveva la voce spezzata. "*Subito*."

Zana tornò di corsa dietro il bancone per infilare in un cesto vuoto i biscotti invenduti.

"E così ti chiami Zana, eh?" Il turista si era appoggiato sul bancone. "Zana, prima che tu vada, vorrei chiederti..."

"Lascia perdere!" Nostro padre diede una manata al cesto, rovesciando tutti i biscotti a terra. "Lasciate perdere tutto. Dobbiamo andare!"

"Che cos'è successo?" chiesi. "Padre?"

"Vostra madre." Ci prese per mano trascinandoci oltre le bancarelle affollate. "Vostra madre ha perso la testa." Quando si voltò a guardare il suo turista sbigottito Zana inciampò, rischiando di cadere, ma nostro padre riuscì a sorreggerla appena in tempo.

Nostra madre era seduta al tavolo della cucina, i capelli sciolti, il volto contratto, le mani strette intorno a una tazza di tè speziato. Le piaceva intenso e dolce; quando ripenso a quel giorno ancora sento quell'orribile profumo. Ci fissò come se fosse sorpresa di vederci, come se avesse dimenticato di avere delle figlie. Poi disse: "Sono appena tornata dalla clinica. Ho la Hrutchma."

Non pianse mai, nemmeno una volta, nel corso di quel lungo pomeriggio. E nemmeno io. Zana si lanciò al collo di nostra madre, poi si mise a piangere coprendosi il volto a mani aperte, e alla fine appoggiò il capo sul tavolo della cucina, le spalle tremanti. Le lacrime di nostro padre erano calde; solo più tardi avremmo compreso cosa nascondevano.

La Hrutchma era una malattia che conoscevamo fin troppo bene. Causava una cosa chiamata iperplasia linfoide, un intenso aumento di cellule all'interno dei linfonodi. La Hrutchma iniziò con noduli nel petto sempre più grossi, le comprimevano i polmoni togliendole il respiro. La notavo quando le veniva il fiatone, nonostante lei ci scherzasse su; dava la colpa ai biscotti di nostro padre, che la facevano ingrassare. Man mano che progrediva, la malattia prese ad aggredire il suo sistema immunitario, portando a lesioni nervose, infezioni, febbri fulminanti. Era morta così nonna Deel, la madre di nostro padre – in preda al delirio mentre scottava come un forno istantaneo. Secondo l'enciclopedia medica sul tell, la Hrutchma è presente solo solo su Sanctuary. Alcuni reietti raccontavano che la malattia si diffuse in seguito a una maledizione che gli Esotici lanciarono sulle antiche pietre, ma non potevamo permettere che quella diceria si diffondesse troppo. I turisti ci consentivano di mettere il pane sotto i denti.

Ricordo di essere affondata su una sedia davanti a nostra madre, cercando di immaginare come avrei potuto vivere in un mondo senza di lei. Non potevo, in parte perché ero troppo insensibile, e in parte perché venivo distratta da Zana. Mia madre si accomodò accanto a me, singhiozzante, e io mi sentii in colpa perché non riuscivo a piangere. Ero senza parole per il modo in cui si tratteneva nostro padre. Mi aspettavo che anche lui provasse dolore. Ma no – sembrava arrabbiato.

Anche Zana se ne accorse. "Padre, cosa c'è che non va?"

"Lei." Emise una risata secca. "È lei che non va."

"È malata!" Zana si passò una mano sul volto umido. "Come puoi incolparla?" Mi domando ora se avesse capito cosa stava per succedere. Conosceva nostra madre meglio di me.

"La Hrutchma posso anche accettarla." Scosse la testa disgustato. "Ma il resto proprio no."

"Puoi accettare che sto per morire?" La voce di nostra madre era affilata come uno schiaffo. "Ho quarantun anni."

"Accetto la volontà della Divina," ribatté lui. "E tu dovresti fare lo stesso. Le nostre figlie sono consacrate a Moya."

Lei distolse lo sguardo per voltarsi verso di noi. "Vostro padre non capisce." Incrociò il nostro sguardo senza esitazione o rimorso. "Andrò a Skytown."

"Per poter vivere." Nostro padre pronunciò quelle parole come un'accusa, ma lei lo ignorò. "Avanti, giaci pure con le loro macchine. Tradisci tutto ciò in cui crediamo. Ma ricorda – non tornare mai più da noi."

"Hai intenzione di eseguire il trasferimento," disse Zana. "Vuoi diventare una replicata."

Nostra madre rabbrividì, come se Zana avesse detto ad alta voce qualcosa che lei non aveva ancora realizzato. Poi annuì. "Non sono pronta a morire."

Partì il giorno successivo.

Nostro padre non parlò mai più di lei. Se qualcuno osava menzionarla, si chiudeva in sé stesso, a volte anche per giorni. Era uno sciocco a pensare che il suo silenzio potesse cancellarla dalle nostre vite. Tutta la nostra comunità era a conoscenza della vergogna che nostra madre aveva portato sulla famiglia e sulla chiesa. Ogni volta che il portavoce Elb parlava dell'abbandono della retta via di Moya, dello smarrimento della nostra umanità, tutti pensavano a lei. Io, almeno, lo facevo. Poi, per mesi, fui ossessionata dal pensiero di nostra madre. Avevo incubi sul suo corpo straziato e abbandonato – che fine aveva fatto? E che ne era della sconosciuta che sapeva tutto della nostra casa, della nostra famiglia – di *me*? Ci era stato insegnato che non c'era alcuna continuità di vita tra un essere umano e il corpo replicato con la tecnologia dei Mille Mondi. In base alle leggi della Divina mia madre era morta davvero. Ma allora chi era la creatura che viveva a Skytown, l'enclave degli abitanti del mondo al di sopra di Sanctuary? Chi era quella persona che ancora diceva di volermi bene?

Lo sapevo perché aveva tentato di rimanere in contatto con noi, almeno con me e mia sorella. Zana mi mostrò il suo primo messaggio, ma io non riuscii nemmeno a leggerlo fino in fondo. In ogni caso, Zana inviò una risposta, nonostante il portavoce Elb ci avesse detto che la nostra falsa madre l'avrebbe portata al peccato. Non sapevo ogni quanto avessero contatti, perché non volevo saperlo. Comunque, mia sorella insisteva nel dirmi come stava.

Dopo la sua replicazione, nostra madre aveva trovato lavoro come inserviente presso l'Istituto di Archeologia Esotica. Condivideva un appartamento con altre tre coinquiline, tra cui la sua vecchia amica Xeni Bluereed, che aveva lasciato la nostra comunità tre anni prima per farsi replicare. Stando a quanto diceva

Zana, c'era una comunità sempre crescente di persone come nostra madre e Xeni che iniziavano una nuova vita tra gli abitanti del mondo di sopra. Più avanti, ottenne un lavoro in un ristorante di Skytown come cuoca, il che era ironico, perché la cucina era sempre stato il campo di nostro padre. La nuova occupazione di nostra madre era ben pagata, e sospetto che lei inviasse a Zana una parte dei suoi guadagni, sebbene non ne abbia mai avuto la prova. Ma a quanto pare nostra madre aveva denaro a sufficienza per visitare l'orbital e acquistare un bot. Stando a quel che diceva Zana, pensava a noi di continuo, eppure sembrava felice. Nonostante le invidiassi i lussi di Skytown, non riuscivo proprio a immaginare come fosse possibile.

Moya non ci chiede di rinunciare a tutte le tecnologie del mondo di sopra, solo a quelle che ci rendono meno umani. Sì, mi piacerebbe avere un bot e una stampante e un'automobile, se potessi permettermeli. Proverei perfino quelle droghe che ti rendono più forte o più intelligente o più felice. Ma Sanctuary è un mondo ormai esausto. Per questo i nostri antenati riuscirono a reclamarlo per la Divina. Gli Esotici avevano usato Sanctuary molto tempo fa, e le loro rovine sono l'ultima cosa di valore rimasta. Cerchiamo di vivere con i loro resti. E per quanto siamo orgogliosi delle nostre rovine, esistono altri esempi di architettura esotica sparsi in tutta la galassia.

Con il passare dei mesi, la nostra famiglia in frantumi fece del suo meglio per adeguarsi al nuovo stile di vita. La pressione turistica mutava con le stagioni, ma ce la cavammo abbastanza bene, soprattutto ora che eravamo solamente in tre. Riuscii a comprare la power-moto e anche un piccolo rimorchio. Zana non prese solo le sue lezioni di anglico, ma poi acquistò perfino un accesso alle banche dati dell'Istituto, in modo da poter imparare di più sui Mille Mondi. Le sue nuove abilità linguistiche la ripagarono in modo inaspettato. Tra gli hotel turistici si diffuse la notizia della bellissima ragazza che non solo vendeva prodotti da forno, ma che parlava anche la lingua comune. I turisti affollavano quotidianamente la nostra bancarella per assistere a cotanta meraviglia. Aiutarono Zana con il suo accento finché non dichiararono che avrebbe potuto presentare il notiziario su Ravi's Prize – non che qualcuno di noi ci credesse davvero. Ovviamente, io non comprendevo una sola parola di quel chiacchiericcio, e quando un giorno i turisti si dileguarono con un ghigno in faccia, sospettai che stessero ridendo di me.

Poi tornò Quin. Peccato che in realtà, come scoprii in seguito, non se n'era mai andato.

Ero sola al banco, il che implicava che per una volta la mia visuale della strada non era ostruita dagli ammiratori di Zana, quando avvistai Quin che vagava nei pressi dello spiazzo. Era passato quasi mezzo anno, ma appena lo vidi lo riconobbi all'istante. Fece una sosta alla bancarella di Twial, sollevò una replica di Mezza Nave per controllarne il prezzo e poi la riappoggiò con la fronte corrugata. Frugò tra gli sgargianti ombrelli di Glif e fece un giro nel nuovo negozio di odori, poi lo vidi accelerare il passo avvicinandosi al nostro banco. Superò la bancarella con gli occhi bassi, come se stesse cercando le crepe nel pavimento. Era ovvio che mi stava ignorando. Ma poi si fermò all'improvviso in mezzo alla strada, rivolse lo sguardo alle mie spalle, verso la mole scura dello Sperone Frastagliato, e infine decise di avvicinarsi.

"Tu sei Jix." Accennò un sorriso che non gli apparteneva.

Gli dissi di sì.

Allungò la mano verso il nostro biscotto più costoso. "E questo è un Blocco di Velluto al Burrobruno."

"Con una spolverata di zenzero."

"Tagliato a forma di rettangolo perfetto." Lo sollevò alla luce per esaminarlo meglio. "Ho studiato la vostra religione. Avrei ragione a dire che il rapporto tra lunghezza e larghezza di questo biscotto è di 1,618?" Sembrò fiero di aver avanzato quell'ipotesi.

"Le consiglio di comprarne almeno due."

Ma non era la risposta che si aspettava. Annuì, corrugando la fronte.

"Desidera altro?," gli chiesi.

"Conosco tua madre. Lavorava all'Istituto."

"Davvero?" Incartai due blocchi di velluto in un pacchetto da portare via. "È lei che la manda?"

"No." Sembrò sorpreso per la domanda. "Sono un archeologo, faccio ricerche sui vostri Gusci."

"Non sono miei." Ipotizzai che volesse rivolgermi delle domande su mia madre. Gli consegnai il pacchetto. "Tre e cinquanta."

Invece di completare la transazione usando i nostri tell come tutti gli altri turisti, si infilò una mano in tasca e ne estrasse una manciata di crediti moiani.

"Mi piacciono le vostre monete." Armeggiò in cerca dei soldi giusti. "Ce ne sono così tante."

"Piacciono anche a me." Mi capitava raramente di maneggiare crediti al banco; li usano solo i moiani, ma i moiani si fanno i biscotti da soli. Mi fissò mentre mettevo in tasca i crediti. Gli diedi il pacchetto e aspettai. Ma lui non sembrava intenzionato ad andarsene. Ricordai allora la sua reazione quando ce ne eravamo andati, quel terribile giorno. "Forse si aspettava di trovare qualcun altro qui?"

"Zana, sì." Sbatté le palpebre. "Ma non avevo aspettative."

"Mi spiace sentirle dire una cosa del genere. Le aspettative sono quel che mi fa sopravvivere alla giornata." Vidi Zana camminare lungo la strada con un cesto di biscotti. "Cerco sempre di indovinare quel che succederà dopo."

"L'altra volta avevate un puzzle votivo," disse. "Posso rivederlo?"

Sorpresa che se ne ricordasse, aprii la mia borsa e glielo porsi.

"Sì." Premette le forme magnetizzate facendo assumere al rompicapo nuove configurazioni con gesti esperti. "È molto ben codificata, la vostra religione. Sapevi che il poligono a forma di stella è uno dei simboli più antichi che abbiamo? Proviene dalla Terra, sai, il mondo d'origine. Rappresentava il sacro femmineo già nel 4000 a.e.c."

"Davvero?" Era ovvio che si comportasse in modo condiscendente con una nullità come me; lui era un turista. Possibile che le buone maniere fossero un tratto che la tecnologia del mondo di sopra non riusciva a replicare?

"Dunque il cosiddetto rapporto aureo..." Disse ignaro. "Un affascinante insieme di tradizione e matematica. Prendi questo pentagono, collega i vertici e ottieni un pentacolo, una stella a cinque punte." Spostò i pezzi del puzzle. "Cinque è nella sequenza di Fibonacci. E il rapporto di qualsiasi diagonale della stella con qualsiasi lato del pentagono è 1,618. Phi, il rapporto aureo. E lo trovi di nuovo qui..." Spostò i pezzi in un'altra configurazione. "E qui." Tracciò una linea con l'indice, l'unghia che strusciava contro il metallo. "E stavi raccontando di quante volte il rapporto aureo si ritrova in natura. C'è in effetti una gran quantità di argomenti a supporto di questa tesi nella letteratura."

"Noi lo chiamiamo Rapporto Divino," dissi. "E in realtà era mia sorella che le stava spiegando tutto ciò. Non è vero, Zana?"

Quin si sorprese quando la vide appoggiare il cesto sul bancone.

"Forse ti ricordi di Quin," le dissi. "A quanto pare viene dall'Istituto. È un archeologo. E conosce nostra madre."

Quello che si scambiarono non era lo sguardo tra due sconosciuti.

"Vedo che non è una novità per te, eh?" Allungai una mano verso il cestino per vedere quali nuovi biscotti avesse portato. "E così ora ci sono dei segreti tra noi, sorella?"

"Oh, nessun segreto," disse Quin. "Abbiamo iniziato a scambiarci messaggi quando...? Tre mesi fa. Mi piace pensare che siamo diventati amici."

"Da poco più di due mesi." Zana sembrava in imbarazzo. "E ci siamo visti di persona solo un paio di volte."

"Motivo per cui avevo pensato di farti una sorpresa," Quin, invece, sembrava soddisfatto di sé.

"E ti ha detto che sta studiando la nostra religione?" Rifornii la nostra scorta di Frollini Tartufati. "Sta pensando di convertirsi, Quin?" Volevo vederla squittire dall'imbarazzo, per avermi taciuto la sua frequentazione.

"No." Appoggiò il mio puzzle votivo come se potesse ustionarlo. "Niente affatto."

"Già, sarebbe imbarazzante, dal momento che non è più nel suo corpo originale. Quante volte è stato replicato, se non le spiace?"

"Gli spiace eccome." Le guance di Zana si tinsero di rosso. "Chiederlo è maleducazione, Jix."

"Oh, scusa." Mi inchinai due volte per sicurezza. "Chiedo perdono, Quin. È solo che pochissimi di voi si interessano davvero alla nostra gente."

Quin strabuzzò gli occhi, come se stesse facendo fatica a seguire la conversazione. "In ogni caso," disse a Zana, "mi stavo solo chiedendo quando... se magari... ti piacerebbe fare quel tour una volta o l'altra? Quello di cui abbiamo parlato."

"Tour?," domandai.

Lui mi guardò un istante e poi fece un cenno del capo verso Shellgate. "So che vivete qui da tutta la vita, ma io ho accesso ai monumenti, perfino a quelli chiusi. Potrei mostrarvi cose che pochi hanno visto."

Zana mi lanciò un'occhiataccia per farmi capire che non ero invitata. Ma me la feci scivolare addosso.

"Io e Zana siamo ragazze lavoratrici," dissi. "Ci sono turisti da sfamare, biscotti da vendere."

Lui annuì. "Shellgate chiude alle cinque. Mi sembra che a quell'ora tutti i turisti tornino nei loro alberghi, non è così? Potremmo andare dopo l'orario di chiusura; ho un accesso illimitato, sapete. Rimane tutto illuminato fino a quasi le otto."

"Grandioso." Sollevai il cesto di biscotti vuoto e gli sorrisi. "Potremmo preparare una cena-picnic."

Zana non era affatto contenta.

"Nostro padre darebbe di matto se sapesse che stai frequentando un replicato."

"Non lo sto frequentando." Zana era un'ombra scura sul letto dall'altra parte della stanza buia. "È un amico, ecco tutto. E fino a poco tempo fa non abbiamo fatto altro che scambiarci messaggi."

"Non fosse che ora fissate appuntamenti per fare dei tour delle rovine."

Casa nostra è sempre stata asfissiante per colpa dei forni, anche a tarda notte, quando nostro padre li spegneva. In estate io e Zana ci stendevamo sui letti con le braccia e le gambe spalancate, il sudore che ci imperlava la pelle. La maggior parte delle notti ci liberavamo dalle lenzuola, a volte faceva troppo caldo perfino per tenere addosso i vestiti. Incapaci di prendere sonno, chiacchieravamo al buio di ragazzi e aspirazioni, la nostra conversazione che tremolava come la fiammella di una candela.

"Ti mostrerà cose che pochi hanno visto." Ridacchiai. "Dove l'ho già sentita questa? Il turista e la bella figlia del fornaio."

"Le cose non stanno così. E poi, a quanto pare ci sarai anche tu, anche se nessuno ti ha chiesto di venire."

"Verrò solo per assicurarmi che tu non faccia nulla di stupido." Non avevamo mai tenuto segrete le nostre tresche l'una dall'altra, perciò questo Quin mi preoccupava. "D'accordo, magari non è un turista, ma comunque non è qui per rimanere." Zana era la mia gemella, e nonostante non fossimo più compagne di giochi, lei era l'unica nella nostra famiglia a cui ero legata. Il silenzio era interrotto dai graffi degli animaletti che correvano su e giù per i muri e il pavimento. Con il bel tempo le lucertole erano attive anche di notte, nel tentativo di procurarsi qualche mollica o di intrufolarsi tra le crepe dei nostri muri in pietra.

"Credi che non riesca a gestirlo?," chiese Zana. "Ho ventun anni."

"E lui ne ha duecento. O magari duemila."

"Oh, ma falla finita."

"Lavora per l'Istituto, Zana. Per guadagnarti da vivere devi schizzare all'interno dei wormhole, devi acconsentire alla dilatazione temporale. La gente come lui si replica, quanto...? Cinque, sei volte almeno."

La sentii torturare il cuscino per dargli una nuova forma, ma quella notte nessuna di noi due riuscì a riposare granché.

"Di sicuro ha un bell'aspetto," aggiunsi. "Capisco l'attrazione."

Le doghe sotto il suo materasso scricchiolarono quando si tirò su a sedere. "Sai qual è il problema di vivere in questa casa?" La silhouette di Zana risaltava contro la finestra, la sua schiena nuda rivolta verso di me. "Non posso mai scappare da voi due."

"Non è giusto. Non ti lascio sempre la stanza quando porti un ragazzo a casa? Esattamente come quando io sono stata con Bibby, e tu sei sparita. E nostro padre non ha la minima idea di tutto questo."

Silenzio.

"Io guardo le spalle a te e tu le guardi a me, ricordi? È questo che fanno le sorelle."

Rispose con un mugugno insoddisfatto.

"Ma se è il sesso che stai cercando, perché non ti fai un umano? Lo sa Moya, se potresti scegliere chi ti pare."

Riuscii a schivare di un soffio il cuscino che attraversò la stanza in volo.

Non portammo biscotti per il picnic. Quando si fa il fornaio di lavoro, si perde il gusto per cose del genere. In compenso, portammo trote golarossa sotto sale dal fiume e un po' di fichi marinati. Una zuppa di zucca fredda. Una selezione di formaggi e una bottiglia di brandy di fata. All'inizio dell'escursione Quin insistette per portare tutto il peso, nonostante io e Zana avessimo trascorso la maggior parte delle nostre vite a trasportare pesanti cesti di frutta e farina e olio e spezie.

A dire il vero, invidiavo il tell inserito nella sua unghia e sincronizzato con i sistemi di sicurezza dell'Istituto di Shellgate. Un cenno della sua mano, e i proiettori si spensero; appena attraversammo l'ingresso, una solida luce blu bloccò di nuovo l'entrata. Non avevo mai visto una tecnologia per le comunicazioni tanto minuscola. Per un istante, Quin sembrò una specie di creatura magica.

Nonostante fossero gestite dall'Istituto, le rovine facevano parte del nostro quartiere. Giocavamo tra i ruderi sin da quando eravamo piccole. Ma quella notte, fu come se ci fossimo lasciate alle spalle Sanctuary per mettere piede su uno dei Mille Mondi. Chiamavamo le varie strutture con i nomi che i primi coloni avevano dato loro; ma Quin identificava le Pietre della Nonna con termini come Segnalatori di Confine da 11n a 11t. Ci spiegò che Mezza Nave e lo Sperone Frastagliato facevano parte di un complesso che lui chiamava Prima Superstruttura Classica del Quadrante Occidentale. Quando noi insistemmo che quegli Edifici Ellissoidali 43, 58 e 70 erano in realtà il Guscio d'Uccello, il Guscio Folle e la Sposa, lui scoppiò a ridere. Disse che dare nomi comuni alle rovine era il modo con cui le persone riuscivano a convivere con la loro paura di tutto ciò che era alieno. Un modo per fingere che comprendevamo la civiltà dei grandi Esotici.

Aveva un talento naturale nell'irritarmi. "Forse," dissi, "assegnare loro dei numeri è il vostro modo di conviverci."

Zana mi lanciò un'occhiataccia, ma Quin annuì, come se stesse riflettendo sulla mia frecciatina. "Potresti aver ragione. Numerare le cose del mondo è quello che facciamo sempre noi esseri umani, non è così?" Eravamo in piedi su un parapetto denominato Panorama Ghiacciato, tutti con lo sguardo rivolto verso i tre Gusci in basso. "Non sono edifici, sapete. Sono sculture."

"Sculture?," chiesi. "Di cosa?"

"Si trovano costruzioni simili in molte altre rovine. Prima di venire qui ho fatto delle soste a Destination e Kenning. Sono certo che i vostri Gusci non sono mai stati abitati. E penso che non fossero nemmeno funzionali. Le mie ricerche mi hanno portato a credere che siano arte propagandistica su scala monumentale, come il Sepolcro di Ravi o il Lubinarium."

"Come la Statua della Libertà sulla Terra," disse Zana. Mi colse di sorpresa. Per quale motivo sapeva delle cose su quel pianeta morto?

"Non la conosco." Quin sollevò il cesto da picnic. "La maggior parte degli studiosi sostengono che le Sculture Ellissoidali siano Post-Classiche, ma io credo che risalgano invero alla fine dell'Era Persistente, poco prima che l'ultimo degli Esotici scomparisse."

"Sculture di cosa?," ripetei. "E che tipo di propaganda?"

"Ho sentito che da lì si gode di una vista particolarmente interessante." Con il mento fece un cenno verso lo spiazzo in cima alla Sposa. "Mangiamo lassù?"

Mentre scendevamo dal pendio disseminato di macerie, ci raccontò del suo lavoro. Nessuno sapeva che fine avessero fatto gli Esotici. La civiltà galattica che aveva sviluppato i wormhole era scomparsa tra i cinquanta e i sessantamila anni fa. A giudicare dalle loro enigmatiche rovine, la civilizzazione degli Esotici aveva iniziato a decadere nell'Epoca Post-Classica, a cui seguì il lungo declino dell'Epoca Persistente. Quin credeva che i gusci di Sanctuary fossero una delle ultime cose mai costruite dagli esotici.

Nel crepuscolo il vento era calato, e passando davanti alla facciata bruciata dal sole del Guscio Folle diretti verso la Sposa, avvertimmo l'edificio irradiare il calore del giorno. "Credo che questi gusci servissero a convincere i Persistenti che rimasero indietro per seguire i loro antenati." Quin appoggiò il cesto sul moncone di un pilastro per asciugarsi il sudore dagli occhi. "Forse per farli vergognare, perché la cultura degli Esotici era progredita. Cosa stavano aspettando?" Aveva parlato in continuazione e adesso era senza fiato.

Io, d'altro canto, mi stavo godendo l'effetto che il calore della nostra estate aveva su questo abitante del mondo di sopra troppo sicuro di sé. "Secondo questa teoria tutti fecero i bagagli per andare dove? In una specie di paese dei balocchi degli Esotici?"

"In effetti le prove indicano una partenza di massa avvenuta in un lasso di tempo molto breve, e un periodo più lungo con i ritardatari rimasti. Secondo alcuni ci fu un suicidio di massa, ma sì, mi piace pensare che andarono altrove. Magari in un altro luogo nel nostro universo, o in qualche realtà progettata."

Zana sollevò il cestino da picnic. "Non riesco a immaginare che qualcuno possa stancarsi di navigare tra i wormhole."

Quin finse di non accorgersi del fatto che mia sorella lo aveva appena alleggerito di un discreto peso. "Non penso che si annoiassero. Una cosa è certa, erano estremamente ordinati. Fu un grande dolore per loro abbandonare i loro mondi." Si tirò la camicia nel punto in cui aveva aderito al suo petto. "Tutte le loro rovine sono costruite a partire da materiali nativi, perlopiù pietra e ceramica. Qualche metallo. Siamo piuttosto sicuri che all'interno non viveva nessuno di loro, ma a dire il vero non abbiamo idea di dove vivessero. Non sappiamo nulla del loro aspetto, della loro biologia, di quello in cui credevano. Erano strutture cerimoniali? Amministrative? Religiose?"

"La cosa sembra disturbarti," commentai. "E per quale motivo? Perché non è giusto nei confronti degli archeologi?"

"Avrebbero potuto lasciarci qualche informazione in più." Sorrise. "Mi piace pensare che ci siano delle risposte, da qualche parte, ma forse mi sto solo illudendo."

Secondo nostro padre, prima che l'Istituto assumesse il controllo delle rovine, i moiani avevano fatto del loro meglio per ripulirle: risistemare le pietre, chiudere i buchi, strappare le erbacce e tagliare i cespugli. Gli abitanti del mondo di sopra avevano bloccato tutte le operazioni e limitato l'accesso pubblico a una minima parte delle strutture. Dicevano che era per preservare i registri archeologici; secondo i reietti era per allontanare i clienti. Qualsiasi fosse la verità, orientarsi tra le rovine era una vera e propria sfida. Gli appigli erano instabili, e gli accessi diretti per qualsiasi destinazione erano spesso ostruiti.

"Dunque Moya cosa..." Avevamo quasi raggiunto la base della Sposa, e Quin era di nuovo affaticato. "... che cos'ha da dire... riguardo tutto questo?"

"Non ci è dato conoscere i pensieri di Moya." Zana scavalcò la lastra di pietra caduta davanti all'entrata grossolana che qualcuno aveva inciso sulla Sposa.

"Avanti," ribattei. "È chiaro che gli Esotici conoscessero il rapporto Divino."

"Credi?"

"Guarda." Gesticolai verso la spirale bianca incisa sulle pietre di rivestimento del muro sopra di noi.

"Immagino sia così." Cercò di ricomporsi per la fatica della scalata. "È matematica, in fin dei conti. Ma voi moiani... voi vedete questo rapporto ovunque."

Tesi una mano per aiutarlo a salire. "E tu no?"

Allungò una mano verso di me, ma mancò la presa. "Non ho la vostra energia." Afferrai il suo polso umidiccio e lo tirai su al mio fianco.

Dopo aver ripreso fiato, Quin insistette per raccontarci che il calcare della facciata bianca della Sposa era stato estratto dalla Piega di Kunlun, anche se lo sapevano tutti. La Sposa assomigliava alle Lumache d'Avorio che alcuni reietti raccoglievano dal fiume per preparare le zuppe. Quelle che sapevano di calzini sporchi. La differenza era che la Sposa era enorme – alta circa trenta metri – ed era capovolta. L'apertura del guscio puntava verso il cielo. Ci chinammo per attraversare l'entrata improvvisata che dava verso l'interno. L'aria era stantia e puzzava come il fondo di un pozzo. Un'impalcatura in legno si inerpicava verso la luce che filtrava dall'alto. Ci chinammo per superare un pavimento scricchiolante pieno di mattonelle rotte cadute dai muri, ciascuna decorata con un motivo mosaicato floreale e a spirale. Alcuni reietti credevano che se si riusciva a trovare una mattonella sana, la persona a cui la regalavi si sarebbe innamorata di te. Purtroppo, le mattonelle integre erano difficili da trovare da quando era stato introdotto il divieto di portare via gli artefatti dalle rovine. In ogni caso, i Naras avevano messo in piedi un vivace commercio di riproduzioni sulle loro bancarelle nei pressi di Rivergate.

Mi chinai per raccogliere una scheggia e la mostrai a Quin. Era difficile distinguerne i dettagli alla flebile luce che proveniva dall'apertura sopra le nostre teste, così il replicato accese l'unghia dell'indice.

"Il rapporto divino." Tracciai diverse forme sul frammento di mattonella. "Nel caso fossi ancora in dubbio sulle conoscenze degli Esotici."

"Già." Spense l'unghia con un rapido gesto. "È già stato detto. Eppure non è esattamente 1,618, vero?"

Mi irritai e lasciai cadere il frammento a terra. "Ci va talmente vicino che è quasi impossibile notare la differenza."

"Già," disse. "Soprattutto al buio."

"Quin si diverte a lanciare frecciatine," disse Zana. "Meglio ignorarlo quando fa così."

"Perdonami," disse lui. "Tua sorella mi ha insegnato le buone maniere, ma temo di non essere un granché come studente."

Mentre ci arrampicavamo tentai di pregare i numeri per calmarmi. Uno, uno, due, tre, cinque, otto, tredici, ventuno, trentaquattro, cinquantacinque... Arrivata a diciassettemilasettecentoundici sentii di essere tornata in me. Quin salì in rapida successione le prime due scalette, ma poi dovette riposarsi su ogni piattaforma. Più salivamo in alto e più tempo ci metteva a recuperare, finché non crollò del tutto al settimo livello, affannato e bagnato come se l'avessimo appena tirato fuori dal fiume. La struttura in legno, ricoperta di muffa a causa dell'esposizione agli agenti atmosferici, lasciò una macchia sui pantaloni di Quin. Zana gli si avvicinò preoccupata, ma lui ci rassicurò dicendo che era stanco solo perché la sua ultima replica era avvenuta su un mondo dove la gravità era 0,68 volte quella di Sanctuary. "E poi non me la cavo benissimo con le altezze," aggiunse.

Riprese vita dopo aver superato l'ultima scala, che ci portò sull'ampio labbro di pietra della Sposa in cima al Guscio. Mentre Zana lo aiutava a sedersi e a spacchettare le nostre cene, io mi avvicinai al bordo per godermi il panorama. Erano passati anni dall'ultima volta che avevo fatto quell'arrampicata. Le rovine in ombra si estendevano ai miei piedi, mentre le luci del nostro piccolo villaggio baluginavano poco distanti. Skytown non era altro che un lontano bagliore all'orizzonte. Nonostante lassù l'aria fosse più calda, fu un sollievo prendere fiato rispetto agli interni appiccicosi della Sposa. Feci un respiro profondo, felice di poter abbracciare tutto il mio mondo con un solo sguardo.

Zana stava sussurrando qualcosa a Quin, non riuscivo a distinguere le parole, ma la sua voce aveva un tono al tempo stesso innocente, sincero e tenero; mi fece rabbrividire.

E se fosse stato qualcosa in più di una tresca da quattro soldi?

Quin riteneva che la trota golarossa sapesse troppo di pesce, ma divorò letteralmente i fichi marinati, e chiese una porzione in più della zuppa di zucca di nostro padre per effettuare delle analisi gastronomiche. Disse che il formaggio era meglio del *framenthakler* che i data-monaci su Encyclopedia stampavano con la loro ricetta segreta. Parlammo molto di cibo. Zana lo incalzò per sapere i suoi piatti preferiti, ma sapevo che era più interessata ad ascoltare le storie sui Mille Mondi di quanto non lo fosse a scoprire la cucina del mondo di sopra. Quin disse che la maggior parte dei replicati preferiva cibi stampati, riproducibili in varietà infinite. Quelli che viaggiavano all'interno dei wormhole si interessavano poco alle culture locali, ma erano sempre molto propensi a provare le ultime ricette.

"A nessuno interessano granché libri e canzoni," disse. "Ciò che vende nel mondo di sopra sono i nuovi menu." Agitò la nostra bottiglia di brandy verso il cielo. "Create un nuovo sapore o un nuovo odore e potrete stampare il vostro biglietto per le stelle personale." Quando si offrì di riempirmi di nuovo il bicchiere, lo coprii con la mano. "Prendete i vostri biscotti, ad esempio. Con la giusta pubblicità, potrebbero pagarvi un modo per lasciare Sanctuary."

Aspettai che Zana sottolineasse che non avevamo alcuna intenzione di lasciare casa. Ma non lo fece, così rimasi in silenzio anche io.

Mi aspettavo che Quin continuasse a parlare quasi da solo, ma a un tratto decise che voleva sapere qualcosa di noi, o almeno di Zana. Ci chiese delle nostre scuole e di quel che ci era stato raccontato del mondo di sopra. Zana parlò di quel che aveva imparato usando il portale dell'Istituto; Quin commentò che aveva accesso a una discreta quantità di dati, ma che non era affatto completo. Si chiese cosa pensavamo delle controversie che imperversavano di continuo tra i reietti e l'Istituto sulla gestione delle rovine. Poi ci fece raccontare alcuni aneddoti sulle stupidaggini che facevano i turisti.

"Non capisco per quale motivo debbano mettersi a contrattare," dissi, "dopo quel che hanno speso per arrivare fin qui. Noi dovremmo vendere una montagna di biscotti solo per poter raggiungere l'orbitale."

"Così gli permettiamo di abbassare i nostri prezzi..." Zana ridacchiò, "... e poi compensiamo la differenza in tasse."

"Ma non ci sono tasse."

"Certo che sì," intervenni. "La tassa sulla stupidità."

Scoppiammo tutti a ridere mentre Zana ci riempiva i bicchieri con il brandy rimasto.

"Poi c'era quella donna fastidiosa che voleva comprare tutta la nostra carta per gli ordini a portar via. Da dov'è che veniva?"

"Diceva che aveva un sapore migliore dei nostri biscotti."

"E poi fanno delle domande stupidissime sul Rapporto Divino."

La battuta mi fece guadagnare un'occhiataccia da parte di mia sorella, ma poi Quin alzò la mano. "Colpevole."

Non volevo che quel replicato iniziasse a piacermi, così dissi: "Tu non credi nella Divina, non è vero?"

Il sibilo di rimprovero di Zana sembrava una cucitura che veniva lacerata.

"Sai che non ci credo," rispose.

Nessuno rideva più, all'improvviso.

"Né credi in qualsiasi altro dio," aggiunsi. Quin mi studiò. Il suo silenzio metteva i brividi.

"Perché no?," gli chiesi.

"Jix" Zana si inginocchiò, ma sapevo che in realtà era curiosa quanto me.

"Hai mai sentito parlare del punto di Dio, Jix?," disse Quin.

"Non esiste." Disse Zana, nel tentativo di porre fine alla conversazione.

"No," dissi. "Che cos'è?"

"Un tempo gli studiosi cercavano il punto all'interno nostri cervelli da cui nascono le esperienze mistiche. Alcuni indicarono il lobo parietale destro, altri la corteccia prefrontale dorsolaterale. In base ad alcune prove si scoprì che i livelli della N.N-dimetiltriptamina nella ghiandola pineale giocavano un ruolo importante. Ma col tempo capirono di essersi sbagliati, e così svilupparono un modello diverso. Non esiste un pulsante nel nostro cervello che si può premere per ottenere una spiritualità istantanea. Le correlazioni neurali sono distribuite in tutto il cervello, nei sistemi che danno vita all'autocoscienza, all'emozione, al senso di sé." Frugò nella tasca della camicia che indossava. "La cosa interessante è che per vivere un'esperienza religiosa non vengono stimolati questi sistemi cerebrali." Scosse la testa. "Al contrario, vengono soppressi. Bisogna inibire quelle aree per creare l'illusione del sé, ed è così che si spalancano le porte del trascendente."

"E allora?" dissi.

Estrasse una siringa dalla tasca e ce la mostrò. "Volete incontrare Moya?"

A volte mi chiedo se quel giorno sia stata Zana a versare il nostro futuro da una bottiglia di brandy di fata. Come potevano due sorelle ubriache sperare di proteggersi a vicenda? O forse stavo sfidando mia sorella mentre lei sfidava me in una sorta di danza alcolica di rivalità tra sorelle? O magari ognuna di noi stava solo cercando di fare colpo sul proprio abitante del mondo di sopra, ciascuna a modo suo e per le proprie ragioni?

La siringa sembrava un pollice di vetro, cilindrica ma con un'estremità piatta. "Non ci vorrà molto." Quin premette la siringa contro il collo di Zana, all'altezza di un'arteria. "Diciamo quindici minuti per oltrepassare la barriera ematoencefalica." La siringa lasciò sulla pelle un gonfiore rosa pallido. "Per quanto riguarda l'esperienza in sé... dipende. Dura circa cinque minuti, anche se dal punto di vista soggettivo potrà sembrarvi più lunga." Si voltò verso di me. "Ma varia da persona a persona. Alcuni sentono di svanire, alcuni diventano uno con il tutto."

Inclinai la testa. "Ed è reale?" Quando mi fece l'iniezione fu come se qualcuno mi stesse baciando il collo.

Scoppiò a ridere. "Questo sta a voi deciderlo." Poi fece l'iniezione a se stesso, e infine rimise la siringa in tasca.

"Avevi pianificato tutto," disse Zana.

"Ne avevamo parlato," rispose, "non ricordi?"

"Non ho mai acconsentito."

Sghignazzò. "L'hai appena fatto."

"Quindi adesso che dobbiamo fare?" chiesi.

Si sedette sul pavimento coperto di mattoni, si voltò verso il panorama e incrociò le gambe. "Aspettiamo l'ascensore."

Ci disponemmo a triangolo fissandoci a vicenda in cerca di qualche segnale. Zana tornò a sedersi sui talloni. La sua schiena era rigida e fiutava l'aria con il naso all'insù, come se si aspettasse di percepire l'odore di Moya da un momento all'altro. Mi irrigidii sul pavimento duro e freddo. Il silenzio mi rese più consapevole di me stessa, non meno. Ero nel giusto? Questa esperienza mi avrebbe cambiato la vita? Dovevo fare qualcosa con le mani?

Quin sembrava divertirsi. "Non vi ho mai chiesto dei vostri fidanzati," disse per distrarci. "Scommetto che ne avete avuti moltissimi."

"Zana sì." Fui sollevata nel sentire il suono della mia stessa voce. "Si è presa tutti i suoi e metà dei miei."

"Non è vero." Si accigliò. "Te la cavi benissimo anche tu."

"Dicono che parlo troppo."

"Teste di rapa." Quin mi diede qualche pacca sul braccio. "Devi stare con uomini intelligenti quanto te."

"E tu?," chiese Zana. "Hai qualcuno a cui tieni particolarmente?"

"Sì e no." Fece una pausa, indeciso su quanto sbottonarsi. "Quando si viene replicati, talvolta le relazioni vengono meno. Sei sempre te stesso, ma anche una persona diversa. Il corpo è diverso, tanto per cominciare, a volte anche molto diverso. Non ci si può opporre ai suoi desideri. Il vecchio te stesso… è come una persona di cui hai letto in un libro. Magari è stata un'avventura molto interessante, e può capitare di ricordare alcune scene in modo più vivido di altre, ma sei arrivato all'ultima pagina."

"Com'è?," domandai. "Farsi replicare."

"Come morire, solo che dopo ti svegli."

"Sei morto?" Non avrei dovuto sorprendermi, eppure ero allibita.

"Tutte le volte," disse, come se stesse discutendo di un'inezia. "Ovviamente in un trasferimento diretto non si rimane morti a lungo. Ma di questi tempi possono replicare qualcuno fino a trenta minuti dopo l'arresto cardiaco e respiratorio, il tutto con una perdita di informazioni minima. Dopo mezz'ora, il cervello inizia a deteriorarsi sul serio. Riguarda le lesioni ischemiche." Rabbrividì. "Quindi sì, Zana già lo sa, ma sono morto in un incidente a bordo di un velivolo prima di venire qui. Non è stata colpa di nessuno, in realtà. Ero con una persona che amavo, ma lui non ce l'ha fatta. I soccorsi ci hanno messo troppo a raggiungerci. Dicono che la mia replica è risultata accurata solo al novantasei percento. È stato molto triste, perché probabilmente sarei ancora con lui se anche la sua replica fosse stata completata con successo."

Zana strinse la mano di Quin tra le sue.

"Perciò sto ancora imparando a essere questo nuovo Quin in questo nuovo corpo." Sorrise con le labbra, ma aveva lo sguardo triste. "Ma è quello che facciamo tutti in fondo, non credete?"

Quando vidi quell'espressione sul viso di mia sorella, una che non avevo mai visto prima, capii che avevo avuto ragione a preoccuparmi per questo abitante del mondo di sopra. L'amore che

Zana provava per Quin era fin troppo visibile nei suoi rapporti perfetti, i doni ricevuti da Moya. La lunghezza del suo volto diviso per la sua larghezza. *1,618*. Il suo sorriso diviso per l'ampiezza del suo naso. *1,618*. L'ampiezza del naso in rapporto allo spazio tra le sue narici. *1,618*.

Ero talmente concentrata su mia sorella da non essermi nemmeno accorta che Quin stava ancora parlando, fino a quando disse: "Farei qualsiasi cosa per te."

Zana chiuse gli occhi. Era la mia immaginazione o stava tremando, per quanto li aveva chiusi forte? Quando li riaprì aveva lo sguardo perso nel vuoto, e l'*1,618* sprigionò in tutta la sua divinità dalla larghezza del suo occhio divisa per il diametro dell'iride.

"No." Si alzò in piedi – per allontanarsi dal suo amante? O da Moya, che l'aveva fatta a sua immagine e somiglianza? La Divina era la ragione per cui la sua altezza era l'*1,618* della distanza tra il suo bellissimo ombelico e i suoi capelli perfetti. I numeri sacri iniziarono a pregare se stessi: *una più una sorella, due sorelle, tre, cinque, otto...*

Quin barcollò fino ad alzarsi in piedi e la strinse in un abbraccio, vomitando un fiume di ardente e incomprensibile anglico. Lei rispose nella stessa lingua, ma con la voce a pezzi. Altre frasi senza senso in anglico, poi altre ancora, e poi iniziarono a urlare. La discussione la fece infuriare al punto che si liberò dalla sua stretta per allontanarsi. Il braccio di Quin penzolò e lui sembrò agitarlo come se si fosse addormentato, ma era troppo lungo, *troppo lungo*, le sue proporzioni erano completamente sbagliate. Quando chiuse le dita a pugno, quell'unghia brillò di un viola sonnolento e magico al tempo stesso.

Una voce gridò dal nulla: "Parlate moiano!"

Zana sentì. "Lo voglio, sì, in tutto e per tutto, ma non posso." Stava piangendo. "È considerato un peccato. E poi come potrei abbandonarli?"

"Possono venire anche loro," disse Quin. "Pagherò io per le repliche."

"Replicare nostro padre?" la risata di mia sorella si fece amara, e la sua bocca si distorse, e i suoi rapporti perfetti si fecero asimmetrici. "Io ti amo, Quin, ma..."

Amore, disse la voce senza rivolgersi a nessuno. Tredici, ventuno, trentaquattro. Lei lo ama.

"Jix, che stai facendo?" L'abitante del mondo di sopra non sembrava più condiscendente ora. "Allontanati da lei, Jix." Con chi stava parlando?

La voce era crudele come una pietra, e triste come il vento. Cinquantacinque, ottantanove, centoquarantaquattro.

"Fermati." Zana cercò di divincolarsi, ma non fu abbastanza veloce. "No!"

E un istante dopo stava precipitando, le braccia perfette che fluttuavano in aria, un urlo fendette la notte. Sulla strada per i Mille Mondi. La verità è che nessuno spinse Zana Ferenc giù dal labbro della Sposa e verso la sua morte.

"Chiama i soccorsi, subito," disse nessuno. "Hai solo mezz'ora."

Non mi sarei aspettata che mia madre potesse essere così bella. Era figlia unica, ma la replica che le avevano assegnato sembrava una specie di sorella più giovane e solare. Mi ricordava mia sorella, quella che non avevo più, stando a quanto diceva mio padre. Si fece da parte e con un sorriso mi fece entrare nel suo appartamento. La stanza era fresca, una sensazione gradevole dopo la lunga escursione dalla chiesa, come fare un tuffo a bomba nel fiume in un caldo pomeriggio estivo. Doveva trattarsi dell'aria condizionata di cui sentivamo parlare tanto spesso.

Non c'erano vere finestre, ma tutto il muro posteriore proiettava un'immagine in diretta delle rovine riprese dal belvedere sulla Sedia del Kai. Il nostro villaggio faceva capolino dall'angolo.

"Xeni e le altre sono fuori," disse mia madre. "Siamo sole."

"Xeni," ripetei. "È la tua coinquilina, giusto?" Mi fermai al centro di quello che a quanto pareva era solo un soggiorno. Due porte alla mia sinistra, una a destra, l'ingresso alle mie spalle.

Avevo così tante cose da dire, tante domande da fare, ma avevo la lingua annodata.

"Mi piace il tuo divano." Era un commento stupido, ma fu tutto ciò che riuscii a tirare fuori. Il divano era a forma di L e coperto da un telo rosso e ruvido. Cercai di stimarne il prezzo in biscotti mentre passavo un dito sul bracciolo esterno. Il materiale era caldo, sembrava di toccare una specie di pelle.

"Siediti un attimo." Mia madre diede qualche colpetto sul cuscino del divano dove voleva che prendessi posto. "Io torno subito."

Ero talmente disperata che non appena fu uscita dalla stanza presi in considerazione l'idea di scappare di corsa. Ma non sarei riuscita a fare un altro passo con tutte quelle notti insonni alle spalle. Avevo bisogno di qualcuno con cui parlare, così mi sedetti. Il vaporizzatore appoggiato sul basso tavolino davanti a me emise una nuvoletta di condensa. Inspirai, una specie di droga ambientale. Profumava di verde. Agganciata sul muro c'era un'antica ruota di bicicletta, il cromo divorato dalla ruggine, la trama sulla gomma consumata fino a lasciarla del tutto lucida.

"È di Xeni." Mia madre tornò con un vassoio. "Lei gareggia, sai. A quanto pare quella ruota apparteneva alla bicicletta che vinse la Salita di Omeo; risale a chissà quando."

Appoggiò il vassoio sul tavolo e si sedette al mio fianco. Spostai lo sguardo dal vassoio a mia madre. "Rimarrò con te?"

"Se vorrai."

Aveva preparato i miei piatti preferiti: grappoli agrodolci, spiedini di fichi e formaggio, pannocchie sottaceto, e qualche fetta di salame con piccole coroncine di mostarda.

Tesi una mano verso gli agrodolci. "Come, niente biscotti?"

Aveva un modo di sbuffare e ridere al tempo stesso del tutto peculiare. "Quelli sono la specialità di tuo padre." Sentire quel suono intimo che solo lei sapeva fare mi riportò alla mente un ricordo soleggiato: noi quattro sulla barca in mezzo al fiume, nostro padre che remava per riportarci a casa dalla chiesetta, e nostra madre che rideva mentre io e Zana tiravamo fuori dei dolcetti squisiti dal cestino da picnic.

"Lui come sta?," chiese mia madre.

E in un istante tornai nell'appartamento di Skytown, la nostra famiglia di nuovo a pezzi. "È amareggiato," risposi. "Sono stata costretta a trasferirmi. Per ora vivo in chiesa."

"Credo che fosse arrivato il momento. Avevi bisogno di stare da sola." Aggrottò la fronte. "Ma in chiesa?"

"Nessuno sa cos'è successo quella sera," dissi. "Nessuno nel villaggio, voglio dire. Credono che sia stato un incidente." Sentivo la lingua pesante come un mattone. "Ma tu lo sai."

Annuì.

Il silenzio si fece denso, per un attimo credetti di sbottare. "Mi piace casa tua." Perché dalla bocca riuscivo a tirare fuori solo apprezzamenti banali?

"Non mi sei mai venuta a trovare."

"No. Mi dispiace." Era un rimprovero che temevo mi avrebbe rivolto, ma in un certo senso non fu male come avevo immaginato. "Ho fatto male." Aveva tutto il diritto di biasimarmi; non sapevo più chi ero o cosa stavo facendo. "Zana è venuta?"

Pronunciò qualcosa in Anglico. Anche io avevo iniziato a prendere lezioni, e mi sembrò di cogliere qualcosa riguardo una *vacanza* o un *compleanno*. Un istante dopo sul muro comparve una fotografia di lei e Zana sedute sul divano, esattamente dove ci trovavamo in quel momento, e con praticamente gli stessi snack davanti. Era la Zana che conoscevo, mia sorella. Non l'altra, la replicata che non avevo mai visto.

"Ha detto qualcosa dopo essere stata replicata?" domandai. "Su di me, intendo?"

"Non molto." Mia madre sceglieva le parole come se stesse camminando in punta di piedi in un mare di vetri rotti. "Non riusciva a capire per quale motivo l'hai fatto."

Avrei dovuto dire qualcosa – mia madre si aspettava che lo facessi. Ma all'improvviso ero di nuovo sulla Sposa, a rivivere quella serata per la milionesima volta, incapace di capire. Avevo sentito la voce di Moya, quindi come avrei potuto peccare?

"Ha lasciato l'orbitale ieri," disse. "Dovrebbe arrivare al punto d'accesso del wormhole venerdì prossimo."

"Ma non ha mandato nessun messaggio? Niente?"

Sospirò. "Dicono che i ricordi più vividi di un replicato siano quelli relativi agli ultimi momenti. Per me, fu solo nebbia, ma per quanto mi riguarda si trattò di un trasferimento diretto. Mi hanno fatta addormentare, sono morta, e mi hanno svegliata. Anche se da qualche parte nel corso del processo, ricordo di aver combattuto con... be', come ho detto. Nebbia." Con un gesto sospinse verso di sé la nebbia che emergeva dal vaporizzatore e inspirò a fondo. "Fu come nuotare, quasi come annegare. Dovevo rimanere dritta, solo che i miei piedi continuavano ad affondare, e io non riuscivo a liberarmi e... be', ci è voluto un po', ecco tutto. Ero pronta a chiudere la faccenda." Scosse la testa come se cercasse di disfarsi di quella nebbia di cui ancora serbava memoria. "Suppongo che i ricordi di Zana fossero più dolorosi."

"Mi dispiace." Sentii un nodo alla gola. Quanti messaggi avevo inviato a mia sorella chiedendole perdono in tutti i modi che mi passavano per la mente? E lei non aveva risposto a nessuno.

Poi scoppiai a piangere, lacrime calde, singhiozzi violenti.

Mamma mi diede qualche colpetto sul braccio. "Credo che lei sappia."

Ma non era solo per mia sorella che piangevo. Piangevo per mia madre e per mio padre e per la vita che tutti noi avevamo perso. E per Moya, che aveva risposto alla droga di un abitante del mondo di sopra.

Finalmente tornai in me. "Ci stava raccontando che era morto in un incidente a bordo di un velivolo," mi asciugai gli occhi. "Quin, quella notte. Perciò se non altro sa che cosa ha passato Zana. Forse ha aiutato."

"Lo spero." Prese una fettina di salame e lo esaminò con sguardo critico. "All'inizio non mi era piaciuto. Era troppo calato nella parte dell'abitante di sopra, sempre a parlare di come avremmo dovuto abbandonare le nostre tradizioni per diventare cittadini dei Mille Mondi. Credo che in realtà desideri inseguire i suoi

Esotici e andare a vivere con loro." Mia madre leccò la coroncina di mostarda con la lingua, poi mordicchiò il bordo come faceva sempre. "Ma le ha fatto bene, le ha perfino pagato il biglietto per Ravi's Prize. Dice che la seguirà non appena avrà finito la sua ricerca. Vedremo. Credo che abbia buone intenzioni."

"Hai una foto di lei?" chiesi. "Del dopo, intendo."

Parlò di nuovo in Anglico. Riconobbi la parola *figlia*.

Una donna mi fissava dal muro di mia madre – non era esattamente una sconosciuta. I suoi occhi erano profondi come il cielo notturno, proprio come me la ricordavo. Ma aveva una carnagione disumana e pallida, e i suoi capelli erano troppo corti e le proporzioni del suo viso erano tutte sballate. Quando compresi che assomigliava più a me che a mia sorella, rimasi senza fiato. La mia gemella.

"Spero," dissi, "che un giorno possa essere di nuovo felice."

"Sì," rispose mia madre. "Prego i numeri che ci riesca."

TABLE OF CONTENTS

INDICE

Progetto grafico Alda Teodorani
Illustrazione di Flavia Sorato e Chiara Mazzotta
Stampato da BD print Srl - Roma